MAGEBORN:

THE LINE OF ILLENIEL

BY

MICHAEL G. MANNING

Cover by Amalia Chitulescu

Map Artwork by Maxime Plasse

Illustrations by Michael G. Manning

Copyright 2011 by Michael G. Manning

First Edition October 2011

Second Edition March 2018

All rights reserved.

ISBN: 9781943481217

Printed in the United States of America

Acknowledgements

For my father, who was the inspiration for Royce Eldridge. His contribution to my life over the years has been difficult to measure, and only now that he is gone do I realize how much I have lost. This one is for you Dad.

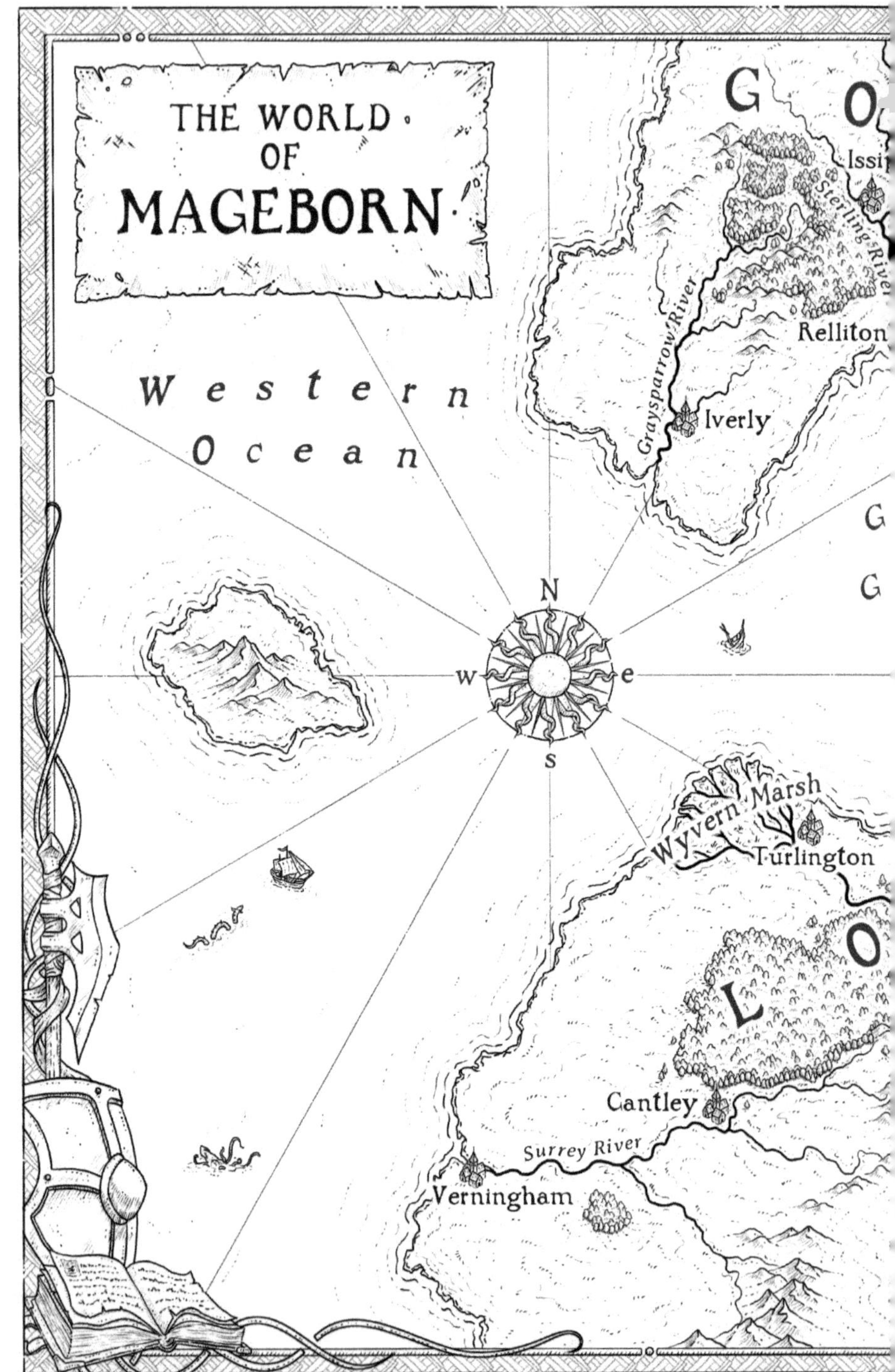

THE WORLD OF MAGEBORN
Western Ocean
G O
Issi
Sterling River
Grasparrow River
Relliton
Iverly
G
G
N
W
e
s
Wyvern Marsh
Turlington
L O
Cantley
Surrey River
Verningham

DUNBAR
DODDIN
SURENCIA
Vergil River
Dalensa
Northern Wastes
Shepherd's Rest
of
ulon
Glenmae River
Cameron
Arundel
Formby Marsh
Lancaster
Elentirs
Malvern
Trent River
THION
Myrtle River
ALBAMARL
Southern Desert
PLASSE
2015

CHAPTER 1

I moved quietly through the darkness, 'til I reached the door I sought. There was no ambient light, nor did I bring any with me; I preferred magesight for this task. Light would only increase the danger. Stretching out with my mind I explored the room beyond the door; my task would be easier if it was empty, but I felt a presence there already. A dangerous aura hovered around the form within, causing me to break out in a sweat as I considered my options. I checked my shield again; making sure the spell covered me fully. Briefly I considered my sword, but I knew it would be useless against this foe.

Carefully I reached for the handle, checking to see if it was locked. It wasn't, naturally enough… the being within the room was waiting for me. The huntress only locks the cage once her prey is inside. Slowly I eased the door open, hoping for darkness within. My foe needed light to see, while I didn't; it was perhaps my only advantage.

The room was brightly lit, dammit.

"Hey sweetie, I didn't expect to see you up this late. You weren't waiting on me were you?" I kept a cheerful tone in my voice, but I knew she wasn't fooled.

"Where the hell have you been?" Penny growled. She had that tired grumpy look on her face that people sometimes get when they have been sitting up half the night. I took it as a bad sign.

No one has ever accused me of being terribly bright around women, so I decided to try honesty. "I was sneaking around behind your back," I replied. Hmm, that sounded even worse out loud.

Penny was exasperated, "If you were doing that at least it would make sense!" Her eyes flicked upward, indicating a place above my forehead, "There's a twig in your hair by the way."

"I was sneaking around!" I protested. "There's this girl see—and she just wouldn't leave me alone! So, I went out..." This was a blatant attempt to make her laugh… she didn't.

"Please! There are several that have been making eyes at you, but you haven't the sense to even know who they are! Don't give me your stupid stories. You went out to the miller's house didn't you?" She had obviously been hanging around with Rose Hightower too long. The woman was a terrible influence. The house she was referring to had lost a child the previous night. It was the third disappearance in less than a week and people were starting to get panicky.

The first had been a young woman, Sadie Tanner, but no one had made much of it. She was a teenager and there were rumors she had run off with a fellow from a nearby village. They became more concerned when a small boy vanished two days later. Some claimed he had been snatched from his bed, but I figured he had been taken while making a trip to the privy during the night; either way he was gone. The last one had been Rebecca, the miller's daughter. She was only thirteen, and no one believed any of it was coincidence anymore.

"To be perfectly honest," I began dishonestly, "I did not go to the miller's house, but I did happen to pass by there."

"Pretty damn close I'd imagine. You have mud on your boots." She gave my boots a disapproving stare. I was tracking mud on our dirt floor. Why she cared that mud might follow me in and get on a *dirt* floor I never understood. We were currently living in a small ramshackle cottage near the gutted remains of Castle Cameron. It was a step up from a wattle and daub hovel, but not a big enough step to have an actual floor. Ah, the luxurious life of a true aristocrat!

"Well I did In fact, walk along the river bank for a while and..." I had already given up hiding my purpose, but Penny enjoys a good interrogation.

"You walked so far you got mud all over your rear end too!" She was standing close now, and looked worried. "Why did you think you had to sneak out?"

"I didn't want you to worry."

"So waking up to find you missing from the bed, after three other people have disappeared, and then waiting up until nearly dawn, *hoping* you would be back—*that's* not supposed to worry me?!" She seemed to be taking it well.

"Hmm… I hadn't thought of it from that perspective exactly. You see the idea was that you would *not* wake up and thus when I returned in the morning you would never have suffered from all the worrying and such." It had made perfect sense when I formed my plan the day before. I had waited until after nine in the evening, and once I heard Penny's distinctive snoring I eased my way out of bed. I spent most of the night walking through the woods near the outskirts of the village, or sitting on the bank near the miller's house, hence the mud on my pants.

Penny wrapped her arms around me and leaned her head against my chest. She was upset, but not the 'throw things at you' sort of mad I had expected. "I would have gone with you if you had just told me," she said softly.

Sure, I would take my fiancée out on dark nights to hunt for a bogey-man that was snatching people away… when pigs started flying. "Listen, Penny, I know you 'would' go with me, but I can't drag you into situations like this. If something happened to you, I don't know what it would do to me."

"Turn that around and look at it from my perspective," was her reply. The conversation didn't go anywhere productive from there but eventually we gave up and went to bed. She hadn't had any more sleep than I had, despite my clever plan, so we both slept late the next morning.

As you might guess already, being the revered Count Cameron had not turned out to be quite the 'happily ever after' I had expected. Actually it was looking more and more like a lot of work. Since my grandfather's untimely demise the estate had fallen into disrepair. The old castle had been gutted by fire; my father's doing I am told. My uncle, the Duke of Lancaster, had taken over the rents and done his best to maintain the basic services required, but he had seen no need to restore the castle himself.

Now the Cameron lands consisted of one small village, and it was quite a stretch calling it a village. Mainly it was a collection of dwellings… most of the farmers traveled to Lancaster to sell their goods and barter. Penny and I had moved there shortly after I had received my title and we were currently in the most exalted building to be found. Luckily the good Duke had been keeping the rents and taxes for the past sixteen years, minus his portion of course. In practical terms that meant he had given me a sum amounting to slightly over nine hundred gold marks.

At first this had seemed a princely sum, especially on top of the two hundred I had won from the late Devon Tremont. How naive I had been! It truly was a lot of money, but the cost of restoring a feudal keep is considerable. I would have been quite happy just upgrading our cottage to a more traditional half-timbered, wattle and daub home with a field-stone foundation. Stone floors and solid walls; who could ask for more? But to my dismay, Penny had been taking lessons from Rose Hightower, who convinced her that this absolutely would not be satisfactory.

There had been a number of positives though, my parents had moved to Washbrook, which was the name of our village. They resisted my attempts to give them money but were more than willing to help in the restoration of Castle Cameron. Having a full time blacksmith in the area had been a boost to the economy all by itself. I had also hired a number of stone masons and carpenters, though I tried not to think about how much it cost.

Penny's father had also moved to Washbrook and I had spent considerable time exploring my new talents repairing the injury to his back, so he was back at work again. The money I was paying to the various workers also seemed to have sparked a boom in Washbrook's fortunes.

Over the past sixteen years the people's taxes had largely vanished with nothing returning to stimulate the economy. Now that I had returned, most of the money that had been paid over those years was now being spent to rebuild and people had new hope. At least until some of those people started vanishing.

One of my responsibilities, as their liege, was protection. Ordinarily that would mean a place to hide in time of war, the castle, and guards to patrol the roads and keep the king's peace. I had neither. The castle was a work in progress, but it was still uninhabitable. Guards? Ha! I could barely afford to pay the workmen I had already employed.

That's not to say I was broke. I still had a sizable sum stored away in a hidden strongbox, more than half of what I had received. Yet my calculations had shown me already what the restoration would cost by the time it was done, and I would have to be frugal to avoid running short before the end.

While we're on the subject, the strongbox was a work of stout craftsmanship. My father, Royce Eldridge had constructed it. Rather than being an 'iron-bound' box, this one was literally an iron strongbox. All kidding aside, he had actually made the entire thing of solid iron. In addition I had been studying magical wards, and my attempt to make it sounder had been successful. I pitied anyone that tried to steal from me. The whole thing, loaded, weighed over six hundred pounds. Breaking it open would require a team of men and with good tools and plenty of time; warded iron is amazingly strong. If someone did manage to force it, everyone in a large radius would wind up sleeping soundly for some time. Being a wizard did have its benefits.

Back to the matter at hand, protection, without guards or keep the only one left to handle our current situation was yours truly. I had no idea what might be behind the disappearances, but I was fairly confident that if I could find the perpetrators I would be able to handle them. My powers had grown during the past year. I spent several hours each day studying the books I had found, and much of the rest of my time was spent applying that knowledge.

I know, you're wondering how? With a castle to rebuild and all the other projects going on you might think I should have been pitching in—lending my back etc... The Mordecai of a year ago would have done just that, but things were different now. Every time I got involved helping with something I found more ways in which magic could assist.

Take the carpenters for example, one of their biggest time consuming tasks was drilling holes for dowels. That took a lot of time with a traditional brace and bit. I had been helping them for less than an hour before I tried applying Devon's spell to the drill bit. The one he had used to cut through my shield during our battle in Lancaster Castle. It worked brilliantly and soon I was drilling holes as quickly as you could slice butter.

That caught the eye of one of the carpenter's apprentices, who promptly asked me to do the same for him. It wasn't long before they all had me spelling their tools. The problem was that it didn't last very long, so back to the books I went. Some additional research and I was soon learning to make wards. Wards involve creating a written sort of spell, using Lycian of course. The results last much longer than magic cast with words, but they still fade over time. There are some advantages to being self-taught however. I didn't know that the art of enchanting, the crafting of permanent magical items, had been lost several hundred years previously.

Hell, I didn't know what *enchanting* was, even though it was what I was attempting. Enchanting is similar to making wards, but it takes more effort, and it lasts forever. You should be familiar with the concept, magical swords, legendary goblets, unbreakable armor, that sort of thing. The problem was no one had known how to manage it for a long time.

Being a complete novice, and unaware of the possible dangers of experimentation, I had forged ahead anyway. My first attempts were simple. I affixed wards to things and made them as strong as I could. One of the kitchen knives I did is still quite sharp, but after a few weeks I could sense the gradual weakening of the magic within it.

My next idea was to make them with a secondary ward that drew energy from the world around it, from sunlight or heat for example. That worked even better, but still the spell to draw the energy showed signs of weakening over time. Once it had worn out the primary spell that depended on it would eventually fail. The spell to use heat had a wonderful side effect though; it made anything near it cold. When I had time I planned to try it on a large box for storing food… but I digress.

The solution, when I hit on it, was surprisingly simple. The wards had to be designed in a circular pattern, such that the beginning and the end were connected. Properly done it held the magic involved within the pattern indefinitely. I did make a serious mistake at one point; once I understood how to seal magic within a ring of symbols I tried it with a spell to draw energy from heat. The combination turned out to be a bad idea. After a day the item had stored more energy than the enchantment could contain and exploded spectacularly. Fortunately the object, a small paring knife, wasn't being used at the time and no one was injured, but it still gave me chills to think what might have happened.

Anyway, I've made my point, I had been learning a lot over the past year. With each new idea came better ways of doing things and more ideas. The carpenter's tools were better than ever now and I spent a considerable amount of time at the new smithy with my father. He was a wealth of ideas regarding how things could be improved and soon we had provided the stone masons with better tools for cutting and dressing stone.

So when I had ventured out last night, I had not been unarmed. I carried the same sword my father had made for me, though I had enchanted it. The thing was so damn sharp it scared me; it could easily slice through thick wood and even metal. Dorian had tutored me some in its use and between that and my own magical protections I was reasonably sure I had little to fear from bandits or night-time kidnappers.

I had spent the better part of the night being still. Not sleeping, though I was tempted a few times. Rather I was still the way a hunter is, waiting for his prey. In the dark my eyes were largely useless but my hearing became acute, and I had other senses. I had spread my awareness as widely as possible, feeling for anything unusual in the night. I could sense animals sleeping in their dens and nighttime hunters like owls finding their food in the dark. Trees moving softly in the wind soothed my watchful spirit, while the sound of the river moving slowly by the miller's house was a balm to my ears.

I hadn't found a thing. Whether that meant the culprit was waiting for another night, or that they suspected I was watching, I had no clue.

Noon came bright and early. Surprisingly Penny still lay sleeping beside me, and I felt a twinge of guilt that she had lost so much sleep over me. She wore a soft linen sleeping gown, much to my annoyance; still it was only a small barrier. A brilliant thought occurred to me; perhaps I could make up for my misdeeds of the night before?

Her eyes popped open as my hand ran over her posterior. "What do you think you're doing?" she asked.

That was a damn stupid question, but I had learned a few things about how to talk to women since last year, "Well when I first woke I thought I must be dreaming to find such a lovely woman beside me, but now my senses tell me that you must be real." I ran my hand up the small of her back.

"Don't think you'll have me that easy," she said as she rose from the bed and started putting on her clothes. She did do me the service of letting me watch her dress—pure evil that woman.

"I still don't understand the point—we're getting married in a few months anyway, and it isn't as though we have never—well you know," I said. Since the events a year ago Penny had instituted a new policy regarding our physical relations, namely that there wouldn't be any.

"Mordecai Eldridge!" she exclaimed. Penny often used my old name when she was lecturing me. "Do you think I want to show up to my wedding in a dress sized to fit a pregnant mare?"

"I told you, I'm fairly sure I can keep that from happening, if you'll just let me..."

"Don't you dare! I don't want you experimenting with—with—*that!* What if I became barren?" she declared.

"No, no—I wouldn't do anything to you! It would be purely a mechanical thing, a sort of shield to keep..."

"Don't mess with that either! I like your tools as they are and I don't trust you not to mess something up. I do want to have children after all." Clearly we had some trust issues concerning my magic.

"Fine, fine, I can wait," I replied. I wasn't really sure about that, but the argument was old. No need to go over it all again, I'd just have to bide my time and catch her at an opportune moment. Hope springs eternal. "I'm going back out tonight," I added. I figured I'd go ahead and get that out in the open ahead of time.

"I know," she answered easily, which set off a warning in my head.

"I understand your feelings, but I'm responsible for these people and I can't just sit around and do nothing," I said defensively.

"You're right."

"I'll take every precaution, and I'll be armed so I don't think I'll be in any real danger," I continued.

"I'm sure you will do everything you can."

I glared at her suspiciously, "Something tells me that your words and your intentions are two different things."

"Nope," she said, "I realize I can't keep you here when there's something dark prowling the night." She did her best to make her voice sound deep and ominous.

"Well—good then," I said. Unusual as it was, it felt good to win one now and then. After dressing we went our separate ways. She had been busy with the architect lately; overseeing the construction of the kitchens and living quarters. I spent the afternoon helping my father. He had been working to produce a serviceable portcullis for the gatehouse.

The day passed quickly and that evening I calmly got ready for my night out. I didn't have anything resembling proper armor but I hardly needed it with my magical shields. Instead I wore dark hunting leathers, buckling my sword on over them. I also carried a staff.

The staff warrants special attention. After discovering the secret of permanently enchanting things I thought I would try to recreate something I had read about in Vestrius' journal. The specific details regarding what sort of staves wizards carried long ago was lost, along with the art of enchanting. Still I was drawn to the idea and I decided to try and create something similar to the descriptions I had read in Vestrius' journal.

Supposedly the ancients had used them to channel and focus their powers to greater effect. I had no idea how they accomplished it but I tried a few things of my own anyway. The first was to enchant the head of the staff so that it would hold any spell I put there indefinitely, sort of a flexible enchantment. I could light it and not worry about maintaining the spell. Potentially I could do other things as well, but that was all I had thought of so far. The second thing I had done was encircle the entire length with a sort of hollow shell of wards and runes. I found that if I channeled my strength along the shaft I could direct my power out to much greater distances, or focus it more powerfully at short range.

Honestly I hadn't had a need to do either so far, but I had great hopes that it would prove useful eventually. Plus it looked pretty nifty. "I'm off to save the village honey!" I shouted toward our bedroom, hoping to provoke a laugh.

"Ok, be careful," she yelled back calmly, not even bothering to step out and give me a good-bye kiss. Obviously she had resigned herself to the situation. I stepped outside, looking around and trying to decide which way to head first. Penny showed up a moment later, walking around from the other side of the house.

She was wearing a soft gambeson and a long chain shirt. She also carried a bow and a slender sword. "Um… Penny, what are you doing?" I inquired.

"I'm going out to hunt for evil-doers," she answered casually.

"You're not coming with me," I said firmly. Once in a while a man just has to put his foot down.

"That's fine, you go that way, I'll work my way south." The smile on her face was positively diabolical.

I rephrased myself, "No… I mean you're staying here."

"Nope," she replied.

She was missing the subtleties of my argument so I decided to try something more direct, *"Shibal"* I said, using a spell that should put her soundly to sleep.

Penny held up the amulet I had made her a few months previously, "Forget about something?" I had made it to protect her from mental assaults such as she had endured previously… such as I had just attempted.

"Goddammit, you're not going out there alone!"

"Fine, you can come with me, but try not to make noise, I don't want to scare them off," she answered. Her attitude was one of indifference.

"This isn't your job Penny," I said stubbornly.

"Like hell it's not! You may be the damned Count, but I'm about to be your wife. If you are responsible then I'm in this just as deeply as you are. Now you can go your own way or we can go together… what's it going to be?" she said with resolve. She could be really beautiful when she was determined, but don't tell her that, she's hard enough to deal with already.

In the end I let her come with me. There really wasn't any alternative, other than tying her up, which I did briefly consider. We headed north of the village, since all the missing persons had lived on that side, and found a nice quiet spot in the forest. Once we got under the trees the darkness intensified; neither moon nor the stars could be seen.

"Oof!" Penny had just tripped over a root and almost went down in a sprawl. I stifled the urge to laugh. I could have provided light but I had the wonderful excuse that we were trying to avoid tipping off our quarry. My magesight gave me a distinct advantage in the dark.

"Stop it," she said.

"What?"

"You're laughing at me… I can tell," she answered.

"I was just wondering how you're going to see to shoot that bow if something happens." It was so dark there weren't even shadows. She declined to answer so I dropped the subject and we kept walking. Soon enough we had reached my spot.

It was a location without anything to recommend it. There was nothing particularly comfortable about it, but it was in a place where, by stretching my senses I could cover most of the area that had lost people. We sat down, back to back and I began to relax. The art of sensing a large area requires a lot of effort, but most of that goes into *not* tensing up. I had to calm myself and let my mind expand, feeling as much as I could around me.

The first hour was the worst, after that we both gave up thinking about our daily lives and it got easier. I wasn't sure but Penny might have gone to sleep. There really wasn't anything else for her to do, and nothing could sneak up on us as we were. I could feel a field mouse moving around half a mile away.

Another hour drew slowly by and I began to wonder if this would be a repeat of the previous night. My thoughts were drifting, but my mind was still alert. If anything had moved I would have felt it, but I had no idea what I was looking for… I would learn that later. Penny had begun snoring, which probably hid the sound of its approach. Even if she had been silent I'm not sure I would have noticed. It was very quiet.

The first indication things were not as they seemed was the sound of a twig snapping not five feet behind me. The sound would not have been so surprising, except I knew there was nothing there, no animals, no life at all. I came awake suddenly and then I felt it, an absolute emptiness. It was as if something had carved a void in the air behind me, a place where nothing existed.

I stood and whirled about, the darkness was absolute so my eyes were useless; yet I could feel the empty place with my extra senses. I reached for my sword but a hand grabbed my arm. It went through my shield as if it didn't exist and when it touched me the world changed. Everything vanished—my sight was gone, and I could sense nothing but a vast void drawing me in. It was absorbing the light within me, and crushing the light from the world as well. A few moments longer and I would have been lost.

Something knocked me sideways, breaking the contact, and the world rushed back in at me. I could sense Penny there, grappling with something so black my mind could not reveal it, something that was sapping her energy. Her life force wavered in front of me, being drawn rapidly away, like a candle guttering in a strong wind.

"Lyet," I spoke, conjuring a ball of light, and then I could see it. In the stark light I saw Penny struggling with Sadie Tanner. Ordinarily Penny would have easily overpowered the smaller girl, but now her strength was waning quickly. Whatever this thing was, it was a mockery of the girl we had known. It looked like Sadie, but the emptiness revealed by my magesight made it clear that she was nowhere within the creature we faced now.

"Sadie?" Penny exclaimed.

"I don't know what that is… but it isn't Sadie," I yelled back, and then I continued in Lycian, *"Stirret ni Pyrenn!"* A line of fire lanced from my outstretched hand. I had learned to focus my power in such a way that it would burn a hole through the thing—yet my fire disappeared the moment it touched the thing.

Sadie, the thing, whatever it was… looked at me then, a hideous grin on its face. With a shove it threw Penny back six or seven feet, to strike a tree, and then it reached for the ball of light I had created. As it touched my spell the light vanished, winking out as suddenly as it had appeared. I felt a sense of shock. This thing, whatever Sadie had become, consumed my magic as quickly as I had summoned it.

I drew my sword and lashed out at her even as the light disappeared. I hoped cold steel would do what magic could not. I felt the blade meet resistance and then it passed onward. Stepping back I conjured more light. My eyes were wide now; fear had replaced my confidence.

The new light showed a hideous scene; Sadie Tanner's body lay in two parts upon the ground, both still moving, struggling to reach me. I tried another fire spell and it disappeared as quickly as the first. The moment my magic touched the grotesque thing on the ground the fire winked out of existence. "Penny! Are you ok?" I called.

"Yeah, I just hit my head," she answered, sounding tired and disoriented.

I moved toward her, making a wide circle around the creature still writhing on the earth. "I think we found it," I said. What an understatement… it had found us. A thought occurred to me and I checked my blade. To my relief the magic within it still glowed in my sight. Why hadn't it been extinguished as well? *This shit just keeps getting weirder,* I thought.

I reached Penny and ran my hand over her, making sure she was still in one piece. As a precaution I examined the landscape around us with my mind, and this time I was looking for holes, empty places where nothing existed. Finding none I began to relax. "I think this is the only one," I said to Penny.

"You don't sound so sure of yourself," she replied.

"I'm not. That thing walked up on us without me sensing anything." I created several more globes of light, spacing them around us at a distance of ten yards each. We wouldn't be surprised again, and then I started thinking.

I took a moment to methodically cut Sadie's body into several more parts, separating arms and legs from the rest of her. There was very little blood, and what did seep forth from the severed pieces was thick and black, like old blood that has already begun to congeal. My sword still showed no sign of being affected by her ability to consume magic. I tried my staff as well, poking the torso, and its enchantments were unaffected as well, yet when I conjured a light globe near the body it went out like a lamp that had been doused. *Maybe it has something to do with the structure of enchantments,* I thought. To test my theory I set a light within the head of my staff, where it would be held by my variable enchantment, and then I touched the torso with it.

Nothing happened, the light persisted; whatever it was, it could eat magic, but not enchantments. I could only guess that the rigid structure that contained their magic also protected them from being absorbed like my normal spells had been.

Penny spoke up, "As interesting as this thing is, we can't leave a bunch of twitching body parts lying around here." I loved her pragmatic nature.

"Alright, I have an idea," I replied. I gathered up some dead wood and leaves, piling them around the still moving body parts. Using my power I set the makeshift pyre ablaze, 'til the wood was burning brightly. The fire consumed the flesh that lay among the wood, and what magic couldn't accomplish normal fire did. We continued to add fresh wood until there was nothing left of Sadie Tanner's body. I learned an interesting lesson that night… it takes a lot of wood to burn a body completely to ash.

"What was it?" Penny asked while we watched, but I didn't have an answer. With more questions than answers we headed back home, too tired to do more that night.

CHAPTER 2

The sun rose entirely too early. I wish I could have found the fellow who arranged that, he obviously had a poor sense of humor. Despite our late night Penny and I both woke not long after the sun came up. I think we were both anxious.

Sleep and some early morning thinking convinced me that there had to be more of those things out there. To begin with, Sadie hadn't been like that before she disappeared, and something had to have taken her. If something similar had happened to the others that meant there were at least three more of those things out there… that we *knew* of. It was a chilling thought.

The only good news was that no one else had been taken, though I felt sure that there would have been, if we hadn't encountered the creature first. Penny and I discussed what had happened but neither of us could understand it. In the end we decided to keep it to ourselves to avoid a panic.

I wrote two letters, one to the Duke of Lancaster, detailing everything that had happened, the second I addressed to Dorian. I hoped he would be free to come stay with us for a while, if magic wasn't effective against this new creature his sword would certainly be more useful. After that I went looking to see if I could find a farmer or someone heading toward Lancaster.

As things worked out there wasn't anyone planning a trip that day, but I ran across Joe McDaniel and he offered to go if it was urgent. Joe was a transplant from Gododdin, the neighboring kingdom. He didn't talk much about his past, or his reasons for leaving, but I gathered it must involve the change in government there.

Technically Gododdin wasn't a kingdom anymore. The royal family had been thoroughly exterminated some time before I was born and the country was now a theocracy, controlled by a cult known as the Children of Mal'goroth. Joe had never had anything good to say about them.

"I don't mind going for ya Lord Cameron," he told me, "I was planning to go in a few days anyway, to order a new cask of ale." Joe was working to build a tavern, the first Washbrook had ever seen. At the moment it consisted of a few benches scattered around his house where he sold beer in the evenings. Being a beer enthusiast myself I had thoroughly supported his efforts.

"Thanks Joe," I said, clapping him on the shoulder. Once he had gone I began walking toward my father's smithy. Someday soon I was going to have to start hiring a staff of some sort, such as regular messengers. It was quickly becoming apparent that I could no longer do everything myself anymore.

"You looked troubled son," my father commented after I came in. He was a quiet man, which might be why he was so perceptive.

"There was trouble last night," I explained, and then I told him what had occurred the previous evening. I also described the creature's effect on my magic. Dad didn't have any magical talent of his own but he was very intelligent and I had come to appreciate his advice when I had been testing different ways to enchant things.

My story alarmed him, but you would have had to know him to tell. He had always been a difficult man to read. Rather than spend his time talking about his worries, he moved on to practical matters. "Looks like we have a lot of work to do," he said and then he walked over and drew out the stack of sheets he used when he was planning a design for something.

Naturally I was curious. "You've already got an idea?"

"You said when it touched you everything went black right?" he replied.

"Yes."

"But… Penny was still able to fight it," he reminded me.

Damn! I hadn't thought of that. The merest touch had rendered me insensible, but although it had been steadily drawing her life out she had retained the ability to struggle.

He went on, "And it wasn't able to draw the magic out of your enchantments, like the sword."

At last it came clear to me. "The amulet! It must have protected her mind even while the creature was sucking the life out of her." That thought had a lot of implications; it meant I had a way to protect people, at least partially. Penny's amulet wouldn't have saved her life, but people would be much more difficult to prey upon if they weren't immediately paralyzed at the first touch of these creatures.

"Not just the amulet Mordecai, you could enchant your clothes, or armor, to more fully protect yourself. Anything to keep them from touching you," he replied.

"There's no way I could enchant enough armor or whatnot for everyone in the village, it would take years!" I argued, for the thought was daunting.

"Not them! For you boy! If something happens to you, none of us will be able to protect ourselves." He gave me a look that spoke volumes, "You've got to start thinking like a lord and less like a footman, you're important now."

I didn't completely agree with him on that, but in any case there was no way we could afford to produce armor for everyone. Besides, no one could work, farm, cook or anything else while wearing armor all day. The idea was ludicrous, but I still wouldn't give up on the idea that we could do something for them. "Alright, I agree with you to a point, but we've still got to do something for the people."

"If I could make enough amulets..."

"You did that in silver and I'm not really set up for that sort of thing, not if you plan to make dozens," he responded.

"It doesn't have to be silver; we could do them in iron."

"That makes it easier, still it will take quite a bit of time, and the shape of it was very intricate. Could you change the shape?" Royce asked.

"Only if we engraved it instead, the symbols are the important part. When I made Penny's I made the entire pendant from the symbols before I infused it," I replied. I knew my father didn't have the right tools to do intricate engraving.

"Hah! I have it," he exclaimed. My hopes went up, for when my father set his mind to something he always found a way.

"What?" I asked.

"If you can borrow Penny's amulet, we'll make a mold, then we can cast as many as we need. How long does it take for you to do your magicking?" Royce waved his hands around comically while swaying side to side as he said this.

I gave him a hard stare, but inwardly he had me smiling, "Not long, maybe half an hour each if they're already formed." After that we got busy, though I had to do some talking to get Penny's necklace away from her, she seemed to think I planned to take advantage of her. I had no clue where she would have gotten an idea like that.

Dad set things up and assured me he would have the molds ready in another day or two, after that he would be able to make them faster than I could enchant them. I worried it might not be soon enough.

I left after that, he didn't need me so I got out of his way. I spent the morning helping the carpenters again but I was interrupted in mid-afternoon when Dorian arrived. "Ho! Mordecai!" he called up to me. At that moment I was standing on some scaffolding on the exterior of the keep.

I was relieved to see him but I hadn't expected him to arrive so soon. I yelled down to him, "How did you get here so quickly?" I began climbing down so we could speak more easily.

"I left as soon as I got your message this morning." Dorian was the most reliable of friends, the sort of man who would walk through fire if he thought it would help someone. He had already saved my life at least once before. "The description in your letter was a bit vague, but I got the impression you're dealing with some sort of monster?"

I hadn't known what to write so I hadn't been very specific, "Yeah, let's not talk about it out here. I haven't figured out what to tell the people yet and I don't want to start a panic."

He blinked at me, "Seriously, a monster?" I could see the gears in his head turning, conjuring up creatures from childhood fairy tales. I also noted that he had come geared for war. He wore chainmail, not just the hauberk… but the leggings as well, complete with a steel cap and aventail. He had also brought both his sword and a long spear.

"I see you took me at my word. Did you really need the barding though? That must be a real pain for your horse." Barding was the term for the armor that partially covered his steed, a great black destrier.

"How should I know? I'd rather come to the party overdressed than arrive and find out later that I should have worn my chainmail knickers!" he answered. As usual his joke wasn't that funny, but I felt a bit less burdened seeing him in full armor. Dorian was the deadliest man I had ever known, and I was glad he was my friend.

Since his horse was tired (wouldn't you be after carrying all that?), we walked him over to the makeshift stables and I helped him clean and groom the massive beast. It wasn't a chore for me as I loved horses almost as much as people. While we combed him down I had a thought, "Take your armor off too, if you're going to help there are some things I can do to improve your chances."

"I'm afraid to ask," he replied, but he started shucking the armor. Once it was off he handed me a very heavy pile of mail. Luckily I was still in good shape from helping Dad now and then at the smithy. As big a man as Dorian Thornbear was the armor probably weighed around eighty pounds or more.

"Bring your sword and spear too," I added.

"I wasn't planning on leaving them behind." He gave me a look that indicated I was crazy to think he would walk about unarmed. "What are you planning to do to my armor? It's very expensive you know." He eyed me suspiciously. I never understood why he didn't trust me.

"I won't hurt your precious mail, never fear. I'm just going to improve it." I tried to give him my best 'wise and mysterious wizard' look, but he merely shook his head.

We had reached my house at this point, although according to Penny it barely deserves the name. I took him around to the back where a small shed served as my workshop. It didn't have all the neat toys Dad kept around his smithy, but I didn't need most of them for my work. My skill with magic allowed me to do a lot of things without recourse to tools. I stretched his hauberk out flat on the table.

"Just be careful, Dad gave me that," Dorian said. His father had died the year before, a fact neither of us liked to remember. I had loved Gram Thornbear too.

"When I'm done I doubt you'll ever have to worry about anyone damaging it again," I assured him. "Would you mind fetching some water? This will take a while and I'm thirsty already." He set off to find a pitcher and I got to work. My request was half to get him out of the way so I could get started. I wasn't sure how he would react.

I took down the papers I had my notes written on, though I had done a lot of enchanting lately the designs were complicated and I didn't want to make a mistake. This one I had tested once before so I was fairly confident that it would perform as intended. Leaning over the mail I extended a finger and began tracing it along the metal rings; as it went the metal changed color, from dull grey to gold.

Dorian returned with the water, but he didn't interrupt me since he knew I was concentrating. A long while later I looked up from my work, "Still got that water?"

"Sure. For a thirsty man you took long enough to stop for a drink," he handed me a cup.

"How long has it been?" I asked.

"You've been talking to yourself and stroking my armor for about three hours now. It'll be getting dark soon," he replied.

"Damn! I didn't even realize. I'm sorry Dorian I've been poor company."

"Don't worry about it, whatever you're doing must be important. I just hope my mail still works properly." He was looking at it over my shoulder.

"Well I'm done with the hauberk now, take a look," I gestured to the table. The mail coat was gleaming. I had removed the gold coloring, which had been a temporary measure to keep from losing track of where I was in the process. The entire coat glimmered now, as though each ring had just been polished while to my eyes patterns of symbols and words still covered it. Dorian wouldn't be able to see those.

"Well it's really pretty, but battle isn't about beauty. Will it still stop a sword?"

"My friend, it will stop everything short of a ballista. It won't rust and you'll never need to oil it again," mentally I hoped that it would improve the smell as well. If you've ever been around men wearing chain armor you know what I mean, rust and sweat are not a good combination. "More importantly, it should also prevent the thing I ran into last night from sucking the life out of you."

A voice came from the doorway, "Aren't you boys getting hungry?" Penny had returned and she carried a basket. I was pretty sure it held food of some sort.

"In a little while, I still have to finish here." I motioned toward Dorian's weapons, his steel cap, and the chain leggings.

"I'm certainly hungry… I haven't eaten since lunch," Dorian answered. It was rare for him to miss a meal.

"At least one of you has some sense then. How much longer are you going to be Mort?" She looked at me questioningly. Lately she had been a bit overbearing when it came to making sure I took breaks and ate food.

"Not long, an hour or two."

"Alright... Dorian if you would be so kind?" She held her arm out and he took it, escorting her into the house like some noble lady. I supposed she soon would be.

I went back to work, starting on the steel cap first. I didn't think it would take too long and soon I was wrapped up in my task as I lost track of time. I finished the cap and leggings and began working on the sword before Penny returned.

"Mort?"

"Huh?" I looked up; Penny was a bit fuzzy around the edges.

"You need to eat, you can finish this later," she said this gently but I had a hunch she was just warming up.

"I can't stop in the middle or I'll have to start all over. Actually while I'm at it go get your chain shirt. I can do it next." I had already returned to my work on the sword. She didn't answer and by the time I looked again she was gone.

A while later I had finished. It was fully dark now but that hadn't been a problem, I had put several globes of magical light around the shop. I wanted to start on Penny's chain shirt but she hadn't brought it back so I went looking for her.

I found her in the house, sitting by the fire. "Where's your chain shirt?" I asked with a fuzzy expression. You would think I'd have more sense, but I've been practicing my stupid.

"Do you know what time it is?" she asked.

What a silly question, I thought, *any fool can see that it's dark.* "It's nighttime," I replied.

"Mort it's almost midnight, and you still haven't eaten. Did you even eat lunch?" She was giving me her best worried expression, but I wasn't fooled. That's just how they get you to lower your guard. Then I remembered what I had planned to do.

"Oh! You're right; I've got to get ready. Where's Dorian? I'll have to eat while we walk I guess." My eyes were a bit bleary, probably from lack of food.

Penny got up and taking me by the hand she led me to the table, coaxing me into sitting down. "You're not going anywhere tonight. You're tired and hungry, and probably too dumb to do much good out there right now anyway."

"No I'm…," I started to reply but she shoved a roll into my open mouth. I might have complained but it was good so I started chewing without thinking. It was all downhill after that… the roll had a conversation with my stomach and the two of them convinced me that they needed a lot more company down there. I made short work of the cold cuts and the rest of the bread. After I had stuffed myself I felt drowsy.

"Thanks honey, I should listen to you more often." Penny scowled at me. I had broken the first rule of women. Never compliment them when they're worried or mad. I didn't let her start on me, though. "Where's Dorian? He can go with me tonight and I'll do the work on your chain shirt tomorrow."

"I already told you, you're not going out tonight. Dorian can stand guard," she replied, hands on her hips.

I gave her a long look, "If something happens to someone tonight I'm responsible."

"You're already responsible for everyone. Things will happen no matter what you do, but going out there like this will only get you killed. Where will those people be then?" Her features softened as she spoke, "Come to bed, Dorian will watch tonight. He's already patrolling anyway."

I should have known—they had already conspired against me. "I won't be able to sleep," I said petulantly.

Penny leaned over and kissed me. Not one of the chaste kisses I had been getting recently either, these were the sort of kisses that made a fellow wake up and say 'hello'… nor was I immune to her charms. "Come to bed now and I'll make it worth your while," she whispered softly in my ear.

I had no fight left in me so I surrendered and went to bed. I couldn't figure out why she was no longer worried about waiting 'til the wedding, but I wasn't about to look a gift horse in the mouth. Bad analogy, I wasn't about to look a—wait never mind, that analogy would have been even more inappropriate. My head was reeling… and the bed seemed incredibly soft after my long day. I decided I really should listen to her more often.

"I'll be right back, I need to put the food away," she said, leaving the room. I closed my eyes to wait on her and when she returned a few minutes later I was snoring soundly. "Works every time," Penny smiled and crawled in beside me. I never even realized I had been cheated 'til morning came.

CHAPTER 3

Marcus Lancaster stretched lazily, enjoying the touch of satin on his skin. He looked over at his companion, the Lady Eleanor Strickland. She was a lovely girl, with long blond tresses and golden eyes that nearly matched her hair. *Talented as well,* he thought quietly to himself.

The night before had been a blur of wine and dancing, which was a common occurrence in the capital of Lothion. Albamarl was a large city and many of the nobility kept residences there, to better keep up with the important social doings around the King's court.

"Time to be off," Marc said to himself, rising silently. Dawn was getting close and it wouldn't do to be caught in the young lady's bedroom by the morning servants. He quickly donned his clothes and gathered up his scattered belongings. Eleanor didn't wake; she had had a long night.

A few minutes later he was walking down a narrow lane that ran between the houses in that part of the city. The street proper was on the other side of the houses, this way being used mainly for servants and deliveries. Marc knew his route well; he had already visited a number of noble houses over the past few months. Being the son of a duke had its advantages and he had enjoyed a large number of dalliances with the young ladies of Albamarl. Despite what Mordecai had once thought regarding Penny, Marcus never took advantage of maids or other female staff, he restricted himself to women of noble birth.

It wasn't that he looked down on the lower class, but he felt intuitively that it was wrong. A woman of low birth could hardly say no to a duke's son. Such a thing would be an abuse, even if the lasses were willing, and he had no problem finding plenty of prey among girls of his own class anyway.

He started whistling to himself as he walked. The sun was starting to peek over the horizon and it looked to be another beautiful day. *I wonder how much longer I should stay in Albamarl?* he thought to himself. After the events last year he had taken a new interest in the future. Lord Thornbear's death had made him painfully aware that his own father would not live forever. Someday he would have to take on the mantle of Duke of Lancaster.

Marc originally came to Albamarl to court and woo, being the heir apparent meant he had a duty to find a wife before he got too old. Although his original intention had been pure, he soon found that none of the noblewomen he met could keep his attention, well not for much longer than a week or two. As a dutiful son he kept searching, and before long he realized that he enjoyed the chase more than the conclusion. Life is hard sometimes.

He was walking along, already wondering where he would find his next conquest, when he heard the sounds of a scuffle. The first noises were harsh thumps, the sound of someone taking a beating, but they were followed by a sickening wet sound. Rushing around the corner he saw three men in a dark alley.

One was standing, looking around anxiously, while the second rifled through the pockets of a young man. The fellow on the ground was leaking blood at an alarming rate. "Cease and desist! I'll have the watch here in a moment!" Marc shouted, reaching for his sword.

It wasn't there; he had left it in the cloak room at the party the night before. *Shit!* he thought. The man standing lookout charged him, a heavy truncheon in his hand. *That's probably what produced the thumping noises*, he observed. He found himself leaping backward to avoid the other man's clumsy swings. Timing them he waited 'til his foe over extended himself, and then he stepped in and delivered a heavy left hook to the thug's temple. The man stumbled, his legs having turned to jelly, and fell. Marc kicked him solidly in the head as he tried to rise.

Snatching up the truncheon he looked for the second assailant, but that one had apparently run when his friend went down. Their victim didn't move. "Hey! Are you alright?" he asked, kneeling beside the fallen man. The fellow had been stabbed in the gut and blood was still pumping sluggishly from the wound. It didn't look good.

"Someone help me! Get the watch, someone find a doctor!" A few curious folk had stuck their heads out when they had seen the fight was over. Marc called to them for help, but he knew it was useless, the man on the ground had little time left. It was doubtful even a doctor could save him at this point. As he looked down at him the fellow opened his eyes and groaned.

"It hurts..." The injured man's eyes were wide with pain, yet he obviously couldn't see clearly. Pain and loss of blood seemed to have robbed him of his senses. "Momma, I couldn't find the fish—I'm sorry." Finally Marc noticed the scattered food on the ground. Apparently the victim had been returning from the market.

Something about the pure ordinariness of it struck a chord within Marc. Groceries seemed like a silly thing to die for, yet this man had been stabbed for nothing more than that and whatever change had been in his pocket. He had probably been an honest man; he wore the silver star of Millicenth, the goddess of the Evening Star. Without thinking Marc reached out to touch the star, "Please Goddess… if there is a way to save this poor man, show me."

Marc had never been one to pray before, outside of weekly services. He knew little of the proper ways to beseech his goddess, but he knew nothing else to do. His emotions built and he felt hot tears forming in his eyes. Still he clutched the silver star, "Please Lady, if this man meant anything—help him. I know I'm not worthy, but this man needs you." It might have been his imagination but he felt a warm glow form around him, and then he saw her.

She was wrapped in a luminescent dress, like starlight made into cloth. Silver hair and bright eyes accented a face so beautiful that he felt like crying at the sight of her. "Long have I waited for this day, Marcus Lancaster. We have much to do," she said with a voice that reminded him of music.

"I don't know what you mean Lady; I just need to save this man. He has wronged no one and does not deserve to die." Despite the beauty of the goddess in front of him he could still feel the man's life fading under his hand.

"If you would save him you must give over your worldly life. Devote yourself to me. I will show you the path of the righteous and through you I will shine my light into the empty hearts of men." She drew closer as she said this, 'til it seemed her face was mere inches from his own.

Marc could feel her beauty like a physical thing and was filled with a sense of the divine, a holy radiance such as he had never known. It flowed into the cracks in his heart, the empty places. The eternal solitude that every human knows from birth… was gone. For the first time in his life he felt complete in her presence. "I will my Lady," he answered, "If you will let me I will serve you all the days of my life, forsaking all else."

"Open your heart to me child," she said, but he had already done so and he felt her pouring into him, like liquid light into a dark vessel. The world vanished into a sensation of such joy and power that he was overwhelmed. Opening his eyes again he became aware of the world in a new way. Light filled everything, and below him he could see the light fading from the man on the ground.

Marc opened his hand and placed it over the wound. He could feel her power flowing through him and as he watched the blood stopped and the flesh closed up again without even a scar left behind. The man on the ground was watching him now, eyes wide, as though he were staring at an angel. "You healed me," he said simply, touching his unblemished stomach.

Marc spoke, "You were healed by the grace of the Evening Star. Her mercy saved your life. Remember that and live with her in your thoughts and actions." Then he stood up and looked around, a crowd had gathered. People were murmuring in amazement. "The Goddess has blessed this man, and she will bless us all, if we but let her," he said. Unable to bear their continued stares he worked his way through the crowd and headed for his father's city home.

First you must go to my temple, to present yourself before the priests there. They must hear my words and prepare to give you a place among them. The goddess spoke within his mind. "Yes my Lady," he answered and then he turned to head for the temple of Millicenth. He had no more doubts about the future.

—⋅—

I woke early the next morning. I had slept more soundly than I had in weeks and for a change I felt fresh and rested. Penny lay beside me, snoring softly… for once. I watched her for a few minutes, marveling at her beauty. I still didn't understand what she saw in me, but I hoped her eyesight never improved. Remembering her promise from the night before, I decided to see if it was still on the table for discussion.

I eased closer to her and began kissing her neck softly, while my hands—well let's just say they roamed a lot. The general idea was to get her into such a state that she would be unlikely to refuse me when she finally awoke. It seemed to be working. When her eyes opened I covered her mouth with my own, hoping a kiss would seal the bargain. For a moment it worked, I could feel her excitement, but then she pushed me back.

"Oh you play dirty!" she exclaimed as she untangled herself from the bed sheets.

"You can't blame a guy for trying." I was in a good mood despite her strength of will. Was she panting? It might have been my imagination.

"You keep that up and we'll be in separate beds 'til the wedding day," she retorted. I was pretty sure she was bluffing.

"You did trick me last night. That was hardly fair," I smiled at her.

"What isn't fair—is you working yourself to death in front of me."

She might have a point there, but it reminded me of my plans. "Oh that's right! Where's your chain shirt? I'll do it first, and then I can go see how Dad is doing with the molds."

"Molds?"

I hadn't had a chance to tell her about our plans yet so I filled her in. She liked the idea and agreed to come along to the smithy with me so that Dad could use her pendant for the molds. Her only condition was that I eat breakfast before I got started. She seemed to think I would starve myself to death if I didn't eat in front of her.

Dorian came in while we were eating. He looked tired. "Got any more of that?" He motioned toward my food.

"Sure," Penny said and she got up to make him a plate.

"You look like shit," I opined.

"This is what you looked like last night, so don't get too cocky," he responded. "I spent the entire night looking for your monsters."

"Well I'm glad you did, I slept better than I have in days," I tried to sound grateful. He ate with us and then I got busy working on Penny's chain shirt. Penny went ahead and took her pendant over to my father before she went to see the architect.

"What are you going to tell people?" Dorian asked. I had just finished with her chainmail byrnie and was preparing to head over to the smithy.

"I don't know. I'm not sure what's worse, panic or fear of the unknown."

"I spoke to some of the townspeople this morning; right after the sun came up. They're worried," Dorian added. "If they don't hear something soon they may panic anyway. They haven't failed to notice me, especially now that my armor sparkles like this. People know you called me for a reason."

Dorian could be awfully smart sometimes. It was easy to take him for granted but he was a careful thinker. "What do I tell them? That some sort of undead monsters are prowling around?"

"You're their lord, they need your leadership. Explain things to them and maybe they'll surprise you," he commented.

"No one else here is capable of fighting those things..." I started.

Dorian cut me off, "You are mistaken if you think that's how this works. Where do you think the Duke of Lancaster gets his power?"

"What does that have to do with anything?"

"Answer me," Dorian said stubbornly.

"The King of course," it seemed obvious to me.

"Wrong. His power comes from those that serve him. A duke, or a count...," he looked at me pointedly, "...receives his power from those who do his bidding. Without them he is just another man."

"I'm a wizard, and they still can't deal with those things," I countered.

Dorian stood up and walked over to a small tree that stood by the house, drawing his sword he swung at it. His newly enchanted blade cut through the sapling as if it were made of paper. It toppled slowly over, narrowly missing my outdoor table. Dorian looked a bit surprised; at a guess I would say he hadn't tested the sword since my efforts to enchant it the day before. He paused, then remembered his train of thought, "Who cut that tree down?" he asked.

Idiot, I thought, *He cuts down my pear tree and then asks me who did it?* "I'm telling Penny," I replied sarcastically, as if we were still kids.

He gulped nervously, but went on, "Come on Mort; answer me... who cut the tree down?"

"When Penny asks I'm telling her it was you, but it was my enchantment that made it possible." I took a sip of water, looking at him over the rim of the cup.

"Who's hand held the blade?" he replied.

"Yours my good friend, it was definitely yours," I said, nearly laughing, sometimes I crack myself up.

Dorian threw the sword on the ground, "Can it cut a tree down now? Get up sword! Go cut that tree down for me!" He was yelling at the blade and pointing at another small tree.

I was beginning to wonder at his sanity. "Come on Dorian… calm down. Obviously the blade can't do anything if you don't hold it. Well technically, I might be able to make it work without holding it—but I think that's not your point is it?"

"Damn right it's not! *I* held the sword. *I* cut the tree down—with this hand," he held his large hand up, making a fist. "And who made the sword, before you enchanted it? Who built this house? Look around you! Everything you see was made by plain old everyday people, *your* people! You can improve on some things with magic, surely, but you are just one man. True power lies in the people around you. As the Count di'Cameron you have been given their trust, it is up to you to use it wisely. Hide everything from them; treat them as children and you throw away your power, you cheapen their strength. Talk to them, trust them, let them help you and you will learn what true strength is."

I had never heard Dorian give such an impassioned speech before, and it cut through my arrogance, touching my heart. "Dorian, you're right." For a moment he reminded me so strongly of his father that it almost brought a tear to my eye. I got up and hugged him. "As long as I have friends like you things will always work out. If it weren't for you and Penny I don't know how I would manage all this."

"I'm glad you realize that," he answered gruffly. He always got a bit uncomfortable when I was overly emotional.

"Let's go see how far Dad is with the pendants, maybe we can help him. When they're ready I'll talk to everyone. I won't tell them 'til I can at least give them some small measure of protection," I said.

"At least you have a plan," Dorian replied. "Any plan is better than none." Together we went to the smithy, there was much to do.

CHAPTER 4

The next few days passed by uneventfully. Dorian took to sleeping during the mornings, since he spent the nights patrolling. His speech had made an impact on me, so I let him do it, while I used the days to make enchanted pendants for the townsfolk. After four days I had over sixty of them ready, which I figured would be enough for everyone to have one. I intended to keep at it though; there would be more people as time went on.

The keep was still a work in progress, but Penny told me that the living areas were finished, so we started moving in. Much of the rest of the interior was still open timbers and unfinished stone, but at least we would have a better place to live. Many of the townsfolk pitched in to help us move our things and get settled, so I took the opportunity to speak to them afterward.

"I appreciate everything you have all done to help us, but there's something I need to talk about. If you could gather your families here this evening, I'd like to tell everyone at once." I felt a bit odd giving speeches, but I guess it comes with the territory. People nodded and soon they had all left to find the others.

Penny spoke up, "Are you sure about this Mort?"

"I have to do it—it's not fair to keep them in the dark."

She had a pensive expression. "If you tell them about Sadie Tanner things could get ugly, assuming they believe you."

She had a point. I hadn't thought that part through fully. Sadie Tanner's friends and family would likely be upset and confused. Scratch that, if I told them I had dismembered and burned their daughter because I 'thought' she was a ravening undead monster—they'd go bat-shit crazy. There was no proof, and no one had heard of such creatures before. Even the relatively superstitious common folk would be more prone to believe I had committed a crime as opposed to self-defense.

"I'll tell them it was a man, but we didn't recognize him. If this gets worse they'll be more able to accept the truth later on. If it doesn't we'll just have to find another way to break the news to her family later on," I said.

My father came over while we waited, bringing the newly made pendants. I was glad for his presence and support, the thought of giving a speech had made me nervous. "Don't worry about it Mordecai, just tell them the truth and it will be alright," he whispered in my ear as people started filing into the room.

We were standing in the great hall, or rather what would be the great hall. Presently it was more like a courtyard, it had been framed in but the roof was still absent. Sunlight filtered down between the towers and onto the wood floor beneath me. It was a beautiful day, belying the dark news I had to deliver.

Once everyone had arrived I stood on a chair. It was the best I could manage. "I've called you all here to talk about the disappearances," I started simply. "I don't know if anyone has noticed, but I've been spending a lot of nights outside, watching and waiting. I called my friend Dorian here to help with that," I told them, gesturing to Dorian. He had worn his armor so he made for a formidable sight.

"I've seen him walking about in the early morning hours," the man who spoke was David Tanner, the father of Sadie. I winced inwardly.

"That's right; I couldn't keep working on things every day and patrolling at night, so he generously offered to help," I continued.

"I wouldn't want to meet him in a dark alley that's for sure," another man chimed in. I realized it was Joe McDaniel. Several people laughed at his remark.

I went on, "The fact of the matter is I think I have an idea, or at least some knowledge of what is going on. A few nights ago I was out, with Penelope, and we met something in the dark." I paused, the next part was difficult.

"What was it? And why were you out there? I thought you were the new Count," that was from a fellow near the back, I couldn't see his face.

"I'm sure you have all noticed, but I don't have much in the way of retainers yet. As your lord I feel responsible for handling this," I could hear a few people muttering in agreement. "What I found that night—or rather, what found me—was nothing natural. I've never seen anything like it. It managed to sneak up on Penelope and me, despite my abilities. That shouldn't have been possible."

Joe McDaniel cut in, "You're not exactly known as a hunter from what I've heard, no disrespect yer lordship."

That took the wind out of my sails. The last thing I could use were doubts at this point, so I decided to put that to rest quickly. "I'm sure you all know by now that I'm a wizard. You've seen what I've been doing with the workmen's tools, but I have other abilities you may not have seen. Joe, would you mind helping me for a moment?"

"Sure sir, just tell me what you want," he grinned. He was an amiable fellow, even if he took more convincing than most.

"I'm going to turn around and when I do, I want you to do something… anything you want. I'll describe whatever you do," I turned my back on the crowd. Probably not the best idea when giving speeches, but I didn't have any better solution.

"Alright, what am I doing now yer lordship?" he called out.

"You're holding up one arm, your right one," I answered promptly. That drew a hushed murmur from the crowd.

"How about now?"

"Nothing, except grinning from ear to ear and scratching your nose… now you're gaping at me," I replied. I turned back around. "I can see things with my mind, not the same way as with my eyes, but it's something I do all the time. The thing that approached me that night… I couldn't see." The crowd was starting to look fearful, though whether it was because I seemed to have eyes in the back of my head or because of what I was telling them I couldn't be sure. "It came on me unaware, and it reached through my shield as though it wasn't there."

"Shield? Like a wooden shield?" I couldn't tell who had asked.

"No, here let me show you," I made my usual shield visible, adding a blue hue to it. I was nervous since some people reacted badly to seeing things so visibly unnatural.

"Holy shit!" someone said. "Merciful lady!" called another. The crowd was shifting now, afraid. Not what I had been trying to accomplish.

"Calm down, I told you I was a wizard already. The important thing is that I'm *your* wizard, same as I am your lord." That helped, I think, so I went on, "The thing that found us that night reached through my shield, and if Penny hadn't beaten it back it would have had me. It eats magic and only physical force worked against it."

"So what happened to it? Is it still out there? Does it have my Sadie?" That was David Tanner again.

"We killed it; or rather I cut it into several pieces, using plain steel. The worst is that cutting it up didn't kill it. It was still moving. We had to burn it completely to be sure of things." The crowd looked uncertain.

"So we're safe now? What about Sadie, did you find her?"

It was Sadie, I wanted to shout. That would have made things worse, but my frustration was rising now. "We never found her. We killed that one, but there may be more, in fact I feel sure there are. That's why I'm here now."

"What did it look like?" Joe piped up. I had to admit it was a good question.

"Like you or me—it looked like a man. Once I had some light on it, it looked just like an ordinary person."

"So how can you be sure it wasn't just a man?" he replied. Obviously Joe wasn't keen on the idea of monsters in the night, or perhaps he wanted to find a way to make things seem easier to deal with.

"With my other sight it looked like an empty hole, like something that didn't exist. It ate my magic, my spells, as if they were nothing. When it touched me I felt as though it might suck out my very life. It was no man." I stopped looking at them. This was the point that worried me most. Fear could undo us all, I had to offer them some hope or panic would break out. "I have found a way to fight them though, and a way to protect you."

My father stepped up then and opened his box, preparing to pull out the new necklaces. I continued, "I've spent the last few days preparing these. Penny has one already, and it is the only thing that allowed her to fight the thing without being paralyzed by its power. So I've made more of them, one for each of you."

"What are those supposed to do?" David Tanner spoke, he looked angry.

"They protect the wearer from magic of the mind. As long as you're wearing it no magic can enter your thoughts, or affect your spirit. It won't protect your body, but at least you'll still be able to fight." I waited to see what their reaction would be. Chaos broke out.

People were shouting at one another, and at me. "You tell us there are creatures out there that don't die when you cut them and we're supposed to feel safe because you have some gewgaws to give us!?" "This town has been cursed since the old Count died!" I was losing control, but old Joe came to my rescue.

"Now pipe down! You ungrateful lot! Are you men or sheep?" the crowd grew quiet. Joe had a lot of respect among the men in Washbrook, and they listened. "This boy has been working hard to do what none of us would. He's been patrolling the farms at night, by himself at first, while we huddled in our beds! Now he's offering us something, a way to defend ourselves."

"We can't fight the dead Joe!" someone shouted back.

"We can and we will! I been in this town since you were a pup Cecil Draper! We used to have a militia and I don't see why we can't have one again," Joe bellowed back, then he looked at me, "if that's ok with you yer lordship."

I could have hugged him. "Damn right it's fine with me!" Things improved after that. We got everyone organized and handed out the necklaces, one for every man, woman, and child. Then Dorian and Joe began discussing the militia idea. Soon enough they worked out a schedule and a chain of command. I would be in charge, but Dorian would handle the militia. He made Joe his lieutenant. I thought it was a good choice; the man had strong leadership qualities.

We talked late into the night and I was tired by the time everyone left. "You did good Mort," Penny told me as we climbed into our new bed.

"I just hope it's enough."

"It will be. You just have to trust them. These are good people and they're tougher than you realize." She gave me a light kiss.

I was hoping that kiss might lead to something more satisfying, but Penny could be as stubborn as a mule about some things. With a sigh I went to sleep.

CHAPTER 5

The next morning was better. People had a purpose and it gave them strength. The workmen continued their efforts to repair the inner keep, and the stone masons turned their efforts to the outer walls, making sure they were sound. When the keep had burned, seventeen years before the outer curtain wall had been untouched. Even the walls of the inner keep were in fairly good shape, though they had tumbled down in places. At the rate they were working the walls and gates would be finished within a few months.

I was at the smithy again, enchanting more necklaces when a rider from Lancaster showed up. It was one of the duke's regular messengers. Every time I saw one of them I reminded myself that someday I would have to have a few as well. It was damned inconvenient trying to find people heading that way whenever I needed to send a message. I walked out to meet him.

"A message for the Count di'Cameron!" he said loudly, his horse was lathered with sweat. I figured his message must be urgent.

"That would be me," I said to him.

He looked at me in surprise. I guess most people don't expect to see a count dressed like a workman and wearing a smith's apron. He recovered quickly and handed me a sealed message tube. I opened it deftly and soon had the paper unfurled so I could read it.

Lord Cameron,

I trust this note finds you well. Unfortunately I have no good news for you. The King, his majesty Edward Carenval sends greetings. You are expected in the capital immediately to swear fealty to him. I have enclosed the letter he sent for you. He wants you to arrive as soon as possible after receiving his command and it would be unwise to delay. I did not think he would require your presence so soon but the matter of your wizardry has complicated things I think.

Regarding the other matter you informed me of, I will send ten of my men to guard Washbrook until you return. I wish that I could send more, but I have few to spare, especially given the vague nature of the threat. Please make haste to Albamarl, and take Penelope with you, he will wish to meet her.

I will meet you at the Capitol. I have also been summoned to answer for the matter of Devon Tremont. His father, Lord Tremont has demanded an accounting for his son's death and I must present my case, your testimony will be helpful.

James Lancaster

I found the other note inside, but it contained no better information. It was beautifully written and sealed with his majesty's personal signet. It annoyed me to think I would have to leave my people at such a dangerous time. The journey would take a solid week on horseback. Thankfully my father had brought his horses; otherwise I would have been afoot. I hadn't had time to buy any horses of my own yet. I asked the courier to wait so I could send a reply with him, then I went to find Penny.

She was busy setting up the interior of our new apartments within the castle. She saw me coming and knew something was going on by the look on my face, "What's up?"

"I just received word from James; we have to go to the capital—immediately." No use beating around the bush.

"Now?"

"Yep, we are summoned by the king himself. James is going as well, to answer for Devon's death," I replied.

"Surely they don't plan to place blame on him? Devon got what was coming to him!" she was already getting worked up. I tried to head her off before she got too far into it.

"I feel sure that it is just a formality. He has to present his case before the king and the council of lords. We will probably have to testify on his behalf as well. The other reason we have to go is that his majesty wants my oath of fealty."

She pursed her lips, "I thought we would have more time. I don't even have anything to wear." Trust a woman to think of that first. I almost smiled.

"What are you smiling at?" she growled. Damn, I thought I had hidden it better than that.

"You," I replied simply. "Start packing, I'll go write a response for James and another for the king."

We got busy after that, I talked to my father to make sure he wouldn't mind us borrowing his horses. Then I went to see Dorian and Joe, they would have to handle things by themselves for at least a few weeks. They seemed a lot less nervous about my trip than I was.

"Don't worry so much," said Dorian, "This place will still be here when you get back." The irony of Dorian telling *me* not to worry struck me as funny. He was generally the most anxious one of all my friends; usually I was the easy going one.

"I know, I know…," I replied, "I've just never had this many people depending on me before. It's not something I'm used to dealing with."

"Just take care of your business with the king and return as soon as you can. We'll make sure there's still something to return to." Dorian clapped me on the back. I was expecting it so I braced myself, sometimes he doesn't know his own strength.

Penny and I left an hour later. Frankly I was amazed at her speed in packing. As lovely as she was it was easy to forget she wasn't some fragile flower raised in a nobleman's home. She had lived a hard life for all her youth and she knew how to get things done when she needed to. We rode two solid palfreys and carried our luggage on a sturdy packhorse.

For the journey we wore plain traveling clothes and I convinced Penny to wear her chain shirt as well. "I still don't see why you want me wearing this smelly thing. It's hot enough already without wearing a lot of heavy metal on top of it all," she complained.

"It isn't that heavy anymore and you know it," I countered. Part of the enchantment I had placed on her armor reduced the weight by half. The shirt had weighed over thirty pounds before, now it was closer to fifteen.

"Why aren't you wearing armor then?" she arched an eyebrow at me.

"You're my guard, I'm just a traveling nobleman," I smirked at her. "Besides, do you honestly think anyone could hurt me?" I said a word and my shield glowed visibly for a moment.

"That didn't work so well the other night with that creature," she pointed out.

"That's why I have my stalwart companion to protect me," I declared loudly.

She snorted, "And here I thought I was your fiancée, so much for my gallant knight!" That remark annoyed me and she knew it. Still I didn't let her take off the chain byrnie. I worried she might need its protection at some moment when I couldn't protect her.

I need not have worried. Our trip passed uneventfully, but the first night we discovered how cold the evenings could be. We were eating cold rations so we hadn't bothered with a fire. Lying on a lumpy bedroll and wrapped in a simple wool blanket we huddled together for warmth.

"It's awfully cold. Couldn't you just 'bippity boppity boo' up a fire for warmth?" she suggested.

"Then we wouldn't have an excuse to snuggle!"

"As if you ever needed an excuse!" she replied mockingly, but her eyes were smiling.

Overall it was a pleasant trip. Rather like a camping vacation. We rode, we ate, we camped and within a span of six days we arrived at Albamarl. We had passed through several villages on the way but we declined to stay in them. Something about the novelty of being on our own, alone for the first time; appealed to both of us. I think we were both a bit regretful that the trip was over when we reached the city gates.

Neither of us had ever been outside of the area of Lancaster or Washbrook, so the sight of the great city was a shock. The pictures and drawings I had seen in books just didn't do it justice. It was so *big*. The road was paved the last few miles before we reached the massive gates. At the entrance the road expanded until it was over thirty feet wide, flanked on either side by two massive towers of stone.

There was a famous quarry near the capital, which produced a lot of rose granite, so everything had been faced with it. This had the effect of making the entire city sort of pink. For that reason Albamarl was sometimes called the 'Rose of Lothion'.

The guards took no notice of us as we entered. I suppose so many people went through the gates each day they couldn't question them all. I stopped to ask one how to reach the royal palace and he looked at me oddly, "Just follow the main street. You'll know it when you see it." He turned away, without waiting to see if I had any more questions. I decided if I ever had guards they'd be trained to be more polite.

His directions turned out to be more than adequate, though. The main road was straight, heading directly into the heart of the city. Various winding streets led away from it, probably circling the great city, but this street went straight to the center, like the spoke of a wheel. We passed stone buildings and houses, shops and businesses, 'til at last we reached what could only be the royal palace.

The gate here was also guarded, but a bit more seriously. "Ho! State your business traveler!" Two men barred our path. Their faces bore looks of extreme disinterest; apparently road weary travelers were rarely welcome.

"I am Mordecai Illenial, the Count di'Cameron and this is my fiancée Penelope Cooper. We seek entrance that we may obey the summons of our king," I answered, using my most disdainful tone. I had been taking lessons from Benchley.

"You'll pardon me *my lord,* if I find that hard to believe. Do you have papers to prove your claim?" He gave me a hard stare but the other guard's eyes widened a bit. He leaned in to whisper in the first man's ear. I couldn't quite make out what he was saying, but I distinctly caught the word 'wizard' and 'Tremont'. Even after a year the story of the battle at Lancaster must still be circulating.

"Certainly," I answered him and drew out the letter from King Edward. As I handed it over I made sure he saw my grandfather's signet ring on my hand. He scanned the document quickly, but I'm not sure he even read it.

"If you will come inside I will have someone escort you immediately, my lord." His tone was suitably respectful now. We were taken in and told to wait for a moment in the courtyard. A moment later two groomsmen arrived to take our horses. One of them assured me our things would be sent directly to our rooms.

Penny leaned over to whisper in my ear, "Doesn't all this make you nervous?"

I smiled at her confidently, "Hell yes. But one thing I learned from watching Marc is never let them see you sweat. Half of being an aristocrat is confidence." In fact, I had never been more nervous in my life.

"If you'll follow me sir," the man who spoke looked as though he might be a close relative of Benchley's. He had that air about him, smug bastard. He led us through a maze of courtyards and hallways, until at last we reached a door. Presumably to our room, if it was a dungeon they were considerably upscale from what I had been led to expect.

He opened the door and passed me the key. The rooms, perhaps I should call them a 'suite', were sumptuous. The first room was a large living area, wide open spaces and furniture for lounging dominated the room. It had several doors leading off from it. Upon investigation I found one led to a large bedroom, the second to a smaller bedroom. A third door led into a private bath! I had never heard of such a thing.

It was like having a small pond indoors. Water ran constantly from a small opening on one wall and drained away where it overflowed through a clever arrangement of drains. I had no idea how it was managed but it seemed like purest extravagance to me.

"Are the rooms to your liking sir?" the servant asked meekly. Inwardly I was sure he was sneering. How could they not be to my liking? Until recently I had lived in a house with a dirt floor and thought myself lucky.

"They're satisfactory," I replied. I could 'snob' it up with the best of them. I wouldn't give him the satisfaction of seeing just how impressed I was. "When will we meet with his majesty?" I asked.

"He has already been informed of your arrival. I should expect he will send for you when he is ready."

"What is your name?" I inquired.

He seemed mildly surprised, "Adam sir."

I liked to know the names of the people I was dealing with, "Adam, could you give me an idea when that might be? I fear I am new to the royal court and have no clue what to expect. I'm sure you possess far more knowledge on the subject than I."

Adam was definitely surprised now; I would guess he wasn't used to being spoken to so directly. "I would venture to say he will probably call for you sometime before dinner. Otherwise you will see him at the evening meal."

"I appreciate your candor, do you know if the Duke of Lancaster has arrived yet?"

"He sent his man over yesterday to announce his presence," Adam replied.

"He isn't staying at the palace?"

"The Lancasters maintain a residence in the city my lord." That was news to me, but then I knew very little about the city. I knew Marc was here somewhere as well, but I had assumed he would be staying at the palace.

"How would I send a message to him? I am loath to leave myself, not knowing when the king's summons might arrive," I asked.

"Simply give me the message sir, or one of the other servants. They will see it delivered promptly," he answered in a tone that made it clear I should already know these things.

"Very good, I'll write a note out and give it to someone shortly. You may go now," I made it clear that I was dismissing him.

After he had left Penny spoke, "You handled that well. You sound more like a Count every day."

"Is that a compliment or a rebuke?"

"I'm not sure; I'll let you know when I make up my mind," she said, winking.

I wrote a quick note for the duke and gave it to a servant I found outside. Apparently the king could afford to have servants just waiting around for that sort of thing. After that I found myself at a loss for something to do.

We couldn't exactly go sight-seeing. It was mid-afternoon and there was always the possibility we would be summoned by the king, which effectively tied us down. I gave serious thought to a nap, but Penny had other ideas.

"Don't lie on the bed! You're dirty," she admonished me.

She was one to talk, "You're not much better." In fact, the chain mail had her smelling significantly worse.

"Let's try out the bath," she suggested. Normally I wouldn't have been a huge fan of that idea, but taking a bath *with* Penny reversed my usual misgivings.

"That sounds like a wonderful idea!" I replied. My enthusiasm showed though, and I could see caution in her eyes.

"You have to behave, or you'll be bathing alone," she said with a warning tone, naturally I agreed immediately. I had no dishonest intentions either, I swear. You believe me right? Yeah, she didn't either. We wound up sitting on opposite sides of the tub. She was more wary than a deer in the forest, so there was little chance I would be able to sneak up on her.

Penny herself was enjoying the warm water and watching Mordecai watching her almost made her laugh. She enjoyed the attention even if she wouldn't admit it. Closing her eyes she leaned back, letting the water wash away her cares. Drifting she could see a blue sky studded with fluffy clouds. It might have been beautiful if not for the smoke spoiling the picture. Glancing around she realized she was standing just outside Castle Cameron. Men in armor were rushing around her, readying weapons and pulling back the wounded.

At a glance she knew it was spring, which seemed odd. For some reason she thought it should be late summer, but she pushed the thought aside.

She looked for Mordecai for a minute before she spotted him. He was standing on a rise, holding his staff and sending lines of fire into the enemy. He cut a heroic figure standing there but he looked tense. She felt an uncommon sense of urgency and she knew he was in danger. Running she reached the top where he was standing and looked down. Thousands of soldiers were arrayed against them, advancing steadily.

Mordecai raised his staff again and a cone of fire surged forth. Cries went up and men died, yet still they came on. The enemy answered with crossbows but few of the bolts found their marks, the men of Cameron were well sheltered. Looking out across the field she suddenly spotted a ballista, a large crossbow-like weapon that fired bolts the size of heavy spears. Somehow she knew its target.

In slow motion she saw the heavy shaft soar out over the battlefield. Light glinted from the steel head as it flew. She opened her mouth to yell, to warn him, but no sound came out. Time snapped back as the great bolt slammed into Mordecai, striking him squarely. It ripped through his chest as if it were no more than tissue paper and drove him back several feet. Falling backward he struck the earth, blood running like water from a broken vessel upon the ground. He was dead within seconds.

***

I watched Penny relaxing in the bath across from me. A better vision I couldn't imagine. Her hair floated in the water as she slid down ever further into the warm water. I couldn't even see her eyes now, she had submerged herself. I kept trying to think of ways to coax her into dropping her silly premarital prohibition but I doubted any of them would have worked.

She hadn't come up for air in a while, which seemed odd. She had been under for nearly a minute now, so I leaned over to check on her. She was lying on the bottom of the huge tub, and she didn't look right. Something told me she was unconscious.

Grabbing her by the arms I dragged her up quickly. She was limp as a ragdoll, which scared me even more. I pulled her out of the tub and laid her on the tile floor, "Penny! Penny! Breathe damn you!" I turned her onto her side and tried to get her to expel the water from her lungs. I didn't have the faintest idea what I was doing.

She drew a great gulp of air and opened her eyes. No water came out but she looked at me, terror marking her face. "Mort!" I realized she hadn't swallowed any water at all, she simply hadn't been breathing.

"What the hell was that?" Fear and anger had me almost shouting. She ignored me and sat up, throwing her arms around me, sobbing. At this point I remembered a crucial factor; women are strange and mysterious creatures. "What's wrong with you?" I asked at last.

She grabbed my head between her hands and looked at me, tears still in her eyes, and then she kissed me. I'll be the first to admit that was pretty much what I had been hoping for when we first undressed for the bath, but this was too strange. I pulled back, "Damnit, will you talk to me? Why are you so upset?"

"Shut up," she replied and kissed me again. Her hands weren't idle either. I struggled with her for a few minutes, but as they say, 'When a woman is willing all any man can do is go along'. I try to live by that motto.

She made love to me with a desperate ferocity that was almost frightening, but I'm nothing if not brave. That's what I tell myself all the time. She wasn't satisfied quickly either and an hour later she had thoroughly exhausted me. I hoped she was tired too. If not I was in trouble.

"Are you ready to talk yet?" I asked.

She started crying again. I have that effect on women. It was particularly unsettling considering I figured I had done a damn fine job of making her every dream come true. Finally she slowed and choked out a few words, "We have to leave Mort. We can't stay here."

"What? I'll be exiled or banished or worse if we run from the king's summons!"

"It doesn't matter; you can't be the Count di'Cameron. You just can't, we have to run. Anything is better than—than...," she started weeping again.

"I can't and won't leave my people. They need me, they need us. We have responsibilities Penny. What brought all this on?" The thing that really worried me was that I knew she wasn't irrational. Whatever had started this she probably had a good reason.

"I had another vision," she said and stopped there.

I waited a full minute before I decided she wasn't just being slow to talk, "A vision of what?"

"We have to leave Mort, there's no future for us if we keep following this path," her eyes were beseeching me. I had never seen her look so desperate.

"What did you see?" She didn't reply so I repeated myself. She had that stubborn look. "I'm not doing anything unless you tell me," I declared.

That got her. She argued for a minute more before she finally gave up and shouted at me, "I saw your death! Are you happy?! Will you listen to me now?"

I was stunned but I stayed calm. "When?" I asked.

"Less than a year I think, sometime in the spring. That's why we have to leave, we can't go back to Washbrook," she was insistent.

"So it happens at home? How?" The question scared me witless and I wasn't sure I wanted the answer.

"I won't tell you that, it's too hard. There was a war, you died during the battle. I couldn't do anything to stop it." She had stopped crying and gave me a hard stare.

"A lot of things can happen during battle, you can't be sure that things will turn out that way. Who were we fighting?" As far as I knew Lothion had no enemies, within or without, other than some crazed cultists.

"I don't know who, but I know what will happen. Mort—I know! There's no avoiding this, I could feel it," she said.

"The future is never fixed."

"Nothing I have ever seen has failed to come to pass," she replied.

"What about the priest poisoning people?" I knew for a fact she had changed that.

"I knew when I saw it that I could prevent it, and I did. Yet everything I saw before and after it still happened. There was no changing what I saw today." There was a cold certainty in her voice that chilled me.

"Let me think for a bit." I walked out onto the veranda. I forgot to mention it before, but the view of the gardens was stunning. She started to follow me but I waved her away. It isn't every day a fellow hears he has only months to live.

I spent close to a half hour out there, watching the trees and listening to the wind. The world seemed a lot more vibrant than it had just a short while ago, so much more worth living for. I wish I could say what moved me to my decision, but it wasn't a thing of words. I simply knew. To alter my course would be to deny myself, to become someone I didn't want to be. I went back inside. Penny was already repacking our things.

"Stop that, we're not leaving."

The look on her face was heartbreaking. I would have given almost anything to take it away from her, but not this. "You can't be serious?" she said.

"I am. I can't abandon them. The duke needs my testimony. The people of Washbrook need our protection. Our parents need us. If I walk away I won't be the man you love, I'll be a mockery of him, a sham. I would rather face the future with my head up, even if it means losing—everything." I was close to weeping myself, but my resolve kept my eyes clear.

Penny stood up and marched up to me, anger written all over her, "What about me? Huh! What about your parents? We can bring them with us! What will I do after you're dead? Did you think about that!? Did you!?" She was shaking like a tree in a storm. "Do you think memories of your noble intentions will keep me warm at night? Think they will make your parents happy?"

"I won't change my mind on this." It hurt to see her like this.

"You selfish bastard!" she swung at me, but I caught her wrist. I would have let her slap me, it might have made me feel better, but I worried she might hurt her hand on my shield. She struggled with me for a moment before jerking her hand away. "I'm not staying. If you're going to do this you can do it alone. I won't watch you kill yourself," her voice was quiet now.

I opened my mouth to reply, *I need you. I can't do this without you,* but the words wouldn't come out. I couldn't force her into this. I didn't have the right. She stepped backward as I stood there, with my mouth half open. She was shaking her head, as if to deny what she saw in my eyes. Finally she turned and walked to the door, and a moment later she was gone. She didn't even slam it.

I sat down on the bed. I couldn't imagine a day gone more terribly wrong.

CHAPTER 6

I sat in the room for almost an hour. I wanted to go after her, but given what she had said I couldn't. If I really was going to die in half a year it wouldn't be fair to force her to watch. Maybe if she got away now she could find someone else, forget… anything to keep it from hurting her so much. Of course I was an idiot to think that, if the situation had been reversed there's no way in hell I could have gotten over it in just a few months, if ever.

One thought lightened my mood. If I knew the approximate time and circumstances of my death, then I could be pretty damn sure that I *wouldn't* die before then. Seen in that light it meant I was damn near disaster-proof for the next six months. There's a certain freedom that comes with knowing you can't die, at least not yet. I tried to focus on that. A knock at the door interrupted my train of thought.

Rising I answered it promptly, to find a servant escorting James, the Duke of Lancaster. He entered as soon as I opened the door. As it closed behind him I could tell he was agitated. In fact, looking at the aura around him he fairly pulsed with rage. I hadn't seen James that angry since the battle in Lancaster Castle.

He paced the room without speaking, so I left him alone and poured myself a cup of wine. I may not have mentioned it before, but the suite had a very nice wine selection laid out in the central room. "Would you like some?" I asked him.

"Screw the cup, bring me the bottle," he replied abruptly.

James was not known for drinking to excess, but I damn sure wasn't going to question him. I handed him the bottle and he turned it up, taking a long draught before sitting down on the couch. I relaxed a bit; now that he was sitting he didn't seem quite so explosive. "You look like your day has gone about as well as mine," I ventured.

"I wouldn't know about that. Did your son just piss all over you and tell you to go to hell?" his tone implied I didn't have the faintest idea how bad his day had been.

"Marc said that?" I was shocked. Throughout our entire lives he had lived only to please his father, not that he always succeeded.

"No, he didn't *say* any of that. He has joined the priests of the Evening Star and disavowed his inheritance, no warning, no word, no reason," he finished and took another long swig from the bottle.

"He wants to be a priest? What the hell?" I couldn't imagine it. The last few years his only interests had been women and wine. I still wasn't sure if I trusted the goddess of the Evening Star anyway. Father Tonnsdale had set a bad precedent for me by poisoning my parents and almost poisoning everyone at Lancaster as well. I tossed my glass back and looked for another bottle. I didn't think I could pry the first one away from James.

"He wasn't at the house when I arrived yesterday. He sent me a note saying he would call on me today. Arrogant pup!" He drank some more. At the rate he was going I wondered how long he would last.

"And today?" I sat down on the couch next to him. I had my own bottle now.

"Today he showed up at the door wearing a white robe, told me he had been 'called' by the goddess. He gave me this," he pulled out a crumpled sheet of parchment. I took it from him and scanned the lines. It spelled out in clear words that Marcus of Lancaster was giving up his inheritance and all claim to the duchy of Lancaster.

"And you just let him?" I regretted saying that immediately after the words left my lips. The wine had overridden my normal good sense.

"Hell no! I raged at him! I was so damn angry I wanted to throttle him right there! But he was unmoved. Calm as a ship in the eye of a storm. That made me angrier than anything I think. He just listened to me, then left." James seemed calmer now, and a little tipsy. "Mordecai, tell me something… and be honest."

"Certainly, Your Grace."

"None of that 'your grace' shit! I'm asking you as one man to another, as a father to his son's best friend," his face was flushed. "Was I a good father? Did I drive my son to this? He always seemed happy, what did I do wrong?"

I was completely at a loss. James had always been a towering figure in my life, the picture of confidence and command; to see him so vulnerable shook me to the core. "Marc loves you James. He always did, but he also feared you, as any son fears and respects his father. I think he felt a lot of pressure to live up to your expectations, but I don't think it was too great a burden. He never gave me any cause to think he wanted to escape like this."

"Then why would he do this?" He had his hands over his face, possibly to hide his tears, but I would never say so.

"James, I don't think this is any reflection on you. Rather it sounds to me as though something has happened with him. He wouldn't do this on a whim, and I'm sure he didn't do it just to hurt you." I leaned over to pat him on the back. Normally I would never have dared be so familiar, but right now James seemed to need a friend more than a vassal.

"Thank you Mordecai," he uncovered his face and leaned back, throwing his arms over the back of the couch. "You remind me a lot of your father, though I didn't know him that well."

I didn't know how to reply to that, so I kept my silence and poured myself another glass. The wine was getting to me as well by now. Idly I wondered what would happen if we were summoned before the king while inebriated.

"Where's that feisty girl of yours?"

"She left me," I replied.

"Well damn! That deserves a drink," he raised his bottle so I followed his example. Wiping his lips he went on, "Why aren't you out chasing her down? I wouldn't think you'd let her go that easy."

"It's complicated."

"It always seems that way. Don't let your brain get in the way of your heart boy. The brain always fucks these things up. Trust me on this. Not that I've ever been able to follow my own advice. Ha!" He took another swallow. Another knock at the door ended our conversation.

I managed a straight line to the door. I answered as I opened it, "Hello?" It was another of the king's messengers.

"His majesty sends word for your lordship and his grace, the Duke of Lancaster to attend him in his quarters," said the messenger. He waited patiently, as if he intended to escort us there.

"James," I said, looking back. The good duke was reclining with his eyes closed, "James!" I yelled.

He looked up, "What?"

"The king wants us."

"When?" he asked calmly.

"Now apparently," I replied.

"Well damn. I should have expected this. Let's go see how much better the day can get eh!?" He rose and knocked the wine bottle off the table in front of him. Luckily it was empty. I started to give him a hand but he waved me off. "Don't worry lad, I can handle it."

We followed the servant down the hall. Neither of us was that steady on our feet but we weren't too far gone either. I gave us fifty-fifty odds of getting out of the king's chambers without causing a major incident. I've always been optimistic.

We arrived at the king's private reception room a few minutes later. A nod from our escort and the doorman let us in without a word. He didn't follow us in. The room beyond the door was opulent, well-furnished without being ostentatious. It reflected the tastes of a man so powerful he did not need to flaunt his wealth. King Edward the First sat reading a dispatch in a comfortable chair across from the entrance to the room.

I had no idea what sort of etiquette was expected of me here, so I followed James' example. We crossed the room partway and then bowed. Later I would learn that in more formal settings we were expected to go down on one knee, but here a simple bow was permissible, for nobility anyway. "You called for us your majesty?" I couldn't detect any slurring in James' voice. I hoped I did as well at covering it.

The king looked at us. He was an older man, in his sixties at least, balding and grey. He looked fit, for despite his age he seemed energetic and trim. Sharp grey eyes looked at us over his papers, "James, you old dog! Come have a seat, this isn't a formal occasion." He motioned to a couple of chairs not far from his own.

"Thank you, your majesty," James took a seat. I moved to sit in the chair next to him.

"Young man, did I give you leave to sit in my presence!" Edward's tone was sharp and it sent a chill up my spine.

"Er… my apologies your majesty!" I jumped up as if the seat had caught fire. I wasn't sure if I should bow again or just stand. I looked at James for help.

King Edward burst out laughing. It was a good laugh and whatever had tickled him so nearly caused him to fall from his chair. "That never gets old!" he exclaimed. My confusion only got worse. "Come, come, young Illeniel, please sit! I was just having a laugh at your expense. You'll forgive an old man for his small amusements won't you?" The fog cleared and I realized I had played the fool. I flushed with embarrassment and sat down.

"Thank you, your majesty." I didn't trust myself to say more. The joke hardly seemed funny to me, especially given that I had no choice but to react as I had. I kept my observation to myself.

"It's been a while since we had a chance to talk James," Edward had already forgotten me.

"Yes your majesty, I haven't been to Albamarl in a while," he answered.

"Just Edward please, I've told you before that you can call me familiar in private," the king told him.

"I remember, but I like to have the reminder before I fall prey to one of your jokes Edward." James gave him a huge grin and they both fell to laughing again. I'm sure they both thought they were terribly funny.

"So what drives you to drink so early in the day my friend?" Edward asked.

"My damn son has decided to join the priesthood of the Evening Star."

"Ah! I should have remembered that. You just heard the news I gather?" Edward's face implied there was a story to be told.

"That's all I've heard so far. Why, did something happen to him?"

"Your boy has become a saint apparently. He healed a man last week after he had been stabbed. Since then people have been dragging their sick to the temple of Millicenth in droves. The priests say that he has been chosen by the Lady of the Evening Star herself."

"That's nonsense! Marcus is no more pious than a stag in rut! He came to the city to find a wife and I've since heard he's done nothing more than dip his wick in every available lady in the city! My only consolation is that he hasn't taken to whoring. Why would the goddess choose him?" Needless to say I was flabbergasted to hear James speak so in front of the king.

"The gods choose who they will. Who are we to second guess them? This does present a particular advantage for you tomorrow, though." Edward didn't seem overly concerned with the duke's colorful use of language.

"How so?"

"I'm hearing Tremont's case regarding his son's death. Marcus will certainly be called to testify. Few would gainsay the word of one chosen by Millicenth." The king smiled.

James still wasn't pleased, "I don't need something like that to clear the Lancaster name, hundreds of people saw what happened. Old Tremont should have just let things be, nothing but more bad blood will come of it."

"He has lost both his sons, he may not be thinking clearly anymore. You were friends once, were you not?" That was news to me. Their conversation was proving to be very educational.

"Yes, when we were younger. He's a good man. He just couldn't stand the fact that Ginny chose me over him, a silly reason to be angry really." By Ginny he was referring to his wife, Genevieve Lancaster. Although she was hardly an old woman the thought of Genevieve as a young lady with two noblemen fighting over her was a startling revelation for me.

Edward chuckled, "It only seems a silly reason to the victor. His current wife is mad as a hatter and now he's lost both sons. Don't underestimate how circumstances may have changed your old friend. He's bitter and nursing a grudge." The king looked at me, "Young Illeniel, I have business with you."

"Yes, your majesty. I am at your service," I answered promptly.

"Assuming you are acquitted of wrongdoing tomorrow I will have your oath of fealty shortly afterward."

"I will give it now if you wish sire," I said.

He shook his head, "No tomorrow will be fine. However there is a serious matter to discuss. Have you given thought to your bonding?"

My what? "Excuse me your majesty; I'm not sure what you mean."

"If the reports are to be believed you showed a great deal of magical prowess during your battle with Devon Tremont. Much like your father, tradition demands you be bound to a partner, your Anath'Meridum," Edward was matter of fact.

"Your pardon sire, I had thought the knowledge of how to create such a bond lost."

"It is not. In fact, the ancients were very careful to preserve the knowledge. We have several books here detailing how it is done. I am not an expert in the matter but your father once told me it was an easy thing to accomplish. The choosing is the hard part," he replied.

"In what way sire?"

"It should be obvious. The person you choose will die when you do, and vice versa. The one chosen should be a friend, or someone close, but it isn't easy to put such a burden upon one you love."

James interrupted, "I thought that part was just a myth."

"Oh no! It's absolute truth, it's the very reason for the bond after all," Edward said.

"Your majesty, if I may? Do I have to choose immediately?" I inquired.

"The sooner the better, there's still a trainer here, from the days when your mother was chosen. He will return with you when you leave, to begin preparing whoever you choose."

That was a surprise, "Did he know my mother?" In my haste I forgot to add the proper honorific, but he took no offense.

"Certainly, he trained her."

"What sort of training is it—Your Majesty?" I remembered my etiquette that time.

"It involves martial training, some meditation, and a lot of history and indoctrination regarding the secrets and reasons for the Anath'Meridum, or so I'm told."

I was having difficulty imagining putting such a burden on Dorian, or Penny if she came back. In truth the thought of having to worry about anyone else dying when I did was—I remembered why Penny had left. I couldn't possibly choose anyone now; it would be a death sentence. "Are there any consequences if I decline to form such a bond with anyone?" It was an ill-considered question but I needed to know.

"Apart from death? I would be forced to rally the kingdom to have you put down. Don't tell me you're considering such a thing?" his eyes grew wary. I could almost see him suddenly regretting the informal setting, the lack of guards.

"No of course not sire! I was just curious. I'm very new to all this and I've never had a teacher, or any formal training." I tried to put as much sincerity in my voice as possible. In my mind I went over his words—*have you put down.* Like a rabid dog? The phrasing made it sound as if I might go mad if I wasn't bonded to someone. Once again I cursed my lack of knowledge.

"Good. I'll introduce you to the trainer tomorrow, assuming you are acquitted of course." He smiled at me, but I could not help but think of my father's old advice, *beware a smile on a dog.*

James and I returned to my rooms after that. The wine had largely worn off, but neither of us felt like dinner in the great hall so we said our goodbyes and he returned to his city home. I managed to get a light supper brought to my room.

While I was eating I realized Penny's things were gone. She must have returned for them while I was out. I guessed she was serious. I lay in bed for what seemed like hours after that. Sleep, when it finally came, was far from restful.

CHAPTER 7

Morning arrived bright and shining; with no regard to my personal feeling on the subject. It should have been raining, if anyone had bothered to consult me on the matter. I took breakfast in my room. The service at the royal palace was definitely a step up from Lancaster. The duke's cook would boil someone alive for requesting a meal in their room, much less between the set meal times. Of course to be fair, the royal kitchen served a lot more people and probably had a whole crew of cooks managing things.

The hearing was set for nine in the morning. A terrible time for me to be sure, but I suspected that the king liked to get unpleasant things out of the way early. Adam showed up to help me dress. He was just as efficient at the task as Benchley had been, but he made sure I knew that true men of quality brought their own man-servants. I was tempted to ask him to empty the chamber pot after that, but I held my temper.

I got directions to the Hall of Lords, where our hearing would occur. I made my way along the corridors alone, without escort or guard, without Penny. When I arrived the man at the door announced me as 'his lordship, the Count di'Cameron' and an usher led me to my seat. I was pleased to find James and Genevieve sitting close by. I suppose as his vassal the seating arrangements put us close together.

The hall itself was large, with a vaulted ceiling and seats on the floor for nearly a hundred people. I say people, but those seats were for the lords and ladies of Lothion. Spectators were allowed to sit, but only in the galleries on either side of the main hall. The king sat in a small box, apart and behind the central dais. Theoretically he could intervene and overrule any decisions made, but James made it clear to me that such things rarely happened. The proceedings and the final decision would be made by the Lord High-Justicer, the Earl of Winfield.

The justicer was not the most highly ranked peer of course, that would have been James, or the Duke of Tremont, but apparently the position was not hereditary. It was by appointment of the king himself that a new justicer was chosen when necessary.

I leaned over to James, "What's going to happen exactly?"

"A lot of rigmarole first, and then they'll call Tremont up to make his case. After that I respond and then the justicer starts asking questions. We take turns calling witnesses if necessary. I hope you stopped by the privies before you arrived," he winked at me.

"Where is Marc at?"

James frowned at that, "No idea, I sent him a message yesterday telling him to be here. I suppose his goddess is more important than keeping his father's trust. Where's Penny?"

"Point taken," I responded. It wouldn't look good for us if half our witnesses didn't appear. The 'rigmarole' that James had mentioned was even more boring than I had imagined. After several minutes of introductions and speeches I was glad it was over. At last Lord Winfield got down to business.

"I believe Lord Tremont has a case to present before the court, please step up and make your claim clear." The elder Tremont took the floor. He was a well-built man, close to James' age, in his early forties at the oldest. He bore a presence of power and confidence around him, reminding me of James.

"I stand before you today to ask for justice. My son was slain while staying with the Lancaster's and his murderer sits proudly here among us, with no shame for his crime," he pointed at me disdainfully. "According to the reports given by Lancaster's own servants, my son was threatened twice by different members of the duke's household. First he was threatened by the man who eventually slew him...," another nod in my direction, "... then by Dorian Thornbear."

I started to stand but James put his hand on my shoulder, "Not yet, you'll get your chance."

Tremont continued, "This man threatened my son for no reason a few days before his murder, then declined an honorably given challenge. Instead he enticed my son into a chess match whereby he swindled him out of two hundred gold marks. Adding insult to injury Dorian Thornbear, another of Lancaster's vassals, threatened to kill my son when he attempted to help the new Count di'Cameron after he had suffered an accident while hunting."

He paused for a moment to survey the room, "I see young Thornbear has declined to appear today. No matter, doubtless his testimony would have only made the case more clear. Not only did he threaten my son's life, but a Miss Penelope Cooper, the fiancée of young Lord Cameron, attempted to assassinate my son just a short time before Lord Cameron succeeded in the deed. She was seen attempting to stab my son with a dagger at the ball that evening. Reportedly it was his act of self-defense that finally drove Lord Cameron to murder him. It has been said that a small army of assassins attacked the Lancaster household that day, but it is my belief that Lord Cameron used the attack as an opportunity to carry out his plan for murder."

Lord Tremont returned to his place and Lord Winfield stood up, "Lord Lancaster, how do you respond to these accusations?" James stood and took the floor.

"I declare them false, in their entirety. Those things mentioned by Lord Tremont that did hold some truth were twisted in their meaning and intention to cast guilt upon innocent. Devon Tremont used my invitation to bring assassins into my home in an attempt to wipe out the Lancaster family. While he was there he insulted my son and young Lord Cameron, which resulted in their disagreement. He attempted to murder Lord Cameron using magic during a boar hunt. Dorian Thornbear prevented him from finishing his task and showed remarkable restraint in not slaying Devon at that point. I invite you to call any of the principals named by Lord Tremont who are present today and I will stand behind their word." James took a deep breath and looked across the assembled lords.

"Considering what occurred it is I who should be laying charges of wrongdoing at Tremont's doorstep, if I were *fool* enough to believe him guilty of his son's crimes." He stepped back.

The justicer responded, "Do you wish to levy counter charges against Lord Tremont?"

"I do not, out of respect for our past friendship and the knowledge that he did not have any part in his son's crimes," James answered.

"How do you answer the charge that Dorian Thornbear threatened Devon Tremont's life, or that Lord Cameron did the same, before eventually making good on his threat?" Lord Winfield would seek an explanation for each particular it seemed.

"Dorian Thornbear is not here to answer that charge, but I will call his friend and the other principal, Lord Cameron to respond," James replied looking at me.

That was my cue so I approached the floor. Earlier I had feared I would be too nervous to speak, but anger had replaced my anxiety. "I am Mordecai Illeniel, the new Count di'Cameron. Devon Tremont insulted my adoptive parents and I did threaten him, but only with a beating. He challenged me to a duel and then agreed to a chess match in its place. He also suggested the wager of one hundred gold marks. I did not swindle him, I merely raised the stakes," I took a moment to breathe and I could hear a few scattered chuckles amongst the crowd.

"How do you respond to the charge that Dorian Thornbear also threatened his life?"

"I am a wizard just as Devon Tremont was. He ambushed me during the boar hunt and almost killed me by paralyzing my horse while she was at a full gallop. Dorian bore witness to this and forced him to surrender before he could finish the deed," I replied.

"There is no record of anyone having sorcerous powers within the family of Tremont. Certainly Devon never displayed any before, do you wish to claim otherwise?"

"I do."

Lord Tremont burst out, "That's preposterous! My son never showed any sign of magical talent."

"How do you support your claim Lord Cameron?" Lord Winfield looked interested.

"Everyone saw him use his abilities in the battle at the ball the night he died. His most visible use was when he tried to burn me alive," I answered calmly.

"Is this true Lord Lancaster?"

"It certainly looked that way to me," James responded.

Lord Tremont spoke up, "He probably did that himself and seeks to cloud the issue by claiming my son had similar abilities."

The justicer spoke, "In the absence of firm proof we will have to set the question of Devon's magical talent aside. It is largely irrelevant to the case at hand. Since your fiancée is not present you will have to answer for her. Did she attempt to kill Devon Tremont during a dance that evening?"

I was on shaky ground now, "She had a premonition of Tremont's plan and given his prior actions she sought to remove the danger he represented." I saw James grimace; I don't think he wanted me to answer so bluntly.

"What prior actions?" the justicer asked.

"I would rather not say your lordship." I knew that answer would cast me in a dark light, but I couldn't bear to share what had nearly been done to Penelope.

"He tried to rape me," a voice spoke from the aisle. I turned and saw her standing there, resplendent in a white dress. She came forward to stand beside me and rush of emotions threatened to undo my calm exterior, but I fought them down.

"Were there any witnesses to this event?"

"Dorian Thornbear and my fiancé, Lord Cameron," she tilted her head to indicate me. I'm not sure if she had ever looked so beautiful before.

Things got heated after that. Lord Tremont started shouting and the questions got out of hand. I almost lost my temper at some of his remarks regarding Penny's credibility. Further testimony only made things muddier and I wondered how Lord Winfield would eventually rule. If I had been in his position I would certainly have been confused. Naturally Marc chose that moment to appear.

He walked down to the floor without being called. Wearing a white robe he seemed out of place amongst the well-dressed lords and ladies. Without being asked he took the center floor and spoke up. Though he didn't raise his voice it carried clearly throughout the room, "The Lancasters and Lord Cameron are innocent." His tone was matter of fact, as if he expected everyone would take him at his word.

"You're a Lancaster! Why should anyone believe your words to be less biased than your father's?" That sounded like Tremont but it was hard to be sure.

"I could give you my testimony but it would do little good. I am here to give voice to the Lady of the Evening Star. She would share her wisdom with you this day." That got everyone's attention.

Things got quiet for a moment, 'til Lord Airedale shouted out, "You expect us to believe you speak for the Goddess?"

Marc looked at the floor before raising his head. Opening his eyes it seemed as though light spilled out from them, illuminating the room. The light enveloped him and then he was gone, replaced by a woman so beautiful she made Penny look drab in comparison. Not that I would ever tell her that. "I am here to show you the truth, and if any man dares gainsay *my* word let him speak now."

Millicenth's voice carried an unearthly harmony behind it. No one interrupted now. The goddess gazed out over the crowd and the most powerful men and women in the kingdom knew doubt. "Devon Tremont sought power through magic. He made a pact with a dark god and brought the Children of Mal'goroth into Lancaster that day, seeking to slay them all," she stared at Lord Tremont, pity in her eyes, "Your grief has blinded you Andrew Tremont. Your younger son slew his brother and you would not see it. His death was the result of his own greed for power. If he had not died you would have been his next victim."

I had never heard the Duke of Tremont's given name before and as I watched he covered his face, overcome with emotion. The goddess walked to him, passing through the crowd while people fell back in awe. She put her hand on his head, for he was kneeling now. "Rise Andrew, for you have done nothing wrong, save letting your love blind you."

He stood, his face wet with tears but he could not bear to look into her face. Turning she strode back toward the center of the room. I thought she would pass by, but instead she stopped when she came to me. I could feel her power radiating outward, encasing me, and seeking entry. Without thinking I strengthened my shield and light flared around me.

For a moment annoyance flickered in her eyes, but she smiled instead, "Child of Illeniel, I see you still refuse me. If you will not accept my guidance, why are you still unbound?"

"I have not chosen who will bear the bond with me yet Lady." I answered her. Sweat stood out on my brow from the effort of keeping her power at bay.

"You should choose quickly, the dark gods will not be as patient as I am. You risk the destruction of your world while you decide," she stretched out her hand toward me and the pressure increased. Lightning flared and crackled around my shield where she touched it and the strain grew almost unbearable.

Anger gave me strength, "Enough! If you would force yourself on me then you are no better than the dark gods you speak of!" My shield flared with red light and she drew back. The pressure abruptly lessened.

"You would do well to watch your words mortal. The time is coming when you will need my aid lest you lose that which you hold most dear." She smiled at me but her grin seemed feral. She turned to address the assembly once more, "I will be watching. This is not the time for discord. The people of Lothion must unite or all will be lost." In the blink of an eye she was gone, replaced by Marc's unconscious form. He slumped to the ground before I could catch him.

The room was silent for a long minute after she vanished. The shock of her appearance had robbed everyone of their power of speech, 'til King Edward spoke, "Lord Justicer, what is your decision?"

"I find for Lancaster. The charges hold no merit," he answered immediately.

I might have cheered but I no longer had the energy. I would have left but for the matter of my fealty. King Edward was kind enough to take my oath without waiting on pomp and circumstance. The room remained silent throughout the rest of the proceedings and once they were done the room emptied quickly.

James and Genevieve took Marc with them. One of the servants assisted James until they got him to the duke's carriage outside. Penny and I were soon left alone.

Neither of us knew what to say so I took her hand and we walked quietly back to my rooms.

# CHAPTER 8

The silence between us stretched out after we reached the rooms. We both sat on the couch, staring toward the veranda. "You look very lovely," I managed at last. I had never seen the dress she was wearing, but it fit her perfectly.

"Thank you." Penelope glanced at me for a moment, her eyes taking in a hundred details at once, "I heard what the king told you."

I almost said, 'about what?', but my good sense caught me this time. I knew exactly what she meant. It didn't help that a god had just reinforced the message. "How did you hear about it?"

"Rose. She went to visit the Lancasters last night." Now I understood… she had gone to stay with Rose Hightower. Where else could she have gone? Rose was a towering intellect framed within a slender woman's body. Obviously she had gone hunting for information not long after Penny arrived on her doorstep.

"Did you tell her why you were there?" I asked.

"No. I started to, but then I couldn't. How could I say I had left you because you would die? It sounded selfish."

"So you changed your mind?" I felt a glimmer of hope combined with fear. If she stayed with me she would only know more pain.

"Sort of… Rose came back with news about the king ordering you to choose someone, to be your Anath'Meridum."

"I haven't decided about that yet," I told her.

"Apparently even the gods are waiting on your choice."

"I wonder about that, it seems as if everyone is trying to push me into this."

Penny gave me a serious look, "You don't have to worry about it anymore. That's why I'm back. I won't have anyone else taking the bond with you."

"What!? Absolutely not! You realize what it means don't you? When I die? Has your vision changed since yesterday?" Without thinking I had stood up and now I was glaring down at her.

She looked up at me calmly, "Yes, I'll die with you. It solves all our problems."

"It solves nothing. I won't accept such a bond," I declared.

"Then you'll be put to death," she stated calmly, "and I wouldn't be surprised if a lot of other innocent people also died trying to protect you. You have no choice." Her voice held a note of resolve and her eyes a quiet madness, the madness of one determined to die with her lover.

"I have plenty of choices; at the very least I could choose someone else. I'm sure Dorian would accept the duty." I didn't like what I saw in her expression and my words kindled a fire.

"No you won't, not if you value my life. You have no idea what I am capable of Mordecai Eldridge. You think murdering a priest in cold blood was easy? That is just the tip of the iceberg!" Her voice had taken on a low growl. I took an involuntary step back; the goddess had been easier to face than the angry woman in front of me now. "If you choose someone else I'll make sure you spend your remaining days *wishing* you were already dead! And to top it all off, I'll kill myself as soon as you die anyway. Do you understand?"

"Fine!" I shouted back, "Have it your way!" In truth I had no intention of agreeing. It was easier to lie now and handle things my own way later. Penny was adept at spotting my lies so I figured I should throw her off the scent. "You want to die with me? No problem, but if we're both going to die in half a year I'll have my way now, in what time we have left." I grabbed her by the shoulders and half dragged her to her feet, planting a rough kiss on her astonished face.

My plan worked better than I could have hoped. What started as a forced kiss turned into a fierce embrace as she responded to my passion. A few moments later I began to wonder what sort of tigress I had taken by the tail. She returned what I gave tenfold over, and the ferocity of her love was a thing to make lesser men shake in their boots. Luckily I am not a lesser man. If I had ever been unsure of that before, she made sure I knew it that day.

A few hours later I decided that dying in a few months might not be so bad. If things continued like this for the foreseeable future I wouldn't survive that long anyway. "There!" I declared after a long breathless moment, "I think I've made my point."

Penny started chuckling beside me and soon we were both laughing. "You can believe that if it makes you feel better, my Lord Cameron."

I grimaced in mock anger and started tickling her but a knock at the door interrupted our battle. Feeling brash I rose to answer it. "Mort! Put some clothes on!" Penny hissed at me.

"Bah! I'll teach that brazen manservant some manners this time!" I went to the door and threw it open, preparing to embarrass the man once and for all.

"Oh my! If I had known you greet all your callers this way I would have visited you sooner Mordecai." Rose Hightower stood in the entrance, covering her mouth with her hand as if to hide a gasp. I turned several shades of red and dashed back to the bed, hoping to cover myself with the sheets.

Penny had already wrapped them around herself and refused to share, "Oh no you don't! You brought this on yourself you cad!" she yelled. I gave up quickly and ran for the bath chamber. Rose stood laughing in the entrance the whole time.

"I may be overstepping, but does this mean you have forgiven him already?" she asked Penny.

Penny blushed, "He was very persuasive."

Rose laughed, "I'll wait here in the hall 'til you're both ready. Unless you would prefer I come back at a later time?"

I wanted to shout that later would be best but Penny answered first, "We'll be presentable in just a few minutes if you don't mind. Thank you Rose." I heard the door close and I peeked out into the main room.

"It's safe," said Penny. We dressed hurriedly and once we were somewhat presentable Penny opened the door. I wasn't quite ready to face Rose so soon.

"I came to ask if you'd been to see your father's house yet," Rose said after we had all sat down.

My first impulse was to answer that Royce couldn't possibly own a house in Albamarl 'til I realized she must mean Tyndal Illeniel, "He owned a house here?"

"Of course, he was a counselor to the king. Naturally he and your mother kept their residence here. You didn't know?" Rose seemed genuinely surprised.

"No, it never occurred to me. I only recently learned who he was and things have been so busy I hadn't thought to ask. Why wasn't the house sold after he died? No one knew I was alive after all." Without an heir ownership should have reverted back to—I wasn't sure who, but someone should have taken possession by now.

"Hah! No one would dare enter his home. Think of what he was! Even robbers and vandals have given it a wide berth since his death," Rose answered. What she said made sense; I would probably have put wards and protections around my own dwelling.

"So it has stood untouched since my parents were there last?" The thought brought a host of fanciful ideas to mind. What had they been doing before they left? What secrets were there? How many of their possessions remained? I had never known them in life yet their home might be full of answers about their lives.

"As far as I know… yes." Rose's eyes twinkled; she seemed as excited by the prospect of exploring the house as I was. She had an insatiable curiosity. Despite her beauty it was impossible to forget that behind her blue eyes lurked a mind as sharp as a razor. "Shall we go take a look?"

"I would love to. You already know the way?" I replied.

"This city is my home. Penny this man's head is addled. If I hadn't seen him naked a moment ago I would still be wondering what you see in him," she teased.

Penny started laughing and I blushed again. I suspected Rose would be using that to embarrass me for years to come. "He does have his talents," Penny added. I wasn't sure if she was referring to my magic or—or my other magic.

I gathered up my sword and staff and we set out with Rose leading the way. Since we had arrived in Albamarl we hadn't had an opportunity to see much of the city beyond the royal palace itself so the walk was educational.

The city was laid out much like a wagon wheel, with the palace at its center. Once we were out of the palace proper we followed the inner hub road until we came to another 'spoke' road that led outward.

At the place where the roads met was a large garden on the side nearest the palace. It was unusual in that its main feature was a massive rock that seemed to thrust up from the very earth. It had to be natural; no feat of men could have moved such a massive stone there to be a garden feature.

Is he sleeping?

"Did you say something?" I asked my companions. I wasn't entirely sure whose voice I had heard.

Penny and Rose had been deep in conversation, so my question seemed out of place, "Rose was just saying that she'd like to stay with us for a while in Washbrook. Haven't you been listening?"

As a matter fact, I had tuned them out. Women's conversation often seems like a sort of pleasant background noise to me, but obviously I couldn't tell them that. "Sorry I thought I heard something else, don't mind me," I replied.

He's awake.

I heard that clearly. This time I knew for sure that the girls weren't the source. I stopped in the street, peering around me. Penny realized immediately that I must have sensed something while Rose looked at me curiously, "Something we should know?" she asked.

I held my finger to my lips, motioning them to silence and with a few words I put a shield around them. I had gotten much better at it over the past year and it hardly took me more than thought and a few well-placed words. "There's something here, but I'm not sure what or who."

Who or what, what or who, he hears us no matter what we do.

It was mental, not a voice at all. That gave me some concern; nothing should be able to speak directly to my mind while my inner shield was up. I stretched out my senses, expanding them to find whoever was playing these tricks.

"Mort, what's going on?" Penny said.

"Someone is talking to me. Give me a moment; I'm trying to find them." I couldn't concentrate and answer her questions at the same time. We stood in the street for several minutes while I searched the area with my mind. I found nothing. Finally I gave up and we started walking again. I explained what I had 'heard' but neither of them had any better idea as to what it might have been.

The fact that I hadn't been able to find the person responsible had me worried. I immediately thought of the creature Penny and I had fought that night two weeks ago. I had been looking for 'holes', though. I should have been able to spot the empty place even if it was one of them. I really needed a name for whatever those creatures were.

Whatever this had been, it managed to speak directly to my mind, despite my shields. That shouldn't be possible. I remained watchful for the rest of our walk, not that it did any good. Soon enough we reached my father's house.

"This is it," Rose said, but I already knew that. The large stone mansion fairly glowed in my sight. Unlike the rest of the city it was constructed of grey granite and every part of it was enchanted. Each stone looked to be individually worked with runes, making them stronger and linking them together. No mortar was in evidence, none was needed. The gaps between the stones were so tiny I doubt I could have slipped a fingernail between them.

The house appeared to be three stories tall; which made it stand out among the shorter buildings in the neighborhood. "The house is not warded," I stated simply, but the fact was hard to comprehend. Enchanting each stone must have taken a lifetime.

"Are you sure?" Rose questioned, "The stories about this house make it sound as if it is guarded by a thousand magics."

"I'm sorry. I wasn't being clear. The house isn't guarded by anything as simple as wards; rather the entire structure is enchanted. How could my father have done this? It would have taken most of his life to build." My awe was evident in my voice.

"He didn't build it. This house was built not long after the founding of Albamarl, some seven hundred years ago. It was built by one of your great-grand-sires," she clarified.

That gave me pause. What would it have been like to be raised here, surrounded by magic? Guided by a father who knew magecraft and the history of our family; life would have been very different. For a moment I felt the loss, the knowledge that could never be regained. I was a stranger to my family's past, picking at the threads of a long frayed tapestry; trying to reconstruct a story of men long gone.

Nothing would be gained standing in the street, so I stepped up to the door. It was a massive oak construction, wide enough for two men to stand abreast. The timbers were so wrapped in runes and symbols that they looked almost gold in my sight. Reaching out I attempted to touch the door-handle, but my hand came up short, stopping several inches from it. An invisible barrier prevented me from even contacting it.

Since that day in Lancaster when I had struggled to get into Devon Tremont's room I had not met a door I could not pass. One of the first things I studied when things calmed down was the art of spelling locks to open. This was not a lock however, it was a magical barrier. Using a few words and a mental push I tried to force my way through the barrier but it resisted me. It felt as though it were as hard as the granite the house was made of, resolute and unyielding.

Penny spoke up, "What are you doing?"

"I'm trying to get in. It seems my father forgot to put a key under the doormat for me." I redoubled my efforts, seeking to pry apart the magic that held me at bay. The air began to crackle with static discharges as I put more and more effort into forcing the barrier aside. I tried subtle tricks to slip past the protections, I tried clever spells to hide my presence, and I tried brute force. Nothing worked. "Goddammit!"

It was frustrating to be so close to such a major part of my past, yet be unable to enter. The thought of the secrets and knowledge my parents might have left inside filled me with yearning. The door didn't seem to care. I lost my temper and attacked it, driving at it with a wedge of pure force, attempting to batter the door down. The house didn't like that. Lightning enfolded me, wrapping me in blue light, burning through my shield and setting my nerves on fire. Screaming I collapsed in the doorway.

I came to in the middle of the road; Penny had dragged me, still twitching, back from the door. "Dammit Mort, if you're going to do something stupid at least warn me first!"

"Let's just assume I'm always doing something stupid. It's quicker and easier for both of us," I replied as I tried to stand up, but my legs had turned to jelly. Penny steadied me.

We can rend it asunder, son of Illeniel. Let us tear it down.

"Who is that!?" I yelled, looking around me.

"What's wrong Mort?" Penny had a worried expression.

"They're talking to me, but I can't find them!" I was staring around me; paranoia was beginning to take hold.

"Who? There's no one here but us," she was talking to me in a soothing tone. I realized she must think I was going mad.

"The voices..." I started, but I decided to let it go. I was beginning to wonder about myself. My legs were feeling better so I pulled away from her and walked toward the door again.

"Let's go back. You're just going to hurt yourself Mordecai." That was Rose. She sounded reasonable but I was tired of being reasonable.

"No, I'm not done yet." I pushed up my sleeves and reached out for the door handle again. Too late I remembered I hadn't replaced my shield. The lightning had burned it away from me. My hand touched the door handle but nothing happened. I stood still for a moment, wondering why the barrier hadn't stopped me. I let go and stepped back. "That's odd."

"What?" Penny asked.

"I just touched the handle, but a minute ago I couldn't even reach it," I responded. An idea came to me and I re-shielded myself. Reaching for the handle I found myself stopped by the invisible barrier again. My hand couldn't get within six inches of the handle. "I'm going to try something stupid," I said, looking at Penny.

"Let me get the fire brigade first," she replied. I'm not sure if she was joking, but I didn't wait. I removed my shield and reached for the door handle. I gripped it without problem and pulled. The door opened easily.

The doorway revealed a large entry hall. The walls were paneled in oak and stained a dark color, contrasting the lighter brown of the wood floors. I stepped inside and a crystal globe hanging above lit up, casting a warm golden light across the room. "Oof!" That was Penny; she had run into the barrier outside the door.

"Oh let me fix that for you," I said and removed the shield I had put over her. "Ok now try." She cautiously tried to enter once more but the barrier stopped her anyway.

"That's odd, when I removed my own shield it let me in."

"Maybe the magics are keyed to allow the descendants of your line inside," Rose put in. As usual her quick insight made sense but a few things still didn't fit.

"I know my mother lived here with him and she wasn't a descendant so he must have had some way for her to enter." Not to mention the protective magics had nearly fried me before I removed my shield. My best guess was that they couldn't identify me while my shield was in place. Still there had to be a way to let strangers and guests inside. "I'm going to look around a bit, I'll be back soon."

"You're enjoying this aren't you?" That was Penny, she wasn't happy about being left outside. I gave her a smile and shut the door.

Before I had gone two steps she started banging on the doorknocker. Apparently she was allowed to touch that. I started to turn back but a voice stopped me.

"There is a woman at the door." It sounded very similar to Benchley but I could tell the voice emanated from the enchantments around the house. I suppose they had people like him back then too. No accounting for taste I guess.

I was in a contrary mood, "See who it is."

A moment later the voice replied, "She says her name is Penelope Cooper and she is accompanied by a Rose Hightower."

Of course, I toyed with my options, but I didn't really know what they were, "What are my possible responses?" I asked.

"You may deny them entry, permit them to enter, or have them eliminated," the dry voice responded. I didn't like the sound of 'eliminated'. It probably entailed the same sort of lightning attack that nearly put me in an early grave.

"Allow them entry," I commanded. The door swung open on its own and I could see an exasperated Penny standing outside.

"Would you please explain to your talking door who I am?" she said.

"Already did, come on in—we'll see what happens this time."

She and Rose were both able to enter without a problem. The door politely closed itself once they were inside. The complexities of the enchantments were beyond anything I had previously imagined but they set my mind spinning with ideas. Meanwhile Penny glared at the door as if she were plotting revenge. "I hope I don't have to go through that every time I come in," she said finally.

"What do you mean?"

With a sigh she answered me, "It's your house now Mort. We'll probably be living here whenever we're in the city."

I hadn't given it any thought before but she was probably right. Assuming we ever returned to Albamarl. I doubted I'd be back within the half a year I had left to live. "Um, 'House' I have a question." I was addressing the enchantments now. It didn't respond. "Door, is there a way to let someone in without my permission?" Still no answer, obviously I had a lot to learn.

"Just forget it for now Mort. Let's see what the house looks like," Penny interrupted.

I didn't feel like arguing with inanimate objects in front of her and Rose anyway so I quickly agreed. We made our way through the entry hall to examine the rest of the house.

CHAPTER 9

King Edward Carenval sat in his reception chamber looking over the man who stood in front of him. The fellow was in his mid-forties and looked like he'd led a hard life. He stood six feet in height with dark hair and eyes, though his hair had gone grey at the sides. He bore no weapons, being in the presence of the king, but something about his stance gave the impression that there *should* be weapons on him.

"Do you know why we have called you here today?" Edward began.

"I would prefer not to make hasty assumptions your majesty, but given my past I would think it might have something to do with the Count di'Cameron." The man looked up from where he knelt, meeting the king's eyes.

"Indeed. We find ourselves in need of your counsel. Who would have guessed that Tyndal's child survived?" Edward rubbed his beard as he spoke.

"It was always a possibility. They never found her body or her child's."

"We understood that if a wizard died his pact-bearer died with him," the king's eyes were curious.

"They severed the bond before his death, your majesty."

"Is that possible? What is the point then?" Edward asked.

"It is possible your majesty, but according to the histories it had never happened before. Both parties must agree to it and the Anath'Meridum are sworn to never relinquish the bond. My guess would be that they agreed to it so that she could flee with the child."

"Cyhan, you were involved in Elena's training, but how would you know she severed the bond rather than having simply died?"

Cyhan answered, "When the bond is formed a gem is created. It is kept by the trainer from that day forward. It glows as long as the bond is intact and crumbles to dust when those bonded die." He reached into his pouch, bringing out a dull red gem. "Tyndal and Elena's gem faded but did not crumble, indicating they broke the bond before he died."

Edward leaned forward to look at the gem, "Why was this not reported?"

"It was reported your majesty," Cyhan looked steadily into the king's eyes without wavering.

"No matter," Edward waved his hand, "we must have forgotten after the news of the Cameron's destruction reached us. You must do better with the new trainee. We cannot afford another mistake such as Elena's."

"I agree your majesty, though if it had not been for that mistake there would be no new Anath'Meridum to train." Cyhan was overstepping his bounds but he had always been brash.

Edward looked at him sharply, "Be mindful of your words lest they lead you to trouble. If Elena had fulfilled her oath we would no longer have to worry about unbound wizards destroying the world. You will meet Mordecai tomorrow. You are to return to his home and see that he chooses quickly. If he refuses send word immediately, before you try to—remedy the situation." He left unspoken what the remedy would be, but they both knew there was only one possibility.

"Yes your majesty, I look forward to meeting him. I understand he has been free for over a year now. Did you see any sign of madness in him?" Wizards were always more difficult to manage if they had already become unstable.

"We would not know what to look for, but he seemed sane enough," Edward answered. "You may go now. You can judge for yourself when you meet him tomorrow."

***

I found the home of the Illeniels was fascinating. The upper floors held at least seven separate bedrooms, several parlors and, much to my excitement, a library. The first floor had a large parlor, a workshop and a massive kitchen. A door from the workshop led down a steep staircase into what seemed to be some sort of basement. The house itself seemed to have a foundation of solid stone, and the stairs had been rough cut from that same stone as they led down. Strangely they came to a dead end within the rock under the house. A casement indicated a doorway but the granite was seamless and unbroken. It appeared to be a false door.

Upstairs Rose was eagerly examining the library while Penny studied the master bedroom. I was alone staring at the strange stone doorway, if it really was a doorway. Unlike the rest of the house there were no enchantments or other magical markings here. The rock was smooth and untouched. I opened my mind to examine the stone, trying to see if there was a space behind it, but the world vanished into the stone. My thoughts sank into it without finding any purchase.

He has come, but does he see?

Great, the voice was back. It was easy to distinguish this from the physical voice that the door had used above. This was a purely mental thing, almost a delusion. I had begun to wonder about myself. I imagined I could feel the stones around me pulse, almost like a heartbeat. *I'm losing my mind,* I thought to myself. A scream from upstairs brought me back to reality.

Grabbing my staff I raced up the stairs, heading for the upper floors where the girls were exploring. I could hear both of them yelling now, followed by a loud crashing sound. When I reached the third floor I saw Penny crossing the hallway brandishing what appeared to be a wooden hat-rack, she vanished through the library door ahead of me.

"Let go of her!" came Penny's hoarse battle-cry as I looked in the doorway. The scene that greeted me would have been comical if not for the seriousness of the situation. A massive creature made of solid stone held Rose upside down by one leg. Her dress had fallen upward to cover her face and revealed a lovely set of gams. Penny charged at the creature holding Rose with her hat-rack lowered like a lance.

She struck it solidly but it ignored her attack. The man-shaped creature's mass was such that she failed to move it at all. "Please desist, intruders will not be tolerated." The voice that issued from it was deep and grating, like the stone it was made of. Penny ignored it and swept her hat-rack back to strike it across the side of the head. The wood snapped, leaving her holding the bottom half.

I had to give her credit, despite her total inability to affect the creature holding her friend she showed no fear. The only sound she made was a low growl as she searched the room for another weapon. She reminded me of an angry cat.

"Let me go you stupid pile of rubble!" That was Rose hissing from beneath her inverted skirts. Meanwhile Penny had found one of the library chairs and was winding up for a swing at the back of the thing's legs.

"Attacks will not be tolerated." It said and I saw long stone spikes sprouting from its free hand. As Penny swung at it the arm lifted, preparing to sweep down. The force alone would crush her, the spikes were overkill.

A quick word and I created a shield around her, the room shook as the massive arm impacted the shield. My knees buckled at the strength of it. Uttering several more words I thrust my arm out and an invisible fist drove it back to slam into the bookcase behind it. Rose screamed as she swung violently back and forth. "Stop!" I yelled.

The creature froze in place. Well hell... if I had known it was that simple I would have tried that to begin with. "What is your name?" I asked.

"Magnus, master," it replied.

"Why are you here?"

"I guard the library," it answered.

"I hate to interrupt, Mordecai, but do you think you could have it release me before you continue your interrogation?" Rose said.

Why hadn't I thought of that? I took one more good look at her legs... no sense wasting the moment after all, "Magnus please release the woman. She is a welcome guest here." It let go of her leg immediately, dropping her unceremoniously on her head.

"Ow!" Rose landed hard, forming a confusing pile of skirts and lovely female limbs. I moved to help her up but Penny beat me to her.

"Back off hero..." she said as she helped Rose to her feet. She gave me a hard stare, "I saw that look."

I was deeply offended by her lack of trust but I figured now wasn't the time to profess my wounded innocence. "Magnus, what are you?" I turned my attention back to the library guardian.

"A golem," it answered simply. That helped, I had no idea what a golem was.

"Please return to your station, you will not be needed further today," no sense admitting my ignorance. "The two women in the room with me are both guests and have my permission to use the library," I added with an afterthought.

"Yes master." It walked ponderously across the room and stood in the corner. Once it stopped moving it looked like statue, a particularly ugly and uninspired one. Its ancient creator obviously hadn't taken many art classes. Then again maybe its creator had been an impressionist. I had never cared much for what they called 'art'.

"Are you ok Rose?" I asked. She was sitting on the floor rubbing her injured leg. The calf and ankle were forming an ugly bruise. "Here let me see if I can help." I knelt down to put my hands on her leg.

Penny whispered in my ear as I passed her, "Careful now, I've got my eye on you." Women! You'd think I was half goat by the way she acted. I gave her a wink to put her at ease.

Placing my hands on Rose's leg I closed my eyes and focused my attention inward, first within myself and then within the leg I was holding. Broken blood vessels and inflamed tissue were the main problem. I repaired as many vessels as I could but the general inflammation was beyond my skill. Hopefully I had limited the extent of the bruising but I couldn't be sure. I also used a trick I had learned the year before, putting the nerves transmitting pain signals to sleep, numbing the sensations from that area.

"How's that?"

"Better," Rose replied, "Thank you." She put her hand on my shoulder and used me as a support while she got to her feet. "Doesn't hurt as much as I thought it would," she mused.

"I numbed it a bit. It will start to hurt more later, but with luck the worst will be over by then."

"I think perhaps I'll stay closer to you while we search. Most of the magics here seem to recognize you as their master." Rose was a wonder. She had just been shaken within an inch of her life and she was already calmly reasoning out the best course.

"That does seem wise," Penny put in, nervous now that it was clear how dangerous the house could be.

A random thought crossed my mind. I wondered how Penny would look hanging upside down. Her legs were easily a match for Rose's. I considered suggesting we test the theory, but I doubted she would take to the idea. Maybe if we used pillows in Magnus' hands, so that it didn't bruise her...

"I don't like that evil grin on your face Mordecai. What are you thinking?" Penny asked.

"Nothing," I replied innocently. "Did you find anything interesting in here Rose?" See, I'm learning the fine art of misdirection. Penny pursed her lips, she wasn't fooled.

"I was just walking around, reading the titles on the spines. I saw one over here titled, *'The History of Illeniel'*, but when I reached up to pull it down your rock monster took offense," Rose responded.

"And that was when Magnus inverted you?" Something about the word inverted just sounded funny to me. I'd have to find more ways to include it in future conversations.

"I'd like to know who *perverted* you Mort," Penny commented dryly.

"Actually I think it meant to warn me away at first, but I was so startled I kicked at it and—well you saw the result," Rose looked almost embarrassed. That was new to me; normally she was rather like a cat, devoid of shame.

I reached up to pull down the volume that had started all the trouble. I had to admit the title was intriguing. The book was inscribed with runes to preserve it against age and decay so it was difficult to judge how old it was, but I had the feeling it was incredibly ancient. The secrets of ages might lie within its pages. Considering the depths of my ignorance the contents of the library were daunting.

Opening the cover I scanned the first few pages. It had been penned by someone named Arador Illeniel. The name was unknown to me, not surprising since I knew next to nothing of the history of wizardry. The year written under his name was 546 A.S., just a few centuries after the sundering. Given that the current year was 1123 A.S. that made the book nearly six hundred years old. My mind reeled at the age of it. I began scanning the first page.

The first to carry the name was known simply as Illeniel. If he had a surname it is no longer known but his descendants bore his name as their surname from that time forward. There were no 'great' wizard lines then, simply men born to power. Over time the families that produced the greatest wizards gained fame and their descendants were watched for signs of it.

Mages were more common then and Illeniel is thought to have been born the son of a farmer. Early accounts claim that Illeniel was the first to hear the voice of the earth and later used this ability to raise the mountains known to modern men as the Elentirs.

Why he did this has been lost over the passage of many generations but some legends claim it was done to end a war between mankind and an elder race known as the She'har.

The age that followed has been called the 'golden age' of man as humankind grew and dispersed across the continents. The wizards of the line of Illeniel and the other great lines: Mordan, Gaelyn, Centyr, and Prathion, developed many fantastic magics now lost to knowledge. Many lesser lines of mages were alive then but only those of the great lines were sensitive enough to hear the voice of the earth, and few among even them.

"You can read the book later Mordecai. We should examine the rest of the house," Rose said, bringing me back to the present. I considered what I had learned in just a few paragraphs. There had been another race before mankind, five great lines of mages had existed, and the first Illeniel had *created* the Elentir Mountains! I was stunned. And what had the book meant by 'the voice of the earth'? Less than a page into it and I was already full of questions.

"What?" I responded. Smart as I was I could only keep track of one conversation at a time and my own internal dialogue had filled that spot.

Penny sighed, "She said we should keep looking around. You can read later."

I balked internally but I knew they were right, "Ok let's finish exploring. You and I will be spending the night here anyway."

Penny turned to Rose, "Would you like to stay the night with us Rose? The house is a bit dusty so you might have to rough it but..."

"Of course!" Rose interrupted. She loved nothing more than mysteries and my new house was chock full of them. "We can make a slumber party of it." She gave me a smile full of mischief, "I'll have some fresh linens brought over for the beds so we don't have to 'rough' it."

They spent several minutes making plans for the evening, a conversation in which I was purely a bystander. I stepped out into the hall and examined the rooms nearby. Across from the library was a short hallway lined with stone alcoves. From the outside it appeared to be the sort of room that might have a variety of statues set into each alcove. Curious I went in.

The alcoves were empty. Where statues might have stood in each recess there was instead a raised stone circle inscribed with magical runes. Having seen something like them before, I knew immediately what they were... teleportation circles. Each alcove had a name written above it, probably listing the destination, but all of them were unfamiliar—except one. 'Cameron' was the name written there.

The more I considered it, the more it made sense. Having married Elena di'Cameron my father would have wanted an easy way to visit her family. The matching circle at Cameron Castle must have been destroyed when fire gutted the keep. It made me sad to think my parents had probably been so close to an easy escape when my father died. I could only imagine how desperate their situation must have been.

I made up my mind then. Before we left I resolved to find the necessary books to build my own circle. There were plenty of examples of well-constructed circles here and once we returned I would build a new mate to the circle here. We would never be more than a moment away from my house here after that was done.

I went back into the hall and found the ladies both patiently waiting for me there. "The golem must have 'shaken' some sense into you," I quipped, since they hadn't gone exploring on their own. They failed to see the humor in my remark. Once again I was saddened that the world would never understand my comic genius.

"Did you find anything interesting in there while you were searching for your wit?" Rose replied.

"Just your dignity," I shot back, "but there wasn't enough left of it to bother with." I'll admit it, that remark was a bit mean, but she started it.

Rose grinned at me and was ready to continue our banter but Penny stepped in, "Let's go look around the master bedroom before I die of a broken funny bone."

"Spoilsport," I said.

We went down the hall to where the bedrooms were located and began poking around. Most of the rooms were quite spacious and despite Penny's statement earlier there was very little dust to be found. I suspected the house had some means of keeping itself clean. Still I would be glad of the new linens Rose had mentioned. No amount of cleaning could keep sheets fresh that had been on a bed for almost twenty years.

I only spent a short while examining the guest rooms. They were lovely rooms but the furnishings were nothing special. Naturally the master bedroom drew most of my attention. It held my parents' things. Entering that room was a strange experience. I knew the last two people to be there were the parents I had never known.

The first thing that grabbed my attention was a large portrait on one wall. The face of a beautiful woman stared back at me. The artist had skillfully captured her expression, a look that held both beauty and mystery. Blond hair stood out against a background of dark green ivy, while her blue eyes drew me in, hinting at intelligence and strong determination.

The picture was unsigned and had no name beneath it so I had no way of knowing for sure who the painting represented, but my heart knew. It was my mother. Unbidden tears came to my eyes as emotions I had not known I possessed came to the fore. Learning my mother's fate years before had stunned me, but still I had not felt sorrow. She was a stranger to me and her tale had evoked only the natural pity anyone might feel. Seeing her now filled me with a wistful sadness as I finally felt the loss of a love I had never had a chance to know.

A soft hand on my back told me Penny was there, but she didn't intrude upon the moment. I looked at the portrait 'til I could stand it no longer, then I turned and put my arms around her. She held me, without words or questions, 'til I had regained my composure.

Rose came in then, as I was wiping my face. Her quick eyes took in the painting and I'm sure she must have understood. She was kind enough to avoid the question and instead asked about the room, breaking the awkward silence. "This must have been your parents' room?" The answer to that was obvious but the question worked.

"I believe so."

Penny walked over to a large wooden wardrobe, "I wonder if they left any clothes behind." Pulling the doors open she looked inside. The interior was half empty but a few dresses still hung there alongside a doublet and a robe. I would have expected the items to be moth-eaten but the house apparently did not tolerate vermin any more than it tolerated dust.

"Oh that's lovely!" Rose remarked, running her fingers down the sleeve of a silken gown. "The style is so traditional."

"It almost looks as if they were just here. Everything is so well preserved," Penny added.

I was opening the drawers of the dresser but there were no surprises there. Just the things you'd expect in a nobleman's house. They had probably taken most of their valuable personal effects with them when they went on their trip. A variety of clothes, socks and undergarments were all that remained. An expensive jewelry box sat on top of the dresser but I saved it for last.

Opening it I was startled at how much it contained. Brooches, necklaces, earrings, bracelets and more sparkled where they nestled in velvet. It looked as though they had left most of their jewelry behind. I had no idea what any of it was worth.

Rose and Penny were both looking over my shoulder. "Do you see that?" Rose pointed at one of the rings.

"Is that what I think it is?" Penny replied.

They were examining a gold ring with a flat engraved top. It showed a dragon with its wings unfurled and circled by seven stars, the signet ring of Illeniel. "Why is it here?" I asked. I had always assumed that Tyndal had been wearing the ring when he destroyed half of Castle Cameron. "Shouldn't it have been with him when he died?" I already wore the signet ring of the Camerons. The old Count had been far enough away from the fire and heat when he died that it had survived and James Lancaster had saved it for me.

"As old as the line of Illeniel is there might have been more than one made," Rose answered. "Either that or he left it here for some reason, but that would be unusual." We discussed it for a while but no better ideas came to us. I tried to put the ring on but it was too tight so I put it on a chain around my neck instead. I would have it re-sized later.

We finished searching the room but didn't find anything else of note. Having determined that the bedrooms were safe I left the girls to making arrangements for the evening and went back to the library. I started to pick up *The History of Illeniel'* again but I noticed a writing desk off to one side. I crossed over to look at it.

The top bore a dried out inkwell and several pens but the drawers of the desk held a collection of letters and other documents. I sifted through them, curious, but most of them were what you would expect. Messages from the king, calling for Tyndal's presence in court were the most numerous, along with notices from a shipping company regarding some business concerns. Wait, what?

I looked over the letters from the shipping company; Trigard Exporters was the name of the business. Most of them detailed deposits at the royal bank here in Lothion. It appeared my father held a large portion of the rights to the business. That of course led to several other questions—if he had an account at the bank how much was in it? Did the company still exist? Who took control of his shares after he died?

The longer I was in Albamarl the more unfinished business I found that needed attending to. I would have to make a trip to the bank before I left. I grew tired of sifting through the correspondence and business papers but before I shut the desk a letter caught my eye. What I had hoped to find in the desk were personal letters but naturally anything my father had written was in the hands of whomever he had sent it to. This letter had the look of a personal letter written to him. What made it stand out was the fact that the outer seal looked like it bore the imprint of the royal arms of Gododdin.

I unfolded it, curious who would have sent my father a letter from that unfortunate country. As far as I knew the royal family there was executed about six years before I was born.

My Dear Friend,

I trust this letter finds you well. I wish I could say the same about things here. The Children of Mal'goroth have not been so foolish to disrupt trade yet, so our mutual concerns here are still doing well.

Vendraccus grows bolder by the day and I fear he has agents even within my home. It is impossible to be sure and paranoia and suspicion are now the rule rather than the exception. Thus far he has done little more than harass and antagonize the church of Celior, but numerous murders and back alley brawls hint that he is not content with civilized debate.

Of more immediate concern, I have sad news to deliver. Your friend George Prathion was murdered and the evidence indicates that Nathan Balabas was most likely responsible. Unfortunately we are unable to find him for questioning, but what would you expect when a wizard commits murder? I doubt we could hold him even if we found him.

As I'm sure you know… George was one of the most outspoken detractors of Vendraccus and the Children. I now suspect that Nathan may have thrown his lot in with the cultists since he had no personal issues with George that I am aware of. That bodes ill for all of us as I'm sure you know how badly Vendraccus would love to have a wizard on his side, even if he isn't one of the old lines.

Take extra caution in your own dealings. Now that George is gone you are the last known descendant of one of the great lines, not that I have to remind you of that.

Please give my regards to your companion, Elena. Though I have not met her I have heard she was good friends with Phillip Balistair. According to all accounts he died well. Had it not been for Nathan's treachery I am sure he would have kept George safe.

Your Friend,

V.

My father had been friends with another wizard of the old families. That shouldn't have surprised me, but then I had never known any of them. More interesting was the name 'Phillip Balistair'. I wondered if he was some relative of Elizabeth Balistair, who I had met last year when she visited Lancaster. From the wording I assumed he was the Anath'Meridum of George Prathion. Too many new facts were rattling around in my skull and I struggled to put them all in place.

More curious was the way the letter was signed, 'V'. The only person with a V in their name of the royal family in Gododdin, that I knew of, was Valerius; the ill-fated last king of that country. That didn't mean much of course, my knowledge of royal bloodlines was next to nothing. The royal Graeling family could have had a dozen members with names beginning in the letter 'v'. I only happened to know Valerius' name because he had been the last king there.

Had King Edward known of Tyndal's connections to Gododdin? There were too many things I was ignorant of. Considering what had happened at Lancaster last year many of those things might be deadly. Ignorance would be no shield if more of my father's old enemies came knocking on my door.

"Mordecai..." Penny's voice came to me from the hall. "Let's find something to eat, the daylight is waning." My stomach agreed with her, so I got up and we went in search of Rose, hoping she would know of a good place to eat.

CHAPTER 10

Royce Eldridge stood quietly by the outer gate. Since his son had left a week gone by there had been two more disappearances. Consequently Dorian had asked all the outlying villagers to sleep within the castle confines at night. It was a pain for the families that had to leave their homes each evening but they didn't complain much. Safety was a welcome trade-off for fear. The new town militia couldn't possibly patrol all the outer farms.

The outer curtain wall of Castle Cameron was still in good condition and encircled most of Washbrook. The families that had to relocate each evening found places to sleep with friends and relatives that lived inside the wall. The few who had nowhere to go slept in the completed portion of the castle garrison.

Dorian and Joe McDaniel had done a good job organizing the men of Washbrook into a passable militia. Most of them kept to their normal jobs during the daytime, while a few would remain on duty guarding the gates. The daytime positions were rotated so that no one's livelihood would be too greatly impacted and they all took turns. At night the men of the village would take up arms and work in shifts to watch the gates, of which there were two. Several would patrol the tops of the walls as well to ensure no one snuck over.

The children were kept busy during the daytime preparing torches and oil lanterns to light the tops of the walls and the areas around the gates. The nighttime shifts and daytime guard positions meant that more work fell on the shoulders of the women of Washbrook but they managed it well. The people of the town were used to hard work. They were a community under siege, but strong organization and constant activity kept fear at bay.

Royce looked over at the other man standing guard at the main gate with him. David Tanner was a lean man, slim and rangy. His work tanning leathers and hides had given him a chronic cough from the fumes but he seemed sturdy enough otherwise. Like Royce he wore a heavy leather jerkin and carried a spear.

David's daughter had been one of the first to disappear but despite his tragedy Royce found it hard to work up much sympathy for the man. He complained too much and had a tendency to fall asleep when he wasn't talking. Royce preferred him asleep as opposed to listening to his constant bitching. *He'd never cut it in a smithy,* Royce thought to himself.

The night was growing darker. No moon and an overcast sky ensured that it would soon be pitch black out. A lantern on a pole some twenty feet from the gate provided most of their light. It had been Joe McDaniel's idea to post lanterns away from gates, that way they provided more illumination of the surrounding area, instead of just highlighting the guards at their posts.

Royce nudged the other man, David had just started to drift off again, "Come on, it's time shut the gate." *You'll be able to sleep better on the battlements anyway,* he thought uncharitably.

"Alright, I'm about tired of standing out here," Tanner responded. Lifting his spear he turned to walk back inside the gate. A third man, Sam Turner stood within, next to the warning bell. "Give me a hand with the doors Sam." Tanner said.

Royce was about to turn and follow him in when he heard a sound. Years hunting deer in the Duke's forest had given him keen ears, but this was no deer. "Who's out there?" he called.

Sam had one of the two gate doors in place and David had his side halfway closed. Once the two met in the center they would throw the heavy bar to lock them in place, but they paused when they heard Royce's voice. Sam looked out to see Royce backing slowly toward the opening. He thought he could see the form of a smaller person approaching from the darkness but it was still indistinct. "Royce, do I need to hold the gate for someone?" Sam asked.

Royce had already recognized the person walking toward them; it was Rebecca Miller, the third person to go missing. She had been gone for almost three weeks now and Royce already knew the full details of Mordecai's encounter with what had been Sadie Tanner. He backed steadily toward the gap in the gate doors, "No Sam, I think we'd best lock up tight as soon as I get through the gate." He never took his eyes off the form of the thirteen year old girl walking steadily toward him. Two more steps and he would be inside. Rebecca was only ten feet away now.

Sam heard the tension in Royce's voice. That and the fact that he didn't turn his head to speak told him everything he needed to know, but David Tanner wasn't so quick to understand. The light clearly showed the girl approaching when David spoke up, "Hey now! Isn't that Rebecca Miller?" He started to step away from the gate but Sam grabbed his shoulder.

"Wait up David," Sam said.

"Will you let me in? I'm ever so hungry and I've had nothing these past few days," came a curiously monotone voice from the girl.

"What's your name girl?" Royce asked. He had stopped backing up since it was clear he wouldn't be able to get them to close the gate doors 'til the girl's identity was settled.

"I can't remember. Won't you help me?" she replied. She was only feet from him now and might have gotten closer but Royce had his spear down, pointing squarely at her chest.

David shook off Sam's hand and stepped out, "It's Rebecca. Dammit Royce, stop pointing that thing at her. She's just a girl!" Shoving Royce's spear aside he reached out to take the teenager's arm, she eagerly clasped his hand.

"Don't touch her!" Royce shouted, but it was too late. David Tanner struggled to pull away from the girl, a look of terror on his face as he felt the dark pull on his spirit. She had both hands on him now and she held him with incredible strength. Royce didn't wait; jerking his spear back into line he impaled the young girl on it, driving the long bladed head through her torso.

Sam saw what was occurring from a few feet behind them, "By the gods! Royce what have you done?!" He started forward but Royce yelled for him to stop.

"Ring the goddamned bell!" he shouted. The girl hadn't let go of David and was pulling him closer as he weakened, his knees buckling. Royce struggled to push her off the other man with the spear but she showed no sign of letting go. The weapon might have gone all the way through her but it was a boar spear and the cross-piece kept it from passing, a good thing as it allowed him to push harder against her. Very little blood issued from the girl's wound, and what there was seemed thick and black.

Sam finally snapped out of his shock and ran back to ring the bell while the men struggled in front of the gate. A dark shadow on the periphery of his vision warned

Royce that the girl wasn't alone and he let go of the spear. Stepping back he drew his sword just in time to meet the charge of a man he didn't recognize. The stranger was unarmed but his slack face and empty expression made it clear he was cut from the same cloth as the girl.

Slashing sideways he severed the man's hand at the wrist as he slammed into Royce. The weight of his body shoved Royce back into the unsecured gate door, causing it to swing wider. At his first touch Royce felt the coldness seeping into him, a dark biting wind drawing his life out. The creature's remaining hand had him by the throat and try as he might he couldn't pull it free. He could hear the bell starting to ring behind him, but help couldn't possibly arrive soon enough.

A lifetime shaping iron had given the blacksmith strength few men could hope to match. Even as he felt himself starting to weaken he slammed the hilt of his sword into the monster's face. The blow had little effect on the creature but it gave him enough room to swing the sword properly and he used the opportunity to hack at the arm holding him. He failed to completely sever it, due to the awkward angle but he cut deeply into the elbow and dislodged the hand from his throat. "Get off me damn you!" he ground out the words as the hand came loose from his throat. He would have backed away but the creature's other arm, the one missing a hand swung up to club him in the side of the head, sending him reeling.

Royce wound up falling sideways onto the hard cobblestones but he kept his eyes on the creature as it turned to follow him. One step and it was to him but he didn't wait for it to fall on him. If it landed on top of him he knew he would never have the strength to get out from under it. Sweeping the sword low to the ground he took the thing's right foot off at the ankle and it toppled away.

Scrabbling backward he looked over to see what had become of Tanner and what he saw wasn't pretty. The other man had collapsed and the thing that was latched onto him was cooing softly, like a small child. The monster that had been Rebecca Miller had a look of rapture on her face while both of her hands were gripping the older man's head. David's eyes had rolled upward and he seemed completely unconscious now.

Royce tried to stand and for a brief moment he considered attacking the girl, but his left leg failed to hold his weight. *Old age, always knew it would be the death of me,* he thought as he saw the one he had been fighting crawling toward him. He raised his sword, wondering if he could take off another appendage before it got to him when a mailed boot swept out and kicked the creature away.

Dorian Thornbear stood over him, his enchanted mail sparkling in the lantern light, "Sorry it took me so long to get here."

"Better late than never." Royce answered as he eased himself up on his good leg and hobbled inside the gate. Dorian was methodically hacking the bodies of the two creatures limb from limb. He was efficient at the task but despite his thoroughness the body parts continued writhing on the ground.

He might have kept at it longer, to see just how many pieces you needed to cut one into before it quit moving, but Royce called to him from the gateway, "Get inside there's more coming!" Looking up Dorian saw several dark shapes approaching in the lantern light. He grabbed Tanner's limp arm and dragged the man back with him, while Royce and Sam shoved the gate doors closed behind them. They all breathed a sigh of relief when the bar was finally in place.

Royce leaned over and checked Tanner, to see if he was alright. David had been alive and healthy only minutes before but he wasn't breathing and there was no pulse. "He's dead," Royce said.

"How? He doesn't have a mark on him!" Sam shouted. The normally reliable craftsman was close to panic.

"When that one touched me a minute ago I could feel it drawing the life out of me. As soon as one of 'em touches you you start to feel weak. I'd guess he got a bit more of that than I did," Royce answered.

"We need to get up on the wall and see what they're doing. The rest of the men will be here in a few minutes," Dorian stated calmly.

"What do we do with David?" Sam asked.

"He might turn into one of them," Royce replied.

"He's dead!"

"So were they, unless I miss my guess," Royce answered flatly. "We probably need to cremate him or something but there's no time right now. We'll figure it out later; if he does turn it probably won't be right away—I hope." He turned and followed Dorian up the stairs to the top of the wall. Not knowing what else to do Sam went with him.

"Dammit!" Dorian said as he looked down from the top of the wall, "They're climbing up."

"How? I cut a foot and a hand off one of 'em," Royce was incredulous, until he looked over the top himself. A crowd of people had emerged from the darkness, gathering at the base of the wall near the gate. Three of them had started climbing the wall, gripping the rough stones in their hands. The walls weren't smooth, and everyone knew an agile child might manage a climb of some distance, if he were foolish enough. Generally though most adults were simply too heavy to manage it with the small handholds the rough stone afforded. That wasn't stopping these things; they clung to the stones with amazing finger strength, pulling themselves steadily upward, hand over hand.

The rest of the militia had finally arrived and began spreading out along the top of the wall. Many carried hunting bows and began firing into the shapes climbing up the twenty foot wall, which had no visible effect. "Stop shooting! It doesn't do any good. Use your spears to knock them loose when they get near the top," Dorian shouted.

Joe McDaniel had reached the wall as well and began organizing the men. "I need five men to return to the other gate, and ten more to spread out along the wall—that way!" he pointed in the direction he wanted them to go. "You— you—you...," he singled out men and sent them out to keep watch along the rest of the wall. "The last thing we want is more of them climbing up while we're all over here."

Within minutes he and Dorian had a good quarter of the militia spread out to watch the rest of the walls, while the rest did their best to keep the things climbing the walls from getting to the top. For the most part it worked; though the creatures were strong even they couldn't maintain a grip while someone with a spear was poking and prodding them loose. The only casualties so far were a few lost spears, whenever one would grab at a weapon before falling.

Royce walked over to where Dorian was watching the progress at one portion of the wall, "I'm damned glad they're too stupid to use bows. They'd be a hell of a lot more effective against us than they were against them."

Dorian's brows went up as he thought about it. After a moment he answered, "I don't know that they're stupid. From what I've seen so far they're more effective without weapons, one touch and they have the advantage. Not to mention they don't seem to fear bodily harm. If we hold them off tonight, though—I wouldn't be surprised if they return with bows. I think they were hoping to get through the gates before we could stop them."

A shout from Joe McDaniel interrupted their conversation, "David Tanner what the hell do you think you're doing? Stop! Have you gone insane?!" Royce looked over and saw what had caused the commotion. David Tanner was standing behind the gate and he had already lifted the heavy bar that kept it shut. The heavy wooden doors were starting to swing open.

"That's not David anymore! He's been turned!" Royce yelled, but it was far too late. Every able bodied man was on the walls, it would take them far too long to reach the gates and shut them. The enemy would be inside within seconds. Royce started to head down the stairs but Dorian shoved him aside.

"Stay alive old man! We'll need your skills if we survive this night." Dorian ran down the steps, jumping the rest of the distance when he was still six feet from the bottom. Several more giant strides and he reached the gate, hoping to shut it before their foes realized the opportunity. He was too late. Before Dorian could stop them hands curled around the insides of the wooden doors, pulling them wider and one of the creatures stepped through.

Dorian switched tactics without missing a step. His sword was out and in his hand; the one that had stepped through fell back, missing its head and a large part of its left shoulder. The enchantment Mordecai had put on his sword made it impossibly sharp and it cut through flesh and bone effortlessly. "Someone shut the gate!" he bellowed as he waded into the undead that surged toward the opening.

The ones climbing the walls gave up and dropped down, to join those rushing at the now open gate. Hands reached out to grasp at Dorian but could find no purchase. Enchanted mail covered him from head to toe, preventing their touch from sapping his strength. Like a wave on a rocky shore they broke against him, giving way before his sword. They might have borne him under by sheer weight of numbers, but for the sword. With each stroke it swept limbs and bodies in twain. Driving forward he cut and sliced, reducing the undead bodies of men, women and children into helpless twitching pieces.

A fierce minute followed as he cut and slashed and eventually even the undead drew back. Unfortunately the gate itself was fully ten feet wide, and some of them would be able to get past him with the next rush. They gathered around him, ten, then twenty, then more, 'til at least thirty stood gathered silently around him. "Shut the goddamned gate!" Dorian was frantic, when they rushed him again he couldn't possibly keep them from getting in, and it would probably only take a few to make a shambles of the lightly armored men inside. The wall was their best defense—but only if the gate was closed.

"I'll be damned before I shut you out there lad!" That was Joe's voice, "Get back in first."

Dorian knew the moment he wavered or turned they would be on him, and pressing against the doors. There would be no way to close it against such a press. "Joe you shut that fucking gate now or you'll wish you were damned! Do it!" As he spoke he saw a glimmer of eyes at the edge of the light, beyond the enemy facing him. A small boy stood there, hanging back from the fight… watching.

The enemy wasn't waiting for Joe to decide and they rushed back at Dorian, now with strength of numbers. He saw one or two pass him, even as he cut at the others and he almost despaired, 'til he heard the heavy thud of the bar dropping down behind him. No longer tied to one spot he began to move, making it harder for them to mass themselves to bear him down.

Fighting wildly it seemed for a minute that they would be unable to stop him. Sweeping slashes removed reaching hands and sometimes whole arms, but no one could fight so many for long. His enemy had no natural fear and they pressed in, surrounding him. At last a hand caught him from behind, pulling at his shoulder and throwing him off balance and within seconds he was down, thrashing under a mass of foes he could not hope to defeat.

The only flesh Dorian had exposed were his eyes and jaw, where his helm didn't cover. He struggled but hands and arms made contact at last and Dorian felt his strength draining away. *I don't want to wind up as one of these things,* he thought to himself, but it seemed that would be his fate after all. He managed to pull his head away for a moment and put his face to the ground, trying to keep their deadly touch from his skin. There were so many on him that he never heard the gate opening.

"Alright boys! Now!" Joe's voice rang out as the men of Washbrook pushed the gate wide and stepped up. Two held casks of lamp oil while the rest carried torches and swords or axes. The two small casks were thrown forward smashing onto the ground a few feet to either side of where the mob of undead held Dorian down. Lamp oil spilled out, washing over the ground and splattering on those nearest where they struck—then the torches landed and the world went up in flames.

Burning bodies thrashed as the flames blinded the undead. Dorian fought his way free of the ones holding him as the militia men waded in, hacking and cutting at the enemy with axes, swords, and in a few cases scythes. Parts of his legs had burning oil on them but it hadn't burned long enough to get through the padded gambeson underneath his mail yet. "Over here Dorian!" Royce called to him, holding a heavy wool blanket soaked with water.

He staggered through the press of men and undead to reach the blacksmith and let him throw the blanket over him. Royce wrapped it around his legs, beating to smother out the flames there. "What the hell is going on?" he shouted.

"We just pulled your bacon out of the fire boy," Royce laughed.

"They can't hold them!" Even now Dorian could see some of the men had already fallen prey to the unnatural creatures. Without enchanted armor such as Dorian wore, it only took a hand on an arm to quickly render a man unable to fight.

"Then you best make sure we do!"

Dorian stopped arguing and went back into the fray. He moved carefully to avoid the worst of the burning bodies, picking his targets. He moved back and forth, hacking away the monsters that had gotten ahold of townsmen before they could drain them utterly. A large number of their enemies were just wildly thrashing bodies, burning silently on the ground now. The rest were soon reduced to helpless body parts.

It finally dawned on him that they had won. *This is what strength is Mordecai. This is the power of the people you are entrusted with,* he thought to himself. He wished Mort could see them now, faces flushed with excitement as fear turned to the thrill of victory. Almost all of them had gotten a taste of the undead touch, and now they understood better what they faced. Having survived, and won, they were full of life. Someone began to shout, "Dorian—Dorian—Dorian...!" and soon they had all taken up the chant.

Long minutes later he finally calmed them down, "Enough! This was your victory, and don't forget it! Now you know what your lives are worth, and more importantly, the enemy knows we won't sell ourselves cheaply." Some of the townsfolk nodded at this, but in their hearts they knew they would have lost but for the burly warrior in shimmering mail.

Dorian turned on Joe, "What were you thinking opening the gate? Everything could have been lost..."

Joe didn't let him finish, "It damn near was, but I wasn't gonna let 'em have you dammit. I'd do it again too and not think twice about it!"

Dorian stared at Joe. He didn't have an answer for the man's stubborn pride. Instead he switched subjects, "whose idea was the lamp oil?"

"That was old Royce there. He's a quick thinking son of a bitch!" Joe slapped Royce on the shoulder, drunk on adrenaline.

Dorian leaned over to Royce, "What are we going to do with him? I thought he was level-headed but he's crazy as a hatter."

The old blacksmith grinned, "Can't fix stupid son, and maybe you shouldn't try."

They spent several hours after that, gathering up the bodies and pieces of bodies. They discovered that the still moving flesh was dangerous yet, but luckily Royce had a surplus of tongs and iron bar-stock in his smithy and they used those to move them. When they had finally created a single pile they used more lantern oil and some deadwood to create a funeral pyre. Nothing would be left of the things that had attacked them.

Once all was said and done the town of Washbrook had lost two men, David Tanner being the first. The second man, Seth Colburn, had gone down during the rush to save Dorian and had died before he could be rescued. From the rough count they made of the enemy it appeared they had dismembered and burned almost twenty eight of the undead. Several had escaped at the end when the fight turned against them.

It was a victory, but a small village like Washbrook could hardly afford to lose anyone and the families of those lost would be mourning for a long time to come.

CHAPTER 11

Irose early the next morning, anxious to check the books in the library once more. I knew I had little time before we would have to return to Washbrook and this would likely be my last chance to examine the writings left here—unless I learned to create a matching teleport circle when we got home.

I started searching the shelves for anything I might find regarding the creation of such circles and by chance I got lucky. A slender volume proclaimed itself to be '*A Definitive Guide on the Creation and Maintenance of Teleportation Waypoints*'. It looked to be just the thing, although the author seemed a bit self-important. I set it aside to bring with me on the trip home.

Having accomplished my primary goal I rewarded myself with some time reading '*The History of Illeniel*':

> *Those powerful enough to speak to the earth came to be called 'archmages' and the arts they employed were fabled to be so great that no modern scholar can rightly credit the truth of the stories about them. The 'shining gods' of humankind were young and weak in those days and wizardry so common that few sought to worship them. The gods of the She'har, now called the 'dark gods' were powerful but malignant to humanity. The loss of their people left them estranged from the new world and they descended into madness.*

The wizards of those times learned to be wary of the dark gods even as they shunned the new gods. None would treat with the dark gods and few paid heed to the shining gods. Mankind controlled its own fate. Things might have remained so had not one young wizard, Jerod, of the line of Mordan given into greed and lust for power.

Jerod had been born to power but was not strong enough to speak to the earth. His jealousy of the existing archmages is part of what led to his downfall and his betrayal of humanity. At that time two archmages were alive, Gareth of the line of Gaelyn, and Moira of the line of Centyr. There were rarely more than two or three archmages alive at any time in history, so this was not uncommon.

Jerod had fallen in love with Moira of the Centyr, but she had eyes only for another, an unremarkable mage from the line of Illeniel. The details of their unfortunate love triangle did not survive the dark times that followed but it is known that Jerod gave in to the temptations of the dark god, Balinthor. Promises of power beyond that of the archmages seduced young Jerod. Believing that greater power might woo the archmage Moira he summoned the dark god and opened his mind to him.

I paused for a moment, thinking, until yesterday I had never heard mention of 'archmages' and I couldn't help but wonder how they differed from the other wizards of the time. The repeated references to the 'voice of the earth' also intrigued me. I could sense Penny approaching so I set the book aside, in the stack I planned to bring with us on our journey.

"Good morning," she said from the doorway.

"Morning," I replied. "I guess we should start getting ready to leave."

"Breakfast first."

That sounded like a wonderful idea, except we didn't have any food. If there was anything left in the pantry I wouldn't trust it to be edible after so many years. "Hmmm, I wonder how we should manage that?"

"There is someone at the door," announced the disembodied voice of the house. I really needed to learn the rules regarding how the enchantments built into the house worked.

"Who is it?" I asked. There was a short pause before the voice replied.

"He says his name is Marcus Lancaster," the voice supplied.

"Wait until I get down to the front door, then let him in." I hurried downstairs. Not long ago I would have simply let him in immediately. Now that my friend was a vessel for a goddess I wasn't sure of his motives. The door opened up as soon as I approached. "Good morning Marc," I said as soon as I saw his face.

"Mort this house is amazing! The door just talked to me," he responded. He looked and sounded like the friend I had always known.

"Yeah I know. I'm still getting used to it myself."

"Can I come in?" he asked.

I suddenly felt a bit bad. I had unconsciously remained in the doorway, my body language relaying the message that he might not be welcome. "I'm sorry, right this way. I'd offer you breakfast but we don't have any food at the moment. We were just sorting that out actually." I stepped back and motioned him inside.

"If you're hungry I know a place where we can get some good bread and sausages," he stepped in and the door closed itself behind him.

"That sounds wonderful, but we need to talk about some things first," I gave him a hard stare. "I thought you came to Albamarl to find a wife, not..." I motioned at the plain robe he wore.

"I did. Life has a way of catching you by surprise sometimes. I never thought I would be chosen by the Lady of the Evening either," he shrugged.

"Your father was not pleased."

"I can understand that, but he'll come around in time. I have a higher purpose now. He has other children to fill that role," he looked around. "This house is interesting! I couldn't see such things before, but every piece of this place is filled with magic."

"Is she inside you now?"

"She's always there, filling the empty parts of me. I was very unhappy Mort. I just didn't realize it because I had nothing to compare it to—now when I look back I can see just how empty it was," he smiled as he said this, but it didn't reassure me.

"So I've lost my friend to a goddess."

"No! I'm still me! I will always be your friend. I'm just a little bit more than I was. I'm complete now, but that doesn't mean I don't still need my friends. You're just as much a part of who I am as you ever were." He seemed very earnest. "I do have some things to tell you however. The goddess sent me with several messages for you, and none of it is good."

I sighed, "How did I know you were going to say that?" I had yet to receive good news from any of the divine beings I had met. Of course I had only met two so far. "Let's eat first; I may not have an appetite after your news."

Half an hour later I was seated at an outdoor cafe with Penny, Rose and Marc. I had actually never even heard the word 'cafe' before that day so it was an educational experience. Who knew a city could be so large that some people could make a living doing nothing but cooking for strangers? In Lancaster the closest thing to it was the tavern, and they only sold food at certain times of day, their primary business was selling ale.

They served us black tea, a heavy brown bread and spicy sausages. I heartily approved. Once we had mostly finished I looked at Marc, "I suppose you might as well get on with the news, I don't think I can eat any more."

"The shiggreth are loose again, and they've begun taking people in Sileby," he said. Sileby was a small town in the barony of Arundel, not far from the western border of my estates.

"Wait, what? Shiggreth?"

Rose spoke up, "Evil minions of the dark gods. Undead creatures that take the form of the men they slay. Before the sundering, Balinthor used them as his servants." I gave her a long stare, lifting my eyebrows in surprise. She looked over her tea with an air of nonchalance, "I read a lot. I never thought the stories might actually be true."

It had never occurred to me to tell Rose about our nighttime encounters. I resolved myself to asking for her advice more frequently. She was a wealth of information.

Marc went on, "Unfortunately what she says is true. The shiggreth are real and they are loose again. If they aren't stopped soon they will overrun the land."

"But what are they exactly?" Penny asked. I nodded as well, wanting to know more about their basic nature.

"I had never heard of them before either, but I have a greater source of information now," Marc replied. "The goddess tells me that they are the shells of men who have had their spirits drawn out. Their bodies live on, in a sort of undying state, while a dark spirit of the void fills them. Their touch can draw the spirit from the living, and when they have done so another dark spirit fills the body left behind."

"Shiggreth means 'eaten ones' in Lycian," I put in.

"I didn't know that," Marc answered. "But it fits."

"Where did they come from Marcus?" Rose asked, "According to the legends they were all destroyed after the Sundering."

"My Lady is uncertain; she can't see the workings of the other gods. Most likely these were created by one of the dark gods. The most obvious suspect being Mal'goroth since he currently holds sway in Gododdin, which borders Arundel, especially in light of my other news."

"Are you sure they were created by one of the dark gods?" I wasn't going to pull any punches even if my friend had become a host of one of the shining gods.

Marc sighed; he knew I didn't trust his goddess. "There is no way for me to convince you of Millicenth's good will, since you obviously don't trust *any* of the gods, but think on this. The shiggreth are a plague, they will consume every living soul if they are not stopped. The shining gods represent what is best in humanity; they are a part of us. Only the dark gods would have a motive in destroying us."

Penny was impatient, "What was your other news? Is it war? Is Gododdin moving against us?"

Marc's face lit up with surprise, "How did you know that? I only just heard it from the Lady herself."

"I saw it, two days ago, but I wasn't sure who it was, or why," she answered and a shadow crossed her face as she remembered what would happen. Her eyes darted to me for a second and I could see despair in them.

Rose looked on with interest, "My… the secrets that are unfolding at the breakfast table this morning! What truly intrigues me, are the secrets still left unsaid. I hope everyone is being forthcoming. The future of the kingdom may hang on the conversation at this table today." Her face was lit with mirth but her voice carried serious undertones. She knew Penny hadn't told her everything.

"Enough," I said, "What did the goddess tell you Marc?"

"That Gododdin prepares for war against Lothion. As you know, simple geography means they'll have to come through Arundel. Cameron and Lancaster will be crushed immediately after if they intend to strike at Albamarl."

"Then the shiggreth are a ploy, to divert our attention from the borders," I stated.

"They are far worse than a decoy. If even one of them escapes it could spell the end for mankind. They can multiply faster than rabbits. Their victims swell their ranks rapidly and they are difficult to fight," Marc answered.

"It doesn't make sense. Why does Gododdin want war? Lothion has done nothing to aggrieve them. Vendraccus has nothing to gain and everything to lose," I said.

"You make the mistake of thinking like a human. Gododdin is not controlled by people, but rather by Mal'goroth. To him their nation is simply a tool to get him what he wants," said Marc.

"What does he want?" I replied.

"The destruction of humankind… his people are long gone, only death and despair drive him now. You are his best hope of destroying humanity. The shiggreth are a secondary means to the same goal," said Marc.

Rose interrupted, "More importantly you need to know 'when'. The knowledge that they plan to attack doesn't help much if we don't know that."

"We have the rest of the summer and the winter to prepare, they'll be in Lothion in the early spring," Penny put in. Marc and Rose both looked at her but no one questioned her information. We had all experienced enough of Penelope's prophecies to know not to doubt her now.

"That doesn't give you much time Mordecai," Rose stated.

"Me? Shouldn't the king be the one to deal with this? I'll help of course, but this sounds like something a lot bigger than one small wizard and the County of Cameron."

Penny gave me a funny look, "Small wizard? I would beg to differ. But you are right, the king will have to be informed, this is a matter for the entire kingdom."

Rose laughed, "True Penelope, he's anything but small." Then she had the gall to wink at me. I turned several shades of red.

"I don't care how big his wizard's staff is. This is going to take a response from the entire kingdom if we're to emerge victorious," Marc added. Apparently being a saint didn't preclude him from making dirty jokes at my expense. I couldn't help but laugh.

"Jokes aside, you underestimate your role in this Mordecai," Rose told me. "You are Mal'goroth's goal. He needs you to create the world-bridge. He's created the shiggreth and manufactured this war to put you in harm's way. He's hoping you'll make a mistake that will put you in his hand. Failing that he'll get what he wants just as surely with the shiggreth. You can't afford to sit back and ignore either situation."

Marc was nodding as Rose spoke, "She's right. You have to plan now."

Rose went on, "First we lay out your advantages. One, you're a wizard. Second, you have land, people and support in the form of Lancaster and hopefully the king as well. Third, you have far more time and warning than the enemy planned for you to have. That means you can determine your response well in advance rather than reacting to events."

I was constantly amazed by Rose's clear headed reasoning, but I felt overwhelmed. "So what do you suggest?"

Rose shook her head, "I'm not making the decisions for you, but I can help with logistics. The Hightowers have had to support many a war." That was certainly true, Lord Hightower was in charge of the defense of Albamarl and in time of war handled planning and supply lines for the army. Some of it must have rubbed off on his daughter.

"The king should be making these decisions," I replied.

"Don't be a fool Mort," Penny said. "The royal army wasn't there in my vision. You have a duty to report this, and to support the king, but you have to plan based on that fact. The king may decide to pull his forces back to protect the capital. Or he may choose a battlefield closer in than Cameron and Lancaster. Either way it means our lands get crushed before the war even gets well under way."

"You don't think he'll send forces to the border to stop the invaders there?" Marc asked.

"I don't know, but I didn't see them in my vision. Whatever happens we have to plan for the fact that at some point we will be facing the enemy in our lands," Penny replied.

I was tired of listening to pointless debate so I cut in, "Alright… so let's make our plans, starting right now, enough speculation. What can we do today?"

"Every war starts with money," Rose stated. "You found out last night that you have more money than you realized. You need to go to the Royal Bank of Lothion and get everything they're holding in your name, you'll need it. Then you have to inform the king. Marcus will have to inform his father, including everything we've discussed here. Lancaster will be your most valuable ally since he stands to lose just as much as you do. I will talk to my father and see what help he can give. No matter what he decides I will gather whatever support and supplies I can to aid you."

"I thought you were going to come to Washbrook with us?" Penny reminded her.

"That was half an hour ago. Things have changed dear," Rose replied. "On second thought Mordecai, don't take all the money out, just take part and leave me a letter of credit to draw on the rest."

"I don't even know how much I have, if anything. How much do you think you'll need?" I asked her.

"It's war sweetheart, we'll need everything you have and more. I plan to use my own savings as well. Fielding an army is expensive."

"An army!?" I know, I should have realized. I just wasn't used to thinking on such a large scale.

"You don't think you're going to stop the armies of Gododdin with your impressively large staff and a charming smile do you?" she replied. I could see I was never going to live down the past. At least she was kind enough to make complimentary jokes—it could have been worse.

I decided to sidestep the joke, "How are you going to explain all this to your father? It seems odd to me that Lord Hightower is going to let his daughter recruit for a war and then go marching off with a private army."

Rose grimaced, "It won't be easy. Fortunately I have lands and titles of my own, modest though they may be. He may not like it but he'll do what he can to aid me, since he can't prevent me from helping you."

"We won't fail," said Marc. "The goddess will support you Mordecai, even though you deny her. Her good grace will open other doors as well. She won't sit idly by and let Mal'goroth ride slipshod over her people," he added piously. I couldn't help but wonder where the goddess had been when the Children of Mal'goroth killed the royal family of Gododdin and enslaved a nation, but maybe I was just being uncharitable. I could certainly use whatever help I could get.

CHAPTER 12

We split up after that. Rose went to see her family, Marc to see his, while Penny and I went to see King Edward. I hoped we wouldn't have to wait long. Even a count has to request an audience. I tried to make it clear to the head servant that our news was quite urgent.

Adam replied with his typical noncommittal tone, "I will make sure his majesty knows you are waiting." The implication being that we *would* be waiting, no matter how important we thought we were.

Half an hour later I was pacing the floor in the small receiving room he had left us in. "We should have just sent a note. We're wasting valuable time here."

"Calm down," Penny tried to soothe me. "We still have months; an extra hour or two won't change anything."

Irritated I started to snap at her but Adam returned and I quickly closed my mouth. "His majesty will see you now." I had to admit, half an hour wasn't that long.

"Thank you Adam," I replied smugly. I had already switched gears, going from irritated to the picture of grace and nobility. Penny and I followed him into the small reception room that Edward used for informal meetings.

After a few formalities I was able to get to the point of my visit, "Your majesty I have learned some things you should hear."

"Feel free to speak, we are all ears," he answered.

I had decided to leave Penny's gift out of the discussion, so I jumped straight to what Marc had told me, "Marcus Lancaster visited me today with a message from Millicenth." Edward's eyebrows went up at that. "He told me that Gododdin prepares for war and will march on Lothion in the spring."

The king held up his hand, "We have received reports that they were preparing for something militarily, training exercises and such. We had not thought they would try something like this however. Gododdin cannot hope to win such a war."

"They do not follow the dictates of reason your majesty, but the insane motives of their god instead," I answered. "There are also shiggreth loose in Arundel and within my lands as well. The goddess believes they were created by Mal'goroth to sow confusion before the war commences." I wasn't sure if he had heard of the shiggreth but I was prepared to explain if he asked.

Edward leaned forward, surprise on his face, "Shiggreth! They are creatures of legend only. Surely you are mistaken. According to the tales they were wiped out after Balinthor's defeat."

"I would find the tale hard to credit your majesty, even coming from a god, but for my own experience before traveling to Albamarl," I spent a few minutes describing the creature Penny and I had slain, as well as the disappearances that had preceded the encounter. Edward was quick to ask questions but his wits were still sharp and he soon had a full grasp of what I could tell him.

"How many men can you muster in Cameron?" he asked.

"I have only begun to restore my mother's estates sire, at present I have no men at arms at all," I responded honestly.

"Then your town is lost. Arundel cannot hope to face so many, and his lands will be the first they cross. Even with Lancaster's aid you could do no more than delay them, and perhaps not even that."

"Surely you will meet them at the border?" I was shocked, even though Rose had warned me this would be his likely response.

"The border itself is indefensible. It would be folly to meet them there. We will consult with Lord Hightower of course, and the marshals, but it is likely that we will face them at the river Trent where the crossing will leave them vulnerable. Unless they plan to turn north and cross the mountains they will overrun your lands and Lancaster as well." Edward was matter of fact, though he spoke of the loss of lives and livelihood for many people.

"Where does that leave my people your majesty?"

"My advice is to abandon your land. Evacuate everyone that can move at the first of spring. Once the war is won you can rebuild." Edward's tone was hard.

"Your majesty, begging your pardon, they will starve. With nowhere to go I cannot hope to find homes and food to feed them while they are dispossessed. Those that survive will return to find their homes gone and their livestock butchered to feed the invader, if we ever get to return," the volume of my voice was perhaps a bit strident.

"Don't presume to teach us our part young lord! We are well aware of the sufferings our subjects will bear if war comes to our lands. Our task is to ensure there is a kingdom left to recover once the war is won. We have more to consider than just Cameron! As it stands we could have you fined for not being able to answer the levy call!" the king was red-faced now. The levy he referred to was the call to arms, in which all the nobles would be asked to provide knights and men-at-arms to fill the ranks of his army. Having none of my own yet I would stand in breach of my oath by failing to respond. "So what will it be?" he asked.

"I cannot abandon my land or the people there that depend upon me," I answered.

"Be wary, you stand close to crossing the line into treason young Illeniel."

"I am the last wizard and the only defense those people have. If no one else will guard them then I shall. The enemy will pay dearly for every step they take into Cameron lands. You may judge for yourself whether that be treason or not!" As I spoke I felt my blood rising and my temper grew hot. For a moment it seemed I could feel the very earth throbbing underneath me, as if some giant heart beat far beneath the ground. Grinding out the last words I brought my foot down heavily and it felt like the earth moved. The sensation startled me and I wondered if it was a product of my imagination. My thoughts were far from clear.

King Edward's face had gone white and a fine trickle of stone dust filtered down from the ceiling above. He gripped the arms of his chair as if he were afraid he might fall out of it. Perhaps I hadn't imagined it. "Very well, we are sympathetic to your plight. If that is your wish so be it, you have our leave to do so." His tone made it clear that the audience was over, but my magesight could detect the fear he carefully concealed.

I bowed and rose to leave but as we reached the door he called out to me, "Mordecai!"

"Yes your majesty?"

"The trainer, Cyhan is his name, is here. Adam will show you to him when you leave. He will remain with you and Penelope until the training and bond are complete. Do you understand?"

"Of course your majesty," I bowed again and left, quietly gritting my teeth. *Of course I understand, you want a muzzle on the dog before it goes rabid and bites you,* I thought.

I left the room with an angry stride while Penny hurried to keep up with me. "You knew this was going to happen… Rose said as much," she reminded me. "Did you make the earth shake back there?" she added.

"I don't know exactly. I felt it, but it didn't feel like I did it—I think. The man just told me he was abandoning our people! It's not *expedient* to help them. What sort of king is that?" My tone was full of anger.

Penny looked around, "Keep your voice down!" she hissed. "We're still inside the royal palace."

She was right of course, but I was too mad to care. Adam stepped up from beside the doors, "If you'll follow me my lord I'll take you to meet the trainer." He was as quiet as a ghost, were it not for my extra senses he'd have startled me half to death.

"Lead the way," I replied without turning to look at him.

We followed him down several long corridors and a flight of stairs, 'til we reached another waiting room. A man waited there. He was big, I'll give him that. He stood slightly over six foot tall, which meant he was looking me eye to eye, but where I was slender he was—not. He carried muscle on him the way a pig wears mud, meaning there was a lot more than anyone should find necessary. He had dark brown hair and brown skin that went well beyond a casual tan.

"So you're my handler," I stated. I was in no mood to mince words. Even as angry as I was I could not help but notice how he carried himself. He gave the impression of a coiled spring, ready to break loose into deadly violence without warning. I couldn't help but wonder how he would match up against Dorian.

He shrugged, "At least we're starting out with no illusions. My name is Cyhan."

I raised an eyebrow, "Just Cyhan?"

"Any other name I had is long dead. If you'd rather call me something else that's fine," the man's face gave away little in expression.

"Cyhan will do. Anything else we need to get out of the way before we get moving? I have a lot to take care of today," I was impatient to get moving.

"Just one," he replied. "Before we start you need to understand how things work between us. I'm not your bodyguard. I'm not your man-servant. I'm not your friend. I'm here to do a job, and that job is all I care about. If it looks like something is getting in the way of that job I'll make sure it doesn't get in the way for long. You cooperate and we get along fine. You don't and this will be a short job." Even as he essentially threatened me, his expression never changed. The effect was altogether chilling, but I'd be damned before I let him see that.

"Is that what you told my father?" I asked.

"Pardon?"

"You heard me. I know you trained my mother, so you must have had a similar conversation with him at some point. I'm curious how he responded to it."

"He was younger than you are now, but he already knew the necessity, so we never had a conversation such as this one. Besides, we had already begun training the candidates. He merely had to choose," he answered simply.

Curious, so he had chosen my mother from a set of candidates. "You trained more than one?"

"Back then there were still a number of wizards alive, we kept a small school going so there were always several ready when needed." He stated it as a simple fact.

My curiosity got the better of me, "What happened to those not chosen?"

"Some became knights, some trained the next generation."

"Like yourself?"

"Yeah, 'cept after your father died we didn't think there would be anymore."

Something in his eyes made me uncomfortable, but I couldn't put my finger on it so I pushed the feeling aside, "Alright, let's go. Daylight's burning."

Cyhan picked up a heavy looking pack and we headed outside. As we went I caught Penny giving him an appraising look and a surge of jealousy went through me. Thinking back to the other day I guess I could understand her feelings about me looking at Rose a little better. I still didn't like it, though. The heavyset warrior spoke up, "Where are we headed?"

"The royal bank," Penny put in.

Cyhan looked her over as if he had just noticed her. His gaze swept slowly up from her feet, taking her in carefully. I didn't care for it. He looked at her in much the same way a butcher does when he's sizing up a side of beef. "Pardon my manners, we haven't been introduced..." he said.

"Penelope Cooper," she answered quickly, "I'm to be his bond-bearer." She pointed at me with her thumb.

Cyhan grinned, a big white toothed smile. It was the most expressive I had seen him be so far and it thoroughly unnerved me, "Pleased to meet you Miss Cooper. We'll have a lot of time to get to know each other after this, but I doubt you'll be glad of it."

"What do you mean?" she asked uncertainly.

The big bastard laughed, "Oh you'll see. No sense spoiling it now." He clammed up after that and refused to answer her questions although she peppered him with them incessantly as we walked.

I decided to change the subject, "Cyhan, I have a question."

"Yeah?"

"Do you know the way to the royal bank?" I asked.

As a matter of fact he did know the way. Several turns and a half hour's walk got us there. A large building with a large stone facade in the front greeted us. "That's it there," Cyhan said.

"Ever been in there before?"

"Do I look like I have money?" he asked. I had to admit he had a point.

"How about me, do I look like I have money?" I turned the question around.

"Not really. We'll see if they let you inside," he replied.

"They turn people away?" It hadn't occurred to me that the bank might be hard to get into.

"Banks are for the rich. If you're not a member of the club they'll have you locked up faster than you can blink. Why are you here anyway? Not that it's any of my business," Cyhan asked.

"I've got a war to fight. For that I'll need all the money I can lay my hands on."

"We'll see," he replied.

I had no plans to go away empty handed. I stepped up to the doors and a uniformed fellow held one open for me. I looked back at Penny and our new 'friend', "Come on." They followed me in. The interior was richly appointed. Vaulted ceilings and dark wood greeted my eyes in every direction. Unsure where to go I walked up to the man at the nearest desk, he seemed very busy with something he was writing, "Excuse me..."

After a long moment he looked up, "Can I help you?" He had the look of someone supremely disinterested in the world around him. Or maybe it was just me.

"Yes, my name is Mordecai Illeniel. I'm here to check into my accounts," I tried to give the impression of honesty and sincerity as I spoke, not that it mattered.

The fellow looked up at me; his spectacles made his eyes seem twice as large as normal. "I don't recall seeing you before. Did you bring your account book?"

I was already uncertain, "I don't have one. I only just arrived in Albamarl and I didn't even know about my inheritance until yesterday, surely someone can help me here?"

"You'll need to talk to Mister Easley, the account manager. He can help you," he responded.

"Excellent. Where can I find him?"

"Check in over at the desk there," he pointed to a desk in one corner where another man was working. I might have said they were twins, but this unfortunate fellow was also bald. I walked over to him.

I addressed him politely, "Excuse me, I'm told I need to see a Mister Easley to discuss the accounts I've inherited."

He glanced at me, "Certainly. Name please..." He held a pen over a blank form.

"Mordecai Illeniel, son of Tyndal Illeniel and current Count di'Cameron. I think I may have more than one account." I tried to look important and patient at the same time. I probably failed at both.

"Very good sir, how does next Tuesday sound, say around one in the afternoon?" He didn't bother to look at me as he asked; clearly the assumption was that any time they could fit me in would be good for me.

"No, I'm sorry. I won't be in the capital then. I need to see someone today."

"Mister Easley isn't in today. I'm afraid you'll have to wait regardless," he answered. His face gave away nothing but his aura flashed with something I might have called 'smug self-importance'. Needless to say it didn't sit well with me.

"Is the bank closed today?" I asked mildly.

"No sir, I think you can see that," he replied bemused.

"Then people can withdraw money, deposit money, or conduct other business here today?" It was a question but I was really just setting the stage for my next remark. My temper was rising rapidly.

"Of course." I could almost see his thoughts as he pondered whether I might be unstable. He wasn't far from the truth there.

"As best as I can ascertain; I have money here, quite likely in more than one account. I need access to it now. Since you are currently open for business I suggest you find someone who can help me," I tried to keep a calm tone but my tension was seeping out.

"I've already told you sir, you'll have to make an appointment with Mister Easley, and he's not here today," the look of indifference on his face was calculated to increase my aggravation.

I leaned over the desk until our faces were barely a foot apart, "Then I suggest you fetch your manager or someone who can handle my business—today." I kept my tone level but with my mind I carefully applied pressure to the back leg of his chair. Doing magic without using words is more difficult but I had energy to spare and nothing better to do with it today. As the last word passed my lips the leg snapped and he fell unceremoniously to the floor. I looked down on him as he sprawled on the floor, "I think you need to replace your cheap furniture."

He got up quickly and brushed himself off. Without a word he left, presumably to find someone with more seniority to 'deal' with me. I glanced at Penny and I could see worry on her face. Most likely she didn't approve of my methods. Cyhan's expression gave away nothing of his thoughts; he might as well have been a statue.

A moment later the weaselly little clerk returned, "If you'll follow me, Mister Aston has kindly agreed to talk to you today." He said it as if they were doing me a favor. I became even more determined to knock a few people down a notch. I had a feeling Penny would be very unhappy with me by the time we left today.

He led us past a row of desks and through a door. From there we went up a large staircase until we reached the third floor, the bank was impressively large. By the looks of things the offices of the higher-ups in the bank were on this floor. A gold plate on the outside of the door proclaimed it to be the office of 'Mister Eagin Aston, Vice-President'. I wasn't sure what the word 'president' meant, but it sounded important, especially if it had a 'vice'. He opened the door for us and let us in.

Inside a red faced and rather corpulent man sat behind the biggest desk I had ever encountered. It was built of some dark red wood and polished until is shone like glass. He looked up at me, "If you would kindly leave your servants outside perhaps I can help educate you better about your financial situation here at the bank." Translation, Cyhan scared the crap out of him. I couldn't blame him for that.

Cyhan walked out without being asked but I could see Penny fuming inside. I might have corrected the man's misapprehension about her, but I had a feeling I might not want her to see our negotiations. "Please step outside if you will Miss Cooper," I commanded solemnly. The look in her eyes warned me there would be dire repercussions later, but she went anyway. It was almost funny but I was too irritated with the bankers already to find it humorous. After they left and shut the door I took a seat across the desk from Mister Aston.

"I am told you claim to be the heir of both Tyndal Illeniel and Miles di'Cameron. Is that correct?" his voice held a hint of doubt.

"I am," I took off both of the signet rings I wore, one of Illeniel and one of the Camerons and placed them on the desk in front of him.

He looked them over carefully then spoke, "These appear genuine, though they do not serve to validate your claim."

I could tell he was going to be difficult but I held my temper, "As I'm sure you know I gave fealty to King Edward just yesterday. Surely you do not take our sovereign for a fool?"

"No of course not, but I still have to properly verify your credentials. If I simply handed money out to anyone that walked in claiming to be this person or that the bank would hardly be a safe place to keep such things. For example, I will need to know your lineage—so I can be sure there are no other heirs with a better claim to the accounts you wish to access." He projected an aura of calm assurance.

I took a moment to explain my line of descent from both since I figured he did have at least one valid argument there. It took me a few minutes but eventually I had told him all the pertinent details. He nodded at me sympathetically, "A very interesting tale and I do believe you… honestly I do. However, I will require a personal statement from the Duke of Lancaster regarding your right to inherit Miles di'Cameron's account. Regarding

Tyndal Illeniel's account I'll need an affidavit from your adoptive parents corroborating your story and a waiver from the King himself to release those funds. I'm sure you understand all of this will take some time." He spread his hands as if to show me he was unable to do more.

I leaned back in the chair and put my feet on his desk. I was done being polite. "You understand that my father was a wizard, don't you?" I asked him.

"Of course, though I'm not sure how that applies...," he gave me an irritated look and stared pointedly at my boots. "I'd appreciate it if you took your footwear off of my desk; it is a rather expensive piece of furniture."

I ignored his request, "How many wizards are left in Lothion do you think, Mister Aston?"

"None, besides yourself, and if you leave your dirty boots on my desk any longer you may find yourself waiting considerably longer to access those accounts," his face had colored and his eyes were narrowed as he looked at me.

"I would think the fact that I am a wizard should be the strongest proof you could have of my line of descent. I would also think you might be a bit more accommodating in light of that fact, rather than making obvious threats concerning *my* property." I had my hands together and made a steeple of my fingers while I stared at him, giving the appearance of a man deep in thought. "I have no intention of leaving here today without a full accounting of my wealth, a proper account book, and a sizable withdrawal."

The fat bastard was almost shaking with rage now, "Lord Cameron, or Illeniel, or whoever the hell you think you are—you really don't think you're the first person to come into this place and threaten the bank do you? Do you think a few magic tricks are enough to frighten me? Right now your guard and your Anath'Meridum are outside surrounded by a rather numerous group of bank guards. If you even think of damaging this facility or harming me you'll be dead before your pact-bearer's head can hit the floor."

That surprised me, I'll admit it. It never even occurred to me that they might be prepared for a situation like this, or that they would so quickly resort to violence. Worse, while I cared nothing for the giant of a man who had come with me I wasn't sure if I could protect Penny. A moment's concentration and I could feel the presence of a large number of men drawing closer from several directions. There would be no easy escape for Penny and Cyhan. I doubted I could get a shield over Penny from the other side of a closed door. He had me dead to rights. But he didn't have to know it; he'd already made one rather large assumption that was incorrect.

I laughed. I tried to emulate the laugh James Lancaster had used long ago to break the tension after I had beaten Devon Tremont at chess. I laughed long and loud, forcing the sound up from my belly. Finally I stopped, "You've made one rather large mistake here my friend. I don't have an Anath'Meridum yet. I am still unbound and while it would probably annoy me even more if you harm my servants, it won't do a damn thing to stop me from bringing this bank down around your ears. I wonder how well you could do business sitting in a pile of rubble?"

Let us shake it down!

Great the voice was back again, I thought to myself.

"Now you're just boasting! What a farce! This building is solid stone and it has stood here for well over four hundred years. You might scorch some of the wood work or damage the furnishings but you don't really think you could bring it down?" Flecks of spittle flew out of his mouth as he shouted. Clearly Mister Aston didn't handle stress well.

Even as he was speaking I could feel a giant heart beating in the earth beneath me. I had planned to use my power to do something mildly showy—like breaking his lovely desk, or tossing some papers around, but the voice and that deep rhythmic beat gave me another idea. I let my mind expand; feeling the heartbeat below as if it were my own—then I directed my thoughts outward. *Go ahead and shake,* I thought at it.

A rumble shook the building, sending a vibration through the floor. It was deep, like a sound too low to hear, and everything began to move. Mister Aston tried to stand as astonishment flickered across his face. He promptly fell as the building gave a shudder and the floor moved underneath him. I was growing concerned myself, dust and plaster were sifting down from the ceiling and my stomach was full of butterflies as the entire building moved again. *Stop! Enough!* I screamed mentally, to who I'm not sure. The rumbling died down and the building grew still, but I could still feel that gigantic heartbeat pulsing far away—below the earth.

I looked at the banker; he was on all fours clutching at the carpet beneath his desk as if to anchor himself. I wasn't sure what had happened but there was no need to let him know that, "You were saying something about how solid the bank is Mister Aston? I don't think I caught all of it. Perhaps you'd like to repeat yourself?"

His face was blank, "Uhh..." He seemed to have lost the power of speech.

"Perhaps you'd better go get those account books so we can get down to business?" I suggested amiably.

"But I can't..." he started.

"Can't is an ugly word Mister Aston. Let's keep a positive outlook. Go fetch the books so I can get out of your hair. I'm sure you have a lot of other work to do," I gave him a reassuring smile.

The blood had drained out of his face. My smile sometimes has that effect. He got up and started to leave the room, "I think perhaps you're right Lord Cameron. Let me get my assistant and we'll sort things out as quickly as we can."

"Please tell my bodyguard and maidservant to come back in on your way out." I had to stifle a giggle at the thought of calling Penny a maidservant, but I managed to keep it in.

Penny and Cyhan came back in immediately after he left. As soon as the door shut she gave me a questioning glance, "What did you do?" She seemed to have forgotten her anger at being called a servant. Meanwhile Cyhan was glaring at me. I got the feeling I had made my situation with him worse, but I couldn't be sure.

I tried to calm her down, "Nothing. It wasn't me! I just heard the voice again and this time I told it to go ahead and shake things up. I had no idea that things would *actually* shake!"

"You're hearing voices already?" Cyhan interrupted. He said it as if he had expected something of the sort.

"Just every now and then, but I'm not crazy. Honestly—I know the voices aren't my own," the more I talked the crazier I sounded. It couldn't be helping my case with him. I wondered what would happen if he thought I had truly lost my mind. Would he try to hurry up the bonding, or just murder me in my sleep? Before we could finish our conversation Mister Aston returned with two assistants and several heavy looking ledgers. I was grateful for the interruption.

The next hour was a confusing mess of numbers and accounting. Having decided to cooperate; Mister Aston had become the very soul of courtesy and helpfulness. My father's company had closed a few years back but they had continued operating for over ten years after he died, while paying in his share of the profits to the bank. The Count di'Cameron had also been a dutiful saver when it came to preparing for the future. Once Aston had finally summed everything up I was stunned at the total. I immediately understood why the bank had been reluctant to let me have the funds.

"Wait, could you repeat that for me?" I asked.

"Twenty six thousand four hundred and twenty three gold marks in liquid assets, plus a six percent interest in the Royal Bank of Lothion," Aston repeated dutifully. "Then you also have to consider your land assets, the mining operations in the southern Elentir copper mines and the wool factorage in Gododdin..."

"Wool factorage?"

"A trading concern there, buying and selling wool, presumably your father invested in it due to the high prices of wool here in Lothion. A good portion of the shipping his other company handled was wool. After the government in Gododdin collapsed the factorage stopped shipping to Lothion, which caused Trigard Export to fall into a slow decline. Although the two nations are no longer trading actively his interests in the wool factorage are still there. I don't have up to date numbers but the Bank of Gododdin should still be keeping records of his profits there, whatever they may be."

In spite of the chaos of a civil war and rebellion the bank was still operating normally? I guess banks could care less about matters of government and religion—business goes on. My mind was still reeling from the shock of what he had told me. "What exactly does six percent interest in the Bank of Lothion mean exactly? Is that interest paid on my cash assets here?"

"Oh no! That's six percent ownership in the bank. Your accounts receive a small dividend on all bank profits each quarter. Now if you'd like to sell off your shares in the bank we could probably find a buyer rather quickly..." Aston's eyes lit up with greed.

"No that's quite alright," I stopped him. "I think I'll leave the hard assets alone for now. The numbers you've been quoting me are a lot more than I expected. Are all the nobility so rich?" I felt foolish for asking but the shock had given my self-control a blow.

Mister Aston snorted, "Hardly! Quite a few are in debt to the bank. You're probably the fourth or fifth richest man in Lothion at present. The king has considerably more, and the duchies of Tremont and Lancaster are doing very well of course. Most of your monies come from your father's accounts. The Cameron accounts were respectable but the Illeniels have been building wealth since the nation was founded."

A thought occurred to me, if I had let—whatever that was—destroy the bank I would have been destroying my own property. I almost chuckled. "I'll need to withdraw some money for my return home, about five thousand marks should do."

The banker blanched at the figure but kept his thoughts to himself, "Very good."

"I also would like a letter of credit written out for Lady Rose Hightower, so that she may draw upon the rest," I continued.

"Excuse me?" he choked.

"Which part was unclear?"

"How much credit do you wish for her to be permitted to draw upon?" he asked carefully. It looked as though he had swallowed a bone.

"The 'rest' would imply all of it, except the hard assets of course," I replied sarcastically.

"But—she could bankrupt you!" he was almost shouting. He might have made me angry but for the fact he was now trying to protect my interests. I thought harder then—he must be protecting his own interests as well. I didn't know much about finances, but at a guess the bank might not have that much in available coin. He might be worried Rose would render the bank insolvent by withdrawing more than their available cash reserves. It would also partly explain his original efforts to slow down my access to my accounts.

"Mister Aston, I understand your fears. I trust Lady Rose implicitly, the bank however I am still not so sure of. I realize that were she to use the entirety of that money it might place the bank in an awkward situation. I do not think she will need to do so, at least not immediately. In the meantime I think it would be best for the bank if it were to spend the next month making sure it has sufficient cash reserves that it is not relying upon the balance in my accounts to remain solvent."

He flushed, "Are you implying..."

I interrupted, "I'm not implying anything Mister Aston. You know your bank far better than I do. Make sure she has access to those funds. If she has any problems drawing on my accounts I will have to return to Albamarl, and I won't be happy." I gave him a hard stare.

"Very well my lord, I think we understand each other," Aston wasn't happy but he could tell when his back was against the wall.

After that he drew up the letter of credit and had it signed and notarized. Getting the five thousand marks out of the bank turned out to be a much larger chore than I had realized. That much coinage weighed nearly four hundred pounds. In the end we had to leave and purchase a couple of mules and some sturdy leather packs to load the money into. For some reason the task put me in a good mood. Something about the feeling of having several hundred pounds of gold, in my 'pocket' as it were, gave me a lighthearted feeling. Told you I'm a fool. Any sane man would have realized how dangerous having that much money around would be.

CHAPTER 13

We went to the Lancaster's city house. I had promised to meet Marcus and Rose there before we set out for Washbrook. Once again we had to rely on Cyhan's knowledge of the city to find it. Neither Penny nor I had ever been there.

Cyhan seemed on edge the entire way. He kept turning to watch behind us. "This is the most foolish thing I've ever known any man to do," he said finally.

"Try living with him," Penny added.

"What?" I could only assume they were talking about me.

Penny's eyes lit on me, "What do you think? We're walking around the city with several hundred *pounds* of gold, casually loaded onto a couple of mules. You're asking for trouble."

Ahh, of course, they were worried about the gold, "As far as anyone knows it could be sacks of grain loaded on those mules. Assuming you can keep your voice down about it." I had already put shields around both of them so I was hardly concerned. I couldn't imagine any street thugs being able to threaten us in any meaningful way.

"Grain isn't that heavy Mort. Besides, plenty of people already know exactly what we carried out of that bank," she replied.

"Such as?"

"Such as Mister Aston and everyone else that works at the Royal Bank, idiot."

"I hardly think the bankers have any reason to rob us, they hardly seemed the type anyway. What would they do? Threaten us with their ledger books?" I laughed.

Cyhan snorted, "Very likely they'd hire someone else to do the deed."

"You can't hire thieves to steal gold. They'd take it for themselves," I pointed out.

"You're right," Cyhan agreed. "They would hire assassins and let them have the gold as a bonus."

"At least you have some sense," Penny put in.

"What would they have to gain from that?" I was genuinely curious.

"Your letter of credit would immediately cease to be of value and the rest of the money would remain safely in the bank," Cyhan answered immediately.

I had to admit they had a point. I hadn't considered all the possible motives. Not that there was much I could do about it at the moment. I expanded my awareness to keep a better watch around us. I would definitely have to give some more thought to our trip back home. They knew we were leaving, they knew where we were headed, and they knew when we would be traveling.

We arrived at the Lancaster's house. I had expected it to be magnificent and I wasn't disappointed. It was actually built slightly back from the road with a small stone wall circling the property to provide privacy and protection for the family. A heavy wrought iron gate blocked access to the property. A bell stood beside it to ring for attention if there wasn't anyone standing watch. Luckily there was someone there so we didn't have to use it.

"Mordecai is that you?" came the guardsman's voice.

I looked at him carefully; he was a man of nearly forty years, slim and sun-browned. "Wallace?" I asked. I wasn't entirely sure, as a boy memorizing all the guardsmen's names wasn't high on my list of priorities.

"Hah! It is you boy! Glad to see you. Hang on I'll get the gate open in a moment. His grace said you would be coming by today." He worked carefully to unlock the gate and then turned a small winch to swing the doors wide for us. He could have used a smaller door built into one side of the gate but the mules were too bulky to fit in that way.

It felt good to see someone who knew me from my childhood days. It took some of the foreignness out of the situation. I hadn't realized how home-sick the capitol had made me until just then. As I relaxed I felt the wind swirling around us and it almost seemed as if it were whispering. The air plucked at my hair and sent small leaves twirling about in the small inner courtyard. I smiled and took a deep breath. As the wind murmured to me I could see the trees along the western edge of the city, where the royal preserve came down to almost meet the city walls. A light rain there had scented the air with the fresh smells of earth and growing things.

Penny's hand on my shoulder interrupted my reverie, "Mort, are you alright?"

"Sure why?" I looked at her, though it took a moment for my eyes to refocus on her.

"You were just standing there smiling and muttering to yourself. Who were you talking to?" her dark brown eyes were full of concern.

"No one, I was just listening to the wind—it was talking about the rain and...," I caught myself. As soon as I had said the words, 'it was talking', her eyes had narrowed. "I mean I could smell the recent rain. It's a lovely day out. I didn't mean to worry you," I finished instead.

"Mordecai!" Marc shouted as he came out of the house to greet us. "How did it go at the bank? When I told father you were going he thought we might need to send a troop of guards to keep them from locking you up. He seems to think they'll be none too happy to see you." For a holy man and a saint he seemed remarkably like the same old friend I had always known.

"Hah!" I answered, forgetting my mistrust and his new profession. "They were only too glad to greet us with open arms and throw open their coffers! They sent us along with this as a token of their kindness," I gestured at the mules and their heavy load.

Penny frowned, "He means they nearly tossed us out before he threatened to turn the bank into a pile of rock and sand."

Marcus laughed, although she hadn't been making a joke. Penny was none too happy at how I had handled things at the bank. I couldn't help but wonder at his good mood. "What's got you so happy?" I inquired. "Did you make up with your father?"

Marc's face fell a bit, "No, he's still mad as hell about my choice, but he's adjusting. I'm just happy in general, though seeing you is always a plus. Since I accepted the goddess I've felt better in every way you can imagine. It's like hearing music for the first time, after having been deaf my entire life."

He did look happy, but his reasons for it soured my own mood a bit. I changed the subject, "Has Rose showed up yet?"

Marc's eyes shifted, showing a hint of pity. He was probably inwardly lamenting that I would never know his goddess' grace. "No she hasn't come by yet. Who's your large and well-muscled companion there?" He indicated Cyhan who was standing silently beside Penny.

"Oh! Forgive my rudeness. Cyhan I'd like you to meet my good friend, Marcus Lancaster. Marcus this is Cyhan. The king has sent him with us to train my bond-bearer." I stepped back and the two of them shook hands quickly.

"By bond-bearer he means me," Penny put in. She was making sure I didn't forget who my choice was.

"The fighting prowess of the Anath'Meridum is legendary. Seeing you I begin to understand why," Marc said as he released Cyhan's larger hand.

"I was never chosen," Cyhan replied, "but I have been involved in the training of several."

"He taught Mort's mother, Elena," Penny added. Cyhan grimaced slightly when she said it.

"Why the face?" Marc asked. "You must be proud to have had such a student. My father tells me that Elena was the deadliest fighter he had ever seen."

"The Anath'Meridum are not judged by their fighting skills, but by how they live up to their oath and their pact. In that Elena was a failure. My shame lies in that I trained the first and only Anath'Meridum to willfully break her oath." Cyhan's statement was devoid of emotion though it struck me like a slap in the face.

"What is that supposed to mean?" My voice was cold.

"Nothing more than what I said. My intention is not to offend, but Elena broke her oath and failed in her trust. There can be no greater sin for one of the Anath'Meridum," the big man replied coolly.

"So you would rather she had stayed and died? That I had died with them? Is that it?"

"It is not my place to judge such matters. She failed and now we face possible war as Gododdin maneuvers to get their hands upon an unbound wizard." Cyhan's face might as well have been carved from stone as he spoke.

"For someone who trains elite bodyguards you seem to feel it would be better for me to be dead." I was angry but I kept my emotions in check.

"You clearly do not understand the Anath'Meridum," the warrior replied.

"You don't understand the first thing about me," I shot back.

"You are angry because I said your mother was a failure. Yet if you examine yourself better you may understand some of my feeling. Your friend stands before you, and yet he has become something very close to what the Anath'Meridum are meant to prevent. Can you still trust him when you know he bears a being within him that hungers to possess you? Has he not failed you in much the same way?" He spoke calmly, which only drove the spike into my heart that much more painfully.

"You arrogant bastard!" I had lost it. Without thinking I drove my fist at him. At close distance and with little warning even someone like me should have connected—but I didn't. Without seeming to move the warrior turned slightly and my fist found only air. With a smile he caught my elbow and his other hand came up to push my shoulder. A few seconds later I was looking up at him from the ground.

"If you want to attack me magic would be a better course of action. Your anger does you no good service." His words mocked me without emotion.

"Like hell," I said and swept my legs across to knock his feet out from under him, at least that was the plan. He was ready for it and rather than let me sweep his legs he leapt upward and toward me. As he came down he drove his right boot into my midsection, even with my shield I felt the force of it. He had meant to drive the wind from my lungs.

Marcus had never been one to stand idly by, when he saw Cyhan's foot hit my belly he stepped up to defend me. He moved gracefully, like a natural boxer, one hand lashing out to strike the bigger man in the stomach. Being quick he almost landed the punch, but the older warrior was quicker, bringing one hand down he knocked Marc's jab out of line. I rolled out from under his feet as they began trading blows. Marc was quick, he had always been a natural athlete but he was no match for the older veteran.

They ducked and wove for several long seconds, neither seeming to have an advantage, 'til Cyhan brought his leg up for a swift kick. Marc's hand instinctively went down to guard his midsection and he turned to avoid it, as he did Cyhan's right hand rushed forward to slam into his temple. He dropped like a felled oak.

I had not been idle, regaining my feet I rushed my foe from behind. With his attention firmly fixed on Marc he should not have known I was coming, yet somehow he anticipated me. Twisting Cyhan spun and I passed through where he had been standing. He didn't let me go peacefully by however; he caught the back of my shirt as I went by and lending force to my rush he sent me headfirst into the building that stood by the gate. Despite my shield I almost went unconscious as I rammed into the stone face first. If it had not been for my protection I might have broken my neck. I wound up dazed and lying on the ground. Woozy, it appeared to me as if two or three separate Penelope's were attacking at least two giant men with large walking sticks. Maybe that was my staff? It was hard to tell, I was seeing double and my vision was blurry.

Wallace had jumped into the fray as well, sword in hand. Cyhan took the sword out of his hands as though he were a child and sent the guardsman down with a simple palm strike. Using the sword he blocked Penny's next swing of the staff. "Time for the lessons to begin," he said smoothly.

"Go to hell! You're just an over-sized bully!" Penny drove the end of my staff at his midsection like a spear but he stepped into it, letting the tip slide by him. Running the sword up along the length of it Penny was forced to drop the staff suddenly, that or lose some fingers. She swung at him with her fist as she let go. You have to admire the spirit of a girl like that.

Cyhan released the sword to fall beside the staff and idly brushed her punch aside. Almost without trying he slapped her across the face with his open palm. I saw her head whip to the side as she reeled from the blow. I was trying to rise but my legs seemed to be made of jelly and I struggled just to stay conscious. Marc seemed to be out cold.

Penny wasn't giving up. She bore a large red hand print on one cheek, but she wouldn't quit. Growling she swung at the burly warrior again. Moving lightly on his feet he let her fist glide past and slapped her again. "Good! You have spirit, I was afraid you'd be a shrinking violet," he taunted her.

They had several more exchanges of blows. Well that might be too dignified a way of putting it. She swung at him and he slapped her—repeatedly. Every time she closed she caught another open palm across the face. She had red marks on both cheeks and as blurry as my vision was I thought she might have a split lip as well. She was watching him carefully, though. The next time she attacked it was a feint, pretending to swing at his midsection. He started to move his feet but she planted her foot down hard on top of his and brought her fist up to strike him solidly in the face.

The blow hardly moved him. Cyhan stopped and looked at her calmly, "Excellent, you're learning already."

An inarticulate howl issued from Penny's throat. I had to give it to her; the girl had an excellent battle cry. Without moving she struck again, but he calmly raised his foot, bringing hers off the ground. A small push and she went over backward to land hard on her derriere. "The lesson is over girl. We'll continue more this evening after you've had time to recover your wits," Cyhan turned away and walked over to check on Wallace who was starting to rise. "Sorry about that, are you ok?" he asked the older man as he offered his hand.

Before Wallace could reply a voice came from the direction of the gate, "Oh dear! Am I interrupting something? Again?" Rose Hightower stood in the open arch. I tried to explain, since I was the nearest to her, "Nothing to worry about Rose, we're just getting the hell beat out of us," but my voice didn't seem to be working properly. All I got out was a gobbledy-gook of mismatched syllables.

Penny spoke up, obviously embarrassed, "Uh, hello Rose. We—ahhh..." She was at a loss for words.

"We were just having a lesson in hand to hand combat while ironing out some personal differences," Cyhan answered for her. He was trying to wake Marc up as he spoke. "I think I may have hit him too hard. Anyone have some water?"

Hit him too hard? He had knocked him cold and then tried to use me as a battering ram. The warrior had a talent for understatement. "Msh goon keek err ash ooo bshtid," I said clearly. I won't bother to translate but you can rest assured it was a dire warning to him.

"Once you cool off you'll rethink that," Cyhan looked at me. He was fluent in 'incoherent-rage' apparently.

Either that or he simply knew whatever I was saying must be a threat.

"What is going on here?" James Lancaster was standing in the yard. I hadn't noticed his arrival but then my powers of observation weren't at their best just then. It took several minutes of explanation to satisfy him. A bucket of water had roused Marc so he was able to answer a few questions. Eventually the duke got enough information to have an idea what had happened, "So you knocked my son on his ass..." He was giving Cyhan a hard look.

For his part the veteran trainer didn't look the least bit embarrassed, "Yes, Your Grace."

"A week ago I might have had you flogged for such an insult," James stepped forward and held out his hand. Cyhan took it and the two men clasped arms. "Thank you," James said. I might have agreed with his sentiment, except that I had just had the sense knocked out of me.

Half an hour later we were all safely ensconced in the duke's house, drinking tea and nursing our wounds. I had gotten the worst of it, my head still felt a bit dizzy. Marc was a bit unsteady as well, but Penny showed the most obvious outward signs. Both of her cheeks were red from repeated slapping and her lower lip was swollen. The looks she gave Cyhan across the table might have burned a hole in the wall. I've never understood how women do that, but having been the recipient of a few similar looks in the past I found it unsettling.

"My apologies for insulting you Mordecai," Cyhan said, quite unexpectedly. "I spoke only truth, but I did it with the deliberate intention of testing you."

"Being tested isn't big on my list of favorite things," I replied. "I hope you learned what you needed. I won't go easy on you next time." By that I meant I wouldn't refrain from using magic against him. It was clear that the man was nearly invincible in physical combat.

He laughed, "I warned you to use magic at the start as you'll recall. In any case I learned what I needed to know."

Rose was intrigued, "And that was?"

"That he's not afraid to take on a larger opponent, if he feels that he has been wronged. Many men shy from such a fight."

I felt a bit better hearing that, 'til Rose continued, "Is that a good thing?"

Cyhan frowned slightly, "In most ways men are measured, yes, if he was to be a soldier or knight, certainly. As a leader, and as a wizard, it isn't so good. He let his emotions take charge of him, overruling his better judgment."

Rose grinned impishly, "Does that apply to the others as well?"

"Not at all," Cyhan answered immediately. "They all fought for different reasons. Marcus for example, he didn't step into the fight until it was clear I might seriously injure his friend. That's a mark of strong loyalty and a sense of fairness. He didn't intervene 'til it was clear I meant to take advantage of his friend once he was down. On the other hand, he fought as if we were in a boxing match. There are no rules in a brawl, such foolishness cost him a headache and a taste of dirt."

"I'm not sure that it would have mattered, you fought like a lion," Marc interjected. "I've never seen anyone move like that."

"You have a lot of natural talent. You could be a real threat with some training," Cyhan said. "Penny on the other hand, was my primary target for the test and I was pleased with the result."

Penny bared her teeth at him. I swear the girl is half wild-cat. "You'll be less pleased next time," she warned.

"You mean in an hour?" he smiled at her.

She lost her fire, "What?"

"From here on we'll be training every evening. While we travel you'll train during the rest stops as well. You showed some good instincts, a quick eye, and a lot of spirit, but you fight like a child. That must change."

"I don't understand why she has to be trained like a soldier," I put in. "We can form the bond without any need for that."

Cyhan raised one eyebrow, "It has everything to do with the bond, but not for the reasons you might think." He stood up, "Follow me; it's time for your second lesson."

I winced, I had a feeling this would hurt.

Back in the yard Penny and I stood side by side, for some reason he wanted us both there. I stared at him uncertainly, "Alright, so what do you plan to teach us, oh wise master?" My sarcasm was legendary. It didn't seem to faze him, though.

"Let us assume, for the present, that you and she are already bonded. Why do you think that Anath'Meridum are taught to fight?" he said.

"Presumably to protect their wizard from unscrupulous thugs," I said, giving him a pointed look. "But I don't need someone else's protection. My magic shields me more effectively."

The big warrior chuckled, "It does eh? Prepare yourself then, I'm going to try to kill you. Put up your defenses and show me how impossible it is." His confidence was unnerving.

I already had a shield around me but I reinforced it just to be sure. As long as he didn't fling me into any more stone walls it would be very difficult to wound me and if I was using magic against him he would never get the chance to do that again.

"Ready?" he asked. I told him I was.

He went from motionless to blinding speed almost before I realized it, but I was prepared nonetheless, *"Shibal,"* I said as he came at me. Nothing happened.

Rather than strike me directly he stepped past and his arm came up. He'd put one leg behind me and his arm swept me from my feet with very little force. I hit the ground hard but my shield kept me safe regardless. "That sort of thing isn't going to be enough," I snapped at him as I rolled away. He didn't reply, but I heard a sharp yelp from Penny.

My eyes took in the scene quickly and I felt a fool. He still stood where he had tripped me but his hand held a sharp blade to Penny's throat. He looked at me without moving the cold steel, "You're dead."

I stared, uncertain while my mind worked out what had happened. His attack on me had been a decoy while he got close to her. Finally he removed the knife and stepped away. "Now do you understand? Anath'Meridum are trained, not to protect *you*, but to protect themselves. Once you form the bond the easiest way to kill you will be her, and there are a thousand ways to do it."

"Why would any wizard consent to such a thing then? It makes no sense," I blurted out.

"Because they were going mad… she's your only hope for sanity. The bond will anchor your mind to hers. Madness drove Jerod Mordan to form a pact with Balinthor and nearly destroyed our world. That is why they agreed to it, to prevent such a thing from ever happening again. The bond will not only ensure your sanity, but will make it impossible for *any* being to enter either of your minds again. Tell me the truth Mordecai—you're hearing voices already aren't you?"

I stared at him blankly. What he said was truth, I'd heard it before, but I hadn't realized he knew about the voices. "Well—no, not exactly."

"The bank shook while we stood inside. I don't know what you told that fat banker, but I'd guess you threatened to destroy the entire place. That's not the sort of thing a sane man would say. Just an hour ago I saw you muttering to yourself when we came in—talking to things only you could hear. Don't lie to me; your sanity is hanging by a thread. What will you do when it is gone? Who will you kill? You might even hurt your friends. *That* is why your ancestors agreed to the bond."

I listened and even as he spoke I could hear a massive drumbeat beneath us. The earth was alive, even if I was the only one that could feel it. *Lies; do not listen, they want to geld you. You cannot trust their words.* I closed my eyes, wishing I could shut out that voice but then the voice of the wind began whispering to me again. In my mind I could see the forest beyond the city, where the wind was capering among the trees while the birds kept up an incessant chatter. Maybe I was going insane.

CHAPTER 14

We spent the night at the Lancaster's house. Cyhan began Penny's training in earnest while I spent considerable time in the room I had been given. I meditated, hoping to calm my mind and shut out the voices that seemed to swirl around me. Most of them were soft and diffused, like the wind, but one voice seemed much stronger, the one warning me against being bonded. That voice was strong and clear, as if someone stood beside me speaking in my ear. The others, I tried to name them according to where they seemed to come from, the wind, the trees, and the giant beating heart of the earth, those voices were less well defined. They weren't human and they used a language that couldn't be understood in words, it was more primal.

The wordless ones calmed me, for they seemed natural and without motive, but the other voice frightened me. It was too human and it had definite opinions. I was afraid that it was a sure sign of my shaky hold on reality.

After dinner we planned our next steps. Marc wanted to travel with us and although I feared his goddess, I trusted him. He seemed to genuinely want to help and apparently his goddess agreed with him. Rose still planned to remain behind. I had given her the letter of credit and explained my thoughts concerning the bankers and their motives. She probably understood them much better than I did. She was certainly surprised at the amount of money that would be available to her.

"Who would have thought that Tyndal Illeniel was so rich?" she said. "He never flaunted it or showed any sign while he was alive. Not that I knew him personally, but if anyone knew he had such a fortune I'm sure I would have heard of it before now."

"The real question is what you'll do with the money, gold won't stop an army," Marc opined.

"As I understand it, Mordecai needs several things, men and weapons, raw materials, supplies and food, and as much of all of them as he can get," she replied. "I will begin sending wagons with materials and supplies as soon as I start making arrangements. I will follow with the men later."

I was still unsure. I had never been a political genius but I had read a lot and mercenaries worried me, "Are you sure sell-swords are a good idea? From what I've heard they're as dangerous to their employers as they are to the enemy, perhaps more so."

Lady Rose's eyes lit on me, "Actually I need to discuss that with you. Mercenaries are much less trustworthy than men fighting for their homes, that is certainly true. I wonder if you would consider offering them more than gold?"

I wasn't sure what she meant, "What else do I have to offer?"

"Land," she stated simply. "Offer them land for farms and homes, with money to build once the fighting is done. There are a large number of men in Lothion who would jump at such an offer: the poor, the unemployed and dispossessed, the younger sons of farmers with nothing to inherit. The chance to become a freeholder with their own land would be a powerful incentive. It would give them a strong reason for fighting to win rather than just to survive long enough to collect their pay."

That had never occurred to me. In fact, most of the Cameron lands were uninhabited, more so now after seventeen years with no lord to maintain them. New freeholds would mean more taxes, more farming, and more men to defend the land in the future, not just today. If Dorian's remarks about a lord's power being built upon the strength of his people were correct then I was a relatively weak lord. More people would change that dramatically.

"I think you may have hit upon an excellent idea," I replied after some thought. *No man can own the earth; merely share it for a while.* "Shut up!" I shouted at the voice. After a pause I realized everyone was staring at me. "I'm sorry, that wasn't directed at you Rose."

Rose studied me for a moment, I could almost hear the gears turning in that keen mind of hers, "The voices are getting stronger aren't they Mordecai?" Concern was clear on her face.

"Not exactly—maybe, I'm not sure. Please, let's move on. I'm fine and we have a lot to decide," I said. The discussion continued but I kept catching my friends giving me worried looks from the corner of their eyes, whenever they thought I wasn't looking.

You aren't mad. It only seems so because they can't accept the truth. Stop denying and accept it, this is what you are. The only insanity is your struggle to deny reality.

I closed my eyes again while everyone discussed what sorts of materials would be most useful for stopping the forces of Gododdin. Tears welled up from the corners of my eyes. *I'm going insane, right in front of them,* I thought. The voice was so clear; I could even tell it was a woman's from the tone.

I was a woman once, the words answered my unspoken question.

What are you now? I thought back at it without meaning to.

I am not sure. Time is different now. No one can hear me, an age has passed and men have forgotten me.

Who are you? I asked. I had given up but shame had the tears flowing freely down my face.

I don't remember. But I loved a man once—he bore your name.

He was an Illeniel? I thought back.

Yes, Mordecai Illeniel was his name. The voice paused but I could almost feel the pain behind the memory, then it continued. *He was much like you.*

Mordecai?

"Mordecai!" I could feel someone shaking me.

"Mordecai look at me!" I opened my eyes. Penny was holding my head in her hands while she crouched beside me. I hadn't seen her look so worried since I had been thrown from that horse a year ago. "Come back to me Mort. Focus—stay with me. Can you hear me?"

"I'm not deaf Penny," I smiled at her.

"You're not normal either. You were sitting at the table with your eyes closed, crying," she leaned in to kiss me, ignoring the eyes of everyone around us. "We have to do something Mort. I don't think you have much time," she said.

I was much calmer now. Something about my conversation with the voice had left me feeling better. I tried to convey that to her, "It's alright Penny. I think I'm better now. I understand a little more. The voice has been talking to me—explaining things. It isn't as sinister as I thought. Given a little time I think we can understand each other."

Cyhan spoke up, "It's almost too late. He's much farther gone than I suspected. You need to form the bond now, before his mind slips completely away."

"But I haven't had any training," Penny said.

"You don't need it to form the bond; he'll do most of that anyway. The training is just to help keep you alive afterward," he replied.

"Honestly, I don't think it is necessary," I put in.

He ignored me, "Do you have a sword Penelope?"

As a matter of fact she did, though we had packed it away after reaching the capital. Rose ran to fetch it from her things while Cyhan pulled a clear gem from a pouch at his side. Marc stepped closer, "Is there anything I can do to help?"

Cyhan glanced at him, "Leave. Your goddess may try to interfere with the bonding. He will be vulnerable during the process. If she takes advantage it could be our undoing."

Marc was incensed, "My Lady is not like that. She bears only goodwill for us. If only men would accept that she could help us!"

"You have a choice," Cyhan answered, "you may leave, or I can remove you." He left it open to interpretation what he meant exactly by the word 'remove'.

Marc left, but he certainly wasn't happy about it. Rose returned a second later with Penny's sword. It was the same slender blade she had carried with her the night we fought the shiggreth together. She passed it carefully over into Penny's hands.

Penny looked at Cyhan, "What do I do now?"

"Nothing, hold the blade up across your palms, as though you were presenting it to him," he replied.

"I don't want to do this yet," I said.

"You don't have a choice. It's either that or I'll see to it that you never walk out of this room alive—understand?" His voice was calm but I could see violence coiled in his large frame. The man was ready to carry out his threat the moment he sensed any resistance.

No! They'll geld you. This is wrong—don't let them do this.

"I understand," I made my choice. "What do I do?"

Cyhan pulled a small scroll from a pouch, "You can read Lycian?" I nodded at him that I could. "She will give you her oath, and you will respond. Place your hands on top of hers where she holds the sword," he told me.

I put my hands over hers, with the sword between our palms. Cyhan reached over and set the clear gem he had been holding on the flat of the blade.

No!

I could hear the voice again, and the earth shook beneath us. The giant heartbeat had sped up. The gem slid off the blade and fell to the ground.

"What was that?" Penny asked.

Cyhan grabbed up the stone quickly, this time he replaced it and wound a long leather thong around it to hold it in place, "I think he's losing control, we have to hurry."

"That wasn't me," I said, but no one was listening.

Don't you understand? This will kill you! the voice shouted at me.

"The voice says this is going to kill me. That can't be true, right?" I asked them.

"Your mind is splintering Mordecai. It's fighting with itself. You have to focus on what we're doing." Cyhan looked worried. It was not an expression that suited him.

"But I can't shake the ground—it's impossible. It's too big, no wizard could do that," I protested.

He had already begun giving Penny her lines and she recited them flawlessly, "I, Penelope Cooper, do give my faith and trust to you, Mordecai Illeniel. My life is yours, to use as you wish. I am your sword; I will protect you and carry your burdens with you. In the light I will walk beside you, to face your foes, and should darkness enter your heart I will..." She faltered for a moment, "should darkness enter your heart, I will be your death." She said the words proudly; looking straight into my eyes, though I could see the last part pained her to say.

Cyhan held the scroll up near me so that I could see it, "Read the response, in Lycian, and put your heart into it."

The earth began a steady vibration that set my teeth on edge, while the house began to shake lightly. *No! You are the last hope! They'll destroy everything if you do this!* A form began to flow up from the floor, taking shape from the very stone of the house's foundation, as if the rock were liquid.

"You'll need to shield us Mordecai!" Cyhan shouted. I spoke and created a shield of pure force around the three of us.

"I keep telling you that can't be me—there's no way I could shake the earth like this. And that...," I nodded at the stone body forming outside my shield, "I have no clue what that is."

"You're much stronger than you realize. Your sleeping mind is fighting to prevent this—start the invocation before it's too late!" he shouted back at me.

Fear and the unknown are strong motivators. I started the response in Lycian, "I, Mordecai Illeniel, do take you Penelope Cooper as my pact-bearer. Our souls will be joined and our lives linked, from now until our deaths..." As I spoke the form outside my shield grew more detailed, until it resembled a young woman.

If you do this I cannot help you. Your life will be short and the darkness coming will devour you along with everything else in this world. Stop!

The floor around us rippled, like water, and then rose up over us to slam into my shield. The force almost made me lose my place in the response, "Your life is my own and I will use your mind for my shield, in return I will give you greater strength. So long as we both live I will allow no evil to shelter within me, and when you die I will join you in the deeper sleep." As I finished I felt the energy flowing between us—through our palms. The gem set upon the blade glowed a deep crimson and light flowed along the steel. I could feel—something, passing between us and I could feel Penelope's heart beating within her chest. The sensation was similar to when we had first briefly linked minds a year ago.

The stone had arched up until it nearly covered my shield on three sides, but now it began to crumble and fall away. The figure of a woman still stood facing us on one side.

"It is done," intoned Cyhan and he began untying the gem. It was still glowing as he placed it into the pouch on his belt. Outside the shield the stone woman still faced us, she had gone still but her face bore an expression of incredible sadness. Tears of pure crystal welled from her eyes to fall tinkling upon the floor, until at last she was motionless again. For some reason I felt like crying with her.

Penny looked at me, "Mort! What happened to your eyes?"

I blinked at her, she looked subtly different. Glancing around the world seemed a little dimmer but I couldn't put my finger on exactly 'what' was dimmer. Then I noticed Penny's eyes were no longer brown—they were blue, "Never mind mine! Look at yours!"

She got up to find a mirror and almost fell over. When she stood she came a half a foot off the floor and was ill-prepared for the landing, "What the hell?" She moved cautiously after that. "Is it safe to go outside now?"

She was gesturing at the stone semi-circle that partially enclosed the area of my shield. I looked at Cyhan to see what he thought, "What do you think?"

"I think now that your mind is your own we will have little to fear. Do you sense anything outside the area of your protection?" he answered.

I stretched out my mind, feeling the room around us but sensed nothing. The stone woman was now merely a statue. "I think she's gone," I replied.

"You keep referring to it as 'she', but it was merely a deeper part of your fractured mind," Cyhan said.

I still didn't agree with that assessment. I knew there was no way I could have moved so much stone so effortlessly. At the very least I would have felt the strain from it. It was hopeless trying to convince him of that, though. I lowered the shield around us and we moved out into the shambles that remained of the duke's breakfast room. The floor had shifted and buckled, overturning furniture and popping the doors from their frames. The expensive glass windows were shattered.

The most astonishing feature of the newly remodeled room was the crumbling stone semi-circle around where we had performed the bonding, that and the statue of course. The statue was a flawless rendition of a beautiful young woman. The details even went so far as to include braids in her hair. Even the nails on her hands had tiny almost indiscernible cuticles. I bent down to gather up the small crystal tears that had fallen to the floor. "I wonder what these are," I mused.

"If I were to hazard a guess—quartz, or perhaps diamond," Cyhan responded. I made a mental note to myself to have them appraised. At the very least they were a notable memento of the occasion.

"Holy crap!" Penny shouted as she ran back into the room. She overshot her mark and ran into a wall before she could stop. She dusted herself off and walked to me more carefully. "I found a mirror Mort. My eyes are blue!" She was almost vibrating with excitement.

"I know—I noticed a minute ago."

"But yours are brown!" she said.

"Huh?"

Cyhan spoke up, "It's a rare side-effect of the bonding. Certain traits are sometimes transferred between the wizard and his Anath'Meridum. Eye-color changes are rare but not unheard of. There are other more deliberate changes you will both notice as well."

"If I find myself fancying men I'm putting an end to myself," I replied pithily.

"I feel different already," Penny enthused, "stronger. And the world looks different. Mort you're positively glowing—everything is so—bright." She smiled at me, "I always wanted blue eyes."

"I liked your eyes the way they were," I groused. She looked almost unnatural with those blue diamonds flashing under her dark hair.

"The bond will make you stronger, faster, and more able to fight than you were before. The effect is in direct proportion to the strength of the wizard bonded. You may be even stronger than me now," the older warrior informed her.

With hardly a thought she slapped him, hard. The motion was so fast I hardly saw her hand move. "That was for earlier," she said.

The warrior grinned as he rubbed his face, "Guess that makes us even."

"Hardly, I owe you about a dozen more, but they can wait 'til we train."

"Don't get overconfident. You're still as clumsy as a newborn pup. It will take some time to adjust to your new-found strength and speed."

I on the other hand, didn't feel any better at all. It seemed like a very one sided deal. The voices were gone, true enough. I could no longer hear the murmuring of the wind, the heartbeat of the earth or the sound of that all too real woman's voice. Now that they were gone I missed them, I had begun to get used to them I suppose. The world seemed emptier now, more sterile, as if the life had been drained from it. Then a thought occurred to me, "Where's Rose?"

We stared at one another. She had been with us at the start but she was nowhere to be seen now. "I saw her step away after she handed me the sword but I wasn't watching her," said Penny.

I cast out my mind, exploring the house around us. I immediately found Marc, his father James, and a number of other people, but Rose was not among them. I examined the room around us more closely and then I felt her, buried under a pile of rubble where one wall had collapsed. Her heart was beating rapidly so I knew she was still alive. "She's over here," I announced and walked over to the tumbled stones and timbers. "She's buried, but alive."

I didn't wait for Penny or Cyhan to start hauling the debris away, instead I spoke a few words and using my will I quickly cleared away the large granite blocks and fallen lumber. Beneath it all was a hard stone shell. It looked as if the floor had flowed up over and around her to form a solid stone shield. I wasn't sure how to undo or replicate the way the stone had flowed so I carefully reached out to explore the layout of Rose's body within the shell.

Once I had a clear image of her body I created a shield of force within the empty space, around her and between her and the stone. Then I applied a sharp hammer-like blow with my mind, shattering the stone sarcophagus-like shell. As the stone broke apart I could see Rose's frightened expression within. The moment the fragments fell away she tried to sit up, only to strike her head against the hard shield I had placed around her. "Ow!" she yelped.

If it hadn't been for the serious nature of the situation I might have laughed. I made a mental note to remember this for future harassment, and then I removed the spell around her. "How in the world did you manage this Rose?"

She started dusting herself off carefully. I could almost imagine a cat cleaning its fur she was so meticulous. "I moved back to watch, and then the floor started moving. I fell down over here and the wall collapsed on top of me. I thought I was going to be crushed."

"Well you survived somehow. How did that stone surround you like that?"

"I think that stone woman did it. When the wall collapsed she saw me, and I think she made the floor rise up around me...or something like that. I'm not really sure, it all happened so fast," she said.

I glared at Cyhan, "My sleeping mind again I'm sure." I don't know why I kept trying sarcasm on him; he seemed completely oblivious to it.

"Most likely," he replied.

I wasn't buying it. Whoever the woman had been she was no fragment of my unconscious mind. She was real, and if her actions were any proof, she could not be malignant. Of course by that logic Marc's goddess was a sweetheart as well. She had a pronounced proclivity for healing the sick and similar good works. I decided I would reserve judgment for the time being. The stone lady might have ulterior motives just as the gods did.

James Lancaster appeared at last, "Is it safe to come in yet?" He looked in through the shattered door-frame. "Damn! Mordecai every time I let you into my home this happens. I suppose you have a good excuse this time as well?" He was projecting mock anger but I wasn't fooled.

"Sorry, Penny was holding hands with me and I got a bit too excited, Your Grace," I replied. Inappropriate? Sure it was, but after everything else that had happened I figured no one would care.

James stared at me blankly for a moment, and then Cyhan started snickering quietly. I had never heard him laugh before, but it set off a chain reaction as everyone's nervous anxiety sought release. James laughed loudest of all, as usual. A great belly laugh, I made more mental notes so I could mimic him better next time.

CHAPTER 15

We started out bright and early the next morning. I offered to pay James for the damage to his home but he declined saying he owed me enough already for saving his life. I argued with him, but we had too many other things to do for me to put much energy into it.

We rode at an easy pace. We might have made better time but the mules carrying the gold couldn't manage anything faster. Penny was back in her 'traveling warrior' garb, chain byrnie over padded gambeson. She wore her sword proudly now, the bond seemed to have improved it. I hadn't enchanted it before but now it was every bit as sharp as the one I had done for Dorian.

I thought about that as we rode. Without being enchanted I assumed that the magic that gave it its sharpness must be continually renewed by the bond between us. That meant that the bond had some perpetual cost, a slight drain upon our personal energies would be needed to maintain it. I wondered what other costs there might be, but I knew too little to have any good guesses.

Penny was in a good mood. Exuberant would be the best description for it. She had been ever since the bond was formed; her new strength and energy had filled her with a joyful zest for life. I'm pretty sure she was looking forward to the evening's training session with Cyhan. She had as much as said she had a score to settle. I hoped the two of them didn't inflict any injuries I couldn't heal.

Cyhan nudged his horse closer to mine, "Keep your eyes open, if they have anyone after us they'll probably make their move tonight or tomorrow."

I hadn't forgotten our previous discussion, "I know. I've been scanning the hills around us. When they get close I'll sense them. We should have plenty of warning."

"Warning would be good, but I won't count on it. Men can surprise you, they may think of some way to avoid detection you haven't come across before," he replied.

Typical, I could have told him they would attack us naked, armed only with spoons and he probably would have warned me how dangerous a spoon could be in the hands of a desperate man. I think he lived in a state of constant paranoia.

Marc leaned over to me, "You need to relax Mort. You seem tense."

"I'm not the one that's tense—or rather I wouldn't be if he wasn't such a worrywart," I replied.

We rode until noon before we stopped to eat lunch. When we stopped Penny made a point of leaping down from her horse, then she remounted with a standing jump. The action delighted her so much she repeated it several times. She was about to try vaulting completely over the horse before she had to stop. Her poor mare had spooked at her strange antics and nearly started bucking. She spent several minutes talking to her to calm her down.

"You're enjoying this entirely too much," I said a few minutes later as we ate our bread and cheese.

"And you my sweet man are jealous," she shot back.

"Hardly, I could make the horse fly over you just as easily, but *I* am too concerned for the poor mare's feelings to put her through that," I replied grumpily.

"If you two are done eating, it's time for my pupil's next lesson. She obviously needs to burn off some excess energy," Cyhan interjected.

The two of them squared off in a small clearing beside the road. I was interested to see the outcome. Penny showed every sign of having far more strength and agility now than any person, man or woman, had a right to possess. My bets were still on the older warrior though, there's something to be said for experience and his constant training had made him just about as strong as any normal human could hope to be.

They were sparring barehanded. Cyhan felt it would be far too dangerous to do any weapons training until she had acclimated to her new abilities. That was as much as an admission that he feared she might injure him, or perhaps that he might be forced to go too far in defending himself. I wasn't too sure which.

As soon as he said, 'ready' she went after him, faster than a jungle cat. She moved almost too quickly for me to follow but a moment later she was sailing past him to land sprawling in the grass. I thought she might pause for a moment after that, but I was wrong. She had barely struck the earth before she bounded up again and headed for him. He was ready for her, and seconds later she was flying off in another direction.

"Pay attention damnit!" he shouted at her. "In a real fight you or Mordecai could wind up dead with all the time you waste charging about and landing on your ass!"

That got her goat; she came off the ground as if it were a trampoline. She twisted as she came up, perhaps she planned to somersault as she came up but she overdid it. She nearly flipped all the way over again, to land face first, but her reflexes saved her. Putting out both hands she caught herself and pushed off again. The end result was a combination tumble and somersault that sent her flying over his head. She landed lightly behind him, but before she could swing at him his back kick caught her squarely in the stomach. I winced as I heard the air driven forcibly from her stomach. She flew back several feet and collapsed, choking and gagging for air.

Cyhan was 'hopping' mad. That would have been a great joke to make, but he truly was angry, and she was in no shape to appreciate my humor either. He took two quick strides and jerked her to her feet by her hair, "That was the dumbest shit I have ever had the misfortune to witness!"

Penny tried to say something but she wound up vomiting on him instead, a nasty concoction of bread and cheese. If I hadn't been so worried about her I might have laughed then too, instead I ran over to help her.

"Goddammit!" he shouted at her. A long string of expletives followed and I wish I had paid better attention, some of them I had never heard before. I was surer than ever that he must have spent some time as a sailor, or perhaps a marine. Quite a bit of his swearing was pure nautical genius.

"Maybe we should take a break from our break..." I suggested.

"You stay out of it!" he roared at me. He looked as if he were ready to beat her and call it 'training' just to get vengeance for the noxious substance she had spewed all over him. Instead he stomped off toward the horses looking for a towel.

"Are you ok Penny?" I tried to help her stand up straight.

"Get away from me!" she shouted, pushing me back. I don't think she intended to push me quite that hard but I wound up flying back several feet to land on my ass. "I don't want your help Mort! I can handle this on my own." She went in a different direction and soon I was left alone, sitting in the clearing.

"What the hell did I do?" I said to myself. Some days it just doesn't pay to try and help your homicidal girlfriend after she's been hurt. Honestly, homicidal isn't too strong a word either. By her own admission she's committed murder before. Granted the circumstances were exceptional.

Marc walked over, he had been watching silently during the bout. "She's always been proud Mort. The best thing to do when someone's pride is injured is to give them space," he commented.

"I only wanted to help."

He sighed, "Listen, ever since you turned up with your magical talents everything has been about you. Then you discovered you were the heir to not just one, but two fortunes; not to mention being a nobleman. How do you think that makes her feel?"

"Happy?" I ventured.

"No, dumbass—inferior. She went from being your equal, to being the girl that just got lucky enough to have her claws in you first," he replied sharply.

"I can't help my birth—or any of the rest of it. None of it matters to me anyway, not without her," I said emphatically. "You know that!"

"Sometimes knowing isn't enough. People think with their heads, but they live by their hearts. This is the first thing she's had to call her own—to make her special. It might be just a burden to you, but for her this bond is an honor. It gives her something to feel good about. Getting her ass handed to her by that great hulk of a trainer is embarrassing. The last person she wants to see it is *you.*"

"Why me?" I complained. "I'm the one person who's cheering her on the most."

Marc shook his head, "How did you get so far in life without understanding the first thing about women?

Why you? Because *you* are the person she wants to impress the most! Not the one she wants to see her being humiliated."

I had to admit, Marc always understood people better than I did, women especially. "So what should I do?" I asked.

"Nothing, if you do watch any more of their sparring bouts keep your mouth shut and your hands to yourself. Give her plenty of space."

"What if she does well? If she's successful I should compliment her right?"

He snorted, "Not now—later maybe. Compliment her on some small achievement now and she'll think you're mocking her. Her self-esteem won't let her believe you anyway. She'll be her own worst critic for a while."

He seemed to be full of good news. "So when will this get better?"

"When *he* compliments her," Marc replied.

Something about having her waiting on another man's approval didn't sit well with me. "So if I encourage her it's mockery, if he does she'll be giddy with happiness?"

"Of course," he replied smugly. "In my wild and loose days, before my new vocation, I used tactics like that to woo women all the time. You start off aloof, disinterested—cold even. Then, when you show them a bit of kindness they get weak in the knees. This is the same sort of thing. Quickest way I know of to get a woman into bed too," he paused for a second, considering what he had just said. "Not that this is going to lead to something like that of course. You've got nothing to worry about with Penny," he amended.

"Whose side are you on here?" I snapped.

"Yours my friend, always yours," he answered, smiling.

An hour later we were back on the road. Our trip was greatly improved by the fact that no one was talking anymore. A sullen silence hung over us like a pall. It was turning out to be a grand journey.

At dusk we made camp. After a quiet meal Cyhan announced that there would be no training that evening. I wasn't sure if he felt Penny needed more time to recover or whether he might not trust himself to spar 'nicely'. In any case I didn't mind the chance for a little extra rest.

"Have you sensed anyone nearby?" he asked me, probably for the tenth time.

"Nope, not a soul all day," I replied.

"That worries me," he said. Big surprise, he'd be worried no matter what I told him. "I'll feel better when it's over. The waiting is the worst part," he added.

That made two of us, although for different reasons. I didn't bother reminding him I would tell him as soon as I found anything. He would keep asking anyway. Personally I was of the opinion that the bankers hadn't bothered to set up anything as sinister as an ambush. "Are we going to set watches?" I asked. I'm not sure why I asked, the answer was obvious.

"Ordinarily I would say let your Anath'Meridum take one watch with Marcus and you take the other with me. Her senses are keen enough now that she should be able to detect any foe almost as quickly as you could," he replied. That surprised me; I hadn't known her senses were heightened as well. He went on, "Frankly though, I don't trust her enough yet so you'll be taking the first watch with Marcus. I'll stay up with her to make sure she doesn't do anything stupid."

"I'm not deaf you know," she responded gruffly.

"I wanted you to hear that. Maybe you'll learn something," he replied.

"Alright, alright—I'll take the first watch. I'll wake you two up after midnight," I spoke quickly. I wanted to head off the beginning of another war between them.

They staked their territories on opposite sides of our small campfire and soon they were both laying still, backs to the fire. Marc and I talked for a while, mostly about the old days, but we had to keep it quiet to avoid disturbing our sleeping companions. Eventually we stopped talking and sat silently on opposite sides of the fire. That left me with a lot of time to think.

I already had an idea of how I wanted to handle the possible thieves, if there were any. But I wasn't sure how well it would work. I took the opportunity to work on the idea and plan out the words I would use when, or if, the time came.

Time went slowly and I soon ran out of things to think about. I got up and walked around the camp a few times to ward off sleep. As I walked I gathered small stones from the rocky ground near our camp. I would need them later if we did get ambushed. I was definitely getting drowsy. Eventually the moon reached a point that told me my time was done, so I went over to wake up Penny first.

I shook her shoulder gently, "Wake up sleeping beauty."

Her eyes opened slowly in the dim light, "Mort?"

"It's me," I said softly.

"I'm sorry about before. I was angry with myself, not you. I shouldn't have lashed out at you like that."

"Don't worry about it. You were under a lot of stress," I told her.

"I just want to learn quickly. We don't have much time."

I knew what she was referring to, "Yeah. Just don't make yourself miserable for what time we have left."

"I can do this Mort, it isn't a waste of time," she said intently.

"I know, but we only have a few months left anyway," I replied hastily, a little too hastily perhaps.

"What is that supposed to mean?" she asked suspiciously.

I would have thought that was obvious. I never have understood why women always look for some deeper meaning in a simple statement. "I mean I understand. It's just that what you're trying to learn isn't easy. You shouldn't push yourself too hard."

"You think I should just give up?" She sounded angry.

How did she get from apologetic to ticked off? "I never said that Penny..." I started, trying to keep my tone reasonable.

She rose from her bedroll in a smooth fluid motion. Her speed was such that she almost tripped stepping out of it. That didn't help matters. "There's your bed. I don't think this conversation is going anywhere," she bit out.

I didn't bother responding. There was little doubt her warped sense of self would turn anything I said into another challenge to her competence. I watched her stalk over to wake up Cyhan before I lay down. I had a bad feeling sleep would be slow to come. *Stubborn girl,* I thought to myself.

CHAPTER 16

It did In fact, take me quite a while to fall asleep, and no sooner had I done so than Cyhan began shaking me awake. "What?" I said groggily.

"It's morning. Time to get moving," he told me.

That didn't seem possible, but the brightening sky confirmed what he said. If morning ever had an accomplice it was Cyhan. The two of them were definitely conspiring to rob me of sleep. I rose and began packing up our things. I wasn't grumpy in the slightest. Honestly.

Penny had a nice hot pot of porridge going over the coals of our fire. My first taste told me that someone had forgotten to pack the sugar and spices. I neglected to mention that to her. After last night I doubted it would improve her mood.

"How's the porridge?" she asked. It wasn't clear if she was addressing me or everyone in general.

"It's passable," Marc answered.

"I've had worse—once," Cyhan said.

"Sorry, I forgot to pack the seasonings," she said apologetically.

"It's not bad. I rather like it," I said, hoping to make her feel better.

"Thanks for the sarcasm, it's bad enough without you being a smart ass about it," she glared at me as she said it.

My mouth dropped open in shock. I truly hadn't been trying to be sarcastic. I looked at Marc for support; clearly I was being wrongly accused. He just shook his head at me in disappointment. Cyhan started chuckling under his breath. *At least someone's in a better mood,* I thought sourly.

Marc offered to help me clean out the bowls when we were done. Since there was no stream nearby we had to use sand from a dry gully close by. "You didn't listen to a thing I said yesterday did you?"

"I didn't think it was too bad," I lied. "No sense in being cruel about it in any case."

"Wrong," he stated.

"So I should have insulted the food? Like Cyhan did?" Now that I thought back, she had actually apologized after he had said that to her.

"No, she's already mad at you. You should have stuck with a neutral response like I did. I don't think you have what it takes to pull off something like what he said."

"Well if being a jerk makes you more of a man then too bad—I'd rather be...," my words tapered off. I could see no good in finishing that sentence.

Marc was too quick to waste the opportunity, "Don't start looking at me like that! Just because I've joined the clergy doesn't mean I like men!" He was laughing as he said it.

I started to reply with something terribly witty and clever, but I was saved by a distraction. Not that it was a good one. I stopped and closed my eyes so I could focus better. I could sense several men in the distance, at the very limit of my range. When we had left Washbrook I had been able to sense things almost a mile off, if I put an effort into stilling my thoughts. Now I found that a half a mile was the best I could manage.

"Hey don't be like that!" Marc said, "...Mort?"

"Give me a second, there's someone out there," I held up my hand. I strained to extend my senses further but it was no use. The figures, there were perhaps five or six of them, moved even further away until I could no longer detect them. I opened my eyes to look at my friend.

"Well? What was that about?" he asked.

"There were people on the road, about a half a mile that way," I pointed in the direction we would soon be traveling.

"Other travelers… or someone waiting for us?"

"No way to know. Let's go tell the others," I replied.

Cyhan and Penny were sparring when we walked back. This time Penny was more cautious, but the results were the same. No matter how quickly she moved and struck she couldn't touch the older warrior. She wasn't giving him a chance to throw her now however.

"You might want to save your energy," I told them.

"Did you sense something?" Cyhan asked as they broke apart.

I explained what I had discovered. "It could be other travelers," I said as I finished.

"It could be," he replied as he began checking his weapons. "But we'll be working on the assumption that there's an ambush ahead."

"Perhaps we could leave the road—circle around this part," Penny suggested.

"Not practical," Marc spoke up. "I've traveled this road many times. The terrain narrows at this part of the road. If we try to go around we'll have to go several days out of our way," he gestured at the hills which rose up steeply ahead of us. "I'm not even sure how to get back to the road if we try."

"Better that than dead," Cyhan said. "I know the wilderness to the north. If we circle the northern hills we'll come to a deep gorge. It will take us tens of miles following it before we can exit, but it's doable. We can afford the time."

"I didn't think you were the sort to avoid a fight," I remarked.

"Then you don't know me," he said bluntly. "I only fight when the outcome is in my favor, or there's no other option. We still have options."

"I'd rather stick to the road," I said, giving him an even stare.

"I don't think you heard me," he replied meeting my eyes.

"I heard you perfectly well. I'm taking the road. If you want to take another route you're welcome to do so."

The tension in the air was palpable. "You're going to meet a bad end boy, and quite possibly hurt a lot of other good people on your way to it."

I turned my back on him and headed toward my horse. Looking over my shoulder I replied, "I've already been promised a bad death, but my appointment isn't for today." I caught Penny's eye as I said it. The only good thing about knowing when you're going to die... is you can be very sure of when you *won't*.

Penny spoke up again, "He's right about that, we don't die today."

"One of your visions?" Cyhan asked. His question surprised me; I hadn't realized she had told him so much about herself already.

"Yes."

"That's fine and dandy, but I don't give a rat's ass about when the two of you die. I'm more concerned with my own demise. I'll bet your vision had nothing to say about me in it," he responded.

"I didn't know you then...," Penny replied uncertainly. "He's right Mort; we could be putting them in danger based on a vision that only concerns the two of us."

Her quick reversal irritated me. A few days ago she had thought I was going insane, yet she would have followed me down that road without a second thought. Now I was supposedly 'cured' and she was my Anath'Meridum, yet she worried more about 'his' opinion than mine. Perhaps I was being irrational, but I couldn't help the feeling.

"Tell you what," I said, "Since I'm certain to survive I'll go alone. I'll come back for you ladies when I've made sure it's safe." Yeah it was a stupid thing to say, but I was starting to get seriously annoyed with two of my companions.

"If you travel more than a couple hundred yards or so from Penelope here you'll both die from the strain on your bond," Cyhan replied.

"What?!" Penny and I said in unison. No one had told either of us about that little drawback before we took the plunge.

"That's ridiculous! Let's undo this. We can't live like this," I said, raising my voice.

"Mort..." Penny said quietly.

"It's possible Penny. We just have to both agree to it and it's over," I told her.

"No Mort. I won't let you. I meant that oath—all of it. It's important," she said and I could see her blue eyes were glistening with incipient tears.

"Besides..." Cyhan started.

I was tired of his constant interruptions. He had already turned my future wife against me, *"Kyrtos!"* I barked at him. It was a spell to silence speech.

"That won't work on me either," he continued. Reaching into his pouch he pulled out the still glowing stone from our bonding ceremony. "As long as I carry this your magic cannot touch me."

Today was just full of surprises. "Anything else I should know?" I bit out. I was angry beyond reason now. He had deliberately kept the consequences of our bond from me. Before he could respond Penny spoke up.

"Yes," she said. "The gem is a keystone, a crucial part of the bond. It will glow for as long as the bond is in effect, but..."

"But what?!"

"She's trying to tell you that if I decide you're a threat I can destroy the gem. It's an extra bit of insurance in case both of you desert your better senses," Cyhan finished for her.

"What happens then?" I asked.

"We die Mort." Penny said, she really was upset now.

"And you knew about this?" I was outraged.

"Yes. It was the only way Mort. You were losing your mind. I couldn't bear to watch it," she said plaintively. "I did it for your own good."

"No need to bother giving me any say in the matter eh?"

Marcus stepped closer, "It isn't as bad as it sounds, you..."

"Like hell it isn't!" I shouted him down.

"Mort, I love you. That's the only reason I would do something like this," Penny added, as if that would make it all better.

"You can take your love and go to hell!" I snapped. I regretted it the moment I said it but I was too angry to let that stop me. "And you can forget about the marriage as well," I pulled a small pouch from my belt. It contained the ring I had ordered over a month gone by. Rose had slipped it to me when she first visited us at the royal palace.

"Here, keep it. Sell it, I don't give a damn. We're done," I tossed it at her feet.

She knelt to pick up the small pouch—her trembling fingers quickly told her what was inside. "Mordecai! No, you don't understand! This doesn't make any sense. I love you!"

"My father and I have one thing in common Penelope. Neither one of us can stand a damn liar," my voice was colder than ice now. "Now unless you lied about your oath as well, you have a duty to perform. I'm going down that road, you'll be coming with me—understand?"

"Don't think your anger will change my mind boy or did you forget something?" Cyhan was holding the gem up between his fingers.

Cold rage swept over me like a freezing wind. Without using words I focused a blast of air at his hand and the gem went flying. *"Grabol ni'targoth. Forzen!"* I said immediately afterward. A hole formed in the ground beneath him and Cyhan fell into a shallow pit, the earth closed around him before he could react. I walked over to casually retrieve the gem.

"What the hell are you doing Mort?" Marcus exclaimed.

"You stay here and watch him. Make sure no one comes and cuts his fool head off before we come back," I said, ignoring his question.

"Mordecai this is insane. Calm down, we can talk this out," Penny tried to calm me.

I walked past her without caring, "I don't recall asking for your opinion. Come with me. It's time to take care of business."

She looked at me blankly, unable to decide what the correct course of action would be. I kept walking. I paused for a moment, "What was it you said the other day?

'My life is yours, to use as you wish', I think that's what you said wasn't it? Time to start your job… unless you've decided that it's time to end my life." I started walking again, not bothering mount up. The horses might be a hindrance if it really was an ambush ahead.

She didn't move to follow for several long minutes, 'til I was almost a hundred yards down the road. Finally she started running, and quickly caught up to me. "You're an asshole," she said when she was within a few feet of me.

"And you're the asshole's bodyguard and executioner," I replied sarcastically.

We continued until we had reached the place in the road where I had sensed the men earlier. As we drew close to the spot I could feel them hidden near the sides of the road another hundred yards or so further on. A rough count told me there were nearly twenty of them. "Stop!" I barked at Penny.

She growled and turned to face me, gritting her teeth, "If you think…"

"Shut up. There's a trap under the road ahead of us, a pit I think." The road ahead was plain dirt, but I could sense a large cavity beneath it. I focused my mind for a second—I could feel the wood and canvas beneath the dirt at the surface. They had done a good job; even knowing it was there my eyes could detect little difference between where the road was solid and where the pit lay.

Feeling contrary, I created a flat shield across the area where the trap was hidden, and then I walked over it, confident it would hold my weight.

"You said there was a trap?" Penny asked uncertainly.

"There is, but we'll see how they feel when they see we can walk across it without trouble. Come on, it's safe," I turned away and kept walking. Penny rushed to catch up.

"What are you going to do if we find them?"

"Talk to them, see if I can change their minds," I replied. I hadn't bothered to mention that they were only fifty yards away now. I used a quick phrase in Lycian to put a shield around Penny. Her mail would protect her from arrows but a lucky shot might still kill her if it struck an unprotected area.

"I think I hear them," she whispered to me. Her ears must be better than mine now; I could hear nothing, though I knew they were less than twenty yards away now, on either side of the road.

"Yep—they're..." I started to tell her they were on either side of us but the thieves didn't wait for me to finish. Arrows struck us from several directions at once, bouncing harmlessly from our shields. Penny had her sword out before I could blink. She was so fast she almost cut one of the shafts from the air, but her timing was off.

"You'll need to practice that later," I remarked, pulling my small bag of stones out. I reached in and pulled out a rock the size of my thumb, rolling it between my fingers. "Who's your leader? I'd like to offer you a deal!" I shouted at the trees on one side of the road. None of the bandits had shown themselves yet.

The only reply was another shower of arrows. "Very well," I said, *"Tielen striltos!"* I blew upon the stone in my hand and it shot away as if it had been fired from a sling. The stone curved as it flew, following an invisible line I held in my mind, 'til it struck the head of one of the archers hidden in the trees. I heard a sickening wet thump and with my extra senses I saw the man's body slump to the ground where he was hidden.

The arrows kept coming, so I repeated the process with three more stones. More bodies collapsed in the leafy darkness. "I really think we should talk! It doesn't have to be like this!" I shouted again. Penny was watching me carefully, uncertain what was happening. She probably didn't realize how effective the rocks were.

A few more arrows zipped out, I made note of their origins and tried to aim specifically for the men who had fired these. Three stones—four—five... I couldn't be sure but I thought I had hit the ones firing. "I'm not going to make this offer again! Lay down your weapons and come out so we can talk!"

I could hear cursing as they began to realize how many of their comrades were already incapacitated. They began running away through the heavy brush. "Shit," I said.

"What's happening?" Penny asked, "Are they running, from stones?"

"It appears so. I didn't want to injure all of them but I can't let them get away. There may be more." The fleeing men were still very close, as far as my magical senses were concerned. Even at a full run it would take them a minute or two to get beyond my range. I carefully sent stones after each of them, one by one, 'til at last they were all still.

"I think that's all of them," I said, putting the rest of my stones back in the pouch. "Let's go see what they look like, maybe we can find out who hired them."

"At once, Your Grace!" she replied acerbically.

"That should be 'your excellency.' I'm a count not a duke," I answered. There was no humor in my tone. Inwardly I felt my heart clench painfully, but I refused to give in to it.

Penny didn't reply, but I could feel her flinch at my cold words. We began searching the roadside. She got to the first of our ambushers before I did. "Here's one Mort—oh! Oh gods!" she turned away, a look of disgust on her face.

As soon as I reached her side I understood why. It was a gruesome sight. The man's head looked like an exploded melon, blood and brains were everywhere. I had put more force behind the rocks than I had known. We searched for the others but it was soon apparent that the results were all the same. Each of them looked as though he had been struck by a slaughterhouse hammer.

At some point it overwhelmed me, and I began retching. I had seen death before, just a year ago in fact, but this was different. The last time I had been struggling just to survive, and I passed out as soon as the battle was over. The bodies had been removed before I saw them. This time they were fresh before me, and their deaths had been particularly brutal. There's nothing quite like seeing a man's brains on the ground to drive the point home.

Even worse, I had done it without being in any real danger myself. Sure I hadn't realized how lethally effective my stones were, but I had picked them off calmly, one by one. They hadn't had a chance. Eventually my stomach was empty and I realized Penny was stroking my back sympathetically.

"It's not your fault," she said softly.

Like hell it wasn't. I knew what I had done, and now I realized even better what I had done a year before. I had killed over a hundred men then and hardly given it a second thought. If her vision was true I would do so again, many times over in all likelihood. I straightened up, spitting to clear my mouth. "It's a good thing I've got you."

"I'm sorry I didn't tell you Mort. I thought you were losing your mind. I would have done anything to stop it," her face was full of concern.

More than anything I wanted to accept her apology, to make up. I needed her love more than ever, but I was full of self-loathing at what I had done. It would have been so easy to let go of it. But I also knew death was coming for me, and I would do worse things before the end. I had the beginnings of a plan—to get rid of the bond before the end came, to save her. I would be doing her no favor by reinforcing her love for me, not when she would be left behind.

"That's not what I mean," I pushed her hand away. The hurt expression on her face was almost more than I could bear, so I looked away and then walked back to the road leaving her standing there. Once my back was to her I spoke again, "I mean it's a good thing I've got you to finish me off—if I turn into a monster." I headed back to our camp without waiting to see if she was following. I didn't trust myself to speak again.

CHAPTER 17

Back at the remains of our campsite Marc was chatting amiably with Cyhan. The large fighter was still buried almost to his neck, so he didn't have much choice in the matter. I might have felt sorry for him but Marc was an excellent storyteller. I doubted he had been bored.

"How was it? Is the road clear?" asked Marc.

"It is now," I said bluntly. I didn't bother asking Cyhan if he would behave, with a few words I opened the earth up around him so he could climb out. I figured he was pragmatic enough to let bygones be bygones, now that the situation was resolved. "Let's get moving. We have a long day ahead of us."

The large man looked me over carefully as he came up out of the hole. A tense moment followed as I waited to see what he would do. "You sure it's wise letting me out after that?" he asked calmly.

"I did what I needed to do," I answered. "I don't see the need to make an issue of it. Would you prefer to go back in the hole?" Despite my bravado I was working hard to keep my voice even.

"At least you're learning," he answered me.

"Learning what?"

"Not to waste your time attacking me with your fists. You didn't hesitate, and you effectively neutralized my ability to threaten you with a minimum of effort," he dusted some of the dirt from his clothing. "If you were my student I would be pleased."

"And since I'm not your student?"

"I'll make sure you don't get the chance next time," he gave me a wicked grin. A smile on the big man was unusual and sight of his teeth made me uneasy, bringing to mind images of a dangerous animal.

A short while later we were riding down the road, mules in tow. When we got to the site of the slaughter Cyhan insisted on stopping to examine the bodies. I didn't bother arguing. They should know what sort of man they were traveling with anyway. Marc joined him but Penny stayed on her horse, she had seen enough already. Neither of us spoke.

When the two of them returned I could see the shock on Marc's face but Cyhan was more reserved. "I've never seen anything quite like that," the veteran commented. "What did you use?"

"Rocks," I pulled one out of my pouch and flipped it in his direction. He caught it deftly.

"Where did you get that idea?" he asked.

"I have an active imagination." Sarcasm is one of my strong suits.

"Some of them looked like they were running."

"I thought they might have friends," I said simply. I wasn't about to show him any of my self-doubt.

"Maybe," he said. "Some of them definitely had families; by their gear and clothing I could tell a few of them were guardsmen from the city."

Guilt shot through me, thinking of their wives and children, but I fought it down. "They should have picked a better way to make extra money." He grunted but didn't say anything else.

We rode in silence after that. Marc tried to start up a conversation a few times but even he couldn't overcome the dark cloud that hung over us. Penelope refused to even acknowledge his questions. Cyhan was less reticent but he wouldn't respond with anything more than one syllable answers. Marc didn't bother trying to engage me.

That evening we made camp without having encountered any more people on the road. Penny sparred with her teacher and even I could see she was starting to improve. She had a serious intensity about her now. After we had eaten Cyhan suggested she take watch with me. In his own way I suppose he was trying to give us an opportunity to make up.

"I'd rather not," she said simply, and that was that.

Once my turn at watch was done I slept restlessly. I woke often, dreaming of the men I had slain. At one point I even dreamt of the stone lady. She was looking down on the bodies of the men I had killed. Slowly she moved from one to the next, leaning down to put her hand on their chests. As she touched each one the earth drew them down, until they were no longer visible. When she finished she looked at me and I could see tears in her eyes, glimmering crystals that fell endlessly to the still earth. She opened her mouth to speak to me but I couldn't hear her words. She was at once both beautiful and sorrowful. Though I couldn't hear her it seemed she was pleading with me, asking for something, but whatever it was I knew it was no longer in my power to give.

I woke suddenly, sweating. Glancing around the camp I saw Penny sitting next to Cyhan. They were talking softly, and he had his arm around her shoulder. He was probably trying to make her feel better but the sight kindled a dark fire in my belly. I closed my eyes to shut out the sight. It wasn't my concern anymore anyway. She would need someone after I was gone. Assuming I could manage to find a way to get rid of our accursed bond.

Dawn came early, as it usually did. We broke camp quickly and set off down the road. Birds were singing and there was a mild breeze, which carried the pleasant smells of flowers and growing things to my nose. In short it was a miserable day. I've never understood why Mother Nature was so clueless with regard to my moods. Women were supposed to have excellent intuition after all. Then again I had long suspected Mother Nature was a bitch by choice.

Penny seemed to have recovered from our fight the day before. She was chatting amiably with Marc, a relief for him I'm sure. It had never been easy for him to be silent. Even Cyhan seemed more sociable, today he had increased the length of his responses from one syllable to several words. Sometimes he even put forth the effort to use whole sentences.

All in all, the lively atmosphere served to highlight my antisocial behavior. At one point Marc rode closer and after a moment I realized he was speaking to me.

"What?" I asked. I hadn't been paying attention.

He sighed dramatically, "I was asking if you're looking forward to getting back home."

"Not particularly," I replied. The thought of home just reminded me that I had broken things off with Penny. My bed would seem extremely empty after more than a year of sharing it with her.

"So what are you brooding about?" he inquired.

The question irritated me. He knew bloody well why I was out of sorts. He would also know that a public conversation was unlikely to improve things. "I was considering various methods for killing people. If war is coming to our lands I'll need plenty of fresh ideas. I'm certain I can't use stones to kill them all one by one, so I was thinking of ways to kill men in large groups."

"That's a really damned morbid way to spend your morning," he commented sarcastically.

"I prefer to think of it as pragmatic."

"It would be more practical if you spent your time trying to figure out how to make up to Penny," he shot back.

I noticed the others were watching us. The last thing I wanted was to discuss my situation with Penny in front of them. "Go on ahead," I waved at them. "I need to iron some things out with my friend here."

"Sure," Cyhan said. Penny pretended she hadn't heard any of it. The two of them kept riding while I stopped my horse and faced Marc.

"You presume that I want to make up with Penny," I told him once they were out of earshot.

He stared at me carefully, "Don't give me that bullshit Mordecai. I'm the king of bullshit and I've known you far too long."

"Is your goddess worried that if I don't make up with Penny it will spoil her plans?" It was nonsense but I wanted to throw him off balance.

"The man I grew up with would never have acted like you did yesterday, not without a reason. Whatever you're planning you need to talk to someone. How else will you know whether you're being reasonable or deluding yourself?" he said, ignoring my insult.

"Why should I trust a god-ridden cast off?"

"Because I'm your goddamned friend!"

Something gave way inside me, "Alright, if you want my thoughts you'll have to promise this stays between us."

"That's the first *real* insult you've given me today," he answered coolly. There had never been any reservations between us before, nor had he ever betrayed my confidence.

"I'm going to die soon Marc. Penny had a vision not long ago."

"What? Are you sure?"

"She's certain, and I believe her—that's part of the reason I didn't want to accept her as my pact-bearer."

Comprehension dawned visibly on his face. He chewed the thoughts over for a few moments before speaking again. It didn't take him long though, he was a quick thinker. "So you think being a jackass will convince her to agree to end the bond?"

"I don't know. Either that or I'll figure a way to undo it myself. In any case when I'm gone it will be easier for her if she's not head over heels in love with me. It will be easier for me too," I finished.

"No it won't. I swear, sometimes you're the biggest idiot I've ever met," he replied ruefully.

"Sometime in the next six months I have to kill an army's worth of people. There's no way we're going to get enough men and supplies in half a year to stop an entire nation. What do you think that's going to do to me Marc? I should be glad I'm dying. Do you think anyone can do that and just go back to living a normal life?" I asked.

"That's precisely why you need her. You are going to need your friends and family. You're going to need her support. If you cut yourself off from everyone you *will* turn into a monster," he said emphatically.

"It doesn't matter! I'll be dead! What part of that are you not getting?" I shouted back at him.

"You don't look dead to me. I don't know what's going to happen in six months. Maybe you will die, maybe you won't. Recently I've come to believe in miracles, if you hadn't noticed. But the most important thing, whether you accept that or not, is that if you cut yourself off from everyone you love, you might as well be dead already. Why rush things? Live! Make the most of the time you have!"

"She's more important than that," I said simply.

"Is that what it all boils down to? Her? Then you're doubly a fool! This isn't the way to get her to agree to break the bond."

"Fine! You're such a damn genius when it comes to women, why don't you tell me how to get her to agree to it!?" I snapped.

Marc gave me a dark smile, "Think Mort, remember the past."

"Huh?"

He leaned in closer, 'til our faces were barely a foot apart and explained, in detail, exactly how to get her to agree. The audacity of his idea shocked me.

"There's no way I can be sure that will happen!" I exclaimed.

"You don't have to be sure. Just lie; you're the powerful wizard after all. No one has a clue what you can and can't do—or know," he gave me another of his most dazzling smiles.

"Lie to her?" I had never considered such a thing. "It doesn't seem right."

"You'll be doing it to save her life remember?"

"That's the same reasoning she gave for lying to me. How is this different?" I asked.

"It isn't. Perhaps that will make it easier for you to forgive and forget in the meantime." He leaned back in his saddle stretching as he looked to see how far down the road our companions were. "Just remember one thing Mort."

"What's that?"

"You have always been my best friend. I think of you as a brother. Hell, I'm closer to you than I am to my brother. I'm on your side so don't shut me out again. If there is anything I can do to change the outcome I will, and I've got a pretty strong ally now. Don't give up hope while you still have life in you," he got down off his horse and walked over to mine.

I dismounted and gave him the hug I should have given him when I first saw him in the capital. Whatever else he was now, he was still my friend. We remounted and rode after Cyhan and Penny, urging our horses to a faster pace so we could catch up.

Neither Cyhan nor Penny asked us what we had talked about, and I didn't volunteer any information. We rode the rest of the day listening to Marc's stories about his adventures among the ladies of Albamarl. For a holy man he certainly had some wicked tales. Penny and I both laughed at a few of them, though we still weren't talking. My heart was a bit lighter now that I had some hope, at least hope for her.

CHAPTER 18

The rest of our trip passed uneventfully and two days later we rode into Washbrook. I was surprised when we found two men at the outer gate. They seemed to be taking their job seriously as we approached.

"Ho the gate!" I called.

"Ho yerself! Who goes there?" One of the two men responded. I recognized him immediately, it was Cecil Draper.

"If you don't remember me after a few short weeks I'll have to question the wisdom of putting you on gate duty!" I responded amiably.

"Your Lordship! Sorry, I was jus' doing my job. I trust all is well with you and the lady?" he nodded at Penelope.

"We're fine," I said, not daring to look at her. "How have things been since we left?"

"We've had quite a bit of excitement," he said.

"What happened?" I asked immediately.

"I think you'd better talk to Lord Dorian or Joe McDaniel your lordship. They'll want to tell you about it themselves," he answered uncertainly.

"Do you know where they would be at the moment?"

"Most likely at the castle," he replied.

I thanked him and we went through the gate. Not much had changed since we had left but there was an air of frenzied activity within. Children were working on bundles of torches in the main yard and men moved back and forth at their assigned tasks. The few women I saw seemed to be extremely busy.

"Let's head home," I announced, turning my horse to head for the main keep.

"You mean your home," Penny said bitterly.

"About that Penny, we need to talk…"

"Don't worry Mordecai, I'll move in with my father," she stated.

"Actually that won't do," I responded. "The requirements of the bond—remember? You and Cyhan will be staying at the keep. There should be plenty of room." I had meant to talk to her about this, but I didn't want to do it in front of the others, especially Cyhan.

"As long as I don't have to sleep near you," she said bluntly.

I held my tongue and we continued on. The gate house leading into the castle was unmanned, which wasn't surprising. There were barely enough people to manage the gates. Honestly I was surprised they were even doing that. People had to eat and every man had something else important to be doing. We were almost to the main door when Dorian came barreling out.

"Mordecai!" he shouted in greeting, and then he looked at everyone else. "Penny, Marcus… am I ever glad to see the two of you! Who's your new friend?" He indicated the giant warrior.

I started to answer him but Penny was quicker, "Oh, Dorian! This is my new teacher, Master Cyhan."

"Teacher?" Dorian was puzzled.

"I had to form the bond with Mordecai. I am Anath'Meridum now. Anyway the important thing is I'm learning to fight under Master Cyhan's skillful tutelage. He's really quite amazing. You two should compare notes. I'm sure even you might learn a few things Dorian. He's been training the Anath'Meridum his entire life," Penny said, practically gushing.

I couldn't recall her ever acting so excited about someone in my entire life. Certainly it had to be for my benefit. That's what my rational mind said; the rest of me was turning green.

Dorian strode up to Cyhan and offered his hand in greeting, "It is an honor to meet you. The fighting skills of the Anath'Meridum are legendary. Their teacher must be extraordinary." The older warrior clasped his hand and they shook. I noted that they stood eye to eye, and it was anyone's guess as to who was bigger.

"Well met Dorian. You do me too much honor, I am but one of a long line of teachers," Cyhan answered.

"You're too modest. Honestly Dorian, he's taught me so much already," she put her hand on Cyhan's well-muscled arm in an almost proprietary way, as if she were claiming possession. Then again perhaps my jealousy was overreacting. Dorian caught my eye for a second, an unspoken question was written in his gaze. Even he could tell something was going on.

"Let's go inside," he said. "Marc I haven't seen you in ages. You must have a hundred stories to tell by now."

A few minutes later we were seated at the high table in the feast hall. I had never presided over an official dinner at the castle yet but the table's size and prominent position proclaimed its future role. "Before we catch up on casual matters, tell me what's been going on Dorian. Cecil indicated that there has been some excitement since we left."

Dorian's expression grew dark, "I finally got to meet your monsters." That got our attention and Dorian spent the next half an hour relaying the story to us. He downplayed his own role in the battle but my father came in before he was done and corrected the omission.

"Don't listen to him son, Dorian here fought like a lion. If it hadn't been for him we'd have been overrun by the hell spawn!" Royce said as he came over. I got up to hug him.

"I would have guessed that even if you hadn't told me," I said.

"Your dad saved my ass Mort," Dorian added. He proceeded to describe Royce's plan to extract him from the mob of undead who had overpowered him. Between the two of them I got a reasonably complete account of what had happened.

"So this was almost a week ago, has there been any sign of them since?" I asked.

"We've had nary a peep from them," my father replied.

"I think your dad scared them off," Dorian laughed.

"I only wish that were true," I said. I gave them what I had learned regarding the shiggreth and their dark origins.

"How'd you learn that?" Dorian asked.

"Marc told me, though Rose knew about them too. Apparently it's one of the finer points of history that I missed out on."

Dorian looked at Marc, "I don't recall you being that keen on history."

"My information came from a higher source," he answered solemnly. That led to a detailed discussion about Marc's new vocation. Dorian was pleased by the news. The Thornbears had long been devout followers of the Lady of the Evening Star and Dorian was no exception. Finding out that one of his best friends had become a saint of the Lady was a thing for celebration in his mind. Royce just grunted noncommittally. He had never had much use for the gods.

"By the way Dorian," Marc went on, "Lady Rose sends you her greetings. She was most interested in your doings since she last visited. She sends her apologies that she had to remain behind."

Dorian's face lit up. He had always been terrible at hiding his emotions. "Is she well?"

"She said to tell you that she is in excellent health and looking forward to seeing you soon. She will be coming to stay here in a few months," Marc replied. He was enjoying his role as messenger far too much.

"Why are you telling me, though? Shouldn't she be giving such messages to Mort?" Dorian had gotten so flustered at news of Lady Rose he had completely forgotten I had been there when she gave Marc her messages. I smiled inwardly.

"He was there Dorian," Marc sighed, "and she was most specific. She wanted me to let *you* know personally that she would be coming and looked forward to continuing her conversation with *you*."

Penny laughed at Dorian's confusion, "Give it up Marcus. He's never going to get it. Not until she brains him with a large club and drags him back to her den."

Dorian glared at her. Uncomfortable with the way the conversation was going he sought to change it, "Penny you'll be pleased when you see your rooms. We finished setting up the furnishings and the workmen completed the rest of that floor as well."

The light in her eyes went out, "I'm sure it's very nice Dorian but I won't be staying there. Mordecai has decided to terminate our engagement."

"What!?" Dorian's shout was exceptional. He managed to draw that one word out into a ten second exclamation of shock and dismay. Across the table my father's face also showed surprise but he kept his silence. He was wise enough to wait 'til later to question me about it. Dorian recovered his voice and went on, "What did you do!?" Naturally he was addressing me. I worried for a moment he might try to throttle me.

"Whoa! Calm down Dorian. We can talk about it later, this isn't the time," Marc interjected, hoping to forestall a messy argument. Dorian looked from Marc to me and back to Marc again. His face was clearly communicating the message that we would need to talk—and soon.

Penny broke the awkward pause, "I'll need alternative sleeping arrangements Dorian. My master...," her eyes shot me a look of utter disdain, "requires that I stay within two hundred yards of his presence at all times."

That riled me up, "Now hold on here, Penelope!" I spit her name out as if it were a curse. "The two hundred yards is a result of the bond you lied to me about, so don't go trying to hang the blame on me for that!"

"I stand corrected. Please forgive me, Your Excellency," she replied in mock obeisance. "As you can see Dorian I am no longer worthy of being in his lordship's exalted presence so I will require a different room."

Poor Dorian was caught in the middle, and ill-equipped to deal with it. "Well, there's not much extra room at the present. I was going to offer to have Cyhan and Marcus stay in your old house, but if you need it..."

"That's too far for her," Cyhan put in, "but for me it would be fine."

"What about the other rooms?" Penny asked. The floor that held our suite also had a number of rooms for guests.

"All the villagers are sleeping inside the walls at night. The rooms have been occupied, though I suppose I could put one of the families in the barracks...," Dean suggested.

"No that's fine," Penny said. "Cyhan won't mind the barracks; he's a military man after all. We can both stay there." Cyhan's eyebrows went up at this.

"I don't mind the barracks either," Marc said.

"You can stay with me," I said. "I will have room after all."

Once everyone had settled upon the sleeping arrangements they started to head out but I had one more announcement, "Before you go… I have some bad news."

"Haven't we had enough bad news for one evening?" Dorian replied.

"I'm afraid this is even worse. The kingdom of Gododdin will invade Lothion come spring. Arundel, Cameron and Lancaster will be the first to feel the brunt of the assault," I informed them.

"How do you know this?" Dorian asked, furrowing his brow.

"One of Penelope's visions and some timely information from the Lady of the Evening Star," I nodded at Penny and Marc.

Everyone began talking at once and I was forced to shout to be heard, "I know this is unexpected but hear me out!" After they had quieted I began detailing what we knew, which wasn't much, other than the time and place. I also shared my conversation with King Edward; they needed to know that help wouldn't be forthcoming. When I had finished the conversation rapidly fell into chaos again.

Royce interrupted. Though he spoke calmly everyone stopped to hear what he said, "I have a suggestion. Why don't we sleep on it? You've told us what you know, but we're still getting a handle on it. We should wait until morning to start making plans, our heads will be clearer then."

That sounded like a good idea so I seconded the notion. Soon people began to drift out and Penny took Cyhan by the arm, "I'll show you where the barracks are."

I'm sure an old veteran would be able to find the barracks without help but I didn't say anything. Marc and Dorian were heading for the stairs. They were giving me glances which I figured meant they planned to grill me back in my rooms. I rose to follow them but my father stopped me. "I need to talk to you for a minute son," he said.

I told Dorian I'd be along in a little while and turned to give him my attention. I had little doubt what he wanted to talk about. I steeled myself, disappointing him had always been my worst fear. He gave me a thoughtful look but didn't say anything. He had a talent for talking without words. After a long silence he finally spoke, "Well?"

"Well what?" I replied. I felt like a rebellious teenager again, which was odd since I had never really had a rebellious stage. I imagined if I were a teenager and rebellious, this was probably what it would feel like.

"What do I tell your mother?" he asked.

"Why isn't she here anyway?"

"Because you didn't bother to stop on your way in and tell her you were back. You're lucky I was here or I'd still be thinking you were in the capital too," his words were a rebuke.

"Sorry I didn't think. I've had a lot on my mind lately. I'll come by in the morning and see her," he already had me apologizing. I never understood how that happened.

"What's going on with you and Penny?"

"I don't really understand it myself Dad. She lied to me about this bond...," I gave him a little background. I don't think he had ever really understood exactly what an Anath'Meridum was before. I also told him about the voices and the stone lady. Before long I was stumbling over my words. It was hard to talk about my emotions. They all seemed so petty when I put them into words before him.

I couldn't tell him about her vision. So I also had to leave out my reasons for wanting to break the bond. Avoiding those things I wound up talking mostly about my experience with the voices, or the onset of madness as everyone else had felt it was.

He listened without comment, until I had run out of things to say, and then he waited a while longer. I began to wonder if he would say anything at all when he finally spoke, "I'm not going to tell you what to do about the girl. You'll have to figure that out for yourself, although I'm sure your mother will have a lot to say about it," he chuckled. "About these voices, though—what were they like?"

I described them, as best I could. For the most part they had been wordless experiences, almost like an extension of my senses, except for the stone-lady. Her voice had been as clear as my father's. I told him about her appearance at the bonding ceremony.

"I don't know much about wizards or magic, but I do know a thing or two about the earth," he held up his rough calloused hands. "I've worked with iron for most of my life. Most men think it to be hard and unyielding, and it is—if you treat it like something to be shaped on a whim. Iron takes patience and strength of will. You have to plan and think—it won't give itself over to be shaped by pure force. No matter how strong you are."

As deliberate as he usually seemed, I couldn't see how this had anything to do with my experiences, "Dad listen, I don't think..."

"Let me finish! Iron is a gift of the earth. What I just said is true of blacksmiths, but it's also true for stone masons and even woodworkers. They're all gifts from the earth. I don't know much about the gods, but I know a bit about the earth. You can trust it. *If* you're sure it was the earth you were hearing," he finished.

My own feelings had been similar to what he was telling me but I had been too uncertain to voice them. Everyone had been so certain I was going mad and the stone-lady had only made it worse. "What do you think about the stone-lady?" I asked.

"Hell I've never understood your mother, much less any other woman. I'd be careful if I were you," he replied.

I laughed, "Thanks Dad." I gave him an awkward hug. He never had been very comfortable with overt displays of affection.

I turned to go but he had one more thing to say, "Mordecai."

"Yeah?"

"Don't be too hard on the girl. You're a fool if you let her go over this, life's too short." He didn't wait for me to answer, just headed for the door.

I stared at the doorway to the great hall for a long minute after he had left. "If only it were that easy Dad." Finally I turned and headed for my rooms. I was expecting another long conversation once Dorian got me alone.

CHAPTER 19

The carpenters and masons had been busy while I was away but much of the interior of the castle was still unfinished. Today that was notable in the fact that my new reception chamber, while completed, still didn't have a table. Instead we gathered at the high table in the feast hall after breakfast was done.

The conversation started with a much more subdued babbling than the day before. My father had been correct; a good night's sleep had given everyone a chance to put their thoughts in order. Now we just needed to figure out how to put the county in order. "If everyone will stop talking for a moment I'd like to start our first planning session," I had to speak loudly to get their attention. It wasn't in my nature to run meetings, but I figured as the new Count di'Cameron I'd better get used to it.

Everyone went silent and I looked down the table. On one side sat Dorian, Marcus and my father, on the other Penny, Cyhan and Joe McDaniel. I had included Joe since he had become Dorian's second hand man in running the town militia and since they were our only 'military' force at present I thought he ought to be in on the planning. In all honesty, the only person at the table with any real standing was Dorian. He had already agreed to stay on permanently as my seneschal in Cameron Castle and handle my garrison (when I had one) and other such security concerns.

The others were there for less official reasons. Cyhan as an advisor obviously, and Marcus too, since he knew much more about the workings of the aristocratic world than I did. Penny was there—well I wasn't sure what reason I could point to—but even now I wouldn't think of leaving her out of something so important.

"As a wise friend once told me, let's start by first cataloguing what we have. Then we'll consider what sort of force we will be facing in the spring. Once we have those two things spelled out as clearly as possible we'll see what can be done between now and then to solve our problem," I stated and then I looked over at Joe, "Mister McDaniel, how many able men do we have in the militia presently?"

Joe coughed to hide his nervousness, "Begging your pardon your lordship, we have thirty two men left in the Washbrook militia. We lost two during the recent attack by the shiggreth."

"No need to be so formal Joe. Understand I was raised a common man, I'm not quite used to titles yet. When we're alone like this please call me Mordecai... or sir if you must," I told him.

"Yes sir, no problem," he answered.

"Dorian how many men can James Lancaster put in the field?"

Dorian's brow furrowed in concentration, "Well—I'm not really certain."

"A rough guess is all we really need," I assured him.

"A little over a hundred trained men at arms I think, and maybe a hundred more when he calls for his levies," Dorian replied. "But that's a very rough estimate."

"Do you have any idea what Baron Arundel might be able to bring to the table?" I asked.

"No more than thirty men at arms, perhaps close to a hundred if you include his peasant levies," Dorian supplied. "I don't know the man that well, though. That's based purely on what my father told me a few years ago."

"He doesn't have a castle if I remember correctly—is that right?"

"It's more of a fortified manor. There's no room for his people if he's besieged, not that it would stand any sort of organized assault," Marcus put in.

I thought for a moment. Cameron Castle was very nearly the same size as Lancaster Castle, despite the smaller size of my lands. Gododdin's army would have to pass through my lands before reaching Lancaster. "I think we should consider using this castle as our first strongpoint. If we fail here we can withdraw to Lancaster. The enemy would be foolish to bypass us and leave us behind them."

Cyhan spoke up, "They will have a considerably larger force than ours. If they assault us here we will probably be encircled, a successful withdrawal will be unlikely."

"If we withdraw to Lancaster at the start James will be overwhelmed with too many mouths to feed and shelter. The enemy will gain an excellent staging area, and Lancaster will be encircled just the same. If they lay siege to us there our combined forces and civilians will be easily starved out," I responded.

The large man's eyes focused on me for a moment. Until then I suspect he had seen me as no more than a stubborn peasant suddenly thrown into politics. I couldn't really blame him though; he had had no evidence to suggest otherwise. "That is true, but either way we face a crushing defeat. The only difference is in the time and place. In one we die more slowly as he isolates us from our allies, in the other he will be able to starve us out more quickly."

"How many men do you think Vendraccus will be able to field?" I asked.

Marcus and Dorian both shrugged but Cyhan spoke again, "If history is any example it will be over ten thousand men. In the last war between Lothion and Gododdin, King Gelleron brought nearly twenty thousand against us."

"But Lothion won that war didn't it?"

Marcus answered first, "Barely, they smashed and burned their way almost to the capital itself before they were stopped."

I had paid little heed to our history lessons when we were younger and I regretted it now, "That war was over a hundred years ago. What happened to Lancaster then?"

"To put it succinctly," Marc responded, "my great great grandfather spent the next twenty years rebuilding Lancaster and Cameron took even longer."

"As much as I've enjoyed rebuilding this castle, the idea of rebuilding the entire county is even less pleasing," I mused out loud.

"You really don't have a choice," Cyhan stated bluntly. "There aren't that many people in your entire county anyway. You should pull out and join the king's forces."

"And lose everything? Just give it to them?" I asked.

"Not everything, you'll still have your lives. If you stay you won't be around to rebuild, nor will any of your people," he countered.

"There is a third option," Penny said. It was the first time she had spoken and everyone's eyes turned to her. "You could capitulate. Put up a token resistance and surrender when he encircles the castle. If we're lucky Vendraccus might leave you your lands and move on with his campaign."

That started an uproar as everyone began arguing at once.

"I'm *not* suggesting we actually do that!" she had to shout to be heard, "I just thought we should be clear on all of our options, even if some of them are distasteful."

"She is correct about that," Cyhan added and she gave him a look of gratitude. My chest tightened at her expression.

"I am not willing to consider that as an option," I said forcefully. "I would rather die first." I met Penny's eyes as I said it. We hadn't looked directly at one another in almost two days now, and I wondered what I would find.

She showed no sign of worry on my account, instead I saw disgust written plainly on her face. "What of the women and children, what is their choice? Will they die for your honor too?"

I could feel my face turning red, "I was thinking we would send them to Lancaster. We could house his troops here and concentrate most of the civilians there."

I saw her nostrils flare as her breathing quickened. "How many more widows will you create before you're satisfied?" she challenged.

My temper snapped, "I can think of at least one woman who won't be a widow!" I was standing now, shouting across the table at her. I don't think I had ever been so angry before.

"I'd rather be dead than be your widow!" Penny yelled knocking her chair back as she stood up. She was leaning toward me, her hands gripping the table.

"You will be dead if you don't undo this ridiculous bond!"

"I'd just as soon beat you to death first! Then we'll both be free of it!" She was gripping the wood so tightly that the edge of the table broke away under her hands. For a moment it seemed she might try to carry out her threat then and there.

"Dammit calm down!" my father said. "The two of you are fighting like cats and dogs. We're here to make decisions, not bicker." Looking down the table I could see everyone agreed with him on that point, though none of the others wanted to get in the middle of our fight.

I took a deep breath, "Fine. You're right. Let's adjourn for a while. We can resume after some of us have had a chance for our tempers to cool." I gave Penny a stern look.

"A break would probably be good," said Joe, relieved that the tension was easing up.

"For us maybe," said my father, "these two need to sort out their differences—in private."

"Now hold on, I've got nothing to say..." I started but Penny cut me off.

"Damn right you don't, coward! You'd rather put families' lives at stake than take a rational approach to anything," she declared.

"I have to agree with Royce," Marcus stood and took everyone in with his eyes. "I think these two need to spend some time alone. Once they've sorted themselves out we can see about the rest of this."

Everyone else began agreeing quickly. A consensus was rapidly reached; Penny and I would be forced to spend the next hour alone. They forced us to retreat to my rooms, "If either of you comes out of there still arguing we'll lock you both in 'til you see sense," my father added.

"What kind of stupid idea is this?" I said as they herded us in through the door.

"Your mother's, ya fool. I was talking to her last night when she mentioned it," Royce growled back at me. I believed him; in my mind I could imagine her saying something like that. He shut the door in my face before I could reply.

Trapped I looked around, Penny stood at the other side of the room with her back toward me. A dark sense of foreboding came over me. It was entirely possible I wouldn't make it out alive. Perhaps I was being overly dramatic, but that's how it felt. I walked over and took a seat on the divan. I figured she probably wouldn't attack me outright if I was sitting down.

The next ten minutes passed in tense silence, before she spoke, "This is stupid. We should just tell them we made up so we can get them to let us out."

"Sounds like a fine idea to me," I heartily agreed.

"Of course you would think so. It's easier than actually *trying* to talk to me isn't it?" she said bitterly.

"It would be easier if you weren't so angry all the time," I shot back.

"That's not true. You were the one who snapped on the trip back. You didn't even give me an opportunity. Just up and cut me off—throwing that stupid ring at me!" she replied.

"I never lied to you Penny. How would you react?"

"Better than that… life happens Mordecai, and people have to work it out. You didn't even try? Do you think people are perfect, like in one of those story books you used to read?" I could sense a speech coming on. She had always been fond of listening to herself talk, I thought to myself angrily.

"I know better than that Penelope. I just expected honesty from you. Is that so much to ask?"

"And what would you have done if I had told you everything? What other choice could you have made? This is just your excuse. It was a shitty situation but you want someone else to blame. I won't be your scapegoat." She was still angry but at least she wasn't shouting any longer.

"At least I would have had a *choice,* a real choice. One based on facts, rather than being spoon fed the information you thought would be good for me, like a child," I retorted.

"And what else could you have chosen? Do you think a thousand years' worth of wizards are wrong? Would you rather risk madness, just for your stubborn pride?" she answered pointedly.

"Maybe I would have. I still don't believe I was going mad. If I had had a little more time I might have been able to figure things out," I said earnestly.

"You wouldn't Mort. No one has, not in a thousand years. Cyhan told me about the Sundering. The wizards of that time were the greatest the world has ever seen, and *they* chose this! You're letting your fear blind you to reason." She had stepped closer as she said this and now we were only a few feet apart. "Admit it! Your real reason isn't that you think the bond is wrong, the real reason is you don't want me to die with you."

"No!" I said vehemently, but then I amended my statement. "Yes and no, I don't want you to die, but I think there is more here than we realize. Just because everyone says something doesn't make it true. I know what I felt! I wasn't going mad. I needed to adjust."

"You pompous—stupid—jackass," she replied quietly. "Cyhan was right about you."

That got me. Just when I thought I might be able to reason with her she had to bring him into it. Jealousy reared up within me like a demon, "So your boyfriend told you I was crazy and you'd rather believe him than trust me?!"

"Boyfriend?" her eyes were wide with surprised innocence, for some reason that only made me madder.

"Yes your boyfriend—you deranged trollop!" The insult was so ridiculous I almost winced as I said it, but I could think of nothing better.

Her hand caught me squarely across the cheek. It would have been a stinging slap but I still had my shield up. Instead I wound up staggered at the force of the blow. Penelope had stopped moving, her hand held motionless in the air where she had struck me. Tears were starting from her eyes. "Take it back," she said quietly.

"Which part?" I asked dumbly. Stupid never dies.

"All of it—take it back," she repeated. The look on her face had me doubting myself suddenly. Anger I could deal with, but now her expression held such anguish I felt ashamed. I had had no idea my words could wound her so deeply.

"I'm sorry Penny, maybe you didn't deserve that," I admitted.

"Maybe? Mort, I have never—ever—looked on another man in that way. Do you really think I would—how could you think that? You are the stupidest man I have ever known!"

"That's as may be, but it's for the best," I said changing tactics.

"What do you mean, for the best?" she stared at me in shock.

"We're done Penny. I know you don't like that but it's best if you just let go of it. I've been thinking about this and I think I have a solution." The words were difficult to say but I kept my face calm. If I showed any sign of emotion now it would ruin my chances of convincing her.

"Oh—a solution?" she asked mildly. "I would love to hear it."

"You're worried that if we get rid of the bond I'll go mad right?" I continued. She nodded her head. "I don't like our current situation but I can understand that concern. According to your vision *I* will die in a few months, but we do have some options. I don't want you anymore Penny, hard as that is to admit. There's no need for you to die with me..."

"I see," she said.

"Wait let me finish. We can wait, 'til near the end. When you think the time is close we remove the bond then. At that point it won't matter if I start hearing voices again. Whatever happens after I die is still uncertain. At the very least you would have a chance to start over, if you can escape the end of the battle."

She watched me carefully, an expression of deep thought on her face. "I hadn't thought about it like that before Mordecai. I guess you're right—there's no good reason why I should die with you, especially if you don't love me anymore. All this time I just felt obligated, I was afraid to share my true feeling for Cyhan. It was just so shameful. But now I can start fresh, right?" Her voice was soft, with a hint of hope in it.

"That's right Penny. You're still my friend, no matter what else. If possible I'd like you to be happy," I said carefully. I hadn't expected her to react so rationally and I still half suspected she might be mocking me. Her acceptance hurt though, I had never thought she could let go so quickly.

"And you don't mind?" she asked.

"Well I don't want to die, but if there's a chance for you to have a normal life I think you should take it."

"And I can marry Cyhan?" her expression brightened.

"Well—yeah. If that's what you want," I almost choked on the words.

"Then it won't matter if I marry him before you die either? I guess we could just go ahead and have it done later this week. So we don't have to wait. You understand I'm sure."

Confusion had me full in its grasp now, "What?"

"For the sex of course—I'd rather not have to wait. Really we wouldn't need to get married either. It's not as if I'm a virgin anymore, but Cyhan is very traditional. I'm sure he would insist on it. It'll be a lot easier to deal with your loss if I'm already in the arms of my new lover. Don't you think?"

I gaped at her, "What the hell is wrong with you Penny?"

"Nothing Mordecai! It's quite simple. Since I'm obviously a great whore I should just face reality and do what I like, right? Maybe after I'm done with Cyhan I can have a run at Dorian and Marcus? I'm sure that would make me feel even better!" her eyes flashed angrily.

I turned my back on her and walked away, "I get it Penelope, no need to be an ass. I was just trying to offer a solution."

She followed me and put her hand on my shoulder to turn me around, "No, I get it now Mort. Look at me..." She had my face between her hands. "No more stupid games, they hurt too much. I love you, and I always will. Don't try to play martyr. You want me to live happily after you're gone, but it doesn't work that way. You're not getting rid of me."

I couldn't take it anymore, my composure broke and I could feel my eyes watering. She was just so damn beautiful standing there, inches away. Even if she did have my face locked between her insanely strong arms. "Damn you," I said sweetly, "I hate you sometimes."

"I hate you too," she answered and then she kissed me. Things got rather more interesting after that and we confessed our hate for one another several times more during the course of it.

A short time later we decided we needed to get back to the meeting. We were in various states of undress so we began putting ourselves back together when I heard a noise at the door. I had been so wrapped up in our 'conversation' I hadn't been paying attention to my other senses and I realized that two men were standing outside my door, Dorian and Marc, naturally enough. Opening my mind a bit more I could tell they had their ears pressed against the wood.

Striding rapidly across the room I flung the door open. I was hoping they would fall on their asses but they caught their balance. "What the hell are you doing?" I demanded.

Dorian's face was a picture of embarrassment but Marc was quicker on his feet, "Sorry Mort we were just talking and I had to confess something to Dorian here...," he faced our large friend with an expression of mock seriousness, hands out to clasp his shoulders. "I hate you Dorian!"

Dorian finally caught on, "I hate you too Marcus!" He puckered up as if he were going to kiss.

"I hate you so much!" Marc exclaimed and kissed him soundly on the lips. That was a bit too much for Dorian and he jerked back.

"Ugh! You didn't have to take it that far!" he declared, suddenly embarrassed. I could hear Penny giggling behind me and I couldn't help but laugh myself.

"Where is everyone else? I'm surprised there aren't more people out here enjoying the spectacle," Penny said.

"Oh they were all here a little while ago!" Marcus said with enthusiasm. "But when you two starting up with all the hating in there Royce decided it was impolite of us to listen in."

"So why are you two still here?" I asked.

"We snuck back up here. It was too good to miss," Marc laughed.

"It was his idea," Dorian hastily added.

"You two are unbelievable. I hate you sometimes," I smiled at them holding my arms out widely.

"We hate you too!" Marc exclaimed and we all wound up in an embrace. Somehow Penny wound up in the middle of it.

"Hey! No need to hug my posterior—Dorian!" she cried in mock outrage. He jumped back with a look of shocked innocence.

"I didn't!" he protested.

"Actually that was me," Marc admitted.

"I thought you were a priest or some such now?" she rounded on him. "Isn't that sort of behavior frowned upon?"

I growled in agreement with her, not that I was really mad.

"I'm sure the goddess will forgive me. After all your derriere is the best proof yet found that the gods are kind and just," he replied clasping his hands together as if in prayer.

"You're impossible!" I said and we began making our way down the corridor toward the stairs. Despite the constant tension of the last month it felt good to be among my friends. I couldn't help but wonder how long it would last. The future looked grim.

"By the way Penny," Marc started, "have you put on weight? I don't remember you being quite so—ample."

"Oooh!" she shrieked. That was followed by the sound of a large thump as Marc struck the wall. She had shoved him and it sounded as if he might get a bruise from that one.

CHAPTER 20

The resolution of my differences with Penelope had taken a bit longer than they had anticipated so we had lunch before returning to the table. Actually that's inaccurate; we had lunch before clearing the table and returning to business, since we were using the same table for both. Everyone seemed much more relaxed now that we had settled things between us.

"Where were we?" I said, starting the discussion again.

"I think we were at the part where we were trying to decide how we wanted to lose," Marc joked. It wasn't particularly funny since it was largely true, but it did set me to thinking.

"You're right," I agreed.

"So you've decided to see sense and join the king?" Cyhan asked.

"Nope, I just thought what Marc said was spot on. We've been going at this from the viewpoint of limiting our losses—planning our defeat. No war has ever been won that way," I stated.

"You don't honestly think there's any hope of us winning do you?" he responded.

"I'm not sure, but I'm not giving up yet. We haven't even finished listing our resources yet, which may be greater than we realize," I returned.

"What else do we have?" Dorian asked.

"Money for one—we have a lot of money, and time to use it," I said.

"Well that's fine—if you're planning to throw it at them," Joe put in, "but all the money in the world won't create an army out of thin air."

"You're right. There's no way we can match their numbers, whatever they may be, but I have Rose Hightower back in the capital recruiting as many as she can find. It might be the case that she can find enough to keep us from being completely overrun," I told them.

"Not many men are going to take your coin to join a lost cause," Marc informed us, "especially when the king will also be opening his coffers to recruit for a far less suicidal battle."

"I'm offering more than the king, remember? Land may draw men that money alone could not tempt."

"That still doesn't get around the fact that it won't be enough men. Even the king won't face them here. The terrain offers no advantage, leaving the battle largely a matter of who brings the largest army," Cyhan said.

"We have something that they don't," Dorian responded calmly.

"What?" the older warrior asked him.

"Him," my friend pointed at me across the table. "We have the only remaining wizard in the civilized world. We have magic—they don't."

"I appreciate your confidence in your friend," Cyhan placated him, "but no amount of magic can stop an army of over ten thousand."

"You weren't there at Lancaster. I was. He killed over a hundred of them in one fell swoop," Dorian replied, unshaken.

"And it nearly killed him," Penny added. "Besides, I don't think Vendraccus will be so kind as to gather his army all in one place where Mordecai could conveniently annihilate them all at once. At Lancaster he had the enemy confined in one room."

"Hah!" Royce shouted. Everyone looked at him wondering at his odd exclamation. "Say that again girl."

"It nearly killed him...," Penny responded uncertainly.

"No, no, the last bit—about the room," my father's sharp blue eyes were piercing as he spoke. I knew the look. He usually got it when he had overcome a difficult problem crafting something in the smithy.

"At Lancaster he had the enemy confined in one room?" she repeated.

"Aye, that was it. You..." he pointed at Cyhan, "you said that the terrain here held no advantage, so the king wouldn't fight here. That may not be true."

"What are you talking about Royce?" Joe asked. A look of hope was forming on his face already. He had a lot respect for the smith's ideas, especially after the fight with the shiggreth.

"The river—here see," he moved a few cups aside and tried to trace out the terrain with his finger on the table top. "Bah, this won't work! Someone fetch me some paper and a piece of charcoal."

I got up to fetch it for him. Paper was in short supply so I doubted anyone else would know where to find a piece large enough. I happened to know where he kept his back at the smithy. He frequently liked to plan his work out with large sketches. Ten minutes later I was back and we laid a large sheet out on the table.

"Alright   look here," Royce started drawing a rough map of the area surrounding Castle Cameron, including Lancaster and Arundel. To the north a long line of mountains formed a rough border between Lothion and Gododdin. South of that were my lands, with Lancaster to the east of us and Arundel to the west. A break at the western end of the mountain range was the common passage between Gododdin and Lothion. A road crossed there and went past the Barony of Arundel, leading onward to Cameron and then Lancaster before turning south to head into the interior of Lothion.

"Here's where they'll be coming from, and they'll have to follow the road past Arundel," he drew a line to represent the road. It went south from the mountains toward Arundel before turning to run eastward past Cameron and Arundel. "You'll notice that the road is paralleled by the Glenmae River for most of its length." He added another line a bit north of the road. "The river runs just a half mile north of the road for most of the valley before it leads back up into the mountains north of Lancaster." The valley itself was very gentle, a sloping grassy plain that stretched for miles between the road and the mountains. A large part of the farming for the three fiefdoms was done there. It was bordered to the north by the mountains and rose again on the southern side where the road ran. Near the road the forest started, stretching for many miles to the south.

"So they follow the road, making short side stops to wipe out Arundel, then us, and finally Lancaster as they go. After that they follow it south into Lothion proper, unless they want to try to drag their entire army through the forest and then into the foothills of central Lothion. I'd say that was unlikely." He looked up from his rough map, catching us with his sharp eyes, "You follow so far?"

I nodded but Cyhan stopped him, "You've laid out a map for disaster. There are no choke points, no bridges, and no narrow passes, just an open gently sloping valley with a road and a river. I don't see how any of that is going to help us."

"Well there is one bridge," Dorian put in, "the small one where the road crosses the river before heading into Gododdin."

"Not that it helps," Cyhan remarked. "The river is shallow enough to walk across in most places. You could burn the bridge and it would hardly slow them. Even the road is almost a joke, most of that valley is so smooth and even you could march across it almost as easily as take the road."

"Let me finish," Royce groused. "The valley slopes gently downward to the river, from the mountains to the north and from the forest and the road to the south. Its source lies in the mountains on the eastern end, north of Lancaster. There's a much smaller valley there, where the mountains come together around the river before it enters the main valley. There are rocky hills that come within a few hundred yards of each other on either side of the river there, roughly dividing that smaller valley from this one."

Joe interrupted, "Not to be rude Royce, but I don't see any reason why they would head up there? Assuming you're suggesting we somehow try to defend ourselves in Shepherd's Rest." That was the name of the smaller valley; Royce had avoided using it for the sake of those who didn't know the area.

"No Joe, you're missing my point," he pointed at the narrow entrance into Shepherd's Rest that the river passed through, "Here—Damn it." He grinned at us.

"Excuse me?" said Penny.

"Dam it!" repeated my father chuckling. He sometimes had an odd sense of humor and he was enjoying his joke.

"Oh! That's genius Roy!" shouted Joe. "We dam it!" He looked around to see who else had caught on.

"You think we should dam the river there?" I said; putting an end to the confusion everyone was in.

"Yep, we dam it there, and turn Shepherd's Rest into a reservoir. Then when those bastards march into the valley we unstop it and watch 'em drown." He put his thumbs in his belt and leaned back, obviously pleased with himself.

Cyhan still had concerns, "Not to get ahead of ourselves, there are still several large problems with your plan. One, the road is too far from the low part of the valley. You're not going to have enough water to wash them away if they're on it. Two, if you try to get them crossing the bridge; you won't be able to time it properly. Your dam is over ten miles from where the bridge is. You'd have no way of knowing when they were crossing, much less figuring out how long the water will take to reach that point. Third, it takes time to fill up a reservoir that large and the Glenmae isn't a very big river. Even if you could snap your fingers and have it dammed today it would still take over a year to fill. Fourth, you can't build a dam instantly, by the time you build it they'll be knocking on your doorstep."

"I've already got that covered," said Royce. "We don't try to get them on the bridge. It's too far like you said already, plus that many men will be strung out for miles on either side. We wait 'til they're on the road, close to here," he pointed at the map marking the point at which the road came close to Washbrook. "We set something up to force 'em to leave the road, make 'em march through the valley there close to the river. That way when we set it loose we catch 'em with their pants down."

"There might be a way to do that," Cyhan mused, "but what about the building time—and the water?"

"We start building right away, and we build from the bottom up. We lay the foundation and the first ten feet or so and then we block the river. We keep building upward from there, trying to stay ahead of the water's rise. You said yourself the river isn't that big, it won't fill too quickly for us." Royce stroked his beard as he thought about it.

Cyhan gave up, "I don't know anything about building dams. It might be possible but I think it will be much harder than you think."

Marcus stepped in, "It will be damn near impossible. You'll need massive stones for the foundation, and those take time to quarry and move. After that if you build too fast and sloppy the water will wash out your upper courses before the mortar can fully set. Assuming you have that much stone ready to lay the upper courses anyway. The base will have to be at least twenty feet thick if not more—I dunno maybe Mort can work that part out. It'll take a lot of math to calculate the water pressure at the base as the dam gets higher. I'm no engineer."

I spoke up, "We won't need mortar; I can probably fuse the stones together. We will have to do some calculating though, to figure out how thick it needs to be. I imagine I can help with the quarrying as well. I'll have to think about that."

"How do we let the water out?" Joe asked, "Are you going to build sluice gates into it? Seems like that would make the construction a lot more complicated."

I looked at my father and our eyes met. He smiled at me. "We blow it up," I said.

"You're talking hundreds, maybe thousands of tons of solid stone. There's not that much powder in the whole kingdom!" Joe remarked.

"He won't need powder Joe," said Marc waving his arms in the air. He was miming some sort of spell casting, either that or inventing a new type of erotic dance. "Boom!" he finished dramatically.

Penny eyed Marc's antics dubiously, "Before we get ahead of ourselves there are certain basic hurdles we have to get past. We need workers to build a dam, and lots of them. There are only so many people available and if they're spending the next few months building a dam they won't be doing much else."

"The dam is the only idea we've had that has any possibility of giving us a victory," I replied.

"And if it doesn't work? If there's a construction failure or the enemy doesn't do what you want, what then? It will take most of our resources and there won't be much left over for a backup plan," she said seriously.

I looked at my father and then back at Penny, "If it can be built he can do it." I pointed at my father. "He's the best damn blacksmith for a hundred miles."

"No disrespect Royce," Cyhan spoke up, "but you're a smith, not an engineer or a stone mason."

Royce wasn't put off, "Where do engineers come from eh? Somebody somewhere woke up one day and said, 'Hey maybe we can build this.' I may not have gone to any fancy colleges back in the city, but I know how to build. My boy here can help with the math. Get me the men, the stone, and enough time and we'll build the finest dam you ever saw."

Cyhan must have seen something in my father's face, "Alright. I believe you. You build that dam. We'll still need to figure out how to make sure the enemy is where we want them when the time comes."

"Let me worry about that," I said. "I have some ideas."

"Such as?"

"Give me a few days to work on 'em and I'll show you all what I'm thinking of," I replied. "For now we need to start moving. The dam has to start immediately if we're to have any chance of finishing it in time." I did a mental head count. "Dorian… head to Lancaster. If James is there tell him we need every able bodied man he can spare. Explain what you can and if he still has doubts tell him to come see me. If he isn't there tell Genevieve, she's not afraid to take the initiative when needed."

"When do you want me to go?" Dorian asked.

"Now," I answered immediately. "Marcus, I need you to visit the Baron of Arundel. He needs to know what's going on, tell him I would be greatly honored if he would pay me a visit."

"I'm not sure if Sheldon will be happy about being 'summoned' by his neighbor," Marc suggested. "What should I tell him?"

"Excuse me?" I said blinking at him.

"What should I tell him?" Marc repeated.

"Did you say his name is 'Sheldon'?" I asked.

Marc laughed, "Yeah he caught a lot of hell over that in his younger days. I wouldn't make any jokes about his name when you meet him though; he's still a bit sensitive about it."

I shook my head, "Alright, at least I had some warning. Tell him there's rumor of war brewing with Gododdin. Given his location I'm sure he'll be more than ready to come discuss it as soon as possible. Don't give him any more information, though. I'll give him the rest when he comes."

"I can do that. He won't be happy about it but that's your problem not mine," Marc headed for the door.

"Hey!" I shouted after him. "I didn't tell you to go yet!"

He spun as he walked, "You were about to!" and kept going. I had to admit he knew me better than myself some times.

"Joe," I addressed the older man next.

"Yes sir!" he snapped to attention.

"You don't have to do that Joe, I'm not a general."

"I did a stint in the royal guard, old habits die hard. Anyway as far as I can see—you're about to be one," he answered without giving an inch. He was still standing at attention.

I sighed, "Fine, whatever—Joe, Rose Hightower is in the capital arranging supplies and recruiting for us. She needs to know what we've decided. We'll need more workmen, lumber, stone masons, food, and—hell I don't know what else. Get with my father he'll have a better idea of some of the specific materials."

"Cyhan I'll want you to go with Joe. I can't risk losing him on the road and the journey needs to be made as speedily as possible," I said looking into the grim warrior's eyes.

For a moment I thought he might argue, "Alright. Have Dorian work on the sword with her while I'm gone. She needs to keep up the training." He nodded at Penny.

Last I looked to my father, "Dad..."

"I'll be taking a horse out to look at the site for the dam," he responded without waiting for me to finish.

I grinned at him, of course he knew his job better than I did, "Penny and I will ride with you. I need to see this myself." The day was already half done so we wasted no more time.

CHAPTER 21

It was almost dusk by the time we reached the area where Shepherd's Rest joined the main valley. I hadn't been there in years but the place looked much as I remembered. The ground was rocky and littered with boulders near the river as it passed through and there was a good fifty yards on the southern side of the river before the hills rose up again. The northern edge of the river was nearly flush against a massive stone face where the mountains met it.

"That's a lot of open ground to fill," I commented.

"It could be worse," Royce answered. "If it was easy everyone would be building dams."

"How deep is the river here?" asked Penny.

"Not sure. Let me borrow that big stick of yours Mordecai," my father said. I could only assume he was referring to my staff.

"No need," I replied. "I can feel it. It's about five feet deep at the middle and maybe two foot near the banks."

"Damn useful talent," my father remarked.

"I wonder how high it is," I mused looking at the rock walls on the northern side. I walked closer and spotted some sage growing a few feet from the river. Never one to waste an opportunity I decided to take some back for my mother. She always needed extra seasonings for her cooking. I was embarrassed to discover I had forgotten my knife. "Hey Dad, do you have a knife on you?"

"I've got my pants on don't I?" he snapped back. I should have seen that one coming. He grinned and handed the blade to me. "Can't believe you forgot your knife. I thought I raised you better than that!"

I cut a large section off and tucked it away before handing the knife back. "It has to be over a hundred feet high on this side," I said looking up again.

"Yeah but it's only thirty or so on the other side," Royce pointed. "We'll have to extend the length once we get over that. Still, it looks promising."

Penny gazed eastward into Shepherd's rest, "The river doesn't look big enough to fill that up in the time we have."

"You're forgetting the spring thaw. Once the mountains warm up the river will be swollen with snow-melt," Royce reminded her. "It's getting dark. I guess we'll have to camp here tonight."

"I can see in the dark," I told them. "If you don't mind riding a few more hours we can sleep in our beds. Besides, I want to be there when the visitors start arriving tomorrow."

◆━━◆

The next day moved slowly at first. I was anxious to see what help we could expect from the Lancasters. When I had last seen James he hadn't yet decided what his response would be to the King's call to arms. He had planned to meet with King Edward the day after we left and I was nervous about the outcome of that meeting.

Chances were high that he hadn't returned yet from the capital, which meant that Genevieve would be forced into making decisions that could possibly go against his wishes. Either way it had the potential to become an awkward situation.

Since I had nothing else to do with my morning I decided to work on my new idea. Our planning session had highlighted the fact that we needed a way to force the enemy to avoid the road and march through the low part of the valley. We also would need a way to destroy our new dam when the time was right. I thought I had something that might achieve both goals.

Last year, during the battle against the cultists in Lancaster Castle I had used a spell I lovingly called a 'flashbang'. I know—the name could use some work, but I had yet to find a better term for it. In short it involved creating a small focused point of energy that would flash outward, producing an intense light and a thunderous sound. It wouldn't actually damage anything nearby, there wasn't any explosive force involved, but it would blind and deafen anyone within a short distance of it.

Of course what I needed now would require explosive force as well. That would be easy enough, my command of Lycian was much better now. I could easily craft any number of variations on the spell, adding fire and a physical explosion would be simple, even if they did require more energy. The big problem was that I couldn't possibly be everywhere I would need to be when the enemy arrived. Driving the enemy from the road would be done primarily at the western end of the road, while at the same time someone would have to be destroying the dam on the eastern end of the valley. I couldn't be in two places at once, and it was at least a six hour ride from one end to the other.

This also ignored the fact that I had a fair idea that so many violent uses of power would exhaust me before I had completed either task. What I needed was a way to set the explosions up in advance. My previous experiments with enchanting had given me an idea, though. I had created a paring knife that drew in heat energy and stored it. Unfortunately it had exploded spectacularly after drawing in more energy than the enchantment could contain. I thought I could replicate that feat by removing the 'heat absorbing' component. Essentially I would set runes upon a small object to store energy, which I would provide, and then release it at the appropriate time. Depending upon the runes I used I thought I could manipulate the type of release, fire, light, etc...

I tried it first using a small block of wood. I inscribed it with simple runes to contain the power and encircled those with a second set of symbols. Hopefully those would channel the energy released into a fiery explosion. Once I had it ready I began focusing my will upon it, pouring as much energy into it as I thought it could contain.

Fortunately I had the sense to try my experiment outside while holding a strong shield around myself. Before I had managed to get half the energy within it that I 'thought' it could contain, it blew up in my face. I was sent tumbling back almost twenty feet while flames raged around me. My shield protected me from the worst of it but two trees nearby lost most of their leaves. I made a note to have them cut down. We would need the lumber anyway.

I tried again, this time maintaining a more respectable distance. It was a bit harder charging it with power from twenty feet away, but I managed without too much difficulty. This one also exploded at about the same time. Although the explosion was impressive, even at twenty feet it knocked me down, it was still nowhere near what I hoped to achieve.

I used a larger piece of wood for my third test, reasoning that perhaps the overall size of the object might be related to the energy it could contain. It did hold a bit more before it blew up, but still I wasn't satisfied. Finally it occurred to me to use a different material, so I tried using a rock the size of my fist.

This time the explosion was powerful enough, even at twenty feet to send me flying. The force of it threw me into a tree and caused my shield to collapse, a shard of stone tore a lovely gash in my cheek. I won't go into what I said when that happened, but I had been studying my swearing diligently ever since the day Cyhan had inspired me with his nautical prowess.

By this time my 'show' had drawn some spectators, my father among them. "You nearly killed yourself that time," he said clapping me on the back. "Keep working at it and you'll succeed I'm sure."

"Thanks Dad," I said sourly.

"Try doing it downhill over there, there's a big boulder you can shelter behind. That way you'll have something stronger to shield you from the blast," he suggested.

I could have kicked myself for not thinking of that already, "Good idea, but I'm still not getting what I want out of this thing." I explained what I had been doing. Although he knew nothing of magic my father was very experienced in many other ways. I thought he might have a better idea. Turns out I was right.

"Sounds like the strength of the material is the key, or maybe the density," he mused, "either way you won't find anything stronger or denser than iron around here."

"I don't want to destroy your bar stock," I told him.

"Nah—just use some of the slag left over from when we made those necklaces of yours. I probably have twenty or thirty pounds of the stuff waiting to be re-smelted," he offered. Slag was the bits of melted iron and dross left over from casting objects. Unless it was re-used it was nearly useless.

After a short search I found a piece the size of a child's fist. It was highly fractured and would probably shatter the first time a hammer struck it but it might do perfectly for my test. This time I gave myself a thirty foot safe zone and hid behind the boulder he had pointed out. I poured power into it for almost fifteen minutes without results. I had already put in twice what I thought I would need for a decent explosion and still it was holding it. That suited me fine since I planned to stop and create a second spell to release the energy on command later, but I thought I should find out what the tolerance was before doing that. I didn't want to have any accidents later by trying to put more in than they would hold.

Another five minutes and it finally shattered. The resulting explosion deafened me and shook the ground. I'm pretty sure the boulder saved my life. When I peeked over the top to look at the result I was shocked. The ground for ten feet around the center was gone, leaving a deep depression. Beyond that the grass and soil had been scoured clean for another fifteen feet. The side of the boulder facing the explosion was blackened and pocked with holes where debris had struck it.

Penny ran up and seemed to be yelling something at me, but I couldn't hear her over the constant ringing in my head, "What?!" I shouted back. I couldn't hear myself either. Eventually she gave up and led me back to the castle where she found some paper to write on.

"Are you stupid?" she wrote in her barely legible script.

"Maybe," I wrote back, and then I added, "I'm definitely deaf."

She began writing again, "I'm not deaf. You don't have to write your answers down for me—idiot."

Our conversation got more colorful after that, but honestly I was enjoying it. I suspect she was too, although she was definitely worried I would kill myself by accident. In the end she convinced me to stop for the day, at least until my hearing returned. I made a mental note to use a sound block on my ears before doing any more experiments.

My hearing returned slowly that afternoon. I had checked my eardrums, thinking they might be ruptured but they were still intact luckily. About the time I began to make out voices again Cecil Draper came running to inform us that Dorian had returned with the duchess. We hastily went down to meet her.

Penny and I greeted her just outside the door to the main keep, "It's a pleasure to see you again Genevieve!" I said.

She answered but I couldn't quite make out what she said. Her voice was muted and unclear. Penny saw my confusion and stepped in to help, "She says she came as soon as she got word!" Then she turned to face Genevieve, "I'm sorry Your Grace, he's half deaf at the moment, you'll have to shout to make yourself heard!"

The duchess flinched at the volume of Penny's voice; she wasn't used to being shouted at herself. She recovered quickly though and replied, "I can tell there's a story here you'll have to share with me!"

I laughed at the picture of the two of them shouting back and forth for my benefit. "Let's go inside, there are some things I need to discuss with you."

A short while later we were sitting in the antechamber to my rooms. Penny had found some wine so we could offer the duchess a bit of refreshment, but Genevieve waved her away, "No thank you dear. It's too early in the day for me. If you have tea that would do nicely, the road left me quite thirsty."

I wasted no time and while Penny was off searching for tea I informed the duchess of our plans. It took a bit of time to relate them all, but thankfully she wasn't hard of hearing, as I was. "I know this puts you in an awkward position, Your Grace, since James hasn't returned yet, but I need your help."

She leaned forward to shout at me, "James wouldn't desert you Mordecai. We haven't forgotten what you did last year; none of us would be here otherwise. This dam of yours reminds me of something you asked me to do back then."

"What would that be?" I asked.

"You want me to help you draw a line again," she replied. She was referring to the line she drew to help create a spell I used to kill the cultists that had attacked us. It was a touching way to remind me of how we had worked together then.

"Exactly," I said.

"What do you need?" she added.

"Men," I said simply. "Every able bodied man and woman you can spare. We have to build that dam as quickly as possible and what we sorely lack is strong backs and sure hands."

"What you ask is difficult. This is mid-autumn, every man I have is busy with the fall harvest. I can spare most of the guardsmen to help you, though they'll grumble at doing menial labor," she pursed her lips as she thought.

I had been thinking on that subject already, "I need them all. I'm planning to buy up all the food and grain I can get my hands on before winter sets in. I believe I can afford enough to keep us from starving before the first spring crop." It had been an exceptional year for farming so I had plans already moving to have Rose purchase as much food as possible before the roads closed in the winter.

Genevieve Lancaster frowned as she considered my idea, "Do you know how much that will cost? You'll have more than a thousand mouths to feed 'til the first harvest next year."

"More than that," I informed her. "I'm also recruiting as many men as I can get, so I plan on buying enough to manage at least two thousand."

"That would cost several thousand marks. Even with as much as James and I have saved we would be penniless if we did such a thing, and that's assuming the king doesn't take offense at your buying up valuable supplies right at a time when he needs them himself," she frowned.

"Frankly I don't give a damn. King Edward and I are not on the best of terms right now anyway. If we don't survive this war it won't matter anyway."

Penny returned with a tray laden with tea and a selection of sweet biscuits. I couldn't help but wonder where she had gotten them. The cook never had sweets around when I came hunting. She set the tray down and offered a cup to Genevieve who took it gratefully. Penny moved to sit down beside me but yelped and almost jumped off of the divan instead. I had stealthily placed my hand under her bottom before she sat down. She glared at me and sat down a bit further away without saying anything. Very likely she didn't want to offend the duchess.

Genevieve raised an eyebrow as she glanced at me over the rim of her cup. I thought I could detect the hint of a smile on her face but she declined to comment on my antics. "Very well Mordecai, I will help you 'draw the line' again. You shall have every able bodied man I have to spare. The women of Lancaster won't be idle either; we'll harvest what we can while their husbands are working on your dam."

"We won't disappoint you, Your Grace," I said gratefully.

"You never have Mordecai. You've always been my favorite nephew. Whether we succeed or fail I will always be proud of you," her eyes misted a bit as she said it. She took another quick sip of her tea before setting the cup down and rising. "I'd better be going."

Penny rose hastily, "But you haven't even finished your tea!"

"The one thing we have is time, but I don't think we can afford to squander it. I'll start making arrangements this evening after I get home." Genevieve leaned forward to give Penelope a quick embrace, whispering in her ear as she did so, "Good luck my dear, I think you have your hands full with this one."

I was confused as Penny and the duchess both glanced at me. I couldn't hear a word for they had spoken too softly. "What?" I said.

Penny gave the duchess a knowing look, "You have no idea!" she said, and they both laughed at that.

CHAPTER 22

Ihad thought I would have time to resume my experiments the next morning but as fate would have it the baron saw fit to show up early that day. I had already changed into my working clothes, plain linen with a leather smith's apron, so I was poorly dressed to greet him. Not that that bothered me in the slightest.

I saw him ride through the gate with two retainers close behind and headed over to greet him before he got to the main keep. "Pleased to meet you my lord!" I said loudly, moving forward to offer him my hand.

He looked down from his horse in obvious horror. He seemed startled that I had approached him so casually. "I am sorry, have we met before?" The young lord kept his hands well away from mine.

I stared at him for a moment, confused by his reticence. Lord Arundel was a slender man in his early thirties, with well-trimmed blond hair. The wind shifted and I caught a scent of lavender in the air. "No, I don't think we have. Sorry for the confusion, my name is..."

"I am here to see your lord, the Count di' Cameron. You'll pardon me if I don't stop to chat," he said brusquely and without further ado he urged his horse forward. I stepped back hastily to let him pass.

I watched him ride on, bemused at his arrogance. Sam Turner walked over to me as I stood there. "What was that about?"

"I have a feeling that Lord Arundel didn't expect to meet a nobleman dressed like this," I replied.

Sam laughed, "He'll be all kinds of embarrassed after you change into your fine clothes."

A wicked grin appeared on my face, "No—I think I'll meet him as I am. In fact, we should probably improve on my humble appearance." I know, I should have been more mature, but I have a devilish side to my personality at times. I'm not sure where I get it from.

My father stumbled upon us a few minutes later, standing beside a horse trough outside the stables. We had dumped some of the water onto the dusty ground to form a muddy slurry. Sam was assisting me as I smeared it liberally over my clothes. "Well you look as happy as a pig in mud," Royce commented dryly.

That started Sam and I to snickering as we explained what we were up to. My father got to chuckling as well. He always had been an excellent role model. "Son you need to stop fooling around and go take care of business," he said. He leaned down to get some mud on his hand before patting me fondly on the cheek. "You don't want to keep the baron waiting."

"Let everyone know to be on their best formal manners, I won't tolerate anyone being overly familiar with me today," I winked at them as I headed for the keep.

Dorian met me at the door, "Mort! Lord Arundel is here, you need..." His words tapered off as he took in my appearance. "What the hell happened to you?"

"Sheldon was a bit rude when he arrived so I thought I'd put on my best clothes for him," I replied smugly.

"The man isn't known for his sense of humor Mordecai. You're sure to insult him." Dorian had his worried look on, it was the face I was most accustomed to seeing on him.

"Don't worry, I'll be the very soul of courtesy," I said smiling. "Tell him I'll be down to meet him in the great hall momentarily." I went upstairs to find Penelope.

She saw me as soon as I entered our rooms, "Ugh! Get out! What is that all over you?" I could tell she was pleased to see me.

"Lord Arundel is here to see us," I managed to get out as she shooed me toward the door.

"Gods! You need to change—and bathe! What will he think if he sees you looking like that?"

I grinned, "He might have to rethink how he greets people at the very least." I took a few minutes to explain our encounter in the courtyard.

"And you think this will improve things?" she exclaimed. "Honestly Mort I worry about you. At times you're absolutely brilliant—and then—there's the rest of the time." She sighed loudly.

I turned and left before she could spoil my fun. "Come down when you're ready, I don't want to keep him waiting."

"Wait! No...," she yelled after me. She might have stopped me if she had grabbed my arm, but I think she was afraid of the mud. I escaped her and went down the stairs two at a time. I reached the door to the great hall just a few feet ahead of her.

"How do I look?" I asked, slicking my hair down with a bit of the mud from my shirt.

"Atrocious, you fool," she replied, giving me her most serious glare.

"Perfect," I said and opened the door.

I found Lord Arundel seated at the high table with Dorian and my mother. I hadn't realized she was in the castle or I might have rethought my hasty plan. Still there was no helping it now. I walked over to greet him.

"Lord Arundel! It's good to see you on such short notice." I held out my arm to him again, but he made no move to take it. Glancing over I saw my mother gaping at my appearance, I worried she might have a stroke.

The nobleman spoke to Dorian first, ignoring my presence, "Sir Dorian, who is this man?! This is the second time he has accosted me."

Dorian's lips had formed a large 'O' as his mind struggled with the situation. Eventually he got his mouth working again, "Baron, may I introduce Mordecai Illeniel, the Count di'Cameron. Mordecai this is Sheldon Arundel, your closest neighbor." Dorian looked as though each word was costing him a year of his life.

It was now the baron's turn to be shocked; his mouth opened and closed several times before he finally spoke, "Lord Cameron, it seems you have made a fool of me."

I couldn't tell if he was upset or not, he still seemed to be in shock. "Nonsense," I assured him, laughing. "You did most of that yourself, I was just having a bit of fun since you seemed confused. Sit back down, have some wine." I gestured to the chair as I took a seat myself.

My mother could hardly contain herself, "Mordecai why are you covered in mud?" She kept her tone calm but I was certain she was fairly agitated. She certainly hadn't raised me to greet lords while looking like a pig in a wallow. Visions of switches rose unbidden to my mind. I suppose we never get past the ingrained fears of childhood.

"Sorry Mother, I was hurrying to catch up with Lord Arundel after our chaotic first meeting and I slipped in some mud near the stables." Her expression told me all I needed to know about her opinion of my truthfulness. I gave her an extra-large smile to put her at ease and returned my attention to the baron. "I appreciate you coming so soon considering we haven't had the opportunity to meet before."

The good baron seemed to be recovering his composure, though his eyes kept straying to the mud in my hair. "Well yes, I thought to make a good impression since we have only recently become neighbors. Might I ask why you were dressed as a serf?"

I felt my hackles rising at the term. Until recently I might well have been described as such, at least by men with no better knowledge. "I keep no serfs here my lord; the citizens of Washbrook are all freeholders."

"Freeholders then, it matters not to me what you call your peasants," he sipped his wine casually. "I am given to wonder if you had not had this prank planned ahead for my arrival."

I was warming up to the baron quickly as it was clear we would get along superbly. "No I am afraid my poor attempt at humor was entirely spontaneous. I was heading to the smithy to work on a project with my father." I could see Dorian shaking his head in a silent 'no' out of the range of the baron's peripheral vision.

"I had heard you were raised in unusual circumstances, this must be your adopted father you refer to?" he asked mildly.

"Yes," I answered. The man's insufferable attitude was irritating to say the least. "I hate to be abrupt, but I have some rather pressing news to relate." I worried that the longer we talked the worse things would get so I decided to get directly to business.

"Please go ahead, I would rather not strain your hospitality further," the baron seemed as anxious as I to have our conversation done quickly.

I gave him the briefest version of what I had learned concerning the unknown threat posed by the shiggreth and the more looming danger of invasion from Gododdin. Even brief as I was it took a quarter of an hour to relate the news and throughout it all the baron showed little sign of apprehension.

"You say you informed the king?" he asked finally.

"I did."

"What was his response?"

"He will face the invader at the river Trent. He plans to call on our levies as soon as spring arrives," I told him. "When I discussed this with him I told him I don't plan to answer that call. Instead Lancaster and I will face them in the valley. We have a plan to..."

"You disobeyed the king?" he interrupted.

"After a short talk he saw the wisdom in letting me attempt to stop them here," I kept my voice neutral to hide my increasing annoyance.

"You plan to face them by yourself—you're either a madman or a fool," the baron's disdain was plain to hear.

"James of Lancaster and I will work together; we have a plan that may lead to success. If you will hear me out I believe you will find some hope in it."

"I think not. Nor do I believe the duke would be part of your foolish schemes." He stood as if to leave.

I was prepared to be labeled a fool if it would gain the baron's aid but it looked unlikely to happen now. "Before you go," I inquired, "What do you plan to do?"

"That should be plainly obvious to anyone but a madman covered in mud. I will take my men and join the king as soon as possible," he replied. He began heading for the door.

"What of your people?" I shouted after him.

The baron stopped for a moment before answering, "I will rebuild when the war is done. As long as there is land people will come."

Everyone in the room was staring at me. Thus far I had kept my calm, though perhaps I hadn't gotten off on the right foot. Now it seemed kind words would have no effect. As he reached for the door handle I considered stopping him but I saw little hope of changing his mind.

"What a bastard!" I remarked as the door closed behind him.

"I don't think your appearance helped any," said Penny. "Though I am surprised you kept your cool. After he mentioned your father I thought you might burn him to a cinder on the spot."

"I wouldn't have wanted his help anyway," my mother added. On that point everyone agreed, but I couldn't help but wonder if the baron's men might wind up being a deciding factor in the coming war. It wasn't as if we were sure of completing the dam on time.

CHAPTER 23

The next day I returned to working on my new explosive enchantments. Since my father's suggestion had worked so well I decided to stick with iron for all my future experiments. I used several pieces to get a more precise feel for how much power could be placed in a specific amount of iron without risking a premature explosion. I was very careful to protect my ears before each test.

Once I had pinned down the amount of energy I could use I switched to my second task, finding a way to set them off from a distance. I could easily do so myself, if the piece was within a range of about five hundred yards, but for our plan to work they would need to be used over much greater distances. The gem Cyhan had used during my bonding ritual had given me the idea I needed.

It was a simple concept; I would include a gem in the initial enchantment to contain the energy within the iron. Afterwards I could presumably remove it and use it to detonate the iron by crushing it. The real problem was that gemstones were in short supply; in fact I had none other than the diamond set in Penelope's engagement ring. I had a feeling she wouldn't be too keen on the idea of me crushing it for a test of my new spell. In any case diamonds aren't known for being easily destroyed.

Eventually I picked glass beads. As far as I could tell there was no reason the activating gem had to actually 'be' a gem. It just needed to be something strong enough to avoid accidentally breaking and brittle enough to be easily crushed.

Oddly enough, glass beads were almost as difficult to come by as gemstones. Washbrook hadn't had an actual glassblower in decades. The small town made do with wooden shutters on windows and handmade pottery for dishware. After a fruitless search and asking various townsfolk I gave up and went inside for lunch.

Penny was studying me as we ate. "You seem deep in thought," she remarked.

I realized I had been silent during most of the meal, "I'm sorry. I've just been trying to figure out a problem with a new spell."

"Perhaps you should bounce your ideas off of me. Let me be your sounding board. Besides I'd like to know what you're thinking before you kill yourself inadvertently." It never ceased to amaze me how much faith she had in my magical experimentation.

Penny had a quick mind and it didn't take her long to understand my problem. "So you just need some glass beads?"

I nodded affirmatively.

"Does it have to be a bead? What about faux jewels, you know—cut glass?" she suggested.

"That would work just as well," I replied, "but I haven't seen much jewelry of any kind around here. Have you?"

"No, but there is at Lancaster Castle," she reminded me.

I was feeling a bit dense. "Where?"

"The chandelier in the sun room, it used to be my job to dust it once a week, it always took me forever," she said. The sun room was an upstairs reception chamber, the same one where I had my original ill-fated conversation with Devon Tremont. I had never paid particular attention to the furnishings.

"Do you think the duchess would part with it?"

"She's already given you every able bodied man on her estate—at harvest time, I would think the chandelier would be a small price to pay," she told me.

"I hate to ask her," I said uncertainly.

"I'll do it. I can ride over there this afternoon," she offered. "I've been cooped up here for days now with nothing to do. I'm starting to feel useless."

"You can't," I reminded her, "Not unless I go as well and I have other things to work on today."

"Why not?" she replied before she remembered our bond. She glanced down at the sword she wore ruefully. "I never thought this would be so inconvenient."

"Who wouldn't want to be stuck with me twenty four hours a day for the rest of their life?" I said sarcastically.

"It's not that," she said. "It's just strange not being able to move about on my own. I guess you'll just have to send a messenger."

That reminded me, I still hadn't set up any regular messengers. The only people I had available to me were the townsfolk, those few that weren't involved in preparing the foundation for the dam. It seemed I was doomed to be perpetually short-handed. "Dorian can handle it. It will sound almost as good coming from him anyway."

Since I couldn't try my next experiments without the glass I spent the afternoon reading the books I had brought from my new 'home' in Albamarl. It had been over two weeks since we had left and I had yet to spend any time perusing them. I found a quiet corner in my room and settled down with '*A Definitive Guide on the Creation and Maintenance of Teleportation Waypoints*'. It turned out to be every bit as interesting as the title sounded, which is to say not at all.

I forced myself to focus and spent the next several hours wading through the basics of teleportation magic. I had assumed it would be easy, but it appeared that creating a pair of linked circles was fiendishly difficult. In theory a mage could teleport without using a circle of any kind, but in practice it required a prohibitive amount of complex mathematics to precisely arrive at any given location.

It would never have occurred to me before that the motion of the world itself would be a factor, but it was. Because of this circles had been designed to create artificial anchors in reality. A circle created a sort of independent location in space that didn't vary in the same way other points in space did. The result was that two circles, properly keyed to one another could be used to teleport easily from one place to another with no risk of a messy 'accident'. Any halfway decent mage could safely use one once it had been created.

People without magical skills could also use them, provided a practitioner provided the magical power to activate it. The possibilities for using the circle in Albamarl to move supplies immediately came to mind. If I could create a circle here to match the one there I would be able to easily move large amounts of materials or people with ease.

I had one major problem however. I had only briefly looked at the circle in the capital, and at that time I had been ignorant as to which parts of it were key to identifying it. The only way I could get the information I needed would be to make another trip there and back again.

I tossed the book aside in disgust and rubbed my temples, I had developed a distinct headache while reading it. I rested my eyes for a few minutes before I looked at *'The History of Illeniel'*. My short time examining it before had left me with more questions than answers, so I was still eager to read it. It had to be more enjoyable than studying teleportation. I opened it again and spent a few minutes finding my place before continuing:

The wizards of those times learned to be wary of the dark gods even as they shunned the new gods. None would treat with the dark gods or pay heed to the shining gods. Mankind controlled its own fate. Things might have remained so had one young wizard, Jerod, of the line of Mordan not given into greed and lust for power.

Jerod had been born to power but was not strong enough to speak to the earth. His jealousy of the existing archmages is part of what led to his down-fall and his betrayal of humanity. At that time two archmages were alive, Gareth of the line of Gaelyn, and Moira of the line of Centyr. There were rarely more than two or three archmages alive at any time in history, so this was not uncommon.

Jerod had fallen in love with Moira of the Centyr, but she had eyes only for another, an un-remarkable mage from the line of Illeniel. The details of their unfortunate love triangle did not survive the dark times that followed but it is known that Jerod gave in to the temptations of the dark god, Balinthor. Promises of power beyond that of the archmages seduced young Jerod. Believing that greater power might woo the archmage Moira he summoned the dark god and opened his mind to him.

Balinthor possessed him completely then, and used Jerod to open a world-bridge that he might cross over into the lands of men. Once he had crossed, Balinthor consumed Jerod's mind and took his body for his avatar.

The creation of the world-bridge drew the notice of many of the greater wizards of the time and they strove to contain the dark god. Led by Gareth Gaelyn they rallied against Balinthor but were unable to prevail. Gareth was slain and the wizards were thrown into disarray.

It was at this time that the 'shining gods' took their place in the forefront of people's hearts and minds. Many lesser wizards and other men who later came to be known as saints made pacts with the shining gods, Millicenth the Evening Star, Doron the Iron God, Karenth the Just, and Celior the Luminous.

The greater wizards and the archmage Moira Centyr remained mistrustful of the shining gods but worked with the growing power of the churches to save what remained of their shattered civilization. Their war against Balinthor and his minions was protracted over many years but it eventually became apparent that they could not win.

Mankind was driven inexorably closer to the brink of extinction until at last only one stronghold of note remained, in a land now known as the Kingdom of Lothion. Moira, the greater wizards, and the saints of the new churches fought long and hard but in the end they knew defeat was close at hand. In despair Moira called upon the earth in a way that no archmage before her had ever done. A great stone rose up, a stone which still stands in what later became the capitol of Lothion, and she treated with the earth.

The wizards then knew that all things, living and unliving, were sentient and aware. The earth itself was the greatest and largest of those things, but its mind was strange and foreign to the minds of men. Archmages past had been able to call upon it to perform great feats but their connection was limited. Moira cast aside her humanity and joined with the earth fully, stepping into the stone that had risen up before her.

The events that occurred afterwards are difficult to accept, but for the physical evidence left behind for modern scholars. A massive stone colossus was birthed by the Elentir Mountains and fought directly against the dark god. Balinthor's power was unrivaled by any mortal creature but he was dismayed by the near unending power the earth's guardian possessed. He was driven back for days and weeks, until he came to a land then known as Garulon.

Garulon was a beautiful country in those days, but it had already been devastated by the war. The inhabitants of the region were all dead or had fled with the remnants still resisting Balinthor. The earth chose that place for Balinthor's grave and there it was that the colossus grappled with the dark god. It bore him to the earth and the land itself rose up over them. A great pit opened beneath them and Balinthor was swallowed up, to be crushed within the earth's bosom. His death released a powerful blast and what remained of the region was torn asunder, leaving a great chasm that was soon filled by the sea.

This was the event known later as the 'Sundering'. Once the god had been slain the remnants of humanity destroyed his servants, dark beings known as the 'shiggreth'. Creatures of unlife, the shiggreth were difficult to root out but eventually they were all undone. Humanity was safe once more.

Civilization slowly rebuilt itself, but there were no archmages left alive and few mages of the great lines remained. The new religions had gained numerous followers during the war against Balinthor and their power grew among the rulers of the new nations. Jerod's action in unleashing the dark god upon humanity was not forgotten and people grew fearful that another wizard might repeat his mistake.

An accord was reached, between the rulers of that time, the new churches, and the remaining wizards of the great lines. To safeguard against weakness and human fallibility each wizard with the strength to potentially create a world-bridge would form a magical soul-bond with another person. The bond would shield their minds from undue outside influences, such as the dark gods, and if they should betray mankind by voluntarily giving themselves over to one of the dark gods the bond-mate would be able end the life of the offender. The bond would link the life of the wizard with his bond mate; the death of one would ensure the death of the other.

In time the bond bearers were named Anath'Meridum which meant 'Pact Bearer' in Lycian. They were the final protection against another tragic mistake. After that time no new archmages arose and the great lines dwindled. The bond meant that any powerful wizard was twice as likely to die due to accident or illness and they were much more vulnerable to assassins, despite the Anath'Meridum's legendary combat abilities.

My head was swimming with the information I had just read. The creation of the Anath'Meridum was the result of some sort of treaty? It sounded as if the remaining wizards left after the sundering had been at a serious disadvantage politically. Even more important, it was clear that wizards had been around for a long time without needing the bond to save them from madness. More and more it was becoming certain to me that the reasons for the bond revolved primarily around the threat of a repeat mistake and the political necessities of the time.

Another thing that truly fascinated me was the term 'archmage'. I had no frame of reference for it, but it sounded as if hearing 'voices' was not such a bad thing after all. From my experience before my bonding I had clearly been able to identify one of the voices as belonging to what I would have described as the earth itself, if so did that mean I was potentially an archmage? Again I found myself cursing the fact that my biological father had never lived to teach me anything. I had no clue what the implications might be if I was, I was still figuring out what it meant just to be a wizard.

That also left me wondering about the stone-lady. She had been very different from the other 'voices' I had heard and I now suspected she might be the archmage mentioned in the book. "Moira Centyr...,"

I mused aloud. If only the book had given the name of her lover. It had said that he was of the Illeniel line, but if his name had been the same as mine I could have been sure that she was one and the same person as my 'stone-lady'. If she really was some historical archmage; still alive after centuries of living within the earth itself—I couldn't begin to imagine what knowledge she might have.

A knock at the door forced me to return to the present, I found Marc standing outside. "Come in," I told him. "I haven't seen much of you the past day or two."

"After I delivered your message to Arundel I found myself called upon minister to the sick," he replied. "There were several there who had suffered injuries during the summer."

"Oh," I couldn't think of anything else to say.

"I thought you should know however, Sheldon returned yesterday evening in a terrible humor. You really made a great impression on him."

I smiled grimly, "The feeling was mutual. What did he say?"

"I won't waste your time with most of it. He's not a very inspired orator, the closest he came to an original insult was 'pig-lord'," Marcus smiled at me for a moment before his face grew serious. "Of more concern is that fact that he is already making preparations to winter in the capital."

"He's leaving already?" I was surprised he had moved so quickly. "What did he tell his people?"

"Nothing, it would almost seem to be a normal trip abroad, except for the fact that he's taking all of his fighting men with him—and packing up every valuable possession he owns." My friend shook his head, "He plans to leave them behind Mort."

My poor opinion of the baron had lowered even more; his sheer indifference to the fate of his people irritated me more than I could say. "Has he left yet?"

"He was still there when I left. I think he plans to start out in the morning."

A plan began to percolate in my head. It probably wasn't the wisest thing I had ever considered doing but my conscience wouldn't let me do otherwise. I went downstairs to make preparations for the next morning.

CHAPTER 24

The good baron was just leaving his manor when we arrived. I think he was surprised to see me, and not pleasantly so, which suited me just fine. Penny rode beside me to my right, while Marc sat upon his palfrey to my left. Behind us were ten men of the Washbrook militia.

"Lord Cameron, I had not expected to see you this day," the baron addressed me. He rode at the head of over thirty guardsmen. I could see heavily laden pack mules with them, as well as an exceptional number of 'spare' horses. He had probably emptied his stables. The fact that he cared more for his livestock than his people did nothing to improve my temper.

"You look as though you are off upon a journey my lord," I replied civilly.

"I plan to winter in the capital. Surely you did not expect me to stay?" his lip curled into a sneer as he spoke.

"I expected you to have the decency to inform your people of the coming war. Only a coward packs his bags and runs without giving his people some warning," I answered coldly. Evidently he hadn't bothered to tell his retainers either—I saw several eyes raised among his men as I spoke.

"Take care with your words Lord Cameron, lest I take umbrage. The affairs of my people are none of your concern." He shifted uncertainly on his stallion but resisted the urge to look at his men, to do so might have shown his fear.

"I see you didn't even have the courtesy to tell your men. Some of them must have families. Did you fear they would desert if they knew you were leaving their wives and children to die?" I raised my voice to ensure it would carry clearly to those listening. Several people had come out of his manor to see what was happening.

"I've had enough of your insults, dog!" the baron's face was red with rage now. "Cut them down..." Before he could finish his order Penny spurred her horse forward and struck him from his saddle with the flat of her sword. Rising from the ground he drew his own blade, "You dare strike your betters?!" he screamed at her.

I had to give the man credit, he might be an ass but he didn't shrink from a fight. Penny dismounted easily and strode toward him. Lord Arundel was obviously well practiced with his sword, but Penny was far too quick for him, she sidestepped his first swing and her hand darted out, wrenching the weapon from his grasp. His face registered shock before she struck him with her fist. A moment later he was stretched out face down in the dirt. She put the edge of her sword against his neck to encourage him to stay there, "I'll dare more than to strike you if you speak again."

The whole thing happened so quickly no one had moved. The baron's men sat their horses with gaping mouths at the sight of him so quickly disarmed. To be truthful I was a bit surprised myself. Penny had always been feisty, but now her speed and agility were frightening. I tried not to show my own surprise, though.

I addressed the guardsmen and the growing crowd of townsfolk who were gathering, "My name is Mordecai Illeniel, the new Count di'Cameron. I have come to give you the news your lord unwisely kept from you and to offer you a choice." I had to shout now to make sure everyone could hear me. Nearly fifty people stood around us now. "Gododdin plans to invade in the spring. I gave your baron this news yesterday, but it seems he would rather hide with his wealth in the capital than safeguard his people."

The gathered crowd gasped at the news and a chorus of hushed voices began talking among them. I worried panic might set in before I could finish. "I am here to offer you a choice. The Duke of Lancaster and I have a plan to meet the invader and defeat him. Any of you who would stay and fight for your homes are welcome to join us."

Poor Sheldon could not stay silent, "You would steal those in my service? The king will know of this outrage!"

"Kyrtos," I spoke and his voice fell silent. I could see his eyes bulging as he realized he was no longer capable of speaking.

"Those of you who wish to stay are welcome to come with me. Those of you who can fight may take employment with me. Those of you who fear the baron's wrath should he return may build new homes on my lands. Where you were 'serfs' to this pitiful excuse for a lord you may be freeholders now."

Someone in the crowd spoke up, "Winter is almost here. It is too late to move now; we would have no place to survive the cold."

I had expected that. "You may stay in your homes for the winter if you wish or you may find shelter in Castle Cameron. I need men and women to prepare for the coming war. I will assist you with building homes in the spring, once the war is done," I answered.

The crowd went silent at that. I suspect many of them were too shocked to know what to make of my offer. I didn't dare give them time for debate. Taking my staff I drew a line in the dirt, "Those of you who wish to take my offer step forward. Those who wish to return to the capital with this piece of trash simply stay where you are, although I suspect he will only take those who were in his original party."

Faced with a sudden choice it didn't take them long to decide. One by one the baron's guardsmen crossed my line. The townsfolk joined in a rush as soon as it was apparent the guardsmen wouldn't be standing against them. In the end only two men remained to the disgraced baron. I motioned to Penny to let him up, "Very well Sheldon. You may leave now." As an afterthought I released the magic that was holding his tongue.

"You will regret this. The king will hear of this outrage," he told me. I noticed he kept his voice low. He motioned to his remaining retainers to gather the pack mules.

"Stop," I declared. "You may take only what is on your person and enough food for you and your two servants to make the journey. The rest stays here."

"So you plan to rob me as well? You are no better than a common bandit," he spat at the ground.

"What you had came from the sweat of your people. You surrendered your right to it when you abandoned them," I replied.

He looked at Penny, "At least return my sword."

Penny glared at him, "It will go to someone who will defend their home."

"You would leave me defenseless on the roads?" he asked me.

"I think you will find the roads clear," I graced him with a cold smile.

We were almost back to Washbrook before Marc spoke, "You understand what this will mean when he reaches the king?"

I kept my eyes forward as I replied, "I have a fair idea."

"You'll be called before the council. He may even strip you of your title," he informed me.

"I know, but I can't in good conscience leave those people to the mercies of fate. Do you think I should have done otherwise?" I asked.

"You could have waited 'til after he had left. Then you would have been doing him a favor, protecting his people in his absence. He'd have been in your debt, rather than branding you a thief."

I glanced at him, "Is that what you would have done?"

"It was never my decision, but if it had been—I don't know. A year ago I might have killed him rather than let him return to the king, but now—I'm not sure. The goddess has shown me a new path, one open to all men. As I am now I probably would have waited until he was gone, though that might not have been the most tactically sound choice." My friend paused for a long minute. If I had not known him so well I might have spoken, but I knew more was coming. "You still aren't comfortable with my vocation are you?" he asked.

"I wish I could say I was. I trust you and I trust your intentions, but the more I learn of magic and the nature of the relationship between wizards and gods the less I trust them," I answered carefully.

I had piqued his curiosity, "What have you learned lately?"

I studied him carefully before I continued. At last I decided to trust my friend and told him what I had read in 'The History of Illeniel'.

After a long pause he spoke, "According to what you read the gods were once weaker than they are today? That goes against all current theological knowledge. What makes you trust it more than the words of the wise?"

"History is written by the victor," I said simply. I didn't need to expand on the statement; we'd had enough debates with his tutors over the years for him to understand my meaning immediately.

"According to what I've learned the victors of the sundering were the wizards of that time," he responded.

"That is true in the most technical sense, but they were left diminished and vastly outnumbered. The religions of the shining gods, by contrast, had risen to much greater power. The wizards that remained had lost the trust of kings and men, while the gods had gained it," I replied seriously. "I think that the bond was as much a political contrivance as it was a safeguard against another wizard opening a world-bridge."

"Your own experience nearly drove you mad," he answered.

"It may have appeared so—but I truly think I was simply adjusting to a new level of awareness. The wizards of old survived for more than a thousand years without a bond to protect them from madness," I said earnestly.

He shook his head, "You seemed like you were losing your mind my friend. Even if I believe that, you can't deny the bond protects you from being taken by one of the dark gods."

"The operative word is 'gods', not dark gods," I said. "When I met your goddess I got the distinct impression she would just as likely have 'taken' me as left me to my own devices."

"I can't believe that, you must have misunderstood her intentions. Besides it puts them at cross-purposes. If the shining gods want you as badly as the dark gods why would they have striven to create the accord that forces you to take a bond-bearer. If they wanted a wizard to create a world-bridge for them that would defeat their own purpose. Why would they do that?"

At first his argument struck me as logical. I hadn't considered it from that angle before, but then a new thought occurred to me, "Perhaps they were afraid. As you pointed out at the start, technically it was wizards who defeated Balinthor at the end. More specifically, it was *one* wizard that killed him, the archmage Moira Centyr. If you were an immortal deity wouldn't you be afraid of someone who could slay a god?"

Marc laughed; the idea that the gods might be afraid seemed plainly ludicrous. "You mentioned the archmages in that history you read, yet you don't even know what one is, do you?"

I had to admit my ignorance on that point, "Not a clue."

"Then why bother thinking on them?" he asked.

"Because I think I was becoming one perhaps, and this bond, which the shining gods helped force upon me—has stopped whatever was happening to me."

Marc gave me an empathetic look, "I think you should be grateful for it. I'm certain it was for your own good."

I didn't reply to that, I had made my argument knowing he couldn't accept it. Still I couldn't help thinking to myself, *I've never liked anything that was done to me for my own good.* It sounded like an excuse. Nevertheless it was an excuse I would have to live with.

◄━━━►

A week had passed since my 'visit' to Arundel and things were proceeding smoothly. The area for the dam had been cleared and dug out so the foundations could be laid below ground level while a large amount of rough stone was being brought in to supply material for construction. At the rate it was progressing my father estimated we would finish within a year—perhaps two.

The problem wasn't raw materials. The surrounding mountains and hills meant stone was available in great supply. We needed more timber but even that wasn't our main issue, it was a lack of sufficient laborers.

I spent several days during the week assisting as much as possible, using magic to do things that were otherwise extremely difficult. Ironically it was the simple tasks that were the hardest for me. I had initially suggested forgoing the use of mortar, thinking I could more easily fuse the stones myself, creating a tighter bond and saving time. How wrong I was!

My idea might have been practical if the stone blocks were much larger, limiting the number of interfaces between separate stones. Unfortunately the blocks were limited to a size of no more than a foot or two on a side; otherwise they took far too much time and effort to move them from where they were cut to the construction site. I could use magic to facilitate cutting and moving much larger blocks, but then I had little time to spend joining them.

As it was there were a vast number of blocks to be joined, and there was only one of me. Whether I spent my time helping to cut, move or join didn't matter. My father, being the practical man he is, chose to stick to building methods that the workers could manage with or without my assistance. "You won't be able to spend every day here helping—you've got too much else to do," he had told me. As usual he was right.

Since they were doing things the normal way, they needed mortar, and that meant some of the work force was occupied producing it. I hadn't realized before then how much work was involved in creating mortar, but I soon learned. Creating mortar first required quicklime; this was made by baking limestone in a kiln. Limestone was in ready abundance, but given the amount of lime needed they were making it by baking the stone in covered pits near where the dam was being built. Apparently plain limestone wasn't sufficient either. One of the masons explained to me that because of the water involved with a dam, a special lime was required; otherwise the mortar would erode quickly.

The details were more than I wanted to learn about the stone-mason's art, but the end result was that fully fifty of our workers were tied up producing the mortar. We had slightly less than two hundred men on a good day, so that slowed things down considerably.

I spent the last few hours of each day producing my new iron bombs. I had perfected the amount of energy to put in each one and the glass jewels had proved excellent for setting them off, but I had other troubles. Although I could produce a similar effect instantly with a few words and a moment's concentration it required a lot of energy. Despite my great potential as a wizard I could only manage it a few times before I was exhausted. Making the bombs was an excellent way to store that energy in advance, meaning when the war started we would be able to produce as many such explosions as we had bombs prepared ahead of time.

The general idea we had worked out was to produce hundreds and have them hidden along the road long before the enemy arrived. On paper it was a great plan, but in practice I couldn't make more than one or two an hour.

My father had set up a temporary foundry to cast the iron in fist size ingots for me to use, but he was able to produce far more than I could possibly charge. In fact, he had already made over a thousand, and almost all of them were still waiting for me to fill them with power. My only hope of doing that would be to devote my every waking hour to the task over the entire winter.

Obviously I couldn't do that, help with the dam, organize the men we had recruited, and prepare the teleportation circles needed for my other plans. You get the point I'm sure. I was working on charging my second iron bomb for the day when my father came over to check on me. He was already done with his shift supervising at the dam.

"You look exhausted son," he said. "Maybe you should quit for the day."

"I can't," I replied, still focusing on the flow of energy into the iron. "I have to get as many of these finished as possible. We only have a few months left."

"You spent six hours today helping at the dam, and I'm sure that must have taxed you. Then you come back here and spend four or five more—you're going to hurt yourself. We can't afford for you to kill yourself before the enemy even gets here." Royce rubbed his beard as he spoke, a sure sign he was worried.

I was already tired and irritated, "Do you know any other wizards who might volunteer to come help out?" I'll admit it. I was grumpy; otherwise I would never have spoken to him like that.

He frowned but didn't snap back, "There has to be some easier way." In all his years smithing my father had learned a thousand tricks to make his tasks easier. He just couldn't accept that there weren't any shortcuts in magic.

"It isn't something I can get around. It takes a certain amount of energy to charge each one of these bombs—and I'm the only one who can do it," I replied sourly.

"Can't you get the energy from somewhere else?" he suggested.

"Huh?" I responded sagely.

He ran his fingers through his beard carefully, "Well millers don't grind their flour by hand. They use a waterwheel to do the work for them."

I sighed, "Dad I can't just hook this up to some sort of magic water wheel! This isn't the same sort of..." I stopped in mid-sentence, staring at him with my mouth open.

He watched me for a moment before commenting dryly, "You're going to start catching flies if you leave your mouth open much longer."

I didn't answer, just shook my head, as if the motion would help put the pieces in my head together. A water wheel draws power from the motion of water, I had no idea how to do that, but some of my earlier enchanting experiments had used heat drawn from the environment. I could conceivably set up a temporary enchantment to charge the iron bombs in the same way. In fact, I had first gotten the idea for storing explosive energy had come from my ill-fated experiment using heat energy to power a ward on a paring knife. It had exploded when the ward had put more power into it than could be held safely.

There was no reason I couldn't do the same thing here. A temporary ward could draw heat to fill the explosive containment enchantment; I would just have to be sure to remove the ward before the limit was reached. I had originally thought of using the heat storing spell to create a device that would chill air—but if I used a stronger version it would work more quickly, and have a greater chilling effect. Perhaps it would be even be great enough to freeze water.

"What would happen if the water behind the dam froze solid?" I mused aloud.

"It might fracture the dam itself. Any water between the stones would expand," my father answered promptly. I had almost forgotten he was listening.

"Would it matter?" I asked.

"Hell yes it would matter. As soon as the water melted the dam would fall apart. Even if it didn't the damage would probably be enough to cause it to fail once the water started flowing through the fractures," he said.

"What if the water didn't melt?"

"Why don't you explain what you're thinking? Instead of asking dumbass questions," he suggested. My father had never been fond of answering pointless questions.

"Alright, this might sound strange, though...," I prefaced.

"Like I'm not used to that already," he snorted.

"What if we used heat drawn from the water to charge the iron? I think I could do it in such a way that it would cause the water to freeze," I told him.

"How much water are you talking about freezing exactly?" he asked.

"I have no idea. But what if we could manage to freeze the river where it met the dam?"

"The water level behind would keep rising, and it would melt your ice. You'd most likely wind up with a mess and a lot of wasted time. Wait, are you suggesting we build the dam itself out of ice?" His face made it plain he thought I had lost my wits.

"Suppose we kept freezing the water as it rose, building higher levels of ice..."

. He shook his head, "You'd have to freeze far more than that—the highest ice would always be at the same level as the water. I don't think it would work."

"Let me think about it," I said. "I'll have something to try tomorrow." I finished the iron bomb I was working on and decided to call it an evening. I had a lot to think about.

CHAPTER 25

The next morning brought its own challenges, Joe had returned from the capital with the first string of wagons and men. I was about to head down to the dam to try out some of my new ideas when they came through the main gate.

"Joe!" I called to him. He was riding with a small group at the head of the procession.

He rode over to me, "Morning your lordship!" He doffed a cap he must have picked up in the capital and executed a bow while staying in the saddle.

"Your trip seems to have been good for you," I remarked.

"Not half so good as it has been to you," he replied. He pointed back along the line of wagons and men. "You can't see the half of it yet. More than two hundred men have signed on, most of 'em hoping for land. I've also got twenty wagons of lumber, seventeen of grain, several more with stock iron and tools—I'll have to make you a list."

"How many of the men are workers?" I asked.

"About half of 'em, the rest are mercenaries, though I bet they'll work a shovel as good as anyone," he winked at me. "Let me introduce you to my new friend here—Angus McElroy. He's a stone mason by trade, and a damn good one. Angus this is our Lord Mordecai Illeniel, the new Count di'Cameron."

The man riding beside him looked short, though it was hard to tell since he was in the saddle. Balding on top he had possibly the broadest shoulders I had ever seen. "Nice to meet you your lordship." He attempted a bow from the saddle as well, though it was a bit clumsier than Joe's had been.

"Excellent to meet you Angus, I've got a rather complicated dam building project at the moment. I don't suppose you have any experience in that area?" I asked eagerly.

"I worked on the pier construction in the port city of Krytos. I've never worked on a dam but I've overseen several large projects in the capital and I'm familiar with the issues of masonry and water," he answered smoothly.

He projected a calm confidence. I took that as a good sign, the one thing we sorely lacked was experience. None of the masons I had working with us currently had ever been involved in large projects, much less managed them. "I'll introduce you to my father; he was about to head over to the build site this morning. He's currently in charge of the project but he could sorely use your help."

"Let the man get settled! He's only just arrived," protested Joe.

"It's fine Joe, the sooner the better. I'll trust you to watch my things," Angus reassured him.

I took Angus aside and introduced him to my father in short order. I had been planning to ride to the dam with him but I figured I'd better stay behind today and help organize the new materials and men. I left them discussing the current state of the dam and returned to help Joe find places to store the materials he had brought.

The rest of the day was occupied with logistics. It was soon apparent that we wouldn't have enough room to permanently house so many people. Rather than assign the new men to the dam I made plans to have them work on building temporary housing for themselves and the other people we expected to be arriving soon.

"Rose thinks we can find a lot more people. You'd best be ready for at least this many over again when the next load arrives," Joe told me.

I had needed more hands, but now that I had them it was clear they brought their own issues, "How are we going to feed all these people?" I explained that we would be relying almost entirely on purchased food and grain to make it through the winter.

"You're going to need a lot more then. If you're feeding the duke's men and all their dependents, plus these, and whoever else Rose finds—you'll need several times more than what I brought," Joe replied.

"I have to have enough to make it into late spring, at least until the first summer harvest comes in—assuming we have a chance to plant," I rubbed my forehead to try and relieve the headache I felt coming on.

"Relax a bit your lordship. Make me a list and give me your best estimate for how many mouths we'll have to feed. That Lady Rose is amazing. She knows more about supplies than anyone I've ever met. She's already thought of things that never occurred to me," he assured me.

"Well her father is in charge of managing logistics for the royal army, in time of war," I reminded him.

"Speaking of which, things seemed a bit tense between her and Lord Hightower," said Joe.

"You met him?"

Joe scratched his head as he answered, "Yeah, he showed up while we were loading the wagons. He was none too pleased about what she'd been doing. I got the feeling it wasn't their first 'discussion' about it."

I was curious, "What did he say?"

Joe laughed, "That he'd have her locked up if she kept at it. Said the king was after him to put a stop to it.

She gave him hell when he told her that. Don't think I'd ever seen her lose her temper before."

I rubbed my chin, I hadn't shaved in over a week and the stubble on my cheek was starting to itch. "You think he was serious?"

"Seemed like it to me, but who knows? He might have just been trying to scare her," Joe started laughing then.

"What's so funny?"

His blue eyes were crinkled with humor, "I ain't never seen anyone like that woman. If there was ever someone that couldn't be scared, it was her. He's wasting his time if he thinks she'll quit. If she was my daughter I wouldn't bother with threats—just lock her up straight away. A woman like that won't listen."

"That's what I was thinking too. I'm sure her father knows it as well," I replied. I was worried Lord Hightower might just do that very thing. "How soon can you be ready to go back?"

"Soon as the wagons are unloaded and the drivers have had some sleep. They'll want a good meal before we get back on the road," he answered.

I felt bad pushing them so hard but time seemed to be the one thing we lacked. "We'll start tomorrow then. I'm coming with you."

Joe's face showed surprise. "I'd be thinking you're more needed here your lordship. Isn't that why Lady Rose stayed behind, to help with arrangements?"

"I suspect that even the formidable Rose Hightower might need some help now and then. My father and that master mason you brought back can worry about the dam for a week or two without me. I'll put Dorian in charge here, he can handle mercenaries as well as I can, better actually." I didn't bother telling him I had another idea as well, since I wasn't sure it would work.

I left Joe eating in the great hall and went to find Dorian. He was out in the yard, already working to organize the new mercenaries turned guardsmen. Cyhan was with him. I caught Dorian's eye and he came over as soon as he was done talking to them.

"Mort! Look at them—worst soldiers I've ever seen!" he seemed rather irritated.

"Well they are mercenaries..." I began.

"Even mercenaries should have some pride! These men are just barely this side of being outright bandits! I'm surprised Rose had the nerve to bargain with such ruffians. I have serious doubts about their usefulness in the spring." Dorian seemed to be his usual optimistic self. I don't think he'd ever gone more than five minutes without having something to worry about.

"Well you have 'til spring to whip them into shape."

"I'd need ten years to turn them into real men," he groused.

"You have a few months, put 'em to work on the housing first. After that, see if Dad needs any help at the dam, if not, start them digging earthworks around the outer wall."

"That's not going to stop Vendraccus," said Dorian.

"It doesn't need to. We don't have enough room inside the outer wall to put all the temporary housing and shelters. Build a palisade and a steep ditch to protect the new quarters, I can't afford to lose men to the shiggreth before the spring gets here," I replied.

"There hasn't been any sign of them since that night but I can't fault your logic there," Dorian agreed.

"I'm going back to the capital with Joe," I told him without preamble.

Dorian frowned, "Why? Is Rose alright?" Leave it to Dorian to immediately think of her. Unfortunately in this case he might be right.

"She's fine," I lied. There was no force on earth that would keep him here if he thought I was concerned about her, and I couldn't afford to have him elsewhere. "I have an idea to speed up the transfer of materials between here and the capital. If it works I'll be back within a week."

"It takes almost a week just to get there Mort," said Dorian dryly.

"Trust me," I winked at him.

"I hate it when you say that. It usually means you're about to do something stupid," he grumbled.

I gave him a looked of wounded innocence, "Have I ever let you down?"

"Yeah remember when you stole those berry tarts?" When we were ten I had stolen three tarts from the kitchen in Lancaster. Dorian's bedroom had seemed the safest place to hide them while they cooled. No one would suspect him I had reasoned.

"Well—technically that wasn't my fault," I protested. It had been Marc's idea, and he had taken another three without me realizing it. The cook had been so incensed they interrogated every boy in the keep.

"The hell it wasn't! You showed up and hid them in my room, 'trust me' you said. Remember what happened? I still have the scars. I couldn't sit for a week," Dorian's eyes lit up. He loved telling a good story, even if it involved childhood pain.

I didn't bother arguing. We'd have gotten away with it if he hadn't blown our cover. As soon as the duchess put him to the question he had frozen up. Eyes wide and face pale they had immediately known he was guilty of something. It was the only time the duchess ever taken a switch to me personally.

"It will be fine," I reassured him, but I had to wonder. If things went wrong this time I would get much worse

than a switching. I went back to my room, I had a lot of
work to do before we left in the morning and I needed a
certain book.

CHAPTER 26

The wagons rolled steadily toward the gates of Albamarl. Joe was driving the lead wagon while I sat beside him. I was carrying a crossbow and dressed as a guard. I had no plans to announce my identity as we entered the city. I couldn't be sure what might have happened since I had been in the city a month past but if Lord Arundel had reached the king's ear my reception wouldn't be warm. Caution seemed the better course.

Penny rode beside the driver of the second wagon and was similarly attired. A woman guard was a bit unusual but shouldn't attract too much attention, unless they were expecting me to return. If they had been alerted to look for a man traveling with a female warrior she might arouse suspicion, but Penny hadn't taken up that role until after we had left. Hopefully it wouldn't have occurred to them. I didn't think they would expect me to try to sneak in to Albamarl anyway. As far as the king knew I should be back at home, preparing for a hopeless defeat.

The guards at the gate let us pass with only a few questions. So many empty wagons attracted attention but they could find no reason to stop us. A few minutes later we were rolling down the streets of Albamarl. "Where to first?" Joe asked.

"The Lancaster house, it should have the space we need. I'll have to make some preparations before we do anything else," I answered him.

The gates to the Lancaster estate were open when we reached it, something that seemed unusual. On my last visit they had been closed and guarded. We rode in and I got off the wagon. "Take the rest behind the house. There should be enough room back there for the wagons," I told Joe. I walked to the front door and opened it.

The house seemed empty so I began searching, hoping to find someone who could explain what had happened. I found James sitting in the breakfast room, he looked tired. The room itself had been crudely repaired and was yet unfinished.

"Mordecai!" shouted James, leaping up from his chair.

"My lord," I answered, "you look rather glum." In fact, the good duke looked downright depressed. It was rare to see him so worn looking, he was generally a man of uncommon health and energy.

"Heh," he said. "You might be right there. If you had been here a few hours earlier you would understand why."

"What happened?"

"The king forced Hightower's hand. He showed up with the royal guard and confiscated everything Rose had bought and stored for the next journey. They took considerably more besides—to be certain they had it all," he told me.

"I noticed there was no guard at your gate."

"They arrested everyone Rose had hired, including my retainers. I thought for a moment they might take me as well, but apparently I am still in the king's good graces," he said.

"I imagine Rose will be a terror when she finds out," I commented.

"Lord Hightower was commanding the guardsmen, he took Rose with him."

"Willingly?" I asked.

"He had her trussed up like wild game, she was far from willing."

"Where is she now?"

"I expect she's under lock and key at her father's house. I rather suspect that's why he took a personal hand in the matter, to prevent her from being locked up in the king's jail. The rest I don't know." James sat down, placing his head between his hands.

"We'll have to do something about that," I remarked.

"Such as? In case you didn't realize it, the king has declared you an outlaw. You're to be locked up as soon as they get their hands on you."

I had expected as much. "He can declare whatever he wants, it won't make a difference," I said.

"What are you planning?"

"I'll explain soon. I have to run an errand, I'll be back in a few hours," I replied.

James was concerned. "Where are you going? If you're going to do something I'd rather know beforehand. We're already in enough trouble."

"I'm going to my father's house. Trust me, I'll be back. In the meantime get your things together, we'll be leaving tonight," I said with a tone of authority. As an afterthought I added, "...your grace," but James didn't seem to notice.

***

Penny and I reached the house of Illeniel after a short walk. Entering was much simpler this time now that I understood how the door worked. I smiled inwardly at the memory of our last visit.

"I'm still not sure why we need to come here," Penny commented. "You already said this isn't necessary for your plan."

"In case we need to come back. Once they figure out what we've done they'll destroy my circle. This house is the one place in the city no one can get into. Plus I'm fairly sure they don't realize that I'll be able to return here at will. It may give us an advantage in the future, but only if I know the key to the circle here," I answered her.

We went upstairs and I got out the writing materials I had brought. My studies of *'A Definitive Guide on the Creation and Maintenance of Teleportation Waypoints'* had yielded good results. Teleportation circles were very specific in their construction; they all shared the same basic design. The most important part however, was the 'key', the part of the circle that identified it. Once that was known another circle could be created to match it. Every circle contained two keys, one identifying itself, and another that corresponded with the key of the destination circle.

Whatever circle had existed in Cameron Castle to match the one here was long gone, but if I knew what the key was I could create another. That would give me safe access to Albamarl, practically at will.

It took me several minutes to copy the keys found within the circle marked 'Cameron'. When I finished I carefully blotted the sheet with sand and folded it away. It wouldn't do to mistake one of the runes due to an unfortunate spot of ink. I tucked the paper into my pouch and Penny and I went back outside.

"Back to Lancaster's house?" she asked.

"Yes, I need to do one more thing there, then we can go get Rose," I replied.

When we got back to the Lancaster residence I didn't bother finding James. I went around the house to find Joe. I found him in the stables, helping to groom the horses that had been pulling the wagons. "Did you find a good place?" I asked him.

He looked up startled, "Oh! Yes your lordship! The duke has a small storehouse here, it's that building over there," he pointed across the yard to a large stone building with double doors wide enough to drive a wagon through. "He said we could use it. Lady Rose had been storing her acquisitions there, before they were confiscated."

"So it's empty now?" I said to clarify the point.

He assured me it was, so I went over and got started. The place was larger than I had realized, at least thirty feet wide and probably sixty feet long inside. The floor was smooth stone which reassured me. I had been afraid it might be simple dirt which would have made my task harder. Penny and I found brooms and began cleaning. She turned out to be much better at sweeping than I was but it still took us almost an hour to get the floor in the condition I wanted it. I decided not to compliment her sweeping skills. She might take it the wrong way given her prior occupation.

Another hour's work and we were ready. I went back to the house to let James know what to expect. "Your grace?" I asked. He seemed to have fallen asleep in a chair.

"Mordecai—sorry I haven't had much rest since yesterday," he apologized. It struck me as strange to hear the man apologize to me. For most of my life he had been my ultimate authority figure, next to my own father.

"Are you ready to leave? I'm going to get Rose and we'll have to move quickly when I return. I'm not sure if there will be any pursuit," I told him.

"I have little to bring other than personal effects. I've already packed those up. Strange, I always took Benchley for granted. I never realized how much work packing could be," he smiled ruefully.

"Did they take him when they arrested everyone?"

"No he's with Genevieve back in Lancaster. I had a different valet here, Percy was his name. Still, I'm missing him already," he laughed.

"Hopefully I'll be able to return with him as well," I said.

"I don't understand what you're planning Mordecai. This is bound to make things worse," he said.

"If things go badly it won't reflect on you. This is purely of my own devising. As far as the king will know you left on your own," I replied.

"He's not a fool. It will be quite obvious what happened and likely enough I'll be declared an outlaw right along with you."

A pang of guilt struck me. I had asked a lot of the Lancasters and now he risked losing everything for helping me. "You're right. Maybe I should do this somewhere else, you've already risked too much...," I started.

"In for a penny, in for a pound," James replied. "Don't think too hard about it. I've already made my choice and now we'll have to live with it."

I couldn't afford to argue the point, I needed his help.

Penny and I headed for the gate to the street; Joe was waiting there. "You're sure about doing this alone?" he asked us.

Penny raised an eyebrow, "Sounds like you think I won't be enough?"

He grimaced, "No lass, it's not like that. I just worry." He had learned enough already to know that Penny had become a dangerous woman when the chips were down.

I bade him goodbye and we set out. I double checked the separate shields I had place around each of us as we went. It paid to be careful, otherwise a single arrow might put an end us both. I had tried to project an air of calm and confidence around the others, but now that Penny and I were on our own my doubts were worrying me. I pulled my cloak closer about myself.

"Feeling cold?" Penny asked as we walked. She hardly seemed to notice the chill air. Winter had begun and it would probably only be another month or two before the first snows.

"A bit," I admitted.

She moved closer to share my cloak, purely for my benefit. Her body put out heat like a furnace. So many things that had changed since we formed the bond, she was hardly discomfited by the cold anymore. I wondered how she would fare in hot weather. Still, it was pleasant to have her so close. I shivered deliberately as the wind blew harder.

"Still cold?" she asked, slipping an arm around my waist.

I nodded and pulled her closer. It was harder to walk that way, but I didn't care. It was worth the inconvenience.

"Mort?"

"Hmm yes?" I answered, smiling inwardly.

"Why is your hand on my ass?"

"It was cold and that seemed the warmest place," I replied with a smirk.

"You are absolutely hopeless. We're about to break into someone's home and face who knows what sort of dangers—and you're still trying to cop a feel." She gave me a look of mock indignation.

"Yep—does that bother you?"

She laughed and placed her own hand strategically over my own posterior, "Not at all, as long as it's just *my* rear-end you're grabbing."

"The duchess certainly found it amusing," I reminded her.

She growled, "I could have strangled you for that! Don't you ever think first?"

"I wouldn't have minded, as long as it was *you* strangling me," I joked.

CHAPTER 27

Lord Hightower's home was easy enough to find. We had ridden right by it on our way into Albamarl earlier. As the commander of the king's guard and the city garrison he occupied the large bailey that guarded the capital's largest gate. As homes went it was a veritable fortress in and of itself, nearly as large as the main keep of Cameron Castle.

From what James had told me I knew his family kept their residence in the top two floors of the bailey. Below that were primarily defensive structures and housing for the guards that defended the city, as well as the mechanisms that controlled the two great portcullises and the gate. Looking at it from the outside I had to pity any invader that might try to force their way through it.

There was a large door that served as an entrance to the interior of the bailey on the left hand side of the inner portcullis. Since there was currently no threat to the city I presumed it would be unlocked, but naturally enough it was still guarded. Two men stood at attention outside the door. Unlike guards I had seen at other points in the city these two looked alert and not the least bit bored. Lord Hightower was known for stern discipline.

I could feel Penny tensing as we drew closer, like a cat preparing to pounce. We were no longer sharing my cloak so I had to lean over to whisper to her, "No need, just relax." Her eyes darted back to meet mine but she said nothing. The tension went out of her stance but I could sense her hand still gripping the hilt of her sword beneath her cloak.

Without pausing we walked directly toward the guards. "Who goes there?" one of them called as we drew close. I didn't bother answering—a whispered word and they both slumped to the ground unconscious. I stepped up to the door and knocked while Penny stood behind me scanning the street.

"You know the drill, you have to identify yourself before you knock!" came a muffled voice through the wood of the door.

"Open up, there's someone here to see Lord Hightower!" I responded.

A small wooden door set at head height opened up revealing a face covered in a very poor example of a beard, "That's not the call sign—honestly the sergeant will have your hide..." I didn't bother with further discussion and a moment later the man slumped down behind the door, soundly asleep.

"Now how are we going to open the door?" Penny hissed at me.

"Watch and learn sweetheart," I replied.

"Last time you tried to force a door you nearly got blown up," she said snidely.

"I doubt that will be a problem here." I put my hand on the door. It had an actual lock which made things easier. A simple bar would have been slightly more trouble for me to move, though not by much. *"Grabol ni'shieran,"* I said softly. With an audible click the mechanism released the bolt and I pulled the door wide. I started to step through but Penny stopped me.

"Fool," she whispered and went ahead of me with her sword drawn. As luck had it only one man was within, and he was already asleep. We dragged the other two in and laid them carefully beside him. "How long will they stay like that?" Penny asked.

"Unless there's an earthquake or someone shakes the hell out of them—several hours at least," I judged. We left them there and moved further in. A wooden stair to the left led us to the second floor. No one seemed to have spotted us yet so we kept going. On the landing to the third floor we saw two more men. They took no notice of us for a moment, seemingly involved in their conversation. I put them to sleep just as one looked at me—a question still on his lips as he collapsed.

"I have to admit, this is a lot easier than I thought it would be," Penny murmured. I had to agree but I thought it was unwise to count ourselves lucky yet. We went on to the fourth floor and seeing no one there continued to the fifth. I was getting distinctly more nervous but I tried not to show it.

The fifth floor seemed to be the final one, so we left the stairs there and started down a wide corridor. The doors on either side looked distinctly more domestic, but I wasn't sure where to look for Rose. I doubted her father would put her in a cell, so my best guess had been he would confine her somewhere within the family quarters. I paused for a moment, stretching out my senses, trying to feel the layout of the floor and locate whatever people might be nearby.

By pure chance the door next to us opened before I could do anything and a startled nobleman's face gaped at us. Strangely he had a black eye. "Who the devil are you?" he asked in a loud voice. Before I could do a thing Penelope put her hand on his chest and shoved. He fairly flew backward, landing in a sprawl inside the room he had been about to vacate. She followed him in, moving too quickly for him to evade her.

"Guards!" he yelled. I was left in awe of his magnificent baritone voice. Every able-bodied soldier within the bailey must have heard it.

"Grethak denu keltis taret," I said quickly. It was a variation of the spell Devon Tremont had once used on me. Unlike his spell I had included an exclusion to let the target breathe. The man went rigid while Penny held him to the floor.

She looked back at me, "You're really taking all the fun out of this," she said, and then her eyes went wide. "Look out!"

I felt something moving toward my head but it was far too fast for me to do anything about it. A guardsman who had been standing just inside the doorway hit me with a heavy mace before I could react. My shield saved me from serious injury but I was sent flying sideways across the room. I struck a heavy chair and fell over, stunned.

From my position on the floor I saw her move, though that word hardly does her credit. She fairly flew across the room, the man who had struck me barely moved before she was on him. He managed one swipe at her with his mace and because of her charge she wasn't able to dodge it. Instead she *caught* it with her left hand, much as you or I might catch a stick swung by a small boy. Her right hand came up and she slammed the hilt of her sword into his jaw. I thought I saw a look of surprise on his face before he fell back to land heavily on the floor.

I struggled upright and made my way over to her. "Goddammit!" she cursed, nursing her hand. "I think it's broken."

"Let me see," I suggested.

"You're both going to wind up in the king's dungeons for this!" said the nearly forgotten nobleman on the floor.

Another drawback of my version of the paralysis spell is that it also allows the victim to speak. I ignored him and reached for Penny's hand.

"Wait," she said. She shut the door and leaned back against it. "There's more coming, I can hear them on the stairs. Whatever you do had best be quick."

I held her hand and closed my eyes, focusing. Two of the bones in her palm had snapped, but fortunately they were clean breaks. Working rapidly I fused the ends back together and as a finishing touch I blocked the sensory nerves at the wrist. Even with what I had done it was badly bruised and would begin swelling rapidly. Hopefully now she wouldn't have to feel the pain, at least not until later. "How does it feel? Can you move it?" I asked.

She flexed it carefully. "It hurts a bit still, but I can move it." The door behind her moved slightly as someone tried to open it.

"Lord Hightower! Are you in there?" a man's voice shouted from the hallway.

Before Hightower could respond Penny answered, "One moment, let me get my clothes back on!" She turned around and put her left hand on the handle.

Beyond the door I could hear them talking, "Was that a woman's voice?"

Penny opened the door calmly, "Do come in, we were finished anyway."

Two men stood there, seeming confused for a moment at the sight of a beautiful woman. One seemed downright embarrassed, 'til he noticed the sword in her hand. Lord Hightower yelled at them from the floor, "You fools! Seize her!"

"*Shibal,*" I said, and they both slumped to the floor.

"Hey!" Penny snapped at me, "I had that under control!"

"I don't want to have to fix anymore broken bones. Not to mention it was much kinder, that other fellow probably has a broken jaw," I replied.

"In case you've forgotten, he tried to put your brains on the floor, not to mention what happened to my hand," she said sarcastically.

"You'll have worse than broken bones once I'm done with you," said Lord Hightower from his exalted position—lying on the floor.

I helped Penny drag the two guardsmen fully into the room before shutting the door. Then I addressed our prisoner, "Lord Hightower, I am extremely sorry for this. I hope you understand that in better times I would never have dreamed of insulting you like this."

"Are you about to surrender? Otherwise you should save your breath," he answered me. I had to admire his nerve; most men in his position would have been ready to bargain. Being paralyzed was a terrifying sensation, I knew firsthand.

"Quite the contrary, I'm here to release your daughter."

He snorted, "I thought you looked familiar, you must be Mordecai. I saw you at the hearing a few months back." He was probably referring to the case put before the Lord High-Justicer.

"I am. Where is your daughter held at?" I didn't see much reason to waste time chatting.

"Two doors down, the key is in that jewelry case over there—by the desk," he couldn't move but he rolled his eyes in the direction he was referring to.

Penny walked over to find the key, "I didn't figure you for a man who would give up so easily," she remarked.

"Well, we're not exactly enemies. I locked her up before the king decided to. Besides, would my men be able to stop you?"

"No," I replied honestly. "Did you really need to lock her up? She's your own daughter."

He laughed ruefully, "You must not know her very well. How do you think I got this?" He winked at me with his black eye. I decided he was right. I couldn't imagine Rose punching her father in the eye.

"How do you suggest we proceed from here?" I asked him. He had become so reasonable I felt it couldn't hurt to get his opinion.

"Lock me in her room and walk out with her. I doubt the guards would try to stop you with her ordering them otherwise." He began scrunching up his face suddenly. "Would you mind scratching my nose—it's got a terrible itch."

I laughed and spoke a word, *"Keltis."* His body relaxed as soon as the paralysis vanished. Lord Hightower sat up and began scratching. "Are you sure we need to lock you up?" I asked him.

"If you don't I'll be accused of helping you. I'm still mad at you for giving me this...," he pointed at his injured eye. I was confused for a moment 'til I understood he was referring to his planned cover story. I was beginning to understand where Rose got her keen wits.

A few minutes later we were marching him down the corridor, at sword point. He had insisted on the sword, claiming it would be easier to explain later if one of his men happened to see us. Soon enough we had the door to Rose's room open. Penny marched Lord Hightower in ahead of us.

As he stepped in a heavy wooden club swept out, catching him in the stomach. He folded over at the waist and sagged to his knees. "Oh Daddy! Oh gods! I'm so sorry!" said Rose, dropping the makeshift weapon.

Penny and I looked on, aghast at the scene. I quietly applauded Penny's decision to lead with the prisoner. I was still slightly shaken from the mace that had struck me earlier. I looked around the room as Rose fussed over her wounded father. On one side was a large four post bed. It looked to be a beautiful piece of furniture but it was now listing oddly to one side. Glancing down I realized Rose's weapon had been the fourth post. I was beginning to wonder how Hightower had survived her childhood.

Rose finally took notice of us, "Penny! What are you doing here?"

"I heard you needed a rescue, but it looks like your captor might have the worst end of this arrangement," Penny said, giving Lord Hightower a sympathetic look.

"I thought it was one of the guards," Rose said sheepishly. "Even so I aimed for the mid-section so I wouldn't hurt them too badly." Hightower groaned where he lay on the floor but he still hadn't gotten enough wind back to talk.

"Where would you hit them if you *did* want to hurt someone?" I asked aloud.

"Pray you never find out Mordecai," said Rose as she helped her father stand up. "Oh! Look at that eye! Did I do that?" I was gaining endless amusement at Rose's startled exclamations. What did she expect to happen when she hit him there? It was a good thing she hadn't become my Anath'Meridum, there would have been a string of bodies between here and the outer door by now.

Several more men came pounding up the stairs. Given the length of time since Hightower's last yell I had to assume these had found the men we had left sleeping below. I stood in plain sight and waited until they had cleared the stairs fully before I put them to sleep. It pays to be careful. A friendly rescue might turn ugly if we 'accidentally' murdered someone in the course of it.

I stuck my head back in the door to Rose's room, "We need to hurry or I'm going to have to put everyone in the place to sleep before we leave."

Her father was able to speak again and he waved for me to come closer, "I want you to realize I don't agree with what you're doing. I think it's foolish and wasteful, but since I can't stop you or my daughter I thought I'd give you some advice."

"What's that sir?" I asked politely.

He leaned close and spoke softly in my ear, "Make sure you have a good escape route planned for my daughter. When the enemy is knocking on your door and you have nowhere else to run she had better not be there with you. If anything happens to her and you somehow survive—I will spend my life hunting you down. You can count on it." There was no humor in his face now. A chill ran through me, for I knew he meant every word.

I looked at him squarely to let him know I took him at his word. "Sir, if something happens to her and I survive there will be no need to hunt for me; I'll present myself to you personally." I turned and left with Rose and Penny close behind.

"What was that about?" Penny wondered.

"Most likely my father gave him one of his 'have my daughter back by nine o'clock' speeches," Rose replied with a laugh. Penny didn't understand the reference at first—not having been courted as Rose had, but Rose explained it to her. Soon they were both laughing behind me. Personally I didn't think it funny; I had meant every word I had said to the man.

We walked with Rose between us until we reached the outer door again. Along the way we met several more guardsmen but had little trouble. I put them all to sleep. Rose protested after the first one, "There's no need to do that."

"Would it be more effective to beat them with a bedpost?" I asked with a chuckle.

Rose grimaced, "I'm sure they'll stand aside if I order them, and that was an accident."

I didn't feel like taking chances, I put every person we met on the way to sleep. Soon enough we were outside and walking carefully away. Running might have attracted attention, so we kept our pace brisk and steady. "How do you plan to get us out of the capital?" Rose asked. "The king's men will be scouring the city for us by morning. They'll probably seal the gates once they know you're here."

"First I plan to recover our property, and then make a leisurely stroll back to Washbrook," I said nonchalantly. Penny sighed.

"Surely you jest Mordecai," said Rose. "Penny, tell me he's joking?"

Penny snorted, "Oh no—he's quite serious. What's more, I'm half convinced he'll succeed."

Rose's eyes went wide, "Only half? The alternative might be quite unpleasant."

"We don't have a happy ending ahead of us Rose, so it's hard to worry about unpleasant alternatives. We have a goal ahead of us, that will have to be enough for now," I told her.

"You were never so grim before Mordecai—I'm not sure it suits you," Rose opined.

"It will suit the king even less," I gave her a feral grin. "Where are the men you hired? James said they were all taken away."

"Those who could afford to pay a small fine were paroled, the rest were locked up in the Crown Tower," she informed me. "Surely you don't plan to attempt a break out?"

"I'll need them to load the wagons. Speaking of which—where would they have taken my goods?"

Rose was alarmed, "Mordecai, this is insane. There's no way this can work. The king will have your head!"

"The goods Rose—you can stay behind if you don't like the plan."

"By now he will have stored them in the royal warehouses. He's been stockpiling grain and other materials there for the spring campaign. All the same things we were buying, it was his primary motivation for seizing the goods at Lancaster's house," she replied. "And I'll be damned if you leave me behind."

I ignored her declaration of loyalty, "I need directions to the Crown Tower. How far is it from there to the warehouses and how far from those to Lancaster's home?" Any other time I might have been less rude, but the stress and anxiety of our situation had begun to wear on me. Our foray into Lord Hightower's home had been nerve-racking, and I had two more places left to force my way into.

It turned out the warehouses were only a few minutes' walk from the Lancaster residence, a fact that would be very convenient for my plan. The Crown tower however was a bit over twenty minutes from the warehouses. I wasn't sure how quickly it would take the city to respond but I had a feeling things would get hairy.

"Rose I want you to go back to the Lancaster residence alone. Joe is there. Tell him to get ready, I want him to have the wagons and drivers ready and close to the royal warehouses," I told her.

It was to Rose's credit that she never even considered complaining about returning alone. Instead she worried about my plan, "Even as late as it is now people will notice if we park a line of wagons in the road."

I had to admit she had a point, "Then have them wait within the Lancaster's yard. I'll come by there first. It should be close enough. If it isn't then I've already attracted too much attention."

She nodded, and a moment later we had split up. I worried for her, walking alone in the dark. Then again after a moment's consideration I decided I should be more concerned for whoever might try to interfere with her. Penny and I began our own walk, striding quietly down darkened streets.

CHAPTER 28

The Crown Tower was dimly lit when we arrived. Although the tower was used for housing criminals it had originally been one of the defensive towers that were periodically spaced along the city wall. As the city had grown a new curtain wall had been built to enclose the outer regions and wall near the tower had been taken down, to allow more traffic between the inner and outer city. The tower itself was a squat ugly structure, built from the same rose granite as the majority of the capital. It rose over sixty feet high and possessed six floors above the ground level.

From what Rose had told me, I knew the first floor was primarily administrative area. The guards that worked in the tower were kept in the main barracks, so at night there would be only a skeleton crew. That suited me just fine.

The outer door was unguarded. Apparently keeping people out was not considered a high priority. I had to assume there would be guards within the doors, though. Penny spoke first, "How are we going to do it this time?"

"We'll just knock and ask nicely," I replied. Under other circumstances that might have been a joke. Not tonight, though—I walked straight toward the door and began rapping heavily upon it.

A small window opened in the door, "Who's out there?"

I focused my mind and I could feel two men on the other side of the door. *"Shibal,"* I said softly and I felt them falling to the floor within. Examining the door I quickly realized it didn't have a lock—it was barred from the inside. I tried a spell to lift the bar but had little success. Someone had had the bright idea to secure the bar itself with a chain and padlock inside the door.

I considered trying to unlock the padlock from the outside but even if I did the chain would still have to be removed. Given a few minutes I could probably do it—but I didn't think I had that much time. "Let's step back a bit," I told Penny.

"Oh jeez...," she complained, "I knew this would happen. If you rouse the entire place you're not going to be able to put them all to sleep."

"I might—but I have an alternative," I replied. I spoke quietly and added a few cosmetic enhancements to the shields around Penny and myself. Soft light flared and blue flames wreathed our bodies.

"Oh this is subtle," Penny remarked looking at her hand as the flames ran up her arm.

"I'm not going for subtle, I'm going for 'scared shitless'."

"This should do it then. I nearly peed myself when you set me on fire just now, next time warn a girl," she said.

"Here we go," I replied. Raising my staff I pointed it at the tower door. I was pretty sure I could manage without it but the enchantments on it would focus my energies more effectively. I thought I might need my strength later. *"Borok Ingak!"* I said forcefully and released the power I held within. An invisible ram struck the door, shattering it with a sharp cracking sound. The force was so great it continued inward and I felt more than saw a wall collapse beyond the doorway.

Penny had tensed and was about to run for the doorway but I put my hand on her arm, "Wait."

Almost a minute passed before three men came out. I thought two of them might be the ones I had already put to sleep. One of them was bleeding badly, probably from the inward explosion of the door. They immediately took note of the two flame-robed people in the street.

"Holy hell!" one of them shouted, stumbling back toward the doorway. I put him to sleep before he could go further.

"Stop!" I commanded, walking toward the remaining two men. Having seen their companion collapse they both stood still. I could sense them trembling as we walked nearer. "Who is in charge here?"

One of the men looked as if he were about to faint but the other retained enough presence of mind to speak, "C..c..c..aptain Gerold sir!"

"Go fetch him for me...," I told him. He hesitated for only a moment before I shouted, "Now!" That was more than enough; he took off at a run. I glanced over at Penny, "Move around the tower, they may have another exit. We can't afford to have anyone running loose."

She looked at me with worry. I could tell she was afraid something might happen to me if I were left alone. Finally she made up her mind. "Alright—don't do anything stupid," she said, and then she sprinted off into the dark near the base of the right side of the tower.

A minute later three men emerged from the shattered doorway; one of them looked significantly less sloppy than the other two. All three approached cautiously. "May I ask what business you have with me, sir?" I had to give their captain credit, even scared and facing a man covered in flames he managed to keep his voice calm.

"Do you have the keys to the cells within the tower?" I tried to sound menacing but I'm not sure if it helped. The flames were more than enough already.

"They're in my desk," he answered nervously. I could see his right cheek beginning to twitch.

"Go get them and release everyone taken from Duke Lancaster's home," I told him.

"Begging your pardon, I'm not sure I know all of them."

"Ask them—open any cell that contains some of them. I want them out here in five minutes, otherwise... Well you won't like 'otherwise', so let's just make sure I don't have to go there," I ground the words out with as much authority I could muster.

It took longer than five minutes but I pretended not to notice. I wasn't really keen on 'otherwise' either. In fact, I didn't have a plan for it. Soon men were emerging from the building, forming a large crowd. One of them shrieked when Penny appeared from the left side of the tower and ran by the milling throng. I had to suppress a smile.

"Someone started to climb down from the top back there," she informed me.

"Did you hurt him?" I asked.

"No he took one look at me below and changed his mind," she replied.

I couldn't blame him. At a guess it had been the guard captain looking for an alternative to violating his orders. I addressed the crowd, "I'm here to reclaim those wrongfully taken from the Lancaster residence yesterday. Is there anyone here that wasn't hired by Rose Hightower?" Since there were more than three hundred people standing in front of me I figured it was a good guess that some of them were just along for the ride. Unsurprisingly none of them volunteered to return to their cells.

I turned to Penny, "If you don't mind, take the good captain and his men inside and lock them in one of the cells." She nodded and began herding them back toward the tower. "Be good and she won't have to hurt you!" I called as they went reluctantly back inside. Inwardly I was nervous, if they turned on her once they got inside things could get ugly. I could only hope their fear was as great as it appeared.

It turned out I needn't have worried. Penny returned a few minutes later without having had any trouble. I extinguished the flames shrouding us; it seemed to be making our new recruits nervous. "Those of you who are ready to work come with me. I have a job for you. I can't promise it will be safe, but those who follow me will be far from the king's reach within a few hours. Those of you who don't wish to come are free to leave, but you're on your own if the watchmen find you."

People began drifting away silently. Mostly those that Rose hadn't hired and I sincerely hoped I wasn't releasing a large number of violent criminals upon the city. I simply didn't have the time to try and be more specific. Of those that remained a voice rang out, "Exactly who are we working for?"

The person speaking was careful to do it from the back. I'm sure whoever it was worried that I might be a lunatic. "My name is Mordecai Illeniel, the Count di'Cameron. The king and I have had a few differences regarding how things should be handled. The end result being that many of you were locked up for nothing more than agreeing to take a job. If you stick with me I will do my best by you. I can't promise it won't be dangerous, though." I lit the end of my staff to make it easier for them to see me in the gloom.

"What exactly does 'dangerous' mean?" It was a different voice but still it came from the back. Given the situation I couldn't blame them.

"I'm planning to recover my possessions from the King's warehouses in the next hour. I plan to be away from the capital in less time than that afterwards. Any more questions? Because I'm really short of time," I answered. I could see lights going on in some of the nearby houses. My antics had not gone unnoticed.

A short man standing in the front spoke up, "Do we have to fight?"

"Not today, not if I can help it, in a few months possibly. You'll have plenty of time to change your minds before then if you so choose," I replied hastily. "Now we really have to be moving. Those of you who wish to come—follow. I will hold no grudge against those that don't." I turned and began striding purposefully down the street. For a moment I had a horrible urge to look back, certain they would be dispersing in every available direction. Magesight comes in handy sometimes—I could feel the majority of them following us.

I spoke to Penny without turning my head, "Looks like most of them are still with us."

She smiled slyly in the dim light, "Most of them I think. We need to move faster Mort. That scene outside the tower had to have drawn attention. Even if none of the guards from Hightower's have reported, someone must surely be taking news to the watch."

Her words echoed my own fears. If the city guard was roused in full force things would not go well. A conflict in the streets would be a loss for all concerned. The men I would be fighting here were citizens of Lothion; any casualties would only weaken us—and further alienate us from the king. I paused to address the people behind us, "We're going to move faster now—follow my light and try not to fall behind." I increased the light coming from my staff to highlight my words.

We began jogging down the streets of Albamarl. It was a surreal experience; my staff cast strange shadows around us, creating odd shapes between the buildings as we passed. The sound of over a hundred feet running behind me was exhilarating in a way that I had not expected and Dorian's words came to mind—he was right, this was true power. *Except you barely have any control here, these men are strangers,* I added mentally.

Two startled watchmen on patrol appeared suddenly from the dark. Their faces were lit with shock and surprise as they saw the huge crowd of people running toward them. I put them to sleep without slowing and hoped they wouldn't be trampled by the men behind me.

Fifteen minutes later we had reached the duke's house. The gate was open and the instinct of those following me was to enter. I held my staff high, "Stop! We wait here for a moment."

Joe had been waiting for us and as I spoke the wagons began rolling out into the street. Rose sat beside him in the lead wagon, a crossbow in her lap. "Are the lanterns ready?" I asked him.

"See for yerself," Joe answered pointing behind him. On each wagon were two lanterns, one sitting beside the driver and another unlit in the bed of the wagon. We would need them in a few minutes.

"Follow the wagons! We're only a few minutes from our goal," I shouted to the crowd. The wagons began moving as the crowd walked alongside them. Penelope slipped her hand into mine as we walked. "Are you alright?" I asked her.

"Nervous," she replied with tight lips.

"There's no way left but forward," I told her.

Her free hand was gripping and releasing the hilt of her sword repeatedly. "I know," she said.

Mentally I hoped things would go smoothly. If a confrontation occurred and got out of control Penny might hurt a lot of people. I worried how that might affect her, but there was little I could do about it.

We entered the warehouse district without trouble. The streets here were wide, to better accommodate wagons, and the buildings were large. The royal warehouses were enclosed by a stone wall, separating them from the rest of this part of the city. Our wagons rolled to a stop as we reached the wide iron gate that gave access to them. Naturally it was closed and locked. Looking through its bars I could see four large buildings looming in the darkness… our goal.

"What are you people doing here?" a voice called from inside the gate.

"Step back from the gate, it's about to open," I told the voice, and then repeated myself to the people behind me.

"You'd best clear off! They'll arrest the lot of you if you try to steal from the king!" Whoever was inside sounded scared. I probably would be too if I were a night watchman facing an unknown mob. I didn't bother to answer this time. I released the power I had been holding, channeling it along the length of my staff. The gates rang like a bell as they were ripped apart by the force of my magic, slamming them inward. One flew back to strike the inside of the wall while the other was torn completely free.

The men behind me cheered and the wagons began rolling in. "If you find any watchmen inside let them go. We're not here to fight!" I called out to the men. At this point I anticipated that whatever few guards were within would be in more danger than my own men. Hopefully they would have the good sense to run or hide.

Rose had gotten down from her wagon and stood beside us now. "You sure that's wise? They'll bring the town guard."

"They'll need a large force to stop us, and that will take time to muster. We should be gone before they can effectively counter us. Chasing down the watchmen would be dangerous and waste time. Very likely some of them would be killed in the confusion. I don't want that on my head," I answered. In the dim light I could see a man's form on the ground and I knew it had to be the man who had been at the gate.

I hastily moved to examine him and I drew a sharp breath. The man lying there looked to be in his late sixties at the youngest. His head was only attached to his body by a bloody bit of flesh and bone, the gate had nearly severed his neck. My only consolation was that he had probably not had time to feel it. A wave of guilt and self-loathing washed over me. I had killed someone's grandfather. Through no fault of his own the man before me was dead. How many people would mourn him tomorrow?

Rose stepped up beside me, "We should put him in the wagon."

"Why?" I asked once I had gotten control of myself.

"If they find his body it will only worsen your situation," she replied calmly.

Penny stared at her, "How can you be so cold?"

If the remark bothered her Rose didn't show it, "We're at war. Anything that distracts from Mordecai's efforts to stop Gododdin will lessen our chances of victory. Something like this could undermine whatever good-will Mordecai has among the people of Albamarl."

Something broke inside me, "I am not at war with these people, and I won't take this man's body to hide my crime. How would his family feel? Never knowing what happened to him? They couldn't even grieve properly, not knowing if he was alive or dead." I bent down to examine his uniform. The cloth was old and thread-worn, the result of many years of wearing and washing. His name had been stitched across the left side, 'Jonathan Tucker' it read. I was sure I would never forget it. It was one more crime I could never atone for.

While I brooded over the fallen watchman the wagons had continued rolling in. Joe had brought a large crowbar and they soon had the doors to the buildings open. Men were moving quickly back and forth, loading the wagons with everything that could be moved. Large wooden crates and sacks of grain were stacked high upon the wagon-beds.

Even with as many men as we had loading it took nearly half an hour to fill the wagons. I couldn't tell for certain what we had taken. There was surely a lot of grain and dry goods. A casual inspection with my extra-senses told me that most of it was food of one sort or another. Many of the crates held weapons and armor, or possibly tools. I didn't take the time to be sure; we loaded everything that would fit.

I counted thirty-nine wagons as they left, heading back toward Lancaster's house. Once the last one went by Penny and I ran to reach the head of the line. I wanted to be there in case we met anyone on our return trip. We were almost to the duke's house when our luck ran out.

CHAPTER 29

A small column of cavalry rode down the street from the opposite direction, at least thirty mounted soldiers armed with long spears. The gate to the duke's house stood fifty yards ahead of the first wagon on the left hand side of the road. The soldiers were at least fifty yards or more beyond that. "Take the wagons inside. Ignore what occurs here. Line them up outside the duke's store house, we'll need to roll them in one by one when I get back," I told Joe.

"What are you going to do?" he asked wide-eyed.

"I'm not sure. Penny stay with him," I commanded and began running toward the oncoming horsemen.

"Like hell I will!" she said, pacing me easily. I should have known better than to try to keep her out of it. I sighed inwardly—outwardly my lungs were working hard to keep me supplied with air as we ran. We reached the duke's gate well ahead of the cavalry. They had broken into a trot when they saw us but were still a good twenty yards away.

I put more power into my staff, causing it to blaze with light. "Stop!" I yelled. The cavalry commander held up a hand and the column came to a halt less than ten yards from us.

"What the hell is that you're holding? Get out of the road fool, this is the king's business!" their leader shouted at me. The light from my staff had left him uncertain; few people these days had any experience with magic.

"My name is Mordecai Illeniel. I am here to reclaim my property and be on my way. Withdraw and no one will have to be hurt," I told them loudly.

"I thought as much," he answered, shielding his eyes from the glare. "Surround the traitor!" he commanded.

I had expected that, *"Lyet ni'Bierek!"* I said loudly. Not that anyone could hear me over the roar of my 'flash-bang'. I hadn't used the spell since my battle in Lancaster Castle, but it was brutally effective here. Then I had faced men on foot—these were mounted. An intense dazzling flash of light went off, right in the middle of the column, accompanied by a sound like thunder. The light and sound were so powerful anyone within twenty or thirty feet of it would be deafened, and blinded as well if they were facing it. Men cried out in shock and fear, horses screamed and reared. Chaos erupted as most of the men were thrown from their bucking mounts.

My spell did no physical damage, but it hardly needed to. Panicked horses trampled some of the riders while others struggled to stand up. Riderless horses ran in every direction, some of them, still blind, ran into buildings. I might have laughed, but I could see a number of the men on the ground were not moving. Those that were able moved poorly, blind and disoriented. I put those to sleep. It seemed a mercy.

Penny was shouting at me but it was hard to hear her. I had forgotten to shield our ears again. "Why didn't you just put them all to sleep at the start?" she yelled.

I shook my head. "I don't think I could get that many at once," I shouted back. In the past I had never put more than five or six to sleep at once, though I thought ten at a time might be doable. I looked back toward the wagons; they had stopped at the gate. Everyone was staring in our direction. I could hardly blame them. I began making motions with my arms, pointing at the gate. "Move your asses! This isn't a show, don't waste time!" I shouted.

That got them moving again. I could only hope we would have enough time to get the wagons out before the rest of the guard arrived. I noticed lights coming from shuttered windows along the street across from the duke's house. I must have awakened everyone within a half a mile.

As the last wagon passed through the gate James closed and barred it. I gave him a nod and kept walking; I needed to get inside the store house quickly. The first wagon was already waiting at the large double doors when I got there. Joe stood next to it. "Get back on that damned wagon!" I told him roughly.

"I need to stay behind to keep the drovers moving," he argued.

"Penny and James can do that, I need you to rouse the militia. This could take some time and I'm going to need men I can trust to keep the king's men on the other side of that wall," I pointed to the wall encircling the duke's city estate. Despite Joe's best efforts the wagons filled the yard with a jumbled confusion of men and horses. It might take us more than an hour to get them all through.

Joe climbed back onto the wagon and drove it into the store house. There in the middle of the open space was a large circle over thirty feet in diameter. I had originally drawn it in chalk but knowing that wagons would be rolling over it had made me fearful it would be damaged. Using my staff I had carefully gone over each line and symbol with an intense line of fire. The circle was now deeply etched into the stone of the floor.

Penny and I stood next to the wagon once Joe had positioned it within the circle. If I had made the jump without her she and I would have died before we realized the mistake of separating ourselves by so many miles. I cleared my mind and channeled energy into the circle around us, activating the symbols written there.

For an unsettling moment I thought I had failed, 'til I realized the walls of the building around us now were wood instead of stone. We were inside the barn I had prepared in Washbrook. I spoke to Joe quickly, "Drive the wagon out, and then go find Dorian. I want as many of the militia as possible armed and ready when I return. Make sure no one stands in the circle. As each wagon comes through I'll need you to hustle them out of the barn as quickly as possible."

"No problem, I'll have the boys here by the time you get back," he reassured me. I sincerely doubted that. It would take him at least fifteen minutes or more rouse the townspeople.

As soon as the wagon was clear of the circle I concentrated again and we were back in the duke's store house. James stared at us dubiously from the doorway. "Well it looks like your spell works. I half expected it might kill you," he said.

I held up my hands, "I still have all my fingers and toes." He smiled at that. "I need you to keep the wagons coming in—one at a time. Once I have Joe back you can cross with the next wagon," I told him.

"I'm in no hurry," he replied. "You men… get that wagon moving!" he shouted back at the man on the seat of the wagon outside the doorway to the store house. Once the wagon was in the circle I repeated the process and it was soon moving through the doors of the barn in Washbrook. Joe had not returned yet (as I expected) so we went back to get the next wagon.

I had moved three more through before I found the militia standing outside barn. Twenty-odd men stood arrayed in heavy leather jerkins and armed with spears and bows. I noted that at some point they had acquired helmets. How my father had found the time for that amidst his other projects I'll never know. Penny and I brought them back with us when we returned to Albamarl.

"Spread out along the walls outside. I want at least five men by the gate. Let me know the moment you see anyone approaching," I told them hastily. "Bring the next wagon in!" I shouted to the driver sitting outside. "James you can come with this load," I added.

"No I'll wait. You may need me to keep them moving 'til everyone is clear. Take Lady Rose instead," he replied.

I didn't have time to debate matters with him. I took Rose by the arm and guided her over to stand by the wagon. She resisted me but I just put more force into it. "I don't want to go yet! You need more help here!" she protested.

I ignored her and as soon as we stood in the circle I took us all back to Washbrook. She looked mildly startled at how rapidly our location had changed. "Keep the wagons moving out as soon as they come through," I told her.

"But! Wait...," she started to argue. I gave her a push and a slap on the derriere. "Oh!" she exclaimed. Penny and I were gone before she could protest further.

Penny glared at me, "You're getting mighty free with those hands Mister."

"Chalk it up to stress. I'm not thinking as clearly as I should be," I said. I would probably pay for that one later. Fatigue was beginning to wear on me. I had used more power in the last few hours than I was accustomed to. Fear gnawed at me; if I couldn't move them all there would be serious consequences.

We kept the wagons moving steadily over the course of the next half an hour. Despite my exhaustion

I had begun to think we would make it without any more 'incidents'. A yell from the wall outside put an end to that hope. "Soldiers coming! Lots of them!"

"Shit!" I exclaimed. I was torn, if I went to help 'discourage' the king's men I would have to stop transporting wagons. If I ignored them they might overwhelm my men on the wall. A surge of fear and indecision paralyzed me, and then a hand settled on my shoulder.

It was James. "Keep moving Mordecai. There are only five wagons left. I'll make sure they don't get in," he assured me. I looked at the man who had become almost a second father to me. He looked old, which seemed strange to me. Still, his confidence made me feel better.

"I'm counting on you," I replied and turned back to move the next wagon. I tried to keep my mind blank; I couldn't afford to think of anything beyond my immediate task.

Each time we returned I heard things that worried me more. Shouting and voices carried loudly on the cold night air. The duke had tried negotiating briefly; to buy us more time, but it didn't seem that the king's soldiers were having any of it. I felt a sense of relief as the last wagon found its place in the circle. One more trip and we would be done. I moved it quickly and Penny and I returned to collect my militiamen.

It was chaos. We left the store house to find the duke's yard filled with running men. Several were down already and I wondered who else had just died for me. The king's soldiers had been unable to force the gate and were now climbing steadily over the short stone walls. The house had not been built with defense in mind; the walls were no more than eight feet in height. Not far away I could see one of my men on the ground—an arrow protruding from the face of his helmet.

James stood in the middle of the yard screaming orders. If it hadn't been for him they might have been lost already. "Get back to the store house! Hurry up!" he shouted. Most of the militia was running in my direction already but I could see some limping behind them. The soldiers crossing the wall were already beginning to follow.

"*Lyet ni'Bierek,*" I yelled, pointing my staff at the wall behind them. Light and sound assailed my eyes and ears. I repeated the process, pointing at different points along the wall, hoping to slow the men swarming into the duke's yard. James turned and started for the store house when he stumbled and fell. An arrow was sticking up from his hip. I felt a cry rising from my throat but there were no words in it, just a primal noise full of pain and emotion. More archers were taking aim from various points around the yard.

One of the men that had come with me turned back to grab the wounded duke, hauling him by main force across the yard. The others had by now reached me and were standing within, waiting for me so we could escape. I ran back to help him drag James back to safety.

Before I could reach them more arrows struck. I couldn't see the man's face because of his helm, but I wondered at his strength. An arrow had lodged in his shoulder yet he pulled the duke along as though he weighed nothing. I grabbed James's feet and we ran for the doorway. Arrows fell around us and I felt several hit my shield. Belatedly I thought to extend it to cover James and his unknown savior. I was so tired I could barely manage even that.

We got inside and several hands helped drag him into the circle. A dozen soldiers were charging for us and I knew they would reach us before I could activate the circle. Fear and rage pushed reason from my mind and I stepped out to face them. *"Pyrren ni'Tragen!"* I screamed. A shockwave of fire and death exploded across the yard. The men charging toward us were incinerated and even those further away near the walls were thrown back. Flames took hold and the single tree in the yard became a bonfire. The duke's house appeared to have caught fire as well.

My anger had gotten the better of me. I stared at what I had done in shock, despairing at the lives I had just taken. A hand on my shoulder brought me back to myself. "Son we need to go. There'll be time for regrets later." It was my father's voice.

Surprised, I looked at the man who had dragged the duke across the yard with me. Recognition dawned as I saw the beard beneath his faceguard. He tugged at my arm and we started back inside. He jerked and made an odd cry as we started back toward our escape.

In horror I saw a second arrow had appeared between his shoulders. I had released the shield around him when I went back outside. I cursed myself for my stupidity. I grabbed him as he fell, struggling to keep him upright as we entered the circle. Fighting exhaustion I took us to Washbrook for the last time.

CHAPTER 30

Our arrival was greeted with cheers by those waiting, but their rejoicing was short lived. James was badly wounded, and my father—my mind went blank as I thought of him. I gently eased him to the ground, shouting at the people around us to move back. I had to lay him on his side because of the arrows protruding from his back.

Penny gave out a cry of shock as she realized who I was holding, "Oh gods! It's Royce!"

My mind was reeling as I tried to think. I struggled to focus, to cast my senses into my father's failing body, to discover the extent of the damage. Someone started shouting in my ear, trying to get my attention. My temper snapped as my concentration broke, without looking I shouted, "Penny! Get everyone back so I can concentrate!" I took a quick look around, glaring at those watching. "If anyone else interrupts me they won't live to regret their mistake," I ground out between clenched teeth.

Starting again it took even longer to regain my inner balance. I fought to calm my heart and suppress the rage boiling up within. After a long minute I regained my focus and began examining my father's wounds. What I found dismayed me. One arrow, the first, had lodged in his shoulder blade. I dismissed that one immediately; it was the second arrow that had done the worst damage.

That shaft had passed between his shoulder blade and spine, the head was lodged beside his heart. It had punctured his left lung and nicked the heart as well. One of the arteries that fed the heart was hemorrhaging badly. The injury was horrifying to my inner sight. I couldn't repair the lung or the artery until I removed the arrow, and I only had minutes at the very most. He was bleeding to death and drowning in his own blood. It would be a race to see which killed him first.

"Someone find Marcus! I want him here immediately!" I screamed. Panic had given my voice an edge of hysteria. Then my father began trying to speak. His words were soft and wet with blood making it hard to hear him.

I leaned closer, putting my ear near his mouth. "Is there any hope?" he said in a quiet wheeze. Tears began running down my face at the words.

"Maybe—hang in there Dad, it's not over yet," I choked before I could say more. His injury was mortal, but the nature of it was something that I could fix—if I could do three things at once. I struggled to think clearly. If it had been my own body it would have been simpler. *I need absolute focus,* I thought to myself. I needed to cast my spirit into him, like I had done with the horse a long year ago. Working from within would be far easier.

I whispered a few words and cast my mind out, staring into my father's blue eyes. For a moment I felt our minds touch as I strove to enter, but then my thoughts snapped back, pulled inexorably back into my own head. I was anchored within my own body—by the bond. My heart cried out in anguish as I realized I couldn't do what was needed. I struggled inwardly, seeking to free myself from the restraint created by the bond. Pain shot through me as I sought to snap it by force and Penny stumbled and fell beside me. I was killing both of us.

Despair washed over me and I gave up, then I heard my father trying to speak again. I held his head up and listened, but even with my ear close I couldn't understand him. His eyes pierced me as he tried to speak. With a finger he traced a shape on the ground, but I failed to understand. He spoke again, but the only word I could make out was 'chandelier'. That made no sense.

"I can't understand… what are you trying to say?" I replied with eyes too blurred to see.

He pointed at James, who was reclining a few feet away, and mouthed the word 'chandelier' again. He seemed so urgent and I was desperate to understand him. "James! What does he mean—chandelier?"

James stared a moment before answering, "I think he means the new chandelier in the great hall, back at Lancaster. He made it for me after your battle." Things had been so chaotic back then I had hardly noticed. I had never known.

Royce nodded at his words and pointed at my eyes, then back at James. A tear rolled down from his eye as he looked at me. "I think he wants you to see the chandelier Mort," Penny said softly beside me.

I nodded in agreement. "Where is Marcus?" I asked her. My only hope now was that his goddess would do what I could not, but time was running out.

Dorian had come in and answered my question, "He's in Lancaster Mordecai. He went yesterday, a child came down sick."

A black wave rolled over me, but I pushed it back. Despair would help no one. I examined the wounds again; I would have to do the best I could from the outside. I began pulling at the shaft of the arrow, trying to seal the damaged lung as the head came out. My father jerked at the pain and the head of the arrow cut deeper against his heart. I was killing him. I felt his heart beating faster, too fast, as it struggled to force blood through his body.

Watching him struggle tore at my heart and I did the only thing left to me—I began damping the pain, suppressing the signals his nerves were sending. There were so many I couldn't be sure of what I was doing, but his body began to relax. The heart slowed and his chest relaxed.

"Royce?" I heard my mother's voice over my shoulder. Looking back I saw her standing there, her face was calm but I could see fear in her eyes, the fear of losing the one person most important to her. It was a look that ravaged my soul, for I knew I could do nothing to prevent it.

She sat down across from me and stroked the hair from his face. I saw their eyes meet, as they had a thousand times before, communicating feelings I had never fully understood. "It's ok darling, I'll be alright," she told him. He tried to speak but his voice was gone. "Mordecai will take care of us, don't worry. I know you love me. Relax, you need to rest."

The words unmade me and I began to weep like a child, hopeless and uncontrolled. The sorrow of a man who knows he can never go home again. My life was changing, and the safety and security my father had given me would soon be gone forever. In a crowd of friends and loved ones I felt more alone than ever.

My father took a long time dying. He had been far stronger than I imagined, and his body struggled to breathe long after he lost consciousness. The pain of watching it was too great, and in the end I gently stilled his heart to speed his passing. Once it was done I sat staring blankly into space, numb and tired.

After some time Penny led me to our rooms. Along the way people spoke to me, expressing their sympathies at my loss, but I barely heard them. At long last I fell into bed, sinking into a deep slumber. One filled with sorrow and unsaid words.

CHAPTER 31

The week that followed was grey and tasteless. Marc returned the next morning and with the aid of his goddess healed the wounded that remained, including his own father. I avoided him for several days, my grief was too great and some part of me blamed him for his absence when my father needed him. It only served to increase my anger at the gods.

A funeral was held and I spoke of my memories, but I could not remember afterward what I had said. It was as if the emptiness in my heart had eaten the memory of it. I returned to working on the iron bombs with a renewed vigor, driving myself as if exhaustion could defeat the demons that haunted me.

Royce's idea served me well. By linking the containment enchantment with a ward to absorb heat I was able to empower multiple pieces of iron with much less personal effort. I developed a routine and soon the only limit to how many I could produce was the time it took me to arrange the enchantment and the linkage. Usually I could manage fifteen or more in an hour.

Angus came to find me a week after the funeral. He was having some issues with the dam. The one thing I was having the most difficulty with, was talking to other people, but the reality of our problems would not wait on my grief. "I need to talk to you about the foundation," he told me.

I was busy creating more iron bombs and Angus was irritating me. "If you need more men or materials talk to Joe. He'll get you whatever you need," I told him brusquely. Since our ill-fated escape from Albamarl our ranks had swelled by another two hundred men. We now had more than enough men for the dam project as well as the building of more temporary shelters for the winter. Food didn't look like it would be a problem either; we had taken far more from the king's ware-houses than we would need, far more than he had stolen from us.

Angus sighed, "It's not more labor I need. It's a basic problem with the base, there's no way we can finish this thing when you want it. The foundation isn't sufficient, it won't hold up 'til spring if we keep building on what's there."

I was annoyed. Since his arrival I had heard a lot from Angus about what we 'couldn't' do. He had the same perfectionist traits that had made my father a skilled blacksmith. But where Royce had been willing to consider what 'might' be possible, Angus seemed only to see what wasn't possible. Of course I hadn't given him any personal support since I had returned. Given the purely mundane resources currently at his disposal it might have been reasonable for him to despair of ever finishing the dam. In a sense his failure was my fault. *Like everything else,* I thought to myself.

"I'll come down and look at it. We can talk about it there," I told him. Today would be as good as any to begin testing my new ideas for the dam. Maybe it would cheer the dour man up, but I doubted it.

Hours later we stood looking up at the dam my father had started. It rose twenty feet now; the stones at its base were large, five foot by five. Above that they were smaller, a foot and a half on each side. Water spilled over in the center where a channel had been left near the top, to prevent the rising water from overwhelming what had already been built. The water behind it was already fifteen feet deep and stretched from one side of the narrow entrance to Shepherd's Rest to the other.

"I can't keep building up," Angus complained. "The foundation isn't big enough to support it. If the water gets any deeper the water will start to seep through and undermine the foundation."

I was feeling contrary, "Why?"

Angus sighed again, "The pressure, the deeper it gets the greater the pressure down at the bottom will be. And that mortar your father used isn't right for building under water, its already starting to erode."

I bristled at the implication my father had made a mistake but I held my temper. "What if the water froze solid?" I asked him.

"What do you mean?"

"I can freeze the water behind the dam," I stated.

"It'll expand and crack the stones. As soon as it melted the whole thing would start coming down," he replied. The tone in his voice implied he was talking to a child.

"It won't melt," I assured him.

"More water will keep coming; it'll still ruin what we've built."

"Then I'll freeze that as well. Imagine this—I'll turn what's behind that wall into something like a glacier. As more water builds up I'll freeze it as well. Then all you'll need to build is a retaining wall, just enough to hold the fresh water at the top 'til I can freeze it as well," I said.

"I'd say that's crazy talk. You can't keep freezing it forever and as soon as it began to melt the whole damn thing would come down," Angus waved his arms as he spoke, agitation clear in his body language.

My temper snapped, "I don't need it to last forever! I only need it to last long enough to kill a goddamn army in the spring. Don't you get it Angus? That's all I care about, killing as many damned people as possible!"

His face blanched as I spoke, "If that thing fails while the men are up there it'll kill people long before the army gets here."

"Then I'll just be a murderer that much sooner," I spat out. "Watch." I walked to the wall and selected the biggest foundation stone, the one that stood in the center, blocking the old river bed. Using the same spells I had been repeating day after day on the iron bombs, I created an enchantment to store energy within the stone. It had become such a habit it only took me a few minutes, despite the size of the stone. After that I modified the wards I used to store heat so they would draw heat from the water on the other side of the stone. I changed it slightly so it would work much more rapidly, then I released the spell to do its work.

At first nothing happened, so I led Angus up onto the dam itself, so we could see the water behind the wall. It was hard to see, but ice was forming below the surface. "I want you to start building a new wall, outside this one. It doesn't need to be strong, just enough to capture any water that leaks through. No more than a foot thick, build it up on the dry side using the foundation that juts beyond this dam."

"It won't be strong enough to hold much," he said rubbing his chin.

"It doesn't have to be. Just build it quickly; I need it as tall as the dam itself within a week, after that it will need to keep up with the rising water. I'll keep freezing the water out there to prevent it from putting much pressure on your secondary wall," I told him.

In the end, he agreed, not that I gave him a choice. I spent the rest of the day enchanting the foundation stones, reasoning that they would be the best place to start. Plus they had the advantage of being the largest stones which meant they could hold more before exploding. Since they weren't meant to be bombs I added a limiter to the heat absorption spell to stop it long before the stones were close to their limit. An explosion now would destroy any hope we had of completing the project before the spring.

The week passed slowly as I worked to freeze the water behind the dam. To speed our trips back and forth I created a teleportation circle at the dam site, with a matching one back in Cameron Castle. I made a side trip one afternoon to do the same at Lancaster, in the duke's own suite. I didn't want to think about the fact that if I had done that sooner Marc might have been able to get back in time to save my father, but I felt the guilt anyway.

Each morning I returned to the dam site. Once the largest stones within the dam were enchanted ice had formed out to a distance of more than forty feet beyond the dam itself. Water quickly began rising over the top and spilling across the center, cutting a channel in the ice there and threatening to washout the new retaining wall, to prevent that I got more ambitious. Moving up the smaller valley I found a massive boulder that was nearly submerged by the rising water. It was irregularly shaped, having formed long ago when the river had cut through the softer stone around it.

I had no way to estimate, but it had to weigh several hundred tons, at least. Working carefully I enchanted it and watched the ice begin forming around it. While I worked on freezing the river over the past few days I had had thoughts about how we would destroy the dam in the spring. The danger of storing so much energy in the stones had one welcome side-effect, it made for a simple method of destroying the dam come spring. I included a glass bead in my enchantment of several of the foundation stones, as well as with the enchantment of the large boulder. I was fairly sure that destroying them would cause a chain reaction.

Winter passed slowly, with a growing sense of trepidation. I added another teleportation circle to the road near Arundel, so I could more easily check on that end of the valley. I also started regular patrols along the western end of the valley. Our plan would be for naught if the enemy came early and caught us unprepared.

By midwinter I had produced more than two thousand of the iron-bombs, each with its own glass activator. Marc, in a moment of inspiration suggested we create a large wooden table, covered with a map of the valley. It took several weeks but once it was complete we added small depressions to it, marking the locations where the bombs would be. As each piece of iron was hidden along the road the glass stone to activate it was placed on the table at the spot the bomb was located.

The change in our dam building strategy freed a lot of men up from laboring there. The smaller retaining wall was much easier to build. The temporary housing had already been completed as well, so I set the free men to digging a massive ditch. As they dug a massive earthen berm was created alongside it. We built a flimsy wooden palisade atop that. As defensive structures went, it was poorly made, but we had no time to build better. If things went as I hoped we wouldn't have to defend it from very many attackers anyway. Pits were dug in the area behind the earthworks and filled with massive stone blocks before being reburied. I had run out of iron, but I had a plan that would require them to be there, should the worst befall us.

Through it all my mother and Penny watched me carefully. I felt their eyes on me as I went about my tasks.

Penny in particular had to be by my side nearly constantly. In her face I could see worry, she didn't like the changes she was seeing. "When was the last time you smiled Mort?" she asked one day late in the winter.

I considered the question seriously, "Hmm, probably the day my father died. Why?"

"You've been quiet. You never smile, or talk—except to give instructions. You seem obsessed with the coming war," she answered with a frown.

"Obsession is a good thing when you're planning a war. I don't have time to be planning dances and parties," I replied sarcastically.

"It isn't that exactly. You just seem unhappy, as if the world has gone dark. There's a shadow in your heart and it makes me sad," she said softly.

"What am I to be happy about? I killed my own father Penelope, and soon I'll kill a lot more people, including you. What part of that should give me joy?" I was gritting my teeth as I spoke.

Penny flinched at my words but she didn't give up. "You didn't kill Royce, Mort. Stop blaming yourself, please." As she spoke she put her hands on my shoulders, trying to rub the tension from them.

I pulled away. "I did. I took them to Albamarl. I killed the king's guards and started that damned fight. My pride insisted we take back what the king had stolen, and my pride refused to leave any of it behind. My own arrogance and self-confidence caused me to remove that shield from him, not knowing it was my own father. It was my anger that sent me back to kill the king's men, and my weakness that forced him to bring me back..."

She started to interrupt, "Mort listen that's..."

"No! You listen!" I shouted. "He walked out to snap me out of my shock. That's why he was shot. And after we had returned I could do nothing for him—because of this gods cursed bond! I *might* have been able to save him then, but that choice was already made. In the end all I could do was help him die." I started walking away. "Exactly which part of that *wasn't* my fault?" I said coldly.

"None of it dammit!" she shouted at my back. "Stop obsessing over it. We still have a few months left to us. Why spoil it blaming yourself for things you couldn't control? Why waste your time thinking only of deaths we can't prevent?"

I whipped back and gave her an icy stare, "Prevent? I'm not trying to prevent any more deaths Penelope. Oh no! History conspires to make me a murderer—but that's fine with me. I'll kill more people this spring than anyone in history," I said fiercely.

"That's not why you're doing this," she argued.

"It is now! I plan to kill every—single—damned—soldier—that enters this damned valley! And when I'm done, I'll make sure I've finished off any of the bastards that were lucky enough to survive, assuming I live that long," I said finally. I left her then, an expression of shock on her face. I could hear her crying before I had gotten out of earshot. *One more thing I'm guilty of,* I thought to myself, but I couldn't go back.

◦——◦

I ran across Cyhan in the castle yard. Considering my conversation with Penny I was in no mood to be chatting, which normally wasn't a problem where he was concerned, but something about his stance told me he had something to say. I stopped a few feet away and waited.

"We need to talk about a few things," he began.

"I can tell," I replied stoically.

"You raided the king's warehouses while you were in the capital," he said, as if that were enough to tell me his thoughts.

"I reclaimed my property. I'm sure the king will give me his thoughts on the matter when he gets around to it," I answered bluntly. "Is that a problem?"

"Perhaps," he said, pausing to consider his words. I had rarely seen him put so much effort into diplomacy. "My orders don't pertain directly to acts of banditry. I'm here to make sure you and Penelope don't forsake your bond. However, I am a servant of the king."

I mentally double checked my shield; things had the potential to go wrong quickly. "You seem to have a conflict of interest then. What do you propose to do?" I responded, giving him a hard stare.

The older warrior did the last thing I expected, something I had rarely seen him do… he laughed. "You've grown a lot since I met you," he said.

The compliment did little to improve my mood and I was impatient to be done with the conversation. "I'll make this easy for you. You can return to the king if you wish… or you can attempt to exact justice on his behalf right now. If you decide on the former I won't stop you, if you try for the second I'll have more blood on my hands. I'd much rather have your help with this war though… I'm not sure if we can afford to lose your assistance," I responded. I kept my voice calm but I could feel the blood pounding in my temples. My anger was dangerously close to the surface now.

Cyhan could probably sense my deadly intent, but if so he didn't show it. "I have been thinking along similar lines. If I had decided to act against you we wouldn't be having this conversation." He made it a statement of fact, as if people discussed cold-blooded murder every day.

"So you're going to stay and help. Excellent… what was the point of this conversation then?" I started to walk around him but he put his hand on my shoulder. I looked at it and then met his gaze, the question in my eyes.

"I just wanted to make sure we were clear about where we stand," he continued. "I think you have a chance in this war, or I would have removed your head already. If you lose, the king's justice will not matter; if you win your case with him will be between the two of you. I will abide by his decision at that point." He removed his hand.

I stared at him for a moment longer. "I think we understand each other perfectly then," I replied before walking away. I could feel his eyes on my back until I had left the courtyard.

My mother found me the next day. Miriam had always been a quiet woman, except when she was arguing with my father, which wasn't often. She found me that day working in Royce's smithy. I was trying to melt our remaining scraps of iron down, to cast a few more iron bombs.

"I spoke with Penny this morning," she began.

I winced inwardly. I could see where this was headed. "Did she send you to talk some sense into me?" I asked.

"No, but she told me how you feel about your father's death," she replied.

"Surely you don't think I'm wrong?"

"I do. Your father made his own choices, the only thing he would have changed is how you feel about it now," she answered.

I grimaced. "I can't help how I feel mother."

"Do you think your father would want you to feel this way?" she responded.

"If he were here I would ask him, but he's not," I said. Anger and sadness were warring within me, but I held them back. Miriam was the one person I couldn't lash out at.

She walked up and put her hand on mine, forcing me to stop my work. "Look at me Mordecai."

I did. Her cheeks were wet. I started to say something but she put her finger on my lips, "Do you know why I'm crying?" she asked.

"For Dad?"

"No. He lived a good life. I'm weeping because now that he's dead, my son seems to want nothing more than to die himself. I cry for the loss of your smile and the joy it always brought me." A tear traced a lonely line down her cheek.

I stared at her for a long moment and something broke loose within me. She held me as my own tears started again. An age passed while she held me, and I cried like a lost child, deep sobs wracking my chest. If anyone saw us standing there they were kind enough to pass on without interrupting.

CHAPTER 32

Spring came at last, bringing with it warmer days. The snow in the mountains began to slowly melt, swelling the Glenmae River. I was forced to add more stones to keep it from overwhelming the dam. I began to hope the enemy would arrive soon, if they waited too long the river would overwhelm the retaining wall and the artificial glacier I had created. I smiled at the irony of that thought.

My mood had improved, which was a great relief to Penelope, though I did have to do quite a bit of apologizing. It was worth it however, the making up did even more to cheer me up. I still held a dark seed of anger and grief within, though. I kept it down, dark and deep, where even I was largely unaware of it. I focused my conscious mind on more pleasant matters, few as there were.

Two weeks after spring had 'officially' begun the riders returned with word that scouts had been seen. The scouts were light cavalry men, riding in pairs to explore the valley and road. We left them alone; I had no plans to interfere with them unless they decided to go near where the dam was located. Fortunately they didn't go that far, stopping ten miles into the valley before returning.

The river at the end of the valley they were entering through was small; we were only allowing a small flow to pass from the dam downstream. I worried they might be suspicious at the low level of the river. Not being native to our valley I was taking a chance they would be ignorant of how powerful it normally became in the spring.

I found Dorian the evening after the scouts had been spotted. "Are the men ready?" I asked him. It was a foolish question; we had done everything possible already. Still, I couldn't help myself.

"As ready as I could make them," he answered. With the addition of the men from Albamarl, and those from Arundel we have over six hundred men able to fight. We would have been hard pressed to arm them all, but some of the crates we had stolen from the capital were loaded with weapons and light armor. I was certain the king was missing them by now; he had to be hard by, trying to arm his own men.

"Six hundred," I repeated. It seemed a pitifully small number to face an army that would almost certainly exceed ten or twenty thousand. "It's time to move the women and children to Lancaster," I added.

Dorian nodded, we had discussed all this before. Everyone not expected to fight would be moved there, furthest from the conflict. If things went badly here as many as could make it would fall back there as well, I had built a larger circle to allow me to transport twenty people at a time to Lancaster, more if they were friendly enough to squeeze together.

From Lancaster I had prepared a second escape, assuming I was alive to use it. It would take them to a location fifteen miles down the road leading to the capital. If I were dead Marc could use it to get them there, he had already demonstrated that with the help of his goddess he could activate it. I hoped it was far enough to keep them ahead of the invaders but I would probably not be there to know.

I went to talk to Penny. I had something important to tell her, before things got out of hand. I found her in the yard, exercising with Cyhan. "We need to talk," I started simply.

"Can it wait? I'm almost finished here," she inquired.

"No, I don't think it can," I replied somberly.

She caught the look in my eyes. This was a conversation I had been holding back for months. I feared the consequences if she read too deeply into my thoughts. "Alright," she answered. "Here… or do we need to go somewhere private?"

"Private."

We went up on the walls since they were close by. The view from there was breathtaking, overlooking the partially forested field leading from Cameron Castle to the valley road. A cool wind tossed the tops of the trees to and fro as we watched. "So what is it?" she asked.

"Have you felt any changes in yourself lately?" I asked. I thought she might be more accepting if I asked for her input first.

"No—Why? I'm getting better, according to Cyhan, but that's to be expected."

"I mean—other things," I glanced downward, staring pointedly at her belly. Unfortunately her stomach was uncommonly flat and hard, a result of her extended exercise and training. For the first time ever I wished she might have gotten a little fatter.

"What are you saying?" she said.

"A few nights ago—while you were sleeping, I felt something. I wasn't sure at first...," I shrugged my shoulders.

"Are you trying to tell me I'm pregnant? Do I look pregnant to you?" her face registered disbelief.

"I think it's very early, I'm not sure. I've never felt something like this before, but I could feel it in your womb last night," I let the fear show on my face.

"You have got to be kidding me," she said. "You honestly think I'm pregnant?"

"Yes," I said plainly.

"You're making it up," she replied, but I could see uncertainty in her face.

"No—I wish I were. This is no time for having children."

"What makes you so sure?" she asked suspiciously.

"I could feel the heartbeat—a second heartbeat Penny. I'm very sure," I put as much sincerity in my voice as I could muster, everything rested on her response.

Her face was awash with warring emotions, 'til at last I could see a resolve forming. "You're lying. You want me to agree to break the bond."

"No! Penny! That's true, but that's not what I'm trying to do. I'm telling you the truth, you're carrying our unborn child, this isn't just about you and me anymore," I told her. I stared at her with a certainty I didn't feel. Then I drew on the image of my father dying, using his memory to bring tears to my eyes. "You have to believe me Penny, I wouldn't lie about this," I lied, letting the tears roll down my face. In one small part of my mind I couldn't help but feel proud of my acting, but despite the deception, my emotions were real.

She began shaking her head in denial, "No, no! You're lying! This can't be true, I would have seen it. I always have visions about important things, why wouldn't I have seen this?!"

"Think about it Penny. Have you had a single vision since we formed the bond? You haven't, have you? The bond is the reason. It blocks your vision just as it blocks the voices I heard. If you don't believe me, ask Marc. Surely his goddess will know the truth of it," I said.

She looked me squarely in the eye, "He would lie for you."

"He would, but he won't lie about what his goddess tells him—he can't. He's told me so before. Ask him!" My lies were growing larger with every breath. I hadn't spoken to him about helping me deceive her, but I had to trust he would know what to do. Some things were more important than the truth.

"Alright," she said. "I will." She started for the stairs leading down to the ground. As I followed her she turned, "You stay here. I don't want you giving him hints. If what you say is true he'll either confirm it or not on his own."

Fear gripped my heart, but I hid it quickly. "Very well, I'll wait here for you."

"You don't have to do that. I'll find you later. Whatever he tells me I'll need time to think," and with that she left. I stared into the distance for some time after, wondering what he would say. Marc was the best liar I had ever met, bar none, but since his calling he had changed. Even though he had given me the idea I wasn't sure he would help. The Lady of the Evening Star had strict rules regarding lying, and there was nothing false about his new devotion.

⟷

She said nothing to me at dinner that evening. The great hall was a good deal quieter now. Almost all of the women and children were already gone. I had spent the better part of the afternoon transporting them to Lancaster, one group after another. We had plenty of time still, so they could have traveled on foot, but I wanted them to get used to the idea. Some took quite a bit of convincing as it was. It was better to make sure they trusted it now than wait until we were pressed for time.

As a result of my efforts I was exhausted by the time I had my meal. Not only had I taken several hundred women and children to Lancaster, I had also returned with the majority of the fighting men that had been living there. Lancaster was now populated almost entirely by women and their dependents, plus the few elderly that had been in Washbrook. Genevieve and Rose were with them, keeping order, though Rose had raised some objections.

I sat at the head of the high table with Penny on my right hand. James Lancaster sat to my left, in the seat that had once been my father's place. The sight of his empty chair had given me trouble for some time and I was grateful to have him filling it. Dorian and Marc each sat in the chairs beside Penny and James. I carefully avoided looking at Marc for fear of revealing my lie. I was sure she had already spoken to him, but she hadn't told me his response. My instincts told me it was better not to ask.

"We're a cheerful bunch this evening," James announced suddenly, breaking the silence. "I haven't seen so many dark faces since—hmm." He rubbed his chin. "As a matter of fact I have never seen so many dark faces. We need to cheer up. Dorian! You first—did anything interesting happen for you today?"

Dorian grunted, "Williams fell on his ass during drill today. Clumsiest man I ever saw, he'll kill himself before the enemy has a chance." I had no idea who he was talking about, but it wasn't very funny. Dorian had a talent for making the funniest of stories a bit dry and flat.

James gave a polite laugh, "How about you Marcus?" His son was his best hope. Marc had a way with stories.

"Actually yes! But I can't tell you," he announced sadly.

"Why not!?" James protested.

"It's a matter of confidence, between man and goddess. I will say that some folks have issues with parts that you would never expect!" There was a twinkle in his eye as he spoke, leaving little doubt what parts he was referring to.

That got a better laugh from all of us, so James looked across to Penny. "How about you my dear? Did anything interesting happen to you today?"

Penelope looked like a deer caught in a trap. She gazed at him seriously for a moment before glancing at Marc and then back to me. Her mouth opened and she started to speak, but her lip was trembling. I could see her eyes watering before she said, "I'm sorry you'll have excuse me." She rose and walked quickly to the door leading to the stairs.

James seemed apologetic, "What was that? Was it something I said?"

Marc put a hand on his shoulder, "No father, it wasn't you. She has a lot on her mind today." He gave me a meaningful look.

"I'd better go check on her," I announced and stood up to leave. Marc rose and caught up to me before I reached the door.

"I told her what she needed to hear," he whispered in my ear.

"Really? Thank you! I—I don't know what to say. It couldn't have been easy for you." I embraced him roughly. "Thank you. No matter what—you'll always be my best friend."

He shook his head at me and let me go. As I headed for the stairs I heard him say something else, but I couldn't quite catch his words, he spoke too softly. I almost thought he said, "I only told her the truth," but that wouldn't have made sense.

—•—

I found Penny in our bedroom, curled into a tight knot and clutching one of the pillows. She had been crying into it. The sheets were a mess and half of them were on the floor. She made no move as I entered the room, though I knew she heard me come in.

"You talked to Marc didn't you?" I asked as I sat beside her on the bed.

She didn't respond, other than to shake her head in what I thought might be a yes. Her hair was a mess. It had been up in a tight bun, but now it was a tangled knot of hair. It looked as though she had tried to pull it loose and given up mid-way through.

"I was right wasn't I?" I said quietly.

She clutched the pillow tighter for a moment, before responding, "Yes." I stayed silent. I wasn't sure what to do, so I held my tongue until she continued, "Are you happy now?" It was as much an accusation as a question.

"Actually yes," I said quietly.

She turned her head to glare at me, "You bastard! This is what you wanted all along!"

"No," I lied again, "but I'm happy that we're going to have a child. I love you Penny, and I had always hoped we would have children someday." Another lie, I had never given it a thought. My idea of happily ever after had never been more complicated than an extended erotic fantasy involving the woman I loved more dearly than my own life. Thinking of children now though, I could see the attraction. I believed she would be a wonderful mother, and the thought of becoming a father brought tears to my eyes. My own father would never see his grandchildren. For that matter I would never see them either, not that any would ever truly exist. I hoped that she would go on someday, to have children without me, but the thought gave me even more pain.

"They would have been beautiful," she said in a sorrowful voice.

"One of them still will be," I reminded her.

"No Mort, I can't do this. It's too much. I won't leave you," she replied.

"You don't have to," I told her, "just stay with me 'til the end. When the time is close—then we'll do it. You can stay with me until it's over."

A small hope blossomed in her face, "Promise me. Promise you won't force me to leave you."

"I wouldn't do that Penny. I already told you," I answered.

"Promise me! Do that and I'll agree to break the bond as soon as the time is near, but you have to promise," she said desperately. It broke my heart to see her beg.

"Well of course I will Penny..." I started.

"No—Swear it! Right now. I don't want any half-empty reassurances. Swear." She gripped my shoulders fiercely.

"I swear it Penelope Cooper. I will not cast you aside, nor will I leave you alone, not until death takes the choice from me. I swear it on my love, and the life of our unborn child," I stared deep into her eyes as I spoke and I meant every word, though I knew there was no child in her womb. I would not betray her trust any further.

She nodded sharply and kissed me, her lips lingering against my own. "Will you marry me Mordecai?"

That surprised me. "I already asked you to marry me," I replied.

"No, I mean now. Right now. There won't be any later, not for you. Marry me now, I don't want to wait any longer," she was emphatic.

Wait for what? I thought to myself. We hadn't exactly been saving ourselves. In fact, we'd been very enthusiastically *not* saving ourselves for several months now. Women are a mystery to me sometimes. I had learned enough to keep from saying something stupid however, "Alright, let's do it."

She bounced up from the bed with more energy than I had seen from her in months, outside of her training sessions with Cyhan and Dorian. She began tearing through the wardrobe, "This is terrible Mort!"

"What?" I was mystified.

She gave me a look filled with horror, "What am I going to wear?!"

I swear, as long as I live, however short that may be, I will never, ever, understand women.

CHAPTER 33

The ceremony was held the next evening, in the small unfinished chapel of Cameron Castle. There on the eve of our war with Gododdin, we gathered for one of humanity's oldest rituals, an affirmation of life and joy. It was a moment of defiance in the face of certain sorrow.

Marc agreed to perform the ceremony, although I had certain misgivings about that. I kept my opinion to myself. Since he was otherwise occupied Dorian played the part of best man. That worked well for me anyway, I would have had trouble choosing between them.

There weren't many guests. James was there, as well as my mother and Penny's father. Cyhan also attended, along with Joe McDaniel and a small collection of Washbrook's citizens. Honestly I was grateful for the small attendance. The wedding we had originally planned, almost a year ago, would have involved a huge guest list. Escaping the pomp and circumstance of such a large wedding was a small blessing in itself.

I waited at the altar while Patrick Cooper walked his daughter down the aisle. With a start I realized Lady Rose would be missing the performance. I was sure there would be hell to pay for that later.

The ceremony itself was a blur. I would later wonder what had happened, for the first part I could remember was the final vows. Marc was staring at me for a while before I realized I was supposed to be repeating his words. My face turned red with embarrassment as he started again, this time I repeated them perfectly. In the end all I could recall were the final "I do's."

I found myself staring into Penelope's blue eyes. She hadn't had a wedding dress so she wore a beautiful yellow dress that Rose had helped choose for her long ago. Someone had helped to braid her hair into a delicately coiffed design, but all I could see were her lovely eyes and lips. Marc said something, but I failed to understand him.

"I said—you may kiss the bride," he repeated more firmly. I could hear some quiet chuckles from the guests.

"Oh!" I said stupidly, and then I did. Cheers and clapping broke out, but I hardly noticed. *I guess weddings aren't so bad after all,* I thought to myself.

A short while later we were enjoying food and what ale Joe could find. He could be quite resourceful when he chose to be. I guess it came from running a tavern. Dorian was well into his cups before the party had even begun. Marc was not far behind him, and both were trying to convince me to match them, mug for mug.

"C'mon Mort! Drink up! It's not every day you get married!" Dorian admonished me.

"You don't want to be the only sober one here do you?" Marc added.

"Well, who knows what we'll be facing tomorrow..." I vacillated. I was truly torn by my desire to drink and my responsibilities.

"Ahem!" said Penelope loudly. "In case you've forgotten this is his wedding night," she told them.

"Well why don't we go upstairs now my love," I told her gamely. "We can get that out of the way and then return to enjoy the evening."

Penny wasn't having any of it. "I don't think you understand. Remember that night in Albamarl, after our fight?" she reminded me.

"Yes," I said uncertainly.

"That was nothing. You'll be begging for mercy long before morning," she replied, arching her brow. "Save your strength soldier."

I looked at my friends gravely, "Perhaps I should excuse myself gentlemen. I believe duty calls."

They gave each other serious looks before raising their mugs once again. "To the dearly departed!" Marc announced.

I laughed and followed Penny to the stairs. My ordeal had just begun, but as a poet once said, 'when a woman has made up her mind all any man can do is go along.' I went along, and quite willingly I might add. In the days to come I would never have such a night again, nor do I think I could have survived one, but I never regretted it. All the joy and excitement of our youth was in it, and when the night was done I grieved for the loss. I would never have such a night again.

Dawn came, with her usual penchant for prematurity. The morning sun stabbed into my eyes, reminding me of the urgencies of the day. I groaned and pulled a pillow over my face. A knock came at the door, and my hopes of a late morning shattered. I sat up, rubbing my eyes, and Penny grabbed my arm. "Ignore it," she told me.

That sounded just fine to me and I fell back into the bed. Unfortunately the knock continued, with increasing insistence. Whoever it was really, really, wanted my attention. With a loud sigh I rose from the bed.

A young man stood in the doorway, looking uncomfortable. "The scouts report that the enemy is entering the valley, Your Excellency," he informed me hurriedly. I didn't recognize him, but I was sorely tempted to tell him to come back a few hours later.

As our plan stood currently, there would be nothing to do for several hours anyway. Watch and wait, that was the heart of it. We wouldn't act until the enemy was where we wanted them. I knew there was no hope for it, though. I looked back at the bed longingly. "I'll be down in a few minutes," I told him.

Once he had gone I returned to sit down at the bedside. Penny was sitting up looking disheveled and absolutely gorgeous. Despite the rigors of the previous night I was strongly drawn to try for an encore. Penny looked at me petulantly. "This is the worst honeymoon ever," she pronounced.

I was inclined to agree. "I know darling," I said instead. "But war waits for no man." I hoped that sounded appropriately important and wise. I had forgotten who I was addressing.

"You are not half so clever as you imagine. I hope you realize this," she told me as she began dressing.

"I know sweetheart, but as long as you don't tell anyone maybe they won't catch on," I replied. Despite her words I was feeling pretty damned clever anyway. Marriage seemed to agree with me.

We went downstairs. I knew with each step we got closer to the end of my good mood. As I entered the great hall I could see men crowding the room in every direction. A small crowd had gathered around the high table where Dorian stood. I admired his calm as he calmly gave instructions to those clustered around him. More than ever it was apparent he had been born for this sort of thing.

I didn't want to think about what I had been born for. *Wholesale slaughter most probably,* I thought to myself.

A hush came over the room as Penny and I made our way through the clustered men. Faces that I had seen a dozen times before looked at me in a new light. I could feel the weight of their desperation and hope bearing down on me, an almost tangible burden. I straightened my shoulders, holding my head high. One thing I had learned from watching Dorian was the importance of giving the impression of confidence. To do otherwise would only sow doubt and confusion.

Dorian seemed relieved to see me. A certain aura hung about him and I could tell that despite his apparent calm he was nervous. "It looks like today will be the start of it," he told me.

"How many are there?" I asked.

His face grew uncertain, "We're not sure yet. The scout just returned, but he said the column stretched back for over three miles that he could see. The head is still a few miles shy of reaching Arundel and the end of it is still emerging from where the road passes through the mountains."

That sounded like an awful lot of men, but I had no idea how to estimate their number. "And that means?" I let my question trail off, inviting him to elaborate.

"The column is marching five men abreast. Using a rough estimate of three feet per man that would be roughly ten thousand men for every mile and a half the column stretches, not considering the gaps between the various regiments of course." Dorian looked extremely uncomfortable.

I did some quick math in my head. "So if the column head is already three miles along the valley road that would be twenty thousand men—at least."

"We're still not sure how much further their line stretches Mordecai. It could be twice that," he added.

A chill ran up my spine. "If it did their column could stretch almost the entirety of the road from Cameron Castle to Arundel, over a third of the entire length of the valley. How could they even hope to feed so many? The logistics of it is boggling."

Joe McDaniel spoke up from beside Dorian, "That's their problem though; we just got to worry about killin' 'em."

Dorian coughed, "Actually no. It is something we should consider. If our plan fails and we wind up in a protracted campaign the nature of their supply line will be vitally important. An army lives and dies on its stomach."

"If this becomes a protracted campaign we're more likely to starve than they are. Our supplies are getting thin after the winter. The spring planting needs to be done soon. If we're besieged we'll starve long before they do," I said.

"Facing that many we wouldn't hold out long enough to starve," Cyhan observed.

I could see men shifting uncertainly at the dark tone our conversation had taken. I raised my voice, "Attend me!" Using a bench as a step I got onto the table. An unfortunate loaf of bread was spoiled but I ignored it. "Today our fight starts! You may be asking yourselves if we can win. You're probably wondering if a bit of land and a new start is worth the risk of your life. Am I right?" I paused to see if anyone would answer. I could see my words had struck a chord with many of them but none spoke.

"Many of you were with me in Albamarl. Others among you were there when we fought the cultists in the duke's castle. Some of you don't have a goddamn clue what I'm capable of, though you may have heard some wild stories," I said loudly. A few men chuckled. I took that as a good sign.

"A good friend of mine explained to me a while back that true power, doesn't come from money or magic. I thought he was a fool! Do you know what he told me?" I paused again before continuing, "He told me that true power lies in the people that follow you."

"But there's a damn sight more people on their side!" someone shouted from the back.

"You're right! But those men down there aren't our real enemy. They're people, just like you, men trying to carve out a living for themselves. Do you honestly think they *want* to be here? They're conscripts, forced to serve by the theocracy that rules Gododdin now. We have a hell of a lot more reason to fight than they do. The real enemy is Vendraccus and the dark god he serves. Forcing those men into this fight is what really pisses me off. Do you know why?"

No one spoke. The room had gone utterly silent as I spoke and I could see the question in their eyes.

"Because I am going to kill every damned soldier that marches into our valley! I have never been a man that likes bloodshed, but today will be the day history remembers me by. The day Mordecai Illeniel became the greatest butcher the world has ever seen," I stopped, staring at them for a long minute.

"There's something I need you to do for me," I cast my gaze across the crowd. "When today is done thousands upon thousands will be dead, but there will be more. The dead will pile upon themselves from one end of this valley to the other, but some will remain. Those that do may well be driven to assault us here. They may still outnumber us. Our women and our children wait on us in Lancaster. I will not be able to protect them. I leave that trust to you. Can I count on you to do that for me?"

The room was silent for a long moment before one man near the front answered, "Yes my lord."

I put my hand to my ear, "What did you say?"

"Yes my lord!" he repeated more loudly.

"I hear your voice, are there any others?" I replied.

"Yes my lord!" several men shouted.

"Louder goddammit!" I admonished them. Soon the room was echoing with cries of "Yes my lord!" They took it up and it slowly became a chant. At some point it changed and before I realized it they were chanting my name. Another day I might have been embarrassed, but not today. They needed hope, and I needed their trust. Chances were that I would lead many of them to their deaths, and for that I certainly needed their trust.

They were still pounding the tables and shouting when I left the room. I stood listening in the empty corridor and each booming cry reminded me of a marching drum, driving me to my doom. Penny walked up behind me, "You were magnificent Mort. They truly believe in you."

The emotions swirling through me were too much, and I began to laugh. An ugly hysterical laugh, a reaction to the tension coiled inside me. "You really think so?" I choked out.

A worried frown creased her brow, "Yes I do."

"We'll see how they feel when the crows and vultures come to feed. We'll see how the survivors feel once they've gained some *perspective*," I replied.

"You really worry me sometimes," she responded suddenly.

"You're not the only one. Come on, let's go see how the enemy is progressing," I said and we headed for the teleportation circles I had prepared.

⊰━━⊱

We sat on two tall destriers near the manor house of Lord Arundel. A large circle was etched in the cobbled patio behind the house. I had created several throughout the valley. With a diameter of fifteen feet they were large enough to allow me to bring both of us along with our horses. Not having access to a better means of viewing the valley I had placed them at spots I thought would prove useful in observing the enemy. The circles that matched them were placed in a large barn we had constructed near the stable in Cameron Castle. I would need good information on the enemy's position to use my iron bombs most effectively.

I had taken us there knowing that the soldiers of Gododdin would already be passing by Arundel—or scouting it. There was a high possibility they would divert to make certain there was no enemy waiting to flank them from the baron's estates. As we rode around the side of the house I spotted two men on horseback in the front yard, their eyes grew wide when they saw us.

I thought for a moment they might charge us, but being scouts they spurred their horses and rode away. Information was more important than engaging and unknown enemy I supposed. I dismounted and plucked two stones up from where they lay. The riders were less than a hundred yards away. A word and a sharp puff of breath sent the stones flying after them. After they had fallen from the saddles their horses continued running. I decided to let them go, they would send a message for me.

I caught Penny watching me. "You seem rather calm," she noted.

"No point in getting worked up over two men. I'll have much worse to atone for later," I replied coldly.

"I don't like what's happening to you," she said.

I remounted and rode close beside her. Leaning over I gave her a kiss. "I love you Penny, but it doesn't matter what happens to me. I won't have long to regret my actions."

She gritted her teeth, "What if I was wrong?"

"Do you think you were wrong?" I asked smoothly.

She didn't reply to that so after a moment I turned my horse and we began riding for the road. I wanted to see the reaction the riderless horses would provoke. As we rode I rechecked the shields around Penny, myself, and our horses. The events of a year ago had taught me a valuable lesson about shielding my horse.

We had covered most of the mile that separated Arundel from the main valley road when we caught sight of the enemy. They were marching five abreast toward us, with small groups of cavalry fanning out to the sides. "What now?" Penny asked me.

I laughed at the question and did what seemed most natural. Standing up in my stirrups I began waving at the approaching soldiers, a broad grin on my face. They came to a halt and I saw their commander ordering the crossbow men to come forward. "Time to go," I told Penny. We turned and began riding hard for Arundel. A few bolts flew by as we rode but the distance was too great for them to have much chance of hitting us. A glance back showed me that their cavalry had decided not to give chase.

They probably thought it was a trap. I couldn't blame them for that.

We returned to Cameron as soon as we reached the circle in Arundel. From there we took another circle to a spot in the valley, on the other side of the road as it passed by the baron's lands. I had been careful to position it slightly more than half a mile from the road. My biggest fear had been putting one somewhere and finding myself in the middle of the enemy when I used it.

From there we had a clear view of the column of soldiers. It stretched now from where the road left the mountains all the way to Arundel. I could see that the last part of it consisted of wagons and what I presumed were camp followers. That meant the column of soldiers was nearly five miles long. "Slightly over thirty thousand men," I mused aloud. Glancing over I could see Penny's mouth agape as she stared at them. "You alright?" I asked.

"There's so many," she said softly.

"Doesn't matter," I reminded her. "Ten, twenty, thirty—it just means more will die."

"Stop it," she replied.

"Stop what?"

"Stop pretending it doesn't matter. You know damn well it bothers you," she told me.

"I can't afford to pretend otherwise. I have to keep my heart hard. If I don't, I'll lose my resolve," I said determinedly.

"But all those men—they must have families, loved ones, people waiting on them," she said.

"Shut—up," I said quietly. Thankfully she did. We watched as they set up a defensive line on the road leading toward Washbrook and Lancaster, while the main column continued to progress into Arundel. They were making sure they weren't surprised while they secured the baron's land. An hour passed while we quietly observed them.

"I think they've noticed us," Penny said casually.

Glancing along the line I realized she was right. A contingent of cavalry was detaching from the main force and riding toward us. That surprised me; our location was well hidden by tall grass and a copse of trees. Perhaps they were merely sweeping the area to make sure it was clear. Either way we would have to move, I couldn't risk them finding us so soon.

Moments later we were back in the barn at Cameron Castle and things weren't as we had expected. Sounds of fighting came from outside, but what was inside the barn concerned us more immediately. The barn was full of soldiers, and I recognized none of them. Heads turned and swords were out, we were surrounded by the armsmen of Gododdin.

A tense moment passed in odd silence as our presence registered on those around us. Penny and I were likewise in shock, and then pandemonium erupted. Our foes started to rush us but I shouted out the words to a spell I had prepared. A circle of pure force erupted around us and swept outward, slamming men against the walls of the barn. Unfortunately the circle started at a distance of ten feet (to avoid hitting Penny). Several were closer than that and their swords reached us easily.

I felt several strike my shield but Penny had already exploded into motion, where she had been sitting upon her mount a moment before she was now leaping above them. Startled heads turned to follow her but they were too slow. She landed behind the men on her side and began cutting a deadly arc through them, her bond-sword slicing through flesh and armor with equal ease.

Those on my side encountered much less resistance and swords began battering me from several directions at once. Worse some of those who had struck the walls were not out of the fight, and rising rapidly they charged toward us. I raised my staff and between the blows striking me I channeled energy down it. A line of searing light flashed forth and I began sweeping it around me, cutting through steel and bone. Men cried out in pain, dying as that terrible line cut through them. I moved it back and forth, raking its awful beam across those nearest and then using it to finish those against the walls.

Turning I sought to help Penny but it was too late, she was already finishing the last of those who had come at her. The sight of so many dead men around her shocked me. Our eyes met and I could see nothing there but adrenaline and the madness of battle. I looked away, for I didn't like what I saw in them.

Before we could leave to see what occurred outside another group of fifteen men appeared beside us, on the circle that led to Arundel. I cursed myself as I realized they had used my own circles to surprise us. I raised my staff, but Penny was there ahead of me and I was forced to withhold my magic lest I hit her. Like a force of nature she went through them, steel flashing while men died and blood spilled onto the floor.

It wasn't even fair to call it a fight; she slew them as a man might kill children. She might have slaughtered them all but for the one in the center, a man who bore a dark aura shining with power. As she neared him he put forth his arm and an invisible hand picked her up, tossing her across the barn to strike one of the main support beams. If not for her shield the blow might have killed her outright.

"Pyrren," I said, and flames roared forth, streaming from my outstretched hand. The men around him died screaming but the fire didn't touch him. He gave me a black smile and I knew I wasn't the only one with a shield. His hand came up again and I found myself flying across the room to slam into the wooden walls of the barn. Stunned, I struggled to pick myself back up. I could taste the iron tang of blood in my mouth.

Penny charged him, she had recovered more quickly than should have been possible, but he waved his hand again, and sent her flying across the room once more. "You obviously don't know how to fight men of power, young Illeniel," he gloated in a voice that sounded as if it crossed a great gulf. I could see the madness of Mal'goroth in his eyes.

I had reached my feet and as he spoke I raised my staff. Without using words I channeled power down its length while I answered him, "And you obviously need to learn when to shut the fuck up and die." The focused beam of light sliced through his shield and cut his body neatly in half. He was dead before he struck the floor, his face registering disbelief. I swept the beam down to destroy the circle that led to Arundel. I wouldn't repeat that mistake again.

"Are you alright?" I asked Penny as she clambered to her feet once more.

"What do you think?" she snapped at me. I took that as a yes. I could still hear sounds of fighting beyond the walls so we paused for a second before opening the door to the outside. I took out a small pouch of stones I had been saving while Penny put her ear to the door. I could have told her there was no one near the other side, but I didn't think she was feeling very receptive to advice at the moment. "You ready?" she asked me.

"Yep," I said and with that she flung the door wide.

Chaos reigned in the castle yard. Men were fighting in tight knots everywhere I looked. There was no firm line, no defensive position. The enemy and the defenders of Washbrook were intermingled in a desperate struggle for survival. There was nothing poetic about it, men cut and slashed and in some places the blood was enough to form mud on the ground. Penny and I exchanged quick glances. "Go," I told her. "I'll be fine." She was running before the words had left my mouth.

I didn't stop to watch her; I didn't want to see her working her bloody art anyway. I began picking targets, taking care to avoid hitting one of my own men. The nice thing about using the stones was that they were highly selective, once I had chosen a target they never missed. One by one my targets fell. Most of them wore helmets but it hardly mattered, the force was enough to knock them senseless. Once they fell, the vengeful swords of Washbrook made sure they didn't rise again.

Within minutes the tide had turned. There were only fifty or so of the invaders within the yard, and they no longer had reinforcements arriving. The castle defenders on the other hand were appearing in ever greater numbers. They had been taken by surprise but the tables had been turned, once Cyhan and Dorian appeared their chances dwindled to nothing.

The enemy was down to ten now, drawn into a tight defensive circle. The look on their faces told me all I needed to know, the fight had gone out of them. "Throw down your swords and you may live yet!" I shouted at them. They paused but a moment before weapons began clattering on the hard earth.

"Take them to the stockade," Cyhan added, addressing our men.

Dorian tapped him on the shoulder, an embarrassed expression on his face. "Actually we never built a stockade," he said as Cyhan turned to him. "It was the lowest thing on the priority list and we never got to it," he added.

The older warrior shrugged, "I guess we'll have to kill them then." His sword appeared in his hand as if it had always been there and his matter of fact expression was chilling.

"Wait!" I shouted, striding forward. "These men have surrendered, we can't kill them."

Cyhan sighed, "Honor is all well and good, *Your Excellency*," he put special emphasis on the last part. "But this is war. We have no place to keep them out of trouble and we can't afford to assign men to babysit them."

"These men are no different than we are, they've got homes and families just as we do. I won't take a man's life after he's surrendered," I told him bluntly.

"What happened to 'I'll kill every soldier that steps into this valley'?" Cyhan asked.

I gritted my teeth and ignored him. "Dorian, take them to the great hall and interrogate them. If they answer your questions freely and honestly we'll release them this evening. They can make their own choices after that."

The reaction of the crowd was a combination of gasps, mutters, and sighs of relief. Clearly opinions were mixed about what to do with them. Some wanted them dead, but others abhorred killing helpless men as much as I did. "As you wish, my lord," Dorian answered immediately. It was the first time I could recall him addressing me that way. I hoped it wouldn't become a habit.

"Find out who their commander is. I also want to know as much as they can tell us about their numbers, troop composition and command structure. After that they can go. If they wish to rejoin their fellows they can die with the rest of them tomorrow." I stared calmly at them as I said the last part.

I saw Joe among the survivors and breathed a sigh of relief. "Joe, assign twenty men with bows and swords to watch the barn. If they discover another of my circles and begin using it I want to know immediately. Kill anyone who appears in them unless I order otherwise. No hesitation, no parley."

"Wouldn't it be safer to destroy them now?" he asked.

"No, I need them. Given their current location the only one they might find is the one I just used. Keep a close eye on it." I took him in and made sure he knew which circle I meant.

I left them then, and headed for my rooms. Weariness had crept over me and a nap was long overdue.

CHAPTER 34

The room was dark when a sound woke me from my slumber. I had only meant to take a short nap but my body had had other ideas. The lack of sunlight told me I must have slept the rest of the afternoon away. I was amazed that no one had come to wake me. A distinctive snore gave away Penny's presence beside me. She hadn't been there when I went to sleep, but she must have needed it as much as I did. I rose quietly so as to not disturb her.

Another rap at the door made me aware of why I had awoken. I crossed the room quickly and opened it, Dorian stood in the entrance. "They've reached the point where the road leads to Washbrook," he said without preamble.

That got my attention. That meant their column would be spread out from that point to Arundel. If they moved further they would escape our trap. The assumption had been they would turn there, to attack us at Cameron Castle. I could only guess whether they had left men in Arundel but it hardly mattered. Whether they had decided to use it as a supply base or left it empty their main body was where it needed to be. "What time is it?" I asked.

"A little past eight o'clock," he replied.

"Hmm," I said wisely, stroking my beard.

"Aren't you going to set things in motion?" he said anxiously.

"Not now, it's too early, or rather late."

"If you wait they'll be out of position once they start moving again, Mort." Dorian's naturally pensive expression was out on full display.

"If we do it now they'll be scattered in every direction. The dark will make them more disorganized. Some will run for the tree line rather than the valley, that would be worse," I told him. "Get some sleep. We'll start the party as soon as dawn arrives."

"As if anyone could sleep now!" he moaned.

"You'd best try. There will be no time for it tomorrow," I advised. "I'll see you before dawn."

"But Mort!" he started. I closed the door before he could finish.

"Was that Dorian?" Penny asked; her voice thick from sleeping.

I told her the news, trying to keep it less exciting than it really was. I figured she could use some sleep. I failed miserably. An hour later we were both still awake, staring up at the darkened ceiling. Eventually we gave up on sleeping and spent our time more productively; since it was obvious sleep wouldn't come.

❖

I woke again with a start. "What time is it?" That seemed to be my favorite question lately.

Penny was already dressed. "A bit after three in the morning," she replied. That meant we had slightly less than three hours before dawn. I planned to act as soon as the sky was bright enough to allow men to see clearly, which would be sooner.

I rose and began dressing. "Think anyone's cooking breakfast this early?"

She laughed, "Dorian's had most of the household up since two. Everyone is on edge anyway. I'm sure they're getting ready to serve now."

We went down and ate breakfast with the others. The mood in the room was a strange contrast between sullen silence and nervous laughter as some channeled their anxiety into joke telling. I ate quickly though I had no appetite. The food sat in my stomach like a rock.

Before we left I went to our map table and took out three small sacks. Carefully I gathered up the glass stones corresponding to the areas of the road I meant to destroy. The largest sack held the stones that would detonate the bombs along the length of the road. The second held those that would destroy Arundel and the third held those that would convince the enemy to flee in the direction we had chosen. I worked mechanically, keeping my mind blank. I couldn't afford to think about what my actions would mean.

On our way to the barn I made a side trip to my father's now dark smithy. The only fires that had been lit there since his death had been my own, and those were few enough. Tonight it was dark and cold. I stepped through the darkened workspace without needing light. Even without my magesight I would have known my way, so familiar was that place.

I took his favorite hammer from the tool rack, a medium weight cross-pein hammer. One side was flat while the other angled in to form a line. He had preferred it for its versatility. I felt a twinge of guilt at using his tool for such a purpose, but I refused to choose another. I was sure he would have wanted to help me, even if it were for something as dark as this.

Hammer in hand we went to the barn, greeting the men who still stood guard there. "Morning gentlemen," I said, though none of them could be said to be gentile.

"Good morning your lordship," Sam Turner responded. He was the only man among them that I recognized. I smiled for a moment as I remembered him helping me cover myself with mud. I hardened my resolve. It was for him, his family, and others like him that I was doing this.

"Today's the day Sam. We should be back soon, but you'll hear the fireworks before we return. Make sure the men don't shoot me when we reappear," I told him solemnly.

"We'd never shoot a lady sir," he replied.

I thought for a moment he was making a joke, 'til I saw him bowing to Penny. I smiled and we took our places on the circle that would take us to our next observation point. I patted my horse gently to soothe it before we jumped. Sometimes the change in scenery unsettled them. A moment later we were in a grassy field on the valley side of the road, midway between Arundel and Washbrook.

I had chosen the place carefully. Almost a mile from the road it had lain in the tall grass undiscovered by their scouts. This circle had no natural concealment for two riders on horseback. Once the sun rose they would be able to see us clearly from the road. I rather doubted they would have much time to worry about us, though.

Penny and I dismounted and I placed the largest sack on a flat stone nearby. The rock hadn't been there originally, but since I had chosen this spot to watch the result of my work I had brought it to simplify my job. *It's a wonder I didn't bring a supply of beer to enjoy the show with,* I thought derisively. I lay the hammer down close by and took a seat to wait on the dawn.

Penny sat beside me in the dark. "How long do you think?" she asked quietly.

"As soon as we can see them clearly from here. I want to make sure they have enough light to run the right direction," I replied.

"What if they don't?"

"I don't think there will be enough to be a threat to Lothion after this. We, however, may be in dire straits. I can't be sure how many will survive but almost any fraction of *that* army would be enough to put an end to us," I informed her.

"If they lose half their army and cannot win in Lothion wouldn't they retreat?" she suggested.

"Possibly, if their commander is a rational man. I see three possibilities. One, their commander is a fanatic, in which case he will prosecute his war as far as possible, even if it is only vengeance against us. Two, their commander is a rational man, but the loss of half his army drives him mad, and he attacks us in vengeance. Three, their commander is rational and keeps a cool head, in which case he withdraws and it's over," I replied.

"So one in three," she mused.

I sighed, "I honestly don't know. I'm just going to kill a lot of people and see what happens."

She caught my bitter tone and stayed silent after that. An hour passed and the sky grew steadily lighter. At first the enemy were just grey shapes across the plain, invisible except when they moved. Eventually their forms resolved until we could see them clearly. It was time—any longer and they'd come calling to ask us why we were watching them.

I picked up the hammer and felt its heft. Before I could strike Penny interrupted me, "Let me do it. You shouldn't bear this alone."

I shook my head. "You have a life to lead after this," I said and brought the hammer down sharply, smashing the glass inside the bag. For a split second nothing seemed to happen and I almost wondered if I had made a mistake somewhere, but then I saw the light flashing on her face. Penny's mouth opened slightly as she drew a sharp breath and then the sound washed over us. It was as if lightning had struck a thousand times, at close range, a tremendous crashing roar that swept everything before it.

Looking up I saw devastation on a scale that I could scarcely comprehend. Fire and smoke were blossoming outward from a thousand places along the road, stretching away from us for almost four miles in one direction. I had spaced my devices thirty to forty feet apart, buried along the road. From what I could see that had been overkill. The sound of it was gone within seconds, and in the silence it left behind all that could be heard were the screams of dying horses and men. Those that hadn't been killed outright were horribly maimed, missing arms and legs. Most of them would be dead within minutes. Only those lucky enough to have been more than forty or fifty feet from the road survived, and many of those were badly burned or otherwise injured.

Smoke and dust obscured our view now, but I could see many of the survivors running away from the road, toward us. I assumed others would be running the other direction, so I set the second bag on the stone and repeated my action. Another roaring wave of sound, almost as great as the first, rolled over us as more explosions destroyed the other side of the road. Only those who ran toward the river would be spared. I took out the third bag, but Penny laid her hand on my arm.

"Enough Mort, no more, please..." she said and I could see her eyes were wet. I should have felt the same, but my own heart had gone missing, replaced by a cold void. Pushing her hand aside I smashed the third bag. It was too far to see, but Arundel was swept by a storm of explosions just as the road had been. I couldn't be certain the enemy had left men there, but it paid to be sure. After a span of seconds we could hear the booms echoing across the valley.

It was time to go, I could see the survivors stumbling across the grassy plain toward us, but I realized that some of the glass stones in the first bag had survived. Not willing to leave the job undone I put it back on the rock and began methodically crushing them all. A few scattered explosions sprang up at distant points along the road. After several swings I had probably shattered all the glass jewels but I kept hammering, pounding the rock until fragments of stone began to fly away. I could hear someone shouting but I ignored them until finally Penny grabbed my wrist, halting the hammer in mid-swing.

It was proof of her strength, the hammer weighed more than ten pounds and she had stopped my swing cold. With her other hand she took it gently from me while I stared at her. Finally I closed my mouth, I had been screaming without realizing it. "We have to go. They're almost here," she told me calmly.

I nodded and stood up. A few steps and a moment's concentration took us home. The castle yard was strangely silent as we walked among the people milling there. Everyone watched me carefully as I made my way among them to the main door. I could see the same question in every face, until at last one man dared to ask, "How did it go, milord?"

I drew myself up. It would not do to show them the pain I held inside. They needed hope, not a man torn by guilt and self-doubt. Taking a deep breath I spoke loudly that all could hear me, "It went even better than I expected. Most of them are dead; those that remain will be mourning their dead during the short time that remains to them."

I paused and a shout went up. I waited for it to die down but they only got louder. Every man in the yard as well as those within the keep began to gather around me. The cheering swelled and became a chant as they repeated my name again and again. I was drowning in admiration. They cheered for a butcher. A hard lump formed in my throat and I knew I would lose control of my emotions if it didn't stop.

Raising my hands for silence I stared at them until they finally wound down. Once the noise was such that they could hear me again I shouted for quiet. Eventually I got it. "We have taken the first step, but there is much you must do this day, and it will not be easy. Lord Dorian and Master Cyhan will be here in a moment to give you your assignments. Most of you will be sent out to watch the enemy. There are bodies strewn along the road for over four miles. Among them are wounded, men who will take a long time dying. Your job will be to show them mercy. You will also ensure that the enemy withdraws to the valley to regroup. Do not thank me until you see the bloody work that lies before you."

I turned and left them there. I needed privacy as a man dying of thirst needs water. I never made it to my quarters however, Dorian caught up to me in the corridor. "Mordecai! Wait up! We need to talk."

Looking back I saw Penny mouthing something silently to him. Probably a warning concerning my mental state, I pretended not to see it. "We talked about this yesterday," I said wearily.

His face was worried, "That was yesterday. You haven't given us the specifics yet. Plans change in the face of the present."

I sighed, "It went better than we expected. Four miles of road will need to be rebuilt once this is over. Arundel is in ruins."

"But what of their army? How many survived?" he asked insistently.

It was a struggle not to shout, but I kept my voice even, "Less than a quarter, beyond that I can't be sure. Those that camped on the valley side of the road were largely unscathed. Make sure you don't engage them. If you see any groups that still remain organized avoid them. Just harass them and finish what wounded you find." I finished and turned away.

"But Mort..." he began.

I kept my back to him, "Just do it Dorian. Go clean up my damn mess! I don't want to see you or anyone else until it's time for me to kill the rest." I left him there without looking back but with my magesight I could feel him looking after me in shock. I couldn't have cared less. I found my rooms and locked the outer door. Penny was still outside but she had a key, not that I really wanted to see her either.

A bottle of wine sat on a table in the front room. *Now that's an excellent idea,* I thought to myself. A moment later I had uncorked it and sitting down I began to drink. The rest of the world could go hang. I glanced at my hands, at some point they had developed a tremor. I wondered how many glasses it would take before the shaking stopped.

CHAPTER 35

Two hours later I had finished the bottle. I might have gone for another but I didn't want to risk leaving my rooms. A knock at the door took the choice from me.

"Go away!" I shouted.

A key turned in the lock and Penny entered, "There's someone here to see you." She had a serious tone in her voice.

"Such as?" I said, taking care to slur the words eloquently.

"An emissary from Vendraccus, he came under a white flag," she answered with a tone of disapproval in her voice. "Have you been drinking?"

"Perhaps," I said carelessly. "I find it to be invigorating. Tell Dorian to accept his surrender and send them packing."

"He hasn't come to surrender and he won't speak to anyone but you," she replied, her frown deepening.

"Fine," I growled. "Clear the hall and have him brought to the high table. I'll meet him there. Tell Dorian to wear his sword, I don't want anyone there besides the two of you."

She gave me a look that spoke volumes. I ignored it and played with the empty bottle. "Are you coming?" she asked.

"I'll be there in a minute," I replied casually.

"What sort of minute?" she asked, "The kind that is just a minute, or the sort where we sit around waiting for you to sober up for half an hour?"

I gave her a look of offended innocence. "If you must know… the sort of minute where I empty my overworked bladder, this bottle didn't just empty itself by magic." I twirled the bottle in my hands but the effect was spoiled when I dropped it. She slammed the door as she left.

Once the door closed I stood and assessed my balance. It seemed good—at least I was able to walk without needing support. I considered my options and decided the balcony was a bad idea, someone might be below. I didn't relish a trip to the privies so with a sigh I found the chamber pot. I chuckled when I thought of what Penny would say later.

A few minutes later I entered the great hall and made my way to the high table. Our guest was already seated there and Dorian stood nearby giving the impression he was but moments from committing a crime against hospitality. Penelope stood by the door; apparently she had thought I might need a hand reaching the table. I shrugged off her proffered aid and made it to the table without assistance.

As I walked I made careful note of our visitor. The emissary carried a dark aura around him, much like the one that had cloaked the man who had used my teleportation circle to sneak troops into the castle yard. Considering I was the only known wizard I assumed he was a channeler, much like Marc, though for a different god. I paused to put a shield around Penny and she gasped for a moment when she felt it settle around her.

She met my eyes and I gave her a look that told her I was worried, then I took a seat across from the man who had so boldly come to parlay with us. "Have you had anything to eat? You must be hungry after such a long journey?" I asked him in a mocking tone.

"I am quite satisfied with what you have already provided," he answered. His voice was far too deep to be normal, which verified my suspicions.

"I don't recall having fed you, Mal'goroth. That is you isn't it?" I asked mildly.

"As much of me as this lowly vessel can handle," the emissary said, gesturing at his body with disdain. "I came to thank you for your work on my behalf."

His tone rankled, and rage burned through the haze of wine. "I would sooner have two sisters in a whore house as do anything on your behalf. Do not think to anger me with poorly considered insults. You have already lost."

He laughed and replied, "Oh but you have done my work. Surely you realize how the 'dark gods' as you term us, work? We are unable to draw sustenance directly from human worshippers, sacrifices are required. Today has been the greatest sacrifice in the history of your wretched race."

I hid my dismay, "Your men made their choice when they chose to serve you. I will not feel sorry for them."

"Some of them, yes. Others had to be persuaded to join the army," he said, giving me a broad smile.

"It's all the same to me," I replied.

"Is it?" he asked. "What if I told you those men's children are held hostage at my temples in Gododdin?" Whether it was the wine, or shock I couldn't be sure, but the room swayed when he spoke.

"If you keep pressing your attack here you may not have many followers left," I said. I could think of nothing better, my mind was still reeling.

"Fool! Kill them all, I care not. Saving your kind has never been my goal. You kill the men, I will kill the children and either way I grow stronger," he said with growing menace.

"Your men will not follow you if you slay the hostages," I stated bluntly.

"That is why I only kill the children of those who fall in combat. I reaped a double harvest this day," he replied with a sickening grin.

I felt ill but I held onto my resolve, "If you hope to undermine my determination you're sadly mistaken."

"On the contrary I am here merely to educate you. I find it unsatisfying to destroy an ignorant foe. You should be honored. Not since your ancestor Tyrion has one of your kind killed so many in one day," he replied smugly.

"Who?"

"How quickly mortals forget. Tyrion Illeniel was the founder of your line, the man who raised the Elentir Mountains. The man who destroyed my people and who set me on the path that has led me now to you, his great grandson many times removed. Did you think you descended from some noble line? The man was a murderer a thousand times over, he slew almost as many of his own people as he did mine. Genocide is a crime that does not go unpunished."

"Why tell me this?" I asked.

His eyes lit with joy for a moment. "To remove one final delusion. You think yourself a hero? You are no better than a common thug. You think you fight to save innocent lives? You do nothing but take them. You think me a mad god of a forgotten age? You are right, but I have fought for a thousand years and more to avenge the murder of my people. Your revered ancestor destroyed the truce that existed between the She'har and humanity for generations. He murdered them for nothing more than pride. I tell you this so that you will know you are no better than he was; so that in the end, when despair has overcome you, you will know that you fight for nothing, and after you have passed I will continue my war until every member of your worthless race is gone."

My face went pale as he spoke, his words hammering into me, showing me the folly of my dreams. I couldn't accept the truth of what he said, for doing so would have destroyed me. I struggled to find a logical response but I came up empty. I was saved from doing so when Penelope's sword lashed out, seeming to come from nowhere. Its magically enhanced edge went through the emissary's shield as if it didn't exist and seconds later his head fell to the floor, still leering at us. Dorian and I stared at her in shock.

Penny stared boldly back. "He talked too much," she said and began cleaning her blade with the dead man's robe.

Her nonchalance broke the darkness that had gripped my heart and I began to laugh. Dorian didn't see the humor, though. "The man was here under a white flag! You can't—you can't do that!"

Penelope smiled at him. "You're just jealous that I thought of it first," she replied. A knock came at the door before Dorian could reply. I rose and answered it to avoid thinking too deeply about what the emissary had just said.

Marc stood at the entrance, looking like a servant, a tray with food and several mugs of ale in his hands. "I thought you might want to offer our guest something...," he began, looking over my shoulder. It was obvious he was merely curious since I had left him out of the meeting. His eyes grew round when he spotted the headless corpse on the floor.

"Our 'guest' isn't feeling well," I told him flatly. "But since you're inclined to play the servant perhaps you would be so kind as to clean this mess up." I gestured at the corpse and then eased past him. Penny came up and took one of the mugs of ale.

"Oh that's very kind of you Marcus," she said and followed me down the hall.

He stared after us for a moment before returning to the kitchen with his tray, leaving Dorian standing alone in the great hall. Dorian gave the dead man's body a steady look. "Well damn," he said to himself.

A few hours later I stood in the castle yard watching Cyhan's group returning. He reined his horse in beside me and looked down. "You did your work well," he complimented me. It wasn't the sort of praise I relished.

"How did it look out there?" I asked.

"At a guess they lost almost eight of every ten of their men. Your magic was most effective. We searched the road for survivors but most were dead before we found them," he told me.

"Were you able to ride all the way to Arundel?"

"No, there were a few groups of cavalry patrolling, we were forced to return or face a pitched battle. They still outnumber us by a considerable margin," he informed me. "From what I could see they are reforming in the valley, much as we had hoped."

I remembered what Mal'goroth had told me and winced inwardly. I couldn't know how much of what he had told me was true, but the knowledge made my task even harder. "How soon before they're able to field an effective force?"

Cyhan's brow furrowed in thought, "It should take them a week at least. Their army is burdened by a large number of wounded. They'll have to reorganize, sending those unable to fight back to Gododdin. Some of the lightly injured will be kept, if they can fight within a few days."

"I'm surprised they still have the stomach to fight."

"Whatever Vendraccus is using to motivate them is highly effective. Any normal army would have routed after today," Cyhan remarked before leading his horse toward the stables.

I watched him go. *Tonight then,* I thought. I couldn't afford to let them reorganize. I went looking for Dorian.

"More bodies for me to dispose of?" he asked me sarcastically when I found him. He was inspecting a group of warriors preparing for the next patrol mission.

Despite my dark mood I chuckled a bit at that. "Not this time, although there are plenty out there that need your expertise," I gestured at the gate and the road that led toward the valley. "I need to know how many men we have left. I'm planning to destroy the dam tonight, so we'll want to prepare for a sortie in the morning."

"Seven hundred and twelve," he answered promptly. I was surprised at his exact count, but then on second thought I shouldn't have been. Dorian had always been meticulous, especially when he was worried, which was most of the time. "I'll have them ready at dawn," he added.

I nodded. "Where do you plan to scout next?" I asked.

"We're going to head through the forest to the east, toward Lancaster. We'll make our way through to the road between here and there," he replied simply.

"There shouldn't be any in that direction," I commented.

"The key word is *shouldn't,*" he said grimly. "It isn't a word I like to hear when it comes to battle. That word has killed more men than any other word, except perhaps one." He waited for my inevitable question.

I sighed and asked, "What word is that?"

"Charge," he replied with a smile.

Dorian left after that, taking fifty riders with him. I hoped they wouldn't find anything.

CHAPTER 36

The day wore slowly on. I had expected Dorian and his men to return within a short span of hours but he failed to appear on time. As each hour passed beyond the time he should have returned I grew more anxious. He wouldn't have delayed unless something prevented him— or he was dead.

Joe stood beside me on the rampart, watching for their return. "Something bad has happened," he stated.

While I admired the man's tenacity, his penchant for stating the obvious was annoying sometimes. "He'll be back," I replied.

"How do you know?" he asked me.

"Because he has to be," I said darkly. In spite of my optimistic words I felt in my heart that something had gone terribly wrong. Another hour dragged by and the sun was beginning to set. I was about to give up my fruitless watch and go inside when I spotted riders coming up the road.

They were too far to make out with my eyes but with my mind I found Dorian among them and breathed a sigh of relief. They were riding hard, as if the army of Gododdin was racing behind them but I saw no others on the road.

A few minutes later I met him in the yard. "What happened?" I asked impatiently.

"They're heading for Lancaster!" Dorian shouted before I finished my question.

"What? How many?"

"All of them as far as I can tell," he replied.

"But the other scouts report they've made camp in the valley," I told him.

"It must be only their wounded. We came across nearly five thousand soldiers on the road. Barely escaped once they caught sight of us. They sent a cavalry detachment after us; chased us halfway back here. I don't think they wanted us to know where they were headed. There's no one but women and children there! We have to send out the men, all of them, try to draw them back." Dorian's tone was full of stress. I had never seen him so close to outright panic.

"Wait, let me think," I replied.

"There's no time to think! We have to respond immediately! Every second brings them closer to Lancaster. There are no defenders there and we'll never lift the siege if they close around them. Not that they could keep them out anyway. They're hauling siege engines behind them Mort!" he was shouting now.

Siege engines? Where in the hell had they gotten those? None had been spotted before now. I suspected they might have had the parts in the supply train, which had largely survived intact, but I couldn't imagine how they had moved them so quickly. I closed my eyes, struggling to think and suppress my own panic.

"Mort! We have to move now!" Dorian shouted again.

"Shut up! Give me a moment!" I yelled back, and then an idea occurred to me. It would be a desperate gamble but the enemy clearly had an idea of my plans already. Knowing that we might be able to fool them into thinking we had more traps ready than we actually did. "How long before they reach the duke's castle?" I asked quickly.

Dorian frowned for a moment; obviously his own mental machinery was also clouded by emotion. Finally he spoke, "From the point we left them—they should get there within an hour, possibly two. The wagons and onagers were slowing them down."

That might be enough time, barely. "Get the men inside and make room, we'll have a lot more people here soon. I need twenty men ready to travel with me, now!" I ran to find Penny. "Have them meet me over here!" I shouted back at him. "I'll be back in a few minutes."

I found the large circle that we had used to transport the non-combatants to Lancaster and stood inside it. A second later I was in a similar barn at Lancaster Castle. I left quickly, looking for Genevieve. I shouted at the first person I saw, a woman hauling water in the yard, "You! Get everyone out here now. Tell everyone you see to come here quickly."

She stared at me blankly for a moment until at last she recognized me, "Yes your lordship." She resumed walking toward the keep, carrying her heavy bucket.

"Now damnit! Drop the bucket and run! There's no time!" I shouted. She let out a startled yelp and dropped the bucket. I watched her run for the keep while I frowned. I found a second woman at work in the stables nearby. A similar tirade sent her running as well.

Within a few minutes people had begun to gather in the yard but Genevieve had yet to appear. "Get the children over here! I'm taking everyone back to Washbrook now. The enemy will be here soon," I told them. Penny and I took the first group of children we could find and transported them back to Cameron Castle. Dorian and the twenty men I had requested were waiting there for me.

I left the children and returned with Dorian and his fighters. Genevieve had emerged when we got back and met me at the barn door. "What's this about the enemy coming?" she asked me anxiously.

"They'll be here within an hour, two at the most. I'm taking everyone back to Washbrook with me," I informed her.

"But what of the food? Half our stores are here! There's not enough room for everyone there," she said urgently.

"That will have to wait. There won't be anyone to starve if we don't get them to Washbrook quickly." I told her.

"Calm down Mordecai, we can close the gates. We'll have hours to move then, even without soldiers to guard the walls. Let me organize things, we can save most of our supplies that way," she replied calmly.

"We're not closing the gates," I informed her.

"What?" she said in dismay.

"Just trust me, help me get these people organized. I need them all back in Washbrook within the hour. Leave everything behind." I turned to Dorian without waiting for her response, "Take your men and make sure the gates are wide open, make it look inviting. Then I need you to help herd everyone over here. Also make sure no one is visible on the walls, the castle needs to look empty if they get here before we're done."

"But Mort...," he started to protest.

"Just do it Dorian! Goddamn, I don't have time to explain everything," I told him sharply. His face flinched for a moment but he took his men and headed for the gates.

"Mort, it might help if you told us what you're trying to accomplish," Penny told me as we guided the next group toward the circle.

"I'll explain as we go," I replied and a moment later we were back in Washbrook. "Vendraccus—or Mal'goroth, whoever is running that army out there—they know I have a trap planned for them." The people with us had cleared the circle so we teleported back to Lancaster. We began gathering another group while I talked, "They must think the next trap is at Cameron Castle, so they're heading here—to bypass us." We continued moving people and I spoke between jumps.

"If they besiege Lancaster we'll be forced to react, in a way that will put us at a serious disadvantage. The only thing we have going for us is that they don't know exactly what or where our next trap is," I said.

"But you only have one more trap," Penny reminded me, "the dam."

"I have two actually, but your point is still valid," I replied.

"How do you know they haven't figured out where they are? They obviously know about the dam," Penny responded.

"No I don't think they do. They left their wounded in the valley, to distract us. It might be a decoy but I don't think they would waste that many people just to fool me."

Penny frowned, "So how does abandoning Lancaster and throwing the gates open help us?"

I gave her a wicked grin, "Arundel."

"What?" she snapped. She had never been a big fan of mysterious explanations.

"I blew Arundel up when they used it for a base camp. Who's to say Lancaster isn't a giant bomb as well?" I transported us again, still smiling.

Penny gave me a strange look, "But there aren't any of your magical traps at Lancaster—are there?"

"Nope," I replied smugly, "but they don't know that."

It took us slightly over an hour to get everyone back to Washbrook, nearly four hundred women and children in total. Once we had them all safely back we returned to

Lancaster. I left Marcus and Cyhan to manage the huge crowd of people and took Dorian and Penny with me. The three of us waited in the barn in Lancaster, watching the castle yard from the partly open door.

It was an hour more before the first riders appeared, cautiously passing through the main gates. Their posture made it clear they expected to be attacked at any moment. I didn't envy them their mission. The strange nature of Lancaster's open gate and empty castle must have left them fearing a trap, which of course was my plan.

"What do we do if they search the barn?" Dorian asked in a nervous whisper.

"Then we teleport back before they see us," I replied. I was hoping they wouldn't search the castle extensively, if we were forced to teleport back I would have to destroy the circle in Washbrook. That might make things more difficult later.

The riders made a slow circuit of the yard, one of them was sent back to report while the others dismounted and entered the now vacant main keep. Another went to check the gate house. Through it all we watched silently, hardly daring to breathe although they never came within fifty yards of the building we were in. Eventually they left.

"What now?" Penny asked.

"Next comes the hard part," I said, "waiting to see if they come back."

"If we stay in here we'll never know if they're gone," Dorian groused.

His irritation amused me, which was a good thing, little else did lately. "Relax… I can sense them within five hundred yards or so. When they get beyond my range I'll slip out and see if I can see them from the walls."

I kept a watch on the men beyond the walls for over an hour. They sent several patrols in various directions, circling the outer walls and exploring the road in both directions. I could imagine their leader's anxiety. The last abandoned estate they had found had blown up in their faces, literally.

Night fell and still they waited. Given the darkness I guessed they had decided to make camp. We would have to wait for morning to see if my gambit had worked. Eventually I sent Dorian back to report on the situation. I knew Marc and Cyhan would be biting their nails back in Washbrook wondering what was going on.

Penny and I spent the night curled up companionably. By companionably I mean she used me for a pillow while I got the dubious comfort of a rolled up cloth sack to cushion my head. We had found it in a corner and it smelled of dust and oats. While we rested I stretched my mind out to its fullest, but I learned little else about the enemy.

—◆—

The night was black and draped the dead men along the valley road in a cloak of darkness. Most were dead but scattered among the corpses were a few survivors, men broken and maimed, unable to move. Even those, few as they were, would have died soon, but for the scavengers that came to claim them. Creatures that walked on two legs like men, but were empty inside.

The shiggreth searched easily among the dead, the spark of life in those that still lived drew them like moths to a flame. Their numbers swelled as the night drew on, for though most of the soldiers were dead hundreds still clung to life. They were in no position to protect themselves from the things that came to feed upon them in the night.

—◆—

Morning sunlight filtered through cracks in the wooden walls when we awoke. I sat up with a start, dislodging Penelope and causing her head to hit the floor with an audible thump.

"Ow!" she said, sitting up herself. "What time is it?"

"It's late," I answered. "Judging by the sunlight coming in I'd say it might be after nine."

"Are they still there?" she asked.

"Yes and no," I replied. "There's a small group, maybe twenty men, camped outside. I don't sense any others. It should be safe to go outside; maybe we can see more from the wall."

"I can't believe we slept so long," she said as we quietly climbed the stairs leading up to the top of the curtain wall around Lancaster Castle.

"I haven't slept well in several days, although it's ironic we would catch up on our sleep while hiding from an army," I replied. "Oh look!" I added. We had reached the top and were carefully peeking between the merlons. In the distance we could see the slower parts of the remaining invaders, traveling back toward Cameron Castle.

"They're not all gone," Penny reminded me. "I see those twenty you mentioned. They must want to make sure we don't sneak back in."

I nodded in agreement. "Most likely they have orders to report as soon as they see anyone returning, they may worry we have another surprise of some sort in store for them."

"The women and children can't come back then," said Penny.

"Not yet, if we kill those men it may alert the enemy. I don't know if they have some sort of scheduled message arrangement but I would expect them to. Let's go back to Washbrook. We'll need to prepare."

Soon enough we were there, in the midst of chaos. Washbrook and Cameron Castle were crowded, and people filled the castle yard in every direction the eye could see. I couldn't imagine what their night must have been like; many of them had probably slept on the ground. We made our way carefully through the crowd, hoping to find news within the castle itself. Genevieve found us first.

"Mordecai!" she shouted to get my attention through the crowded press. People automatically made room for her as she approached me. "This won't do. There are too many here. Last night was a horror."

"I'm sorry, Your Grace," I replied as politely as I could. "I hope we can send everyone back soon, but you'll have to bear with it for a bit longer. How is James doing?"

Her husband had developed a slight limp after the arrow wound he received in the capital. Apparently even Marc's goddess didn't always heal things perfectly. Genevieve frowned at me. "He's fine, as you should know. He went out with Cyhan on that last patrol," she told me.

Actually I was surprised. I had been so busy with other matters I hadn't noticed his presence. Nor did I realize he was taking turns on the patrols. Knowing the man I should have guessed, though. James was never one to sit idle. "The enemy is returning here. When they arrive and start their siege I will have these people returned to Lancaster. I want you to take James with you when you go back," I informed her.

"That stubborn man won't leave a battle," she laughed. "There's no way you'll get him to return."

"There is a small guard left, watching Lancaster. Someone will have to remove them before the people can safely return. I'll make sure to send him for the job," I replied smiling.

"Just make sure it's soon nephew. These people can't live like this for long before they start to sicken," she told me.

I thought for a moment. "Tonight I hope. I don't want to send anyone to Lancaster until I'm sure that Vendraccus has committed himself against us here."

CHAPTER 37

By late afternoon the last of our patrols were forced to retreat to Cameron Castle. The enemy had reached us and begun digging in for what might be a long siege. I considered sending men out to harass them as they prepared their camps but Cyhan convinced me it was an ill-advised plan. They had at least five thousand able men and a large portion of them were holding ready to repel us should we attempt to sally.

Their numbers were enough for concern, since they outnumbered us almost ten to one, but what truly had me worried were the siege engines. I could see a variety of devices at the rear of their lines; machines I had seen in books but never imagined would someday be arrayed against me. There were small onagers and ballista, mounted on wheels and drawn by teams of horses. The onagers were simple affairs, with a throwing arm and a small bucket that could be loaded with various types of ammunition, such as rocks or firebrands. The ballistae were essentially giant crossbows and appeared to be loaded with large spear type bolts.

More frightening was the taller construction near the back. Unless I missed my guess it would be a large trebuchet when completed. The trebuchet had a much longer throwing arm with a sling like cup at one end to hold a projectile. The short end near the axle would have a heavy counterweight when it was finished. It was too large to be moved easily so they had brought the parts and were assembling it as we watched. Given its large size it would probably be able to throw rocks weighing several hundred pounds over a distance of hundreds of yards. The walls would never be able to withstand the assault once they had their range.

Dorian and Marc stood with me on the wall watching their progress. "I'm starting to feel under-dressed for this party," Marc commented.

Dorian laughed, "It's looking more and more like we are going to be on the receiving end of a lot of nasty siege weaponry. Can't you do something about those things Mort?"

"Not while they're that far out. How far do you think they can shoot?" I asked.

Dorian thought for a moment. "The ballista and the trebuchet will be able to fire from five hundred yards or so, perhaps further if they don't mind missing more often. The onagers will need to get within three hundred yards at least."

I didn't like his assessment. Since Penny and I had formed the bond my best range for destructive magic was close to five hundred yards. The onagers probably wouldn't be a problem for me but I doubted I would be able to do anything to disable the trebuchet at that distance. I would have to adjust my plans. "How long before they attack?" I asked.

Dorian's answer was immediate, "Tomorrow."

"You're sure?"

"They won't advance until their position has firmed up and the siege weapons are ready. They also have to worry that the king may be sending a relief force so they won't waste time. If I was their commander I would start as soon as possible, and that would be tomorrow at dawn." There was little doubt in my friend's voice.

"Marc—tonight I want you to take the women and children back to Lancaster. You remember how to use the circles right?" I asked him.

He sighed, "You've asked me that about a dozen times. Yes I can remember, and even if I couldn't my Lady would provide the necessary knowledge. It's her power I am using after all. But why me?"

"It will take a lot of trips back and forth," I told him. "I don't want to exhaust myself the night before the assault begins. By the way, I'm sending your father with a small force to eliminate the small group they left behind to watch your home. Your mother requests that you not bring him back with you."

"I can see I'm about to become more popular with him," he laughed. "You certainly picked an unpleasant task for me."

I grimaced. "I'm afraid there are no pleasant tasks," I said sourly.

❖

That night things went as smoothly as could be hoped. Marc took his father and a group of about fifty men back to Lancaster. I didn't go with them but apparently they were able to eliminate the enemy scouts without too much trouble. Five of the men were injured but Marc's goddess healed them almost before the battle was done.

After that they sealed the gates and Marc began transporting the women and children back as quickly as he could manage. Despite the fact that his goddess provided all the energy it still exhausted him. He explained to me later that although his Lady's energy was limitless (according to him) his body limited what she could do. The more he channeled her power the more it cost him in terms of fatigue and exhaustion. I filed the information away as being of possible future use. After all I had already faced two channelers working for Mal'goroth and there might be more.

Penny and I retired early. Neither of us was tired but I figured the more time we gave ourselves to 'attempt' to sleep the better our chances were of succeeding. As it was we slept fitfully but we did manage to get five or six hours of good rest. I was sure we would need it come morning.

***

By the time dawn arrived we had already been up for several hours. I watched the sun lighting the horizon to the east with Penny. We were standing on top of the curtain wall trying to make out the enemy's arrangements as they became steadily more visible. Most of our warriors were positioned behind the wooden palisade which stood a full hundred yards beyond the outer curtain wall. We planned to hold the enemy there as long as we could before retreating within the more defensible stone walls. At least that is what I had told them. I hadn't shared my true plan with anyone yet.

Penny's eyes grew wide as the dawn sun brought greater clarity to the field laid out before us. Her eyes darted back and forth, from our earthworks to the enemy lines and their siege weapons beyond that. A gasp escaped her lips almost inaudibly. I turned to look at her face but she put her back to me to hide her expression.

"It's today isn't it?" I said calmly. Some inner intuition had told me what caused her to react like this.

She didn't answer immediately. She kept her back to me and hugged herself. I didn't press, waiting instead for her to find the words. After several long minutes she looked back at me. "Yes," she answered simply. Her eyes were wet.

"How do you know?"

"I've had a feeling of deja vu since we walked out here this morning, but I wasn't sure until I saw that," she gestured toward the enemy encampment. "It looks almost exactly like what I saw in my vision. It can't be more than—more than, a few hours...," her voice broke as she spoke forcing her to leave the sentence unfinished. I gently drew her to me and she shook as I held her, crying softly into my shoulder.

I felt strangely calm as she wept. The events of the past few weeks had been a wild jumble of emotions but now I felt numb. There was nothing left for me but to finish what I had started. When she finished I held her at arm's length gazing solemnly into her eyes. "If it is today, then I have several things to tell you. Things you will have to finish for me," I said slowly.

Her eyes narrowed for a moment, "You've been keeping secrets again."

"Just a few... Nothing dire, but you will have to play my part if I die before the time is right," I told her.

"What is it?" she asked.

"Not yet, we have something else to take care of first," I said meaningfully.

"We don't have to do that yet," she protested. "There are at least several hours still."

"Yes we do. I don't know what will happen from here on out. There may not be a chance once things get chaotic. We do it now, and then I'll tell you what you need to know," I said firmly.

"You kept those secrets just to have a bargaining chip didn't you?" she said sharply.

In fact I had, there had been no reason to hide my final plans, other than to make sure she would cooperate near the end. "Not intentionally," I lied, "but now that the time is here I'm glad I did."

"You really are a bastard sometimes," she replied sweetly. "Fine, how do we do this exactly?"

That was the one part of the bond I had paid close attention to back when Cyhan had been instructing her. "First you take out your sword and we hold it between us, then you simply ask, formally and in all seriousness for me to release you. You have to mean it. I will respond formally as well and then we have to let go of one another—in here," I pointed to my chest. Her eyes started watering again when I gestured to my heart.

"Alright," she replied, letting her head droop downward. She drew out her sword and held it across her palms facing me. When I had placed my hands over hers she spoke, "I, Penelope Illeniel, would break my oath and I ask you to release me from this bond we share." Her hair had fallen, blocking my view of her face, but I could see wet spots appearing on the stone between her feet.

I took a deep breath and answered her, "I, Mordecai Ardeth'Illeniel, do release you from your bond." I invested the words with power and inwardly I felt our spirits separating. A part of myself that I hadn't realized had been her, slipped away from me. For a moment I was left with a feeling of incredible emptiness as for the first time in months I was just myself, alone. The sword we held glowed brighter for a moment and then shattered, as if it had been made of glass.

We stood quietly for a minute, neither of us daring to speak. We both knew the distance between us had become much greater than the scant inches separating us physically. Finally I broke the silence. "How do you feel?" I asked.

"Much weaker," she said ruefully. "I had forgotten what it was like to be normal. How about you?"

"I feel empty. Like a man living alone in a house that has become much too large for him," I replied honestly.

She gave me a serious look, gazing steadily into my eyes. Despite what we had just done I could see incredible strength of spirit within her. Every time I looked at her it was as if I had fallen in love all over again. "Your eyes are blue again," she said wistfully.

"I think you look better with your natural brown," I told her in return.

"So what secrets do you have to share?" she said, changing the subject.

I opened the heavy leather pouch I wore at my belt. As I looked inside I saw the gem that had been used when we created our bond. It was no longer glowing. I ignored it and brought out two cloth sacks that had been marked with ink. "This pouch holds the stones that will destroy the dam," I told her. "When the time comes, destroy them. I had hoped to drive the enemy back into the valley first, but you'll have to use your own judgment since I won't be here."

"What about the other pouch?" she asked.

"I'll hold onto this one for now, but if I die before using it you need to claim it quickly. It holds the keys to the bombs beneath the field out there," I pointed to the ground before us, between the curtain wall and the palisade.

"But that's inside our line, why?" she said, confusion in her eyes.

"The palisade is a trap. I didn't have iron but I had the men bury large stones beneath the earth, both inside and outside the palisade. I didn't tell them what they were for, though. They extend out to about a hundred yards from our earthworks. The closest ones are about sixty yards from the walls here. I was afraid if they were any closer they might destroy our walls," I told her.

She shook her head, "I still don't understand. Why not put them further out?"

"We had run out of iron. The stones are much larger and heavier. I didn't have enough time to have the men dig great holes everywhere, and haul stones to them. The further out you go the more area there is to be covered. The only place I could be sure the enemy would be is here," I pointed down to the area below us again.

"Then why bother building the palisade at all?"

"All part of the deception. The enemy probably won't commit his men to a head on assault until they have breached our walls. The earthworks give them the impression that we are serious about defending the castle. Once they breach them they may assault us right away. However, if they wait until they have brought down the gate or one of the walls we have to hold them before they enter the castle yard itself," I stated carefully.

"Why?" she asked.

"I don't want to use our trump card until they've committed most of their men to the attack. We have to wait until most of them are at the walls here before we use it, otherwise we waste our only advantage. So if they breach the curtain wall before that point we have to hold the line here until they commit all their men," I said.

"You should just let me have that pouch now," she suggested.

"I'd like the chance to spit in their faces and blow them to hell myself. If I have to die I want to go with a bang," I smiled wickedly. "You can take them from my cold dead hands if I don't get to use them."

"I really wish you wouldn't talk like that," she complained.

CHAPTER 37

My heart felt lighter than it had in months. Despite the empty place it felt as if a burden had been lifted from my shoulders. "If I can't joke about my impending death what can I joke about? Would you rather I go moping about?"

She laughed a bit, 'til her tears started again and then she held me. I felt a twinge of pain for her; it was easier to be the one dying. My journey was almost over, but she still had a long lonely road ahead—without me. For the first time since Marc had first given me the idea of lying to her about her 'condition' I felt guilty. I hoped she would forgive me someday when the truth finally came out.

They began the bombardment once the sun was fully in the sky. Now that I was free of the bond I found I could sense things at a much greater distance again. When the first stones came hurtling toward us I sensed them long before they arrived. On a whim I spoke a word and swept my hand sideways, striking one of the large boulders from the sky before it reached us. I was amazed at the clarity of my senses. After months being half blind my power seemed easier than ever to use.

"Did you see that?" Marc elbowed me. "One of the stones just went flying sideways. Was that you?"

I smiled. "We'll see how they like facing me now that I've got my kid gloves off," I replied smugly.

"Your eyes are blue again—does that mean what I think?" he asked.

"Your idea worked beautifully. No matter what else, you have my thanks for that," I told him.

"I thought so," he said. "Did she tell you what I told her?"

"Yes, and I appreciate it. I know it must have cost you dearly to say it."

He frowned. "It didn't cost me a thing, anyway, congratulations."

It struck me as odd that he would congratulate me on the day of my impending demise, but I dismissed it as another of his odd jokes. "Just promise me you will make sure she's alright, once I'm gone."

His face tightened, "You didn't have to ask me, Mort. Dorian and I will do everything we can for her, you know that."

More rocks began falling, striking the palisade and bouncing across the ground behind it. So far none of our men had been struck, but I knew our luck couldn't hold forever. The enemy troops were advancing now, approaching to within two hundred yards. The onagers were brought up behind them, allowing them to strike the palisade more easily. Some of our archers fired, though they had been told to save their arrows. Most of their shots fell short, and those that didn't missed their marks.

I raised my staff and with a word I focused energy through it, a line of fire lanced outward and struck one of the onagers. It went up in flames. Repeating the process I began systematically destroying them until none were left. I considered doing the same to the men on the field but I knew I would exhaust myself long before I had made a dent in their numbers. I thought of the other pouch on my belt, the one I hadn't told Penny about, but I quickly dismissed the idea. It wasn't time for that yet.

The enemy withdrew to four hundred yards once the onagers were gone. I could still reach them at that range but I didn't feel the need to tip my hand yet. Things settled into a dull rhythm as both sides waited. I had hoped they might try a premature rush but they seemed content to wait while trebuchet did its work. The only other activity in the interim was the occasional ballista shot. Their crews were disturbingly accurate. Once they had gotten used to the range they began picking their targets carefully. At five hundred yards they missed as often as they hit their mark but when they were successful the result was gruesome. Several of our men were impaled before they learned to stay out of sight.

A deadly stalemate ensued, punctuated only by the thrumming sound of their trebuchet every few minutes. Each time it fired a rock weighing several hundred pounds would come hurtling overhead. The first shots fell short, but they methodically adjusted the machine until the stones were consistently striking the stone curtain wall that surrounded Castle Cameron.

Dorian found me watching the steady destruction from the ground outside wall but within our palisade. "Can't you do something about that damn machine?" he said.

"It's too far away," I answered calmly. "I might be able to misdirect the stones it throws but that would defeat my purpose."

"You want them to knock the wall down?" he asked incredulously.

"Actually yes, they won't try a full assault until they have a clear way in," I replied.

He gave me a suspicious look, "What are you planning?"

"Something big," I said. "Make sure the men are ready to withdraw after a token resistance at the palisade. Also—is there any way to stop them getting through the gap in the wall if they knock part of it down?"

He grunted, "Yeah, but it involves a lot of dying. I've already got them preparing a temporary barricade behind the section that infernal machine is pounding on."

Another giant boulder struck the wall, sending chips of stone flying. "When they finally charge, I want the archers to keep firing until they're almost to the earthworks. Once they're within fifty yards or so they should run for the gate," I told him.

"The palisade will hold longer than that," he argued. "We should make them pay for it. Once we're inside we won't be able to hold that gap in the wall more than a few hours."

I gave him a serious look, "Would it seem suspicious if we ran for the gate sooner?" I had wanted to preserve as many lives as possible but now I was rethinking my plan.

"Suspicious?" he said, "Well of course! If we just surrender our outer defense and let them head straight to the breach it would be strange. If it were me commanding them I'd think we had either a fool for a leader or a trap planned."

I drew a deep breath and replied, "Very well. Do as you see best, just try to keep as many men alive as possible." It didn't sit well with me that men would die defending ground I had no intention of holding.

Dorian gave me a strange look, "What is it that you haven't told me?"

"Trust me," I said smiling.

"Oh no! Absolutely not, you've said that before. If you expect me to defend this castle I need to know what the hell you are planning to do." Dorian set his hands on his hips in a stance that told me he was feeling stubborn.

"We need to concentrate as many of the enemy outside the walls as possible. I think I can eliminate most of them if we can get them to commit to a full assault," I replied.

"How?"

"Something similar to what we did to them on the road," I answered.

"You're telling me that my men are standing on top of more of your bombs?" he yelled.

I tried to quiet him down, "Yes, keep your voice down. If you spook the men we're done for."

He closed his mouth suddenly as he realized how loud he had been. After a moment he spoke again, "I'm going out there Mort. If anyone gets blown up I'll be among them. Understand?"

I nodded. "Just make it look real. Everything is riding on this Dorian. If they don't fall for this we've lost. I don't have any other tricks up my sleeve."

"Don't you worry; it will be so damn real you might think we're dying out there. The blood that flows won't just be theirs," and so saying he turned and left.

CHAPTER 38

The morning went slowly onward. The trebuchet had reduced the upper section of the curtain wall near the bailey to rubble. What remained there was sagging inward and looked as if one or two more good hits would bring it crumbling down. Ordinarily we might have tried to brace it from the inside but we ignored the damage. The sooner it came down the better.

The men behind the wooden palisade looked increasingly nervous. They could sense the impending rush that would come once our defense was breached. Dorian and Cyhan walked among them constantly, doing their best to bolster their confidence.

Penny followed me constantly, refusing to get more than twenty foot away. *She's starting to remind me of a vulture,* I thought uncharitably. I could hardly meet her eyes anymore; every knowing glance brought her near to tears.

Through it all the one thing that worried me most was the lack of any sort of magical attack from the enemy. I had already faced two of Mal'goroth's channelers, so I had a good idea he probably had more. I searched among the enemy constantly with my mind, seeking the dark aura's that might alert me to their presence, but I found nothing. Even with their limited abilities they should have been able to pick off some of our men if they tried, yet none had. That made me anxious because it meant the enemy might be planning something.

Another great stone went whistling overhead. This one struck solidly at the base of the weakened portion of the curtain wall. For a second nothing happened, and then the wall collapsed inward. An area more than twenty foot wide was open now, with nothing more than a pile of stone rubble to prevent a man from entering. "That should be it," I said to myself.

Penny tugged at my sleeve, "Don't expose yourself."

"I don't plan to," I replied. "Do you think it will save me?"

"Just don't do it, maybe I was wrong, maybe...," her eyes were wide with fear.

"I'll do my best, but I've learned to trust your visions. Whatever happens... happens," I told her.

A shout went up from the men along the palisade. The enemy had begun their advance. I left her there and went to stand beside them, watching the approach of the men of Gododdin. "Hold your fire damnit!" screamed Dorian. Some of the men had begun shooting early. "Wait 'til I give the order!"

The footmen were running toward us across the field, growing closer with each step. The tension in the men around me was nearly unbearable. They held their bows with arrows nocked, waiting for the order to fire. After what seemed an impossibly long time Dorian finally gave the command, "Fire at will!"

Five hundred men rose up and began loosing their shafts. The enemy was only a hundred yards distant now and the steel headed arrows fell among them with deadly effect. Men fell only to be trampled by their companions. More arrows flew and more fell, but the men of Gododdin came on anyway. At fifty yards few missed and now we could hear the cries of the fallen. Still they came on and after one more volley they reached the palisade.

Running down into the ditch men stumbled and struggled to rise. Our arrows were still striking them with lethal effect. Within moments those behind them were climbing up, struggling to get past the sharpened stakes that guarded the mound of earth we stood behind. Their ballistae began firing again, sending deadly bolts three feet in length into the defenders.

The enemy was pressing against the short palisade walls now, the sheer weight of their numbers beginning to push it over in places. The defenders of Washbrook had switched to spears, stabbing at those trying to get past our defense. In the end it was a futile effort. Desperate fights broke out at various points as the flimsy wall collapsed and the enemy began streaming in among us.

"Fall back! Into the castle!" Dorian yelled above noise of the fighting men.

I brought up my staff and began sweeping the enemy near where I stood with lines of fire, clearing the area for twenty feet near where I stood. Stepping up to the top of the earthen mound I looked over the field of men. I reached into my pouch brought out a handful of small iron spheres. Each one was no larger than the end of a grown man's thumb. With a word and a puff of air I began sending them out to strike various points along the outside of what remained of the palisade. As each reached its destination I spoke again, releasing the energy held within it. Each one blossomed into a small explosion of fire, killing everyone within ten feet of it. I hoped to give the men enough time to retreat.

Arrows fell around me, and some struck my shield, but to no effect. There was little they could do to stop me. I felt an evil laugh bubbling up from somewhere inside as I killed men by tens and twenties. I hardly noticed the flare of purple as the channelers among the enemy suddenly became active.

Penelope Illeniel watched the men streaming past her as the defense began to fall apart. She only had eyes for one man, the one standing madly atop the earthen mound, sending fire and death out to greet the enemy. *You idiot!* she thought to herself, *I told you not to expose yourself.* She started to run towards him, to pull him down when a new vision blinded her.

She stood transfixed for a minute, unable to move as her gift showed her the future. It was much the same as before, but now it held a choice, where before there had been nothing but unstoppable fate she could see a new path; one that would lead to a different outcome. She made her choice without hesitation. Blinking she took in the scene around her and began running toward Mordecai once again. *I have to hurry!* she thought. A hand on her arm stopped her.

"You're going the wrong way!" Cyhan yelled at her. His grip seemed impossibly strong, especially now that she no longer had the bond.

She shook her head, "No! I have to tell him something! Let go!" She struggled to break the big man's grip. As she did she met his gaze, and as she looked on his face his eyes widened.

"Your eyes," he said suddenly. "What have you done?"

"What I had to do!" she screamed at him. With a twist she broke free and backed away, trying to get closer to where Mordecai still stood.

Cyhan's sword was out and there was a dangerous look in his eyes, "You've betrayed your oath girl." He took a step toward her and his sword flicked out, seeking her head.

Penelope's old sword was gone, but she had taken a new one, and she met his blade with her own. Though she no longer had the strength and speed the bond had given her she still had learned much about swordplay. "What are you doing?" she demanded.

"What you should have done," Cyhan answered tonelessly. His sword struck again, almost beating her frantic block aside, and before she could recover his foot snaked forward to sweep her from her feet. Leaping past her he ran for Mordecai's unsuspecting back.

With a strength born of desperation Penny reached out and caught his ankle, causing him to tumble and fall. As he fell she pulled herself up and struck him solidly in one kidney. Cyhan gasped and twisted catching her across the jaw with a poorly aimed swing. She flung herself at him like a madwoman fighting with all the strength she still possessed.

The fight was over in seconds. The larger warrior caught her by the hair and planted a fist in her belly, doubling her over with pain as the air was forced from her lungs. He rose while she struggled to breathe and spat at the ground, "I taught you better than that." Before he could strike again, a voice from behind stopped him cold.

"Whose side are you on?" Dorian asked… a quiet fury in his tone.

"Get out of my way Thornbear, your wizard has crossed the line," Cyhan warned him. Fire flared and an explosion nearby underscored his words.

"Are you alright Penny?" Dorian said, looking past his opponent.

Cyhan struck the moment Dorian's eyes left him, his sword sweeping up to catch the younger man before he could defend himself. He didn't count on his opponent's speed however. Dorian sidestepped the thrust and brought his own blade to bear. Steel flashed as the two men began to fight in earnest.

Penny rose and began to make her way toward Mordecai, keeping a wary eye on the deadly struggle playing out before her. The two warriors seemed evenly matched to the untrained eye, while Cyhan possessed skill and grace obtained over a lifetime of training Dorian had a natural talent with the sword and his youth and speed made up for what he lacked in experience. Penny knew better though, her own training had taught her to read the flow of a battle and she could see that Dorian was close to losing. With each exchange he was left slightly off balance, struggling to get his sword back into position in time to meet the next sweep of Cyhan's blade.

The two men had practiced together before this, but their faces were a picture of deadly determination now, this was not a practice bout. A silence fell over the field as they fought, as though the war itself had stopped out of respect for their individual battle, then Penny realized what had actually happened. The explosions had stopped. Looking up she could see Mordecai had gone still, his body tense, as if he were struggling against some titanic force while he stood in plain view of the enemy. With a cry she began running, trying to reach him before it was too late.

Meanwhile Dorian continued his losing battle. The man he faced was more skillful than anyone he had ever met and despite his best efforts he couldn't keep Cyhan's blade from reaching him forever. Another pass of their swords and sparks flew as the older man's blade ran along his arm striking the mail Mordecai had enchanted for him. In that moment Dorian knew what he had to do. *You better have been right about this armor Mort,* he thought silently. Dorian slipped and almost lost his footing, leaving himself wide open on his left side. Quicker than thought

Cyhan's blade was there driving in at Dorian's unprotected stomach. The force of the thrust was such that it should have gone through Dorian's armor, but the enchantment held. Instead Dorian felt a blow, as if he had been punched in the stomach, but he had been ready for that. Catching the end of the sword in his mailed fist he swung his own sword downward at the trapped blade and his enchanted steel cut cleanly through it, leaving the older warrior holding a foreshortened stub of a weapon.

Surprise lit Cyhan's face for a second and Dorian's sword swung back. If it had connected it might have severed his head but he threw himself backward before it reached him. He was left with a deep cut across his cheek and nose. Gritting his teeth in pain he cast about seeking a weapon as Dorian advanced on him again. He never saw the heavy pole that struck him from behind. He collapsed wordlessly to the ground.

Marcus dropped the heavy pole he had taken from the fallen palisade and gave Dorian a smile, "I owed him one." His smile vanished as he saw what was happening atop the earthen mound.

CHAPTER 39

My attention shifted as I realized I was no longer the only magic worker on the field. Deep purple auras had sprung up around no less than five men, spread out amongst the advancing soldiers. The closest was no more than fifty yards from me. Before I could react lines of amethyst shot forth to envelope me from different directions.

Sounds of fighting came from behind, but I had no time to think on it. The lavender energies playing over my shield were driving inward with crushing force. Individually none of them would have been much of a threat, for they didn't seem to be powerful channelers, but together they were more than I could handle. Sweat stood out on my brow as I strove to keep their dark energies from penetrating my defense.

In the distance I could hear singing and a deep drumbeat tone, much like a giant heart. Almost instinctively I knew it was the heart of the earth. In desperation I called out to it, *help me!* A surge of power rose up from the ground at my feet, coursing through my body and with an exultant cry I shattered the lines of force pinning me. I felt more than saw a massive ballista bolt go hurtling past. It had missed by scant inches as I stood paralyzed in my own battle for survival.

Raising my staff I pointed it at the nearest channeler and flames roared outward. This was no focused line, flames raced outward in a massive cone, incinerating the channeler and everyone within thirty feet of him. The thrill of power erased my fear and I turned to engulf the second channeler in flames. The other three renewed their assault but they were no longer enough to contain me. I refocused the power in my staff and burned them down, one by one, with a tight beam of light and fire.

Before I could move again something struck me hard and I went flying backward, tumbling down the inside of our earthen mound. In shock I saw Penny rise up from where I had been standing, and I realized it had been her that struck me. She shouted something at me, but I couldn't make out the words. She took a step toward me before the ballista bolt struck her down from behind.

It was a frozen moment of horror as I saw the wide bladed bolt head erupt from Penny's chest. Crimson blood flew outward as it ripped through her and she stumbled and fell forward, shock and pain on her face. My mouth was open in a wordless scream as I ran back to her, but no sound came out. She lay in a heap, the thick wooden shaft had struck the ground first and her body slid slowly down the thick wood, toward the earth beneath her.

With strength I didn't know I possessed I pulled her up, dislodging the spear head from the ground. I could feel her heart still beating but blood was pouring from the wound in a red tide. Somehow she was still conscious and her eyes met mine while her lips silently mouthed the words, "I'm sorry." A second massive bolt whistled by as I awkwardly lifted her up and began running for the castle.

I became aware of Dorian and Marc running beside me, dragging what appeared to be Cyhan's unconscious form between them. The enemy was swarming through our flimsy defenses on all sides now, forcing their way into the enclosure. Arrows from the defenders now on the walls flew out killing some of those that sought to reach us. Death was everywhere now but I had no time to spare for anything but forcing my legs to carry me faster toward the castle gate and safety.

What seemed to be an eternity passed as we ran for the stone archway, but in actuality it was only seconds. As we passed through men formed up within, holding spears to keep the invaders from entering 'til the last of our people had made their way in. A minute later the great doors began to close and the massive iron portcullis came down behind them with an echoing boom. Not daring to go further I eased Penny down and sent my mind out to examine her wound.

The internal damage was incredible. Her spine had been partly severed and a large artery in her abdomen was bleeding freely. Somehow her heart had been missed but one lung had collapsed and the other was damaged. Without pausing I sealed the artery to stop the loss of blood but I knew it was only a temporary measure, the organs it fed would soon die if I could not restore normal blood flow quickly.

Marc stood beside me and I looked at him with hope in my eyes, where my father had died for his absence, perhaps now Penny could be saved. "Please help her!" I begged. He nodded and I saw his focus move inward as he sought his Lady's aid for Penny's sake.

The cold voice that issued from his throat a moment later chilled me to the bone, "You have betrayed us wizard. Your bond is broken."

I stared at him in shock, "She doesn't have time for this. Please—you must save her!"

"She dies in your place, a fitting punishment for an oath-breaker. You should be dead as well," said the voice of Millicenth without sympathy. Though the voice was hers I could see Marc's face twitching as he began struggling with her internally.

"Damn you Millicenth! If you do not help her now I will see you and all your kin dead by my own hand!" I shouted at him. It was an empty threat, but I was beyond reason now.

"You have chosen your fate," she answered. "We can only hope death finds you before Mal'goroth does." Marc's face was twisting now into a rictus of agony as he fought against his goddess' will. Tense seconds passed and then I felt more than saw her leave him. He fell to his knees beside me, with despair written on his face.

"She has abandoned us," he said in a voice that held no hope.

I ignored him and returned my attention to Penelope. As with my father, I was faced with an impossible task. The shaft had to be withdrawn while at the same time her artery and damaged organs were repaired. It wasn't something I could do from the outside. I looked up at Dorian, "Cut the head from the shaft," I said, pointing to the wide steel point of the ballista bolt.

Drawing his sword again he severed it cleanly with one stroke. "What are you going to do?" he asked.

"Something stupid, if it doesn't work we may both die. I want you to count to thirty and then withdraw the shaft," I replied. I turned to Marc, "Hold her for me, I'm about to let go." He nodded silently and moved to brace her as I released her body. "Lay her next to me, so I can see her face," I added. He did so and Dorian crouched behind her, his hands on the thick wooden shaft. Lying beside her I looked into her pale face and spoke one last time, "Start counting Dorian." I added a few more words in Lycian and then the world vanished as my mind left my body, spiraling into the dying form of the woman I loved.

Pain nearly overwhelmed me as the signals from Penny's torn spine tore at me. Agony coursed through me as I sought to balance myself, to find a quiet place within her. I could feel her heart's labored beating as it worked sluggishly to keep blood flowing through her. The first thing I did was to block the onslaught of impulses coming from her torn nerves and damaged spine, giving myself a respite from the pain. Then I focused on the wooden shaft that passed through her body. It had gone through her liver and the steel head had severed the artery that fed into it. It had also ripped one lung open and cut into numerous other organs as it passed.

I had already sealed the artery, to prevent her bleeding to death, but it would need to be reconnected. I didn't dare do any of that until the wooden shaft was removed however. While I waited I drew the blood from her damaged lungs and mended the large cut that was there. Then I felt a great pulling as the wooden shaft was drawn out. New pain shot through her body, threatening to drive me into unconsciousness with her. If I lost control now we would both die.

Drawing on a strength of will I hadn't known I possessed I ignored the pain and began closing the wounds left behind as the bolt was drawn. The liver itself was fairly simple but the large artery gave me trouble. Blood began rushing outward as I fought to reconnect the two separate parts. Panic threatened to destroy my resolve but I held firm, until at last the artery was whole again.

Once that was done I began fixing the numerous smaller injuries within her abdomen, repairing smaller vessels and restoring her other organs. One thing that had been miraculously undamaged was her womb. As I focused my attention there a shock ran through me, for a second heart beat within it. She was pregnant. My intentional lie had been an unintentional truth.

The life inside was tiny but strong. I could feel something akin to fear coming from it. Reaching out I soothed it with my mind, trying to reassure it. *You're safe, daddy's here,* I thought to myself and the unborn child seemed to respond. Emotions I had never imagined before ran through me and I determined I would do everything possible to save them both.

Only one task was left to me now, but it was the most daunting. If Penny was ever to live normally again I had to fix her spine, but the intricate complexity of the nerves there were beyond simple comprehension. I began slowly sorting through the damaged endings, trying to match them with their proper mates but the sheer number was too much for my mind. Fear ate at my confidence as I realized I could never hope to fix the damage there.

I paused, focusing on the now steady beating of her heart. As I listened to it I heard again the deeper beating of the earth below us, a deep primal sound that had existed long before either of us had been born. Reaching out with my mind I called to it again, *please help me, I can't fix this,* but if it heard me it had no answer for me. I had been a fool to think something so vastly different could help me to heal a human being.

I can hear you now Mordecai, came the voice again. The voice of the stone-lady, though I had no eyes to see her with.

I know your name now, I answered mentally. *You were Moira Centyr.*

Yes! her triumphant response came. *I had never hoped to remember that name.*

Can you help me? I do not know how to fix this, I told her.

No. You must do it, but I can show you how. Relax your spirit. The mind cannot heal something so complex, you must feel it. Send your feelings through her; they know where the nerves should lead. Use that sensation to make it as it once was. Thinking will only bring your effort to ruin.

I focused on her words and sent myself along the channels that represented Penny's spine. Relaxing I felt a light welling up from within and sensations began to flow again from her feet to her brain. An age passed as I lay within her, bathing in the light and feeling my way through every nerve in her body. I found more damage than I had known was there, things that had previously gone unnoticed. I fixed those as well.

Eventually I knew it was finished and I lay exhausted inside her body. My senses had gone dark and I could no longer feel anything beyond her flesh. My mind drifted and I wanted nothing more than to relax and sleep. I could feel a cool wind drawing my spirit away—calling me to some other place.

Stop! Moira's voice came to me again. *You must leave; you have been too long in this body.*

I'm tired. I don't know how to find my body anyway. Just let me sleep, I replied.

Use her eyes, wake her up!

Grumbling mentally I did as she asked, sending impulses into Penelope's brain, rousing her from unconsciousness. Confusion swept through her, for she could feel me within her. Opening her eyes we could see my limp form lying on the ground beside her. A feeling of mutual affection passed between us and then I threw myself outward, seeking my own body. Darkness came over me and I drifted into oblivion, unsure if I had found my proper place or not.

CHAPTER 40

I woke slowly. Opening my eyes I could see I was back in my own bed. Penny lay quietly beside me, awake and staring back at me. Neither of us spoke for long minutes, content simply with the fact that the other was alive.

"I felt you," she said softly. "I was dying but you wouldn't let me go."

A lump formed in my throat, "I couldn't."

"You almost died with me," she said.

"Better that than the alternative," I replied. "You really are pregnant by the way."

"You told me that before," she answered with a puzzled face. "Is the baby alright?"

"Yes, he's fine," I smiled.

Penny had always had a quick mind. "You lied before didn't you? You didn't know I was pregnant."

I sighed, "Yes, but things worked out didn't they?"

"You really are a bastard sometimes," she replied, and then she kissed me to emphasize the point.

I pulled away for a moment, "You should be thanking me."

"I think we came out even in this exchange," she replied. "I saved you first."

"Not that, I made some improvements while I was healing you," I said with a smirk.

"What?"

"Don't your breasts feel a bit different?" I added.

She sat up suddenly and brought her hands up to her chest. The sight of her frantically cupping herself made me laugh. "What did you do?" she said loudly.

"Well I always thought they could stand to be a little larger, so I added a bit to them," I lied. The look of shock on her face was priceless. She began struggling to get out of her chain byrnie, writhing to escape the heavy metal and the padded tunic beneath it. Sometimes jokes work out better than you expect.

"They look just the same! What sort of game are you playing at?" she demanded once her torso was bare.

My laughter was uncontrollable now. "Relax I didn't change a thing. They were perfect already anyway," I reassured her.

"Then why would you say something like that?" she said. My eyes ran down her shoulders and over her beautiful curves. She was much more attractive without the mail and blood soaked tunic covering her. The look told her everything she needed to know. "You are unbelievable!" she shouted and picking up the bundle of heavy mail she dropped it on my face.

"Ow!" I exclaimed as I pushed the gory bundle off and stumbled out of the bed. "You didn't have to do that!"

Her thoughts had already shifted. "How long do you think we've been up here?" she asked suddenly.

"I don't even know how we got here. I suppose some of the men brought us," I replied. Stepping to the window I looked out. The view would answer most of our questions more quickly than speculation.

Reality returned in a rush as I saw the men fighting for their lives outside. The army of Gododdin was pressing inward like a great wave against a rock. Most of their forces were clustered against the outside of the curtain wall as they sought to force their way past the defenders holding the breach in it. My eyes focused on the knot of men clustered atop the rubble there, where the fighting was most intense.

Sunlight glinting from shining silver armor showed me Dorian among them. Like a lion among lambs he slaughtered any who came near, his sword sweeping heads and limbs away as easily as a scythe cuts grass. Among the men who had fallen beside him I thought I could see Marc's brightly colored surcoat. If it was him he wasn't moving.

Penny stood beside me now, shrugging her way back into her torn and bloodied armor. She held her head proudly but I could see her limbs shaking as she struggled to get dressed again. "You're not going back out there," I said. "Your body is in no condition. It will be weeks before you get your strength back."

With a sigh of frustration she finished pulling the byrnie over her head before her exhaustion forced her to sit down on the divan. I winced inwardly. The blood on her armor would ruin it. She caught my look and glared at me. "Don't say it," she warned.

Instead I drew out the pouch of glass stones that were keyed to the trap I had placed around Castle Cameron. There was no more time for delays. My father's hammer was back in his smithy and there was nothing suitable close at hand, so I focused my will and with a word I formed a tight, hard shield around the small bag. Clenching my teeth and mind at the same time I used it to crush the glass within and the ground lurched beneath my feet.

The world beyond the walls of Cameron Castle exploded. Soil and stone were thrown hundreds of feet into the air while flames engulfed everything. Thousands perished in an instant, some burned to a cinder while those further from the explosive centers were tossed, broken and mangled, into the air. Dorian and those fighting in the broken gap of the wall were thrown back and tumbled to the ground, along with the men they had been striving against.

I headed for the door and Penny shouted at my back, "Wait, I'm coming too." She stood up but I could see her swaying on her feet.

"No you're not," I said and went back to her, lifting her from the ground. With the armor she was almost more than I could handle, but I managed anyway, carrying her to the bed. She struggled to rise but I gently pushed her back and reached down to pull her enchanted pendant from her neck. A sharp tug and the chain broke. *"Shibal,"* I said and left her sleeping.

As I ran down the stairs my own fatigue threatened to send me stumbling, so I reached out with my mind, calling to the earth once more. I could feel a power there beyond anything I had ever imagined and I drew upon a small portion of it, filling my body with strength and vitality again. I was fairly sure the effect would be short lived, but I didn't have time for proper rest.

When I reached the yard the men there were still recovering from the shock and violence of the explosions. "Get up!" I shouted at them. "There's no time for wasting!" Long minutes passed as I rallied the remaining defenders. All told they numbered little more than two hundred men. More had died holding the breach than I had realized. Dorian and Marcus were not among them but I had no time to search for them.

Driving them by pure force of personality I took them out through the ruined wall. The devastation there was daunting. Great holes had been torn in the earth were the stones had been hidden under the ground. Nothing remained of the buildings and shelters we had built there, nothing but charred wood and broken timbers. I kept them moving and we went beyond the shattered remains of the palisade to find what might be left of the enemy.

For a hundred yards out the earth was covered in bodies and rubble. In the distance the few who had escaped the destruction stood uncertainly. At a glance there appeared to be almost a thousand men left, but their spirits had been shaken and I didn't intend to give them time to recover the will to fight.

The men gathered around me and I remembered Dorian's speech, and the one word that had possibly killed more men than 'should'. "Now's the time! Let's show these whoresons what the men of Lothion are made of!" I shouted. "For Lothion!"

"For Lothion!" they responded.

"For Cameron!" I screamed.

The cry came back again and I could feel their hearts pounding in time with my own. I opened my mouth and roared with everything I had, "Charge!" Like one great beast we began moving forward at a run, our pace eating up the ground between us and the enemy.

For a moment one of the enemy captains tried to rally them. Standing in his stirrups he tried to organize them to receive our charge. *"Lyet Bierek!"* I shouted as I ran and light blossomed over his head. A great cracking boom sounded and his horse reared, throwing him to the ground. Those nearest him were blinded and began running in confusion. In seconds the morale of the rest fell apart and the army of Gododdin was routed.

From that point our charge turned into a long chase. Neither we nor the men we pursued could run for long and soon we were walking after them. Some stumbled and fell, and those we caught died quickly. Those among the defenders who faltered simply stopped and rested, or fell in their tracks. Hours went by and we followed them to the valley road before stopping. I watched as the ragged remainder of Gododdin's once great army rejoined the wounded men camped there.

A sharp pang of guilt passed over me as I drew out the last bag of stones. Our victory had been won, but I needed to be sure. We would be in no shape to fight again if those that were left somehow rallied against us on the morrow. Gritting my teeth I pushed my sympathies aside, there was little place left in me for mercy. A word and a sharp focusing of my will crushed the bag in my hand.

The ground jumped beneath us, throwing men to their knees. I would learn later that the shock was felt even in the capital, Albamarl. A great plume of fire and superheated steam rose up from the end of the valley where my father had built his dam. Rocks and great chunks of ice were thrown for miles. One even landed in the castle yard in Lancaster, crushing a cart that had been left out. Seconds later the sound reached us, a subdued roar at that distance.

It was minutes before the water arrived, a sweeping torrent of roaring water that washed the enemy and their wounded from their makeshift camp. Men cried out in fear as the water struck and many perished as it threw them against rocks and trees. The rest drowned before the waters began to recede. An hour later all that was left was a mess of flotsam and jetsam. The dead bodies of men and horses were scattered from the center of the valley to its western end.

It was the greatest single day of slaughter that history had ever known, and I was its chief architect.

EPILOGUE

A month had passed since the day of our victory and bodies were still being found. There were so many that most were left where they lay. We didn't have the man power necessary to gather, much less bury or burn so many. In the end we settled for disposing of those nearest to Washbrook, piling them together to be burned. The smoke left a smell that lingered for days afterwards and I'm sure no one who experienced it would ever forget the noxious odor.

Despite the large number of bodies that we burned, and those that were found scattered throughout the valley I was fairly sure that a fair amount were never found. Worse, although we had nothing close to an accurate count it appeared that a large number of bodies were missing. I hoped they had been washed all the way to the Formby Marsh, but I had a bad feeling about it. Plus some of my late patrols had reported seeing men moving at night. Because of that we continued bringing everyone inside the walls at night… the war might be over but we still had plenty of things to fear. Repairing the palisade and preparing a larger more permanent wall around Washbrook were among my top priorities.

Dorian was found, alive and uninjured in the castle yard. The blast from the explosion around Cameron Castle had sent him flying against a rock and rendered him unconscious. He was most displeased to have missed the final charge.

Marcus was discovered among the dead defenders of the wall, badly wounded but conscious still. A sword had pierced his leg and an arrow was protruding from his shoulder. I healed his wounds later but he complained of pain in his leg from that day forward. I was sure I had done a thorough job so I began to suspect he only complained to annoy me. His demeanor had changed after his goddess had betrayed us. He was darker now, less prone to laughter and given to quiet moods. I worried he might never recover completely.

Over three hundred of our men had died defending the breach in the wall. Men from Lancaster and Washbrook, and men who had only recently come to call my lands home, but their families survived. In time we would grow and flourish again.

Cyhan was locked away in a cell at Lancaster, since I still had nothing to keep prisoners within Cameron Castle. His condition was a dark reminder to those of us who had come to respect and rely upon him. I still had hopes he could be released, but there had been no time to devote to him yet. Eventually I planned to offer him a place among us, or a return to Albamarl, depending upon his decision.

No messages had come from the king but his scouts had been spotted near Lancaster so I suspected he had some knowledge of the outcome of our battle. I wasn't certain what the future held with regard to him, but I was sure it wouldn't be pleasant.

It was a warm day in mid-spring when Penny and I visited Lancaster again. James and Genevieve met us in the front hall. Dispensing with formality I hugged them both, then I stepped back and addressed them, "I'm sure you both remember Penelope," I said in mock seriousness. "Please let me introduce her again, now as my wife, and the Countess di'Cameron. Penelope Illeniel I present to you their graces, the Duke and Duchess of Lancaster." I gave a bow and held up her hand for James to take.

James laughed, for they both had long known of our marriage the month before. "Mordecai, I hope you know how to treat a lady," he said as he bent to kiss Penny's proffered hand.

"Don't tease him James," Genevieve told him. "Some things should be done properly." She took Penelope's hand as well and stared long upon her before drawing her into a gentle embrace. "I have heard that you will soon have a child," she said once they separated again.

Penny smiled shyly, "That's what I've been told and my body seems to agree." She placed her hand unconsciously on her belly which had finally begun to show a slight bulge.

"Have you thought about how you want to decorate the nursery?" Genevieve asked with visible interest. Of course Penny had already been talking about it to me at home. I never could understand the fascination. My own ideas regarding such topics were non-existent. I figured anything above a straw filled box would probably be sufficient. Naturally I had kept that information to myself.

The two of them began talking animatedly about the possibilities, leaving James and I to our own devices. "They never get tired of it," he told me when they were out of earshot.

"Really?" I asked. His viewpoint as an experienced father of three seemed invaluable to me.

"With each of our three children, Ginny had to decorate the nursery all over again," he replied sagely.

"Why didn't she just leave it the same as when she had the first?" I said curiously.

"I'll never know," he replied with a chuckle. "I can tell you this, don't argue about it. When she wants to redo the whole thing for your second child, just smile and nod. Asking her why her tastes have changed will only bring you trouble."

I shook my head. The mysteries of women were beyond me but I resolved to remember his advice. "I'll be sure to do that," I replied.

"Doesn't matter," he told me.

"Why?" I asked again.

"You'll find some other way to rile her up. I've seen the way you two bicker. You have a real talent for it. No use wasting your talent," he said with a grin.

I laughed as well. We talked for a bit about the issues we were facing presently. Food had become a pressing problem. The flood had ruined part of the spring planting and what harvest we could still expect would be barely sufficient to get our people through to the next crop. My mind was on something else though, and after a short while I finally brought it up.

"You remember the day my father died?" I asked him.

His face grew somber, "Of course, I wouldn't be here now if it weren't for your father's strong arms dragging me back."

"He mentioned a chandelier that he made for you, before he died," I said simply.

"I remember. I should have thought of that sooner. Let's go take a look now; the hall should be empty at the moment. Better now than when they start getting ready for dinner. I'm sure you'll want some privacy." His eyes were full of sympathy.

We walked together and I was reminded again of how much I had come to value the duke's friendship. "Your father was very good to me," he said as we walked. "He had a lot of hidden depths."

I nodded in agreement, not knowing what to say.

"Most people didn't notice, because he didn't waste a lot of time talking, but I could tell the first time he did some work for me," he continued.

"What was it?"

James chuckled, "A broken axle on one of our wagons. It had broken a month before, on a trip to Arundel. I let the smith there fix it, but his weld didn't hold up. Your father had some colorful things to say about that."

That I could well imagine. He had always had firm opinions about shoddy craftsmanship. "I'm guessing he refused to re-weld it."

James' eye lit up, "That he did. Said it would need a newly forged axle and the old one should just be tossed in the scrap pile. I wanted him to just patch it up like before, but he wouldn't hear of it. I thought he was just trying to get me to pay more, so I argued with him about it. You know what he told me?"

I had a fair idea what he might have said but I didn't want to spoil the story. "No sir," I said.

"He said if I wanted a 'shitty job done' I could damn well find someone else to do it. I thought he might spit fire when he said it."

I started laughing, "What did you do then?"

"I had it taken to another smith. I was fairly angry with your father then. You have to understand, being a duke, and young, I wasn't used to being talked to like that. At the time I seriously considered having him punished for insolence, but I held my temper. Two months later the axle broke again." He paused for a moment as we went through the door into the great hall.

As we entered I could see the new iron wrought chandelier hanging above the high table. "What did you do then?" I prompted my host.

"I swallowed my pride and took it back to him. He never said a word about it, but his eyes told me all I needed to know of his opinion regarding my foolishness. I paid him double what he asked for when it was done. I never used another smith after that," he smiled at the memory.

"I hadn't heard that story before, but it sounds just like him," I agreed. Staring upward I could see why my father had wanted me to come here.

Most people don't think of iron work when they think of art, and in truth Royce had never been an artist, not in the strictest sense of the word. He simply did very good work. The chandelier above was simply designed, with long elegantly curved bars rising up to meet in the center, supporting a ring of lamps. I knew enough of his craft to guess where the welds were, but they weren't visible. The metal had been lapped and hot welded carefully before he polished away any imperfections in the joins.

To an inexperienced eye it was merely functional, but my eyes could see the meticulous care he had put into creating it. It was perfect in every detail. I stared at it for long moments, 'til my vision grew blurry and I was forced to wipe away tears.

He hadn't made it for me, or for anyone else. As with everything else, he had built it simply for the joy of making it. His message was clear, even to me. Once again I could hear his words, for he had said them to me often, *if something is worth doing, it's worth doing right.*

My father hadn't always succeeded, for he was no more perfect than I was, but he had tried, in everything he did. I could only hope to live up to his example.

Afterword

It bears noting that my own father died just as I was starting to write this book. His passing had a large impact on the tone of the later story. Much of what was written here about Royce Eldridge was written remembering him and the things he told me during my own childhood. By necessity I had to change some of the language, but the spirit was there. His last scene in the story, and the epilogue were directly inspired by my own experiences during his last days. I can only hope he would have approved.

The Story Continues In:

The Archmage Unbound

Stay up to date with my releases by signing up for my newsletter at:

Magebornbooks.com

Books by Michael G. Manning:

Mageborn:
The Blacksmith's Son
The Line of Illeniel
The Archmage Unbound
The God-Stone War
The Final Redemption

Embers of Illeniel (a prequel series):
The Mountains Rise
The Silent Tempest
Betrayer's Bane

Champions of the Dawning Dragons:
Thornbear
Centyr Dominance
Demonhome

The Riven Gates:
Mordecai
The Severed Realm (coming summer 2018)
More to be announced

Standalone Novels:
Thomas